Set your fields on fire.

WILLIAM THORNTON

WESTBOW
PRESS®
A DIVISION OF THOMAS NELSON
& ZONDERVAN

WestBow Press books may be ordered through booksellers or by contacting:

WestBow Press
A Division of Thomas Nelson & Zondervan
1663 Liberty Drive
Bloomington, IN 47403
www.westbowpress.com
1 (866) 928-1240

Because of the dynamic nature of the Internet, any web addresses or
links contained in this book may have changed since publication and
may no longer be valid. The views expressed in this work are solely those
of the author and do not necessarily reflect the views of the publisher,
and the publisher hereby disclaims any responsibility for them.

Any people depicted in stock imagery provided by Thinkstock are models,
and such images are being used for illustrative purposes only.
Certain stock imagery © Thinkstock.

ISBN: 978-1-5127-2196-6 (sc)
ISBN: 978-1-5127-2197-3 (hc)
ISBN: 978-1-5127-2195-9 (e)

Library of Congress Control Number: 2015919772

Print information available on the last page.

WestBow Press rev. date: 11/30/2015

Also by the author

Brilliant Disguises
The Uncanny Valley

"Judge not, that you be not judged. For with what judgment ye judge, ye shall be judged: and with what measure ye mete, it shall be measured to you again."

- Matthew 7:1-2 (KJV)

I

The Raw and the Cooked

1

"The twenty-first century, my friends, is about debt."

Alterman says the words to the room of faces that have no idea what he's talking about. The lights are out, the only illumination provided by the projector and the screen radiating light back on crags in their perplexed features. This is a standard speech he gives his clients - one of the better ones he carries around by his estimation. All for Shiloh Church at the Point, a modern, glass-and-steel temple feeding off three subdivisions of six-figure homes for its congregation.

They wanted his expertise, and if they know him, they understand this is part of the package. They might as well sit back and enjoy it, because he is going to give them their money's worth.

"Debt," he continues, his voice provoked by the silence of his audience. "Piles of it. Mounds of it. Mountain ranges and peaks and valleys of gorgeous, fatty, pulsating debt. The twentieth century was about the accumulation of old debts, old vendettas, old hatreds. This one will be about running up new ones that aren't really new."

Oh, how they are going to *hate* him for this one, once they hear it. Not as they are hearing now, but later on, during the drive home, when they'll finally catch the nub of what he is saying. Alterman knows he has a voice that carries, not into the next room, but into the next hour. They'll hear him long after he finishes talking, his words pitched at a tone just above the sepulchral.

"What did Our Lord say, during His prayer? 'Forgive us our debts, as we forgive our debtors.' By this, even the Son of God proclaims that we do not forget debts. We *forgive* them, as though they are an offense before the Almighty. What do we say when someone leaves prison? That he has paid his debt to society. Debts are meant to be *paid*."

Alterman can see their faces darkening, even if he can't clearly make out anything. The *room* is darkening, in mood. They did not expect a sermon.

But if they didn't expect a sermon, Alterman thinks to himself, they shouldn't have come to a church.

"Even now, this glorious house of worship has a significant amount of debt that must be disposed of if the business of Heaven is to continue. The Lord does not withdraw, my friends. He invests. He *saves*."

Alterman pauses here, just to let his next words sink in. As he speaks, he runs through a range of motions and gestures. He brings his left fist down into the open palm of his right hand like a tent revivalist. He rubs his thumb and index finger together as a croupier would at a Las Vegas table, asking one side to kindly pay up. He raises his hands over his head as would any stickup victim. He is all of these characters, but he is more focused on how the words *sound*, rolling off his tongue with elegant meter and precision.

"I realize that you probably don't want to think of it this way. You don't want to …as it were, *cheapen*…what you feel is a very holy business. And I respect that. But you also hired me to do a job. And part of that job is that occasionally, I have to preach from the Gospel of Plain Truth so that the Truth can set you free. So let me tell you, with all due respect, that to pay this debt off, you've got to have bodies coming into this church."

Alterman sees there are a few here starting to nod their heads. That may surprise his partner, but it doesn't surprise him. Alterman expects a few of them to agree with what he's saying.

"Unless these coffers are overflowing with offerings, you're not going to be able to pay back what you owe."

This, of course, proves too much for one of the faces he cannot make out. It is a man who speaks, finally, with the challenge Alterman expects.

"I think what you're saying is shameful!" the voice says. Alterman's eyes dart into the darkness but cannot pinpoint the source. "You're saying that we need to draw people into this church in order to get their offerings so that we can pay off our debt! That's not the mission of this church!"

Ah, they always make it easy for him, don't they?

"Indeed it is not, my friend!" Alterman's manner is genial, but he does not smile. Alterman never smiles. "But I didn't say that you need to bring more bodies in here to soak their hard won dollars."

"Then what are you saying?"

"I'm saying that I've done a full audit of this church for the past three months. Longer, actually. And the problems here are much deeper than I think you realize."

The pastor, who has been politely silent up to this moment, now has a reason to speak. "I hope you'll be getting to that part soon."

That's not enough for the voice in the back though. It must belong to Chaffey. "Wait a minute. I want to know what all this rigmarole has to do with why you were hired."

"I was getting to that…" Alterman begins.

"You were hired…at great expense…to come in and observe every aspect of our ministry. The same way somebody scouts a business or a hotel or a resort or whatever, I was told. A 'mystery worshipper,' they called you. Now you've got us in here listening to you rattle on about our debt. What has this got to do with why you were hired?"

Now it's time for Alterman to go into his wounded routine. *The very idea of alleging that he isn't doing his job now! Why, it's insulting. And it isn't that great an expense either.* So Alterman takes out the report that he's prepared. He does this very deliberately. Anyone watching probably thinks that he was planning on handing it out after his little talk, but now it appears he's ditched that plan. It's time to defend himself. He hands the pastor one, and then passes copies out among the people in the room. It's thick - more than 400 pages easily. A lot of people probably didn't expect anything more than his talk. He's giving them enough data to occupy them for the rest of their lives.

Then, Alterman eyes his partner in the back, and launches into his defense.

"Did you not, my friends, vote to borrow money to build this worship center? And did you not do it because you felt you were accommodating this community, which at the time was growing more and more every year? Didn't you think it was an act of faith to borrow all that money and believe that God would find a way to grow you out of debt?"

The room is darkening even more now, because the words are recognized. A few of them probably remember what they said at the meetings, and still others remember what they heard. That was weeks and months ago, many, many offerings ago, and they *had* moved on to other acts of faith, Alterman figures. A few of them skeptically look at the report in their hands and likely conclude that if what's inside resembles what they're hearing, they may never open it.

"Are you not actively engaged in bringing people to this new sanctuary? And they've got to believe in the mission of this church. Correct? So why else did you hire me? I'm here to audit everything that you do, in every way that you do it."

That seems to satisfy a few of them. *Okay, so maybe he has a point. He doesn't have a lot of tact, but he has a point*, they're probably saying to themselves. All but the pastor. He still looks uneasy.

"What about those *deep* problems you mentioned? What are they?"

Alterman is pleased, because this is what he's been waiting for. "I didn't go into this really in the report, because you asked me to audit what is going on right now. But I think it has some bearing on how you're doing things. As I understand it, you've had your present pastor for only about two years, correct?"

The pastor nods, a little unsure of what this means.

"And you...you came on after the building project was already underway, correct?"

The pastor nods again.

"And the man who was here before? Did he leave to pastor another church?"

There is silence. A few people shift in their chairs. A few chairs shift on the floor, sounding like the cries of captured beasts.

"Anyone?"

"He left," is the reply, from that voice in the back of the room.

"Left," Alterman repeats.

They understand that he is dissatisfied with the answer. "He was asked...*politely*...to leave."

"Asked?"

"There was a problem," comes another voice, a little warmer, from behind the pastor. "It was all very amicable."

"I see," Alterman says. He pauses for a second or two, to wait in vain for another, truer explanation. "He was, in fact, let go, because of a matter of background checks, I believe?"

A head nods near the front, vigorously. "Yes. Business with the music minister."

"The music minister had a prior criminal record that had gone unreported?" Alterman says, waiting for the heads to nod again. "Yes, and this came about at the time that the building plan was being voted on, correct?"

No one says anything.

"Of course, I'm sure the two had nothing to do with each other," Alterman says. "Just as I'm sure that your last pastor," he pauses, as though trying to remember the name, "a Reverend Templeton, was it? He was mistaken when he said that one of the reasons he was let go was because he was overweight."

"That wasn't the only reason," comes a reply, then a head shaking violently. "He deliberately misled us about the music minister. It was the simplest thing in the world. All he had to do was check the man's background."

"Did *he* hire the music minister?"

"No, that was done by committee," comes another response, this time from someone who hasn't spoken. This voice sounds as though it sees where Alterman is headed with his line of questioning, and is silently thrilled.

Alterman nods. "Yes, but it's the pastor's duty to make sure about such things? Or at least it was?"

Another voice feels the need to clear the air. "Brother Templeton knew about the music minister. The music minister was arrested while he was at seminary for drunk driving. The music minister told the pastor this in confidence. Brother Templeton didn't mention it to anybody else."

Now both sides are suddenly at each other's throats in the darkness, giving each other rehearsed, ancient arguments hardened in place.

"He had a responsibility to tell anything he knew!"

"It was a confession! He told Brother Templeton something he was ashamed of."

"With good reason!"

"What has this got to do with the state of our church *now?* Brother Templeton didn't want the new sanctuary. There were several reasons why he was let go. Some people felt he misled us. His weight was embarrassing, but beside the point. None of that has anything to do with us *now!*"

Alterman smiles. "But it does. You see, you still have the same problem. You're not doing proper background checks on your staff."

"What?" the pastor says.

"There's a man here right now about whom I doubt any of you know the truth. And his presence perfectly illustrates the reason why this church can't pay its debts, can't fulfill its mission, can't see why it has any problem at all!"

As Alterman says the words, there are a few people on staff who begin looking around to see if they can pick up any guilt in the darkness. Anyone with a wounded expression. Nothing. Just a sheepish smile on the face of the children's director.

"If there's a problem, let me know about it," the pastor says. "But we should be discreet about any issue like this."

"Don't worry, brother," Alterman says. "This isn't about you. It's about your children's director." He points at the man with a finger that brings down guilt just as the lights go up. "Your children's director has only been here for three months. Potentially the most sensitive position in the whole church. The future of the faith right there, under his guilty fingers, and you weren't even aware that everything he put on his resume was a fraud!"

All the eyes in the room now turn to the children's director, the man everyone calls B.D. All of the staff pick up on it instantly. There's something about him that looks cool, as though he expected Alterman to bring this up, but he's got a foolproof defense.

"Mr. Satva, is it? That's your real name? That's what you'd have these fine people believe?" Alterman demands.

Satva doesn't move a muscle.

"Listen to me," Alterman says. "I don't care what you think about this man, but everything I'm telling you about yourselves is laid out in my report. If you really are serious about what you want to do, and I think *some* of you are, then you'd better pay attention to everything in there. I can assure you the conclusions in it were arrived at through lots of hard work and very careful prayer. But brothers and sisters, our friend here with the false name is indicative of what's wrong with this church. You allowed him to sneak in here and do whatever it is he's been doing, unaware of who he really is and what he might be up to. You've got a serious problem here."

"What has he done?" the pastor asks, genuine horror in his voice.

Alterman puts both hands on the pastor's shoulders. "Brother, you're not the one to blame. You had no idea what you were walking into here. I think that if this church is to grow, you're the man to do it."

"What is it that happened?" the voice in the back demands.

Alterman looks at Mr. Satva. "You want to tell them, or should I?"

Satva gestures with his hands, as if to say, *it's all yours.*

"Very well. You see, for me to do this job adequately, I've got to be able to gather lots of information and do it when people don't realize they're being watched."

"Which means…?"

"Which means that we've been spying on you for the past three months. Mr. Satva is one of my operatives. He hasn't been doing anything to the lovely children of this church. He's merely been one of my spies. That's all. But the fact that you didn't pick up on it shows how bad this problem still is."

The darkness in the room suddenly dissipates, like a bank of fog evaporating in the open sunlight. A few men laugh. A few breathe heavy sighs. As Satva stands up, his grin is now even broader. A few of the people clap, as if to say *well done*.

"You'll find inside my recommendations on how this could have been avoided," Alterman says. "This kind of thing is potentially more harmful than unpaid debt. But…there's something else you should know about Mr. Satva."

At this, Satva begins unbuttoning his shirt. Satva is a man that is easily 50 pounds overweight, but he has all this time insisted on wearing an undersized shirt that seems to accentuate his girth. The buttons bulge from the too-tight front even as he removes it, to reveal padding beneath. He discards the padding to show a very fit and remarkably chiseled chest. He buttons the shirt. Then he reaches up to pull both of his eyebrows off, with much cleaner, thinner ones underneath. There is a gasp of recognition from the room just before Satva pulls off the thick glasses he wears, the false teeth that gave his voice a lisp, the wig he has worn for the last three months. In the space of less than two minutes, B.D. Satva has revealed himself to be Steve Templeton, the deposed former pastor, now remarkably thin and back to pay a visit.

"I'm sure most of you will recognize my partner, the Rev. Templeton. He and I have been in business together for almost the whole time since he left your church. I would have expected at any time that you would have caught on. Oh, but I forgot. After all, he is *thinner* than he was before. But that didn't stop you from hiring him for this job when you thought he was heavier. Hiring him a second time, as it turns out?"

There is an outraged silence in the room, the silence of people who realize they are being judged - most mercilessly, by themselves.

"And I doubt your present pastor need feel his job is in any jeopardy because he didn't know *your* committee had hired his predecessor as the children's minister."

Templeton, now revealed, walks to the door behind Alterman. He has a feeling they may need to leave immediately, but he is having too much fun watching all this. The tension of the last three months has proved worthwhile, if just for this moment. He couldn't believe it when Alterman told him they had been hired by his old church. Surely they knew where Templeton was these days? But they didn't. The idea that they didn't care offended him, and Alterman had seen that. In the space of about 10 seconds, that was all the time Alterman needed to hatch this latest and greatest audit of his career.

"You see, my friends, this *is* all about unpaid debts. When someone does you wrong, what do you say? You say, I *owe* you. It's a debt. You got rid of my partner here and didn't even pay him what you agreed to in his original contract. Why? Because *you could.* You wanted to borrow money, and he didn't. I have to congratulate you too. This kind of incompetence would have rated you a bonus on Wall Street. I mean, you didn't even research the names on my staff!"

Alterman gives Templeton an eye, pauses, and forges on.

"Did it ever occur to you that maybe he had a point that things might not always grow around here? Maybe it isn't because of his lack of faith? Maybe it's leadership when a man says things which aren't what the rest of you want to hear? Did you ever stop to think that maybe the Lord was trying to tell you something through your pastor, something you needed to listen to?"

Alterman's voice now is low and threatening, and Templeton has given enough sermons to know this is the tone a pastor adopts when he is about to issue the invitation to salvation. This is the business voice, not the one designed to wake up the deacon in the back who stayed up too late the night before watching football. *This is the pin-drop voice.*

"Well, listen to this. Your church can't grow, and it won't grow, as long as you are careless with what you have. How did you construct a building this big, and yet leave no room for the presence of the

Living God? This church isn't yours, any more than it was Brother Templeton's or your present pastor's. It's *His*. You can't just sack people you don't like any more than you can borrow money and expect everything to pay for itself. When the devil tempted Our Lord, Satan challenged Him to throw Himself from the Temple and dare the angels to rescue Him. He tempted Him with carelessness. You're careless people. You can't be careless with *this*. You can't."

Alterman is finished. He nods as if to thank the stunned people in the room, and turns to leave. He gives Templeton a loving pat on the shoulder as they move toward the door. A few of Alterman's thick reports have dropped to the floor from incredulous hands.

"Look here!" says the voice in the back, stirring. Alterman thinks, this is the guy who did Templeton in. Chaffey probably. It's always the ones who don't show themselves. "What you're doing is deceitful! You've probably destroyed this church on a whim! Just to prove a point that's already settled?"

Alterman turns to the voice, with a smile on his face.

"Yes, it's deceitful," he says. "You think *we're* bad? You don't think the devil worries about something like that, do you?"

As Alterman shuts the door, he hears someone who hasn't spoken for the whole meeting demand, "Whose idea was it to bring them in?"

As the two of them are walking out of the church, Alterman says, without looking at Templeton, "You know, I've got something. Something big. We may need to get everybody together again for this one."

"That's good. Once word gets out about this, we may not be able to ever get another…"

"Are you kidding? We'll have to fight them off with sticks after this."

"Are you talking about clients or mobs?"

"This is big," he said, ignoring Templeton and reassuring him at the same time. Alterman makes a mental note – he must send out the bill for this job tomorrow. He wonders if it will be paid.

"You had this in mind all along, didn't you?" Templeton asks. "You were waiting on this particular job to open up, weren't you?"

"Weren't you?"

2

In just four busy years, Alterman's name has become legend in the mystery worshipper industry, which is larger now than when he started. He left New York after he passed his forty-first birthday and realized early on, so the stories say, that he had missed his life's work all this time. So his new career began in the early part of 2009 when he hired himself out to an Ohio would-be megachurch that noticed its membership rolls were not increasing at the same rate as the population in the suburb that was its home.

Alterman prepared a 96-page report that practically sang. Even the footnotes. He looked at the young families moving into the area, visiting their soccer camps and wandering through the grocery aisles, quizzing the young mothers and fathers who had just moved into the fresh subdivisions. Alterman figured out the youngsters weren't as interested in new statements of faith as they were in building stronger families in a more traditional worship setting. Therefore, it was time to turn back the clock. His report flew in the face of four decades of reliable church growth mantras. He recommended the church scrap its contemporary service's praise music and go with old school hymns. He told them that instead of baptizing new converts in the expensive fount behind the pulpit, on warmer days, they might hold them in a pond just across the road.

Not all his ideas were retro. He told the church to get rid of the old marquee it had out front, repaint the trim on the building, and revamp its website. But every once in a while, read from the King James in services, he said. If your music minister's position should come open, hire an older guy in his sixties who exudes a grandfatherly image. Within months, the church was growing at twice the rate of the population moving into the area. Observers were astonished. It proved, said some, the old adage that the Lord knows how to grow the church but it isn't always willing to listen.

Right after this auspicious beginning, Alterman snatched up Templeton, newly divorced from his old church and in need of a job. A few wags sniffed that if Templeton was such an expert, he would be leading a church instead of telling others how things should be done. Alterman heard this criticism and gave Templeton a raise on the spot.

Over two years, they assembled a crew of manically loyal assistants to tackle the churches of America and preach the gospel of clean toilets and trimmed lawns. The bunch of them with their checklists and tape measures and exacting eyes are as remorseless as a cloistered cell of Russian revolutionaries.

There is Bobby Ingersoll, the seminary dropout who came on board shortly after Templeton. He's the one who occasionally poses as an atheist to test the resolve of some Sunday School teachers. He is so convincing, Alterman says, that he insists Ingersoll make professions of faith at each church he audits in order to ensure his salvation.

Not long after Bobby was hired, Templeton recommended Cherie LeFevere, a single woman with three degrees, none of them theological. She has a talent for disguising herself, or so go the stories. She has been a grandmother in a wheelchair once to test a church's handicapped accommodations.

Whitlow Mountain, or Whit for short, is older than all of them, and a retired pastor. Alterman hired him to give the firm a little more credibility in the face of its rather spectacular publicity. That didn't keep Whit from jamming the radio frequency of listening devices for the hearing impaired at one church to see how long it would take the staff to sniff out the problem.

The stories are repeated endlessly in the industry and to the ends of the Christian world. Alterman once lived as a homeless man for two weeks to test whether a church's outreach program was delivering adequate care in winter. He was later treated for frostbite, word had it, but was sent home after doctors determined he was *always* that cold.

Templeton joined a church and impersonated an out-of-tune choir member until the music director took him gently aside to ask if he could perhaps play an instrument. The same music director got a raise after Templeton rendered his verdict in the church's report, and Templeton in the process learned how to play the piccolo.

There is an apocryphal story that Alterman and Templeton once infiltrated a church's marriage counseling ministry as husband and wife with one of them in drag - the details were vague about which one - to see if the ministry had unrealistic expectations about putting couples back together. Most doubted this story simply because neither man could plausibly pass for a woman. But the tale has enough recognizable truth in it to be endlessly repeated. They have neither confirmed nor denied that they occasionally contract a dwarf to spy on some preschool and nursery ministries.

They sabotage sound systems during services to see if the pastor can be heard in the balcony. They surreptitiously commission senior adult field trips just to confirm if the buses work properly. They bug the teen services to find the young adult worshippers ripping the youth minister in unchurched language when he leaves the room. One operative memorably impersonated a drunk visitor to test not only the quality of a church's security, but its alcohol counseling ministry. They earned the ire of another church when they recommended it start a fitness program after correctly estimating the weight of its deacons. One of them got a concussion during a family roller skating night trying to thoroughly ascertain if the place had a reliable first aid kit. Alterman himself denies the story that he faked a kitchen fire to see if a particular church's volunteers knew where the extinguishers were. "I did it because I wanted to see if the sprinkler system worked," he corrects. "Besides, the exits weren't clearly marked. And the fire wasn't faked. But it wasn't that big anyway."

In the process, they make churches dust corners and clean cobwebs in areas where worshippers haven't gone since bricks and mortar were thrown up. They savage worship centers with fading parking stripes and rickety basketball hoops. They thumb through pew Bibles looking for missing pages and count the used chewing gum accumulating under those pews like stalactites. They count points off for churches that put pithy messages on their marquees without bothering to check the spelling, or the theology.

And as a result of all that manic nitpicking, they have streamlined services and staffs and harnessed spiraling budgets and reintroduced churches to the communities they had supposed they were still catering to. They have broken ancient cliques in churches where young pastors went to watch powerless as their careers died. They have *probably* prevented more church splits than they inspired. Alterman brags that they have bruised and bullied and inevitably bettered scores of churches of different denominations into remembering Who they serve and what they believe.

The legends inevitably collide with reality when Alterman brings his show to a church, but occasionally the people who call him come away thinking the stories go too soft on him. Alterman's answer is typical. "Jesus is described as carrying His winnowing fork in his hand, cleansing the threshing floor," he says. "Does that sound like a pleasant experience?"

3

"This can't go on forever!"

Ingersoll does not recognize the man shouting at him behind the glass doors, pounding to get in.

"Don't you read your Bible!" answers the woman inside, unintimidated by him. "The *Church* goes on forever! We'll be here to welcome Christ when He walks through this door!" This is Rita, a 55-year-old widow who, up until the appearance of the man at the church door, had been halfway through a paperback romance novel. Rita stands in a jogging suit and sneakers and has drawn all of her five-foot-two-inch frame up to the height of the man on the other side of the glass, who is at least a foot taller. From the way the man is dressed, Ingersoll is sure he is a priest of some kind, but he doesn't recognize him. This guy must be new.

Ingersoll is standing next to Rita in the foyer of St. Sossius Catholic Church, which survives in its corner of the city, as it has for 120 years, despite the influx of immigrants at the beginning of the twentieth century and the ongoing decay of the urban area around it. Three years ago, the archdiocese ordered the church to close because of dropping attendance, financial problems among its sister churches, and the after-effects of a clerical abuse scandal elsewhere. The members of St. Sossius, most of them middle-aged or elderly, immediately began a siege to keep it open. After Alterman read about it on the Internet, he dispatched Ingersoll there to help.

As he faces down the screaming man through the door, a smirking Ingersoll is wearing a T-shirt that reads, "Behold, I stand at the door and knock."

Ingersoll's original mission was to stay for only a few weeks and render assistance. But within a month he began renting an apartment here where he keeps his clothes and receives his mail. The bulk of his living has been here, among the militant members of St. Sossius, like Rita. At night, he and other members of the church stand guard, lest some official from the archdiocese comes to padlock the doors and end the church's ministry.

Within a day of arriving, some 1,742 days before, Ingersoll saw why Alterman had dispatched him there. It was obvious - a church whose members were adamant that it stay open, so adamant that they set up cots and took shifts to occupy the church, raised money to keep its lights on and became so vocal that membership increased. It was only when the threat of the church's disappearance became real for its members that its members awakened, as if from a long, terminal slumber, and seized control.

The devotion at some services reminds Ingersoll of things he has seen in clapboard churches in the rural South. The situation seized Ingersoll's imagination, and he wasn't content to simply help plan their strategy and leave town. Ingersoll flies in wherever he is needed because he has something invested in St. Sossius, though he isn't exactly sure what it is.

Ingersoll has long suspected that Alterman sent him here, knowing how the young man would react. That was just the sort of perversely right thing Ingersoll expects from his boss. Alterman probably searched the whole world for just the right church with members willing to die to keep it open. Luckily he didn't have to leave the country.

Rita looks as though the glass is the only thing keeping her from attacking this latest man to come and challenge them. They've seen lawyers, policemen, reporters, all kinds. They know better than to allow anyone in at night, unless that person is a member who has signed up to sit. There was a wrecking ball crew that showed up once to chase them away, but the members correctly sniffed out that the archdiocese wasn't going to risk the effect of televised images of destruction, lest someone get injured.

This latest comer walks away, still miffed at Rita's promise of infinite vigilance.

"I ain't scared of him," she says, still looking at the man as he eyes her over his shoulder, walking away into the night's darkness. She adjusts her sweatshirt as though she's thrown a punch. "I'm not letting this place go! It isn't sick. It isn't dying. *It's alive!*" The words are just as inspiring to Ingersoll now as they were the first 150 times he heard them.

Ingersoll is surprised at the ease with which the man is dispatched. It reminds him of the church's namesake - Sossius, a 30-year-old deacon of Misenum, who was martyred in 305 A.D. during the Diocletian persecutions. Arrested as a Christian, he was sent to be killed by wild bears in the amphitheater at Pozzuoli on the Italian coast. Instead, the animals fell at his feet and refused to harm him. He and others were later beheaded near the volcanic vents of Mt. Vesuvius, the air alive with sulfur as they were gathered to their fathers.

"There's been more of them lately," Ingersoll says.

"Yeah," Rita says, like a cop on a beat noticing an uptick in robberies in her precinct. "They really want this place to go."

"They've got a lot invested here," Ingersoll says.

"It belongs to us! Not them!" Rita then rolls her eyes, crosses herself, and clears her throat. "It belongs to God! They didn't care about it until they thought they could make a buck off it! And it galls them that they snapped their fingers and we didn't have the decency to just let it die!"

Ingersoll pauses for a second, before he says, "You know, he's right. This can't go on forever."

"What do you know? You're not even a member here, Bobby!" Ingersoll expects this observation, as it is true. He has never joined. He isn't even Catholic. It took him awhile to overcome the suspicions of others. The priest knew Alterman and could vouch for Ingersoll's reliability.

"Rita, how long have I been here with you?"

"I know," she says, but her demeanor is like a mother disappointed in her son. *I expected better from you*, she seems to be saying with her eyes. "But if you don't believe in what we're doing here…"

"I'm here, Rita. I wouldn't be if I didn't believe."

"Still, if it gets too hot for you, I can unlock that door and you can just go back where you came from."

"And leave you here alone, Rita?" He pauses, and smirks. "I couldn't do that to that guy, if he comes back. You're liable to kill him."

She laughs. "Smart boy." Her hand goes up to muss his hair.

That's when Ingersoll's phone buzzes within his jacket pocket. He checks the screen and sees the text message from Alterman. Once his shift is over, Ingersoll will have to catch a plane. He quickly texts back a response, just before the lights go out.

"What now?" Rita says.

"That's probably the guy who was just here. He shut the power off."

"How did he do that?"

"I think that's what he was trying to tell you. They've got a court order."

"But we paid the bill!"

"Maybe the court ruled it's their power to cut."

"It's not *their* power!" Rita's hands go up, as if she expects to receive tongues of flame from the empty air. "What now?"

Ingersoll pats her shoulder. "Listen, go up to the sanctuary. Let me see what I can do."

"What are you going to do?"

"Get the power on."

"What am I supposed to do up there?" Rita asks.

"Pray," he says, smiling.

Thankfully, she starts up the red carpeted steps to the altar on the floor above them. Her lips are already moving silently.

Ingersoll takes out his phone again and looks for the programmed number. He had assumed this would happen one night, so he began preparing months before. That was something he learned from Alterman. The will of God operates in the residue of preparation.

The number dialed, Ingersoll waits for the answer.

"Marty," Ingersoll says. "I need that favor."

"Already? I thought it wouldn't be so soon."

"Yeah, I think they got the judge they were looking for."

"That's no problem."

"You think you can do something?"

"Sure. We can keep them on until your lawyer wakes up in the morning."

"Not too much trouble?"

The lights, as if in answer, blink on again. Through the glass door, Ingersoll can hear a shout of astonishment. He is fairly confident Rita is upstairs weeping.

"You got any other problems?" asks Marty, who was baptized at St. Sossius when he was fourteen years old.

Alterman taught Ingersoll to always ask, whenever meeting anyone even for a few minutes, if they went to church and, if so, where. There's always an opportunity, even if the person is an irregular attendee who is ambivalent about the leadership of the archdiocese.

"So, will I see you in church Sunday?" Ingersoll asks.

"Thinking about it."

"Stop thinking about it and just come," Ingersoll says. "We'll leave the light on for you."

4

"I'm Cherie LeFevere, and you're in big trouble." He hears the words as he enters the room, and his attention is automatically focused on the woman. She is tiny; perhaps not even five feet tall. She is sitting down though, which makes her look even smaller somehow. Her voice is anachronistically sweet. It takes him a moment to register just what she is saying, and the fact that he should be offended, even as she gestures toward a chair for him. She is behind a desk, but it makes her look like a grade-schooler, and he is sure her feet are not touching the floor.

He winces as he closes the door, at first wondering if he is in the right room. "Well, it's nice to meet you too, ma'am. And just what trouble would that be?"

"I think you know why I'm here." Her voice is mildly pleasant - so much so he doesn't feel threatened.

"Well, why don't you inform me? Just as a matter of courtesy. I have to tell you, I'm not used to being talked to like this."

"I'm sure you're not. But just so you don't think I'm picking on you, mind if I ask you a few questions?" That voice again. He sits down because he's sure she's joking.

She glances down at a clutch of papers but doesn't seem to need them. "You are the Rev. Walter Naismith, is that correct?"

"Yes."

"And you have been, for the past 22 years, the pastor of Everlasting, a church with about 2,500 members."

"We prefer to call Everlasting a community ministry, but that's correct."

"So it's not a church?"

"It *is* a church, though not in the traditional mold."

"So you're *not* a pastor?"

"Yes, it is a church, and I am its pastor. What I mean to say is that we have such a wide range of activities, calling it a church is rather limiting."

"I see. And is one of those ministries your church basketball team?"

"Yes. Yes it is. The Everlasting Praise." He is proud, and he tries not to smile and fails. The problem is that he can see himself in a mirror behind her.

"I thought so. This would be the same Everlasting Praise that has won the Metropolitan United Gospel League championship for the past eight years? What they call the MUG, is that right?"

"Nine. Nine years. Yes, we're awfully proud of them."

"And this would be one of your players, right?" She holds up a picture of a tall, thin man with close cropped hair, in his early-thirties. "That would be Frederick Davis?"

"Yes. Yes. Brother Fred is our junior associate pastor. We just got him last year. Great jump shot."

"That's what I heard." She smiles, even as she glances down to read a text message. "Now, the reason I've called you here is because a few of the teams that take part in the MUG have raised some questions about Mr. Davis and his position in your church. Never mind where the accusations came from. That's not the issue right now." Her voice is reassuring, though he can't tell whether he is perceiving something or imagining it.

"Well, I can vouch for him myself. He's a very gifted man of God."

"I'm sure he is. But let me just run you through some of the complaints that were brought to our attention."

He lifts a hand to stop her. "Just a moment, Miss..."

"LeFevere."

He continues to smile, more out of politeness than any genuine impulse. "Just what exactly is your position in this? And who is *we?*"

"I was asked by the MUG to investigate this matter."

"Asked?"

"They asked me to."

"This was never brought before the board."

"That's correct."

"Then who hired you?"

She looks down at the page again and smiles. "Could I go over some of these charges with you first? I'll be glad to answer any questions you have."

"Well, I'm just being accused here, and..."

Her voice is easy and cheerful. "Are you aware that your church is known in the metro area as 'that church that always has the tall associate pastor?'"

He smiles, nodding.

"Just a quick check finds that in the last seven years, your church has hired four junior associate pastors, all of whom are at least six feet six inches in height with backgrounds in basketball?"

"Yes."

"And, as I'm sure you know, the MUG was formed ten years ago from church leagues in the metro area for church competition?"

He nodded again.

"And that the winner of the MUG championship gets a portion of the proceeds for use in its mission activities. Is that right?"

"The Lord has blessed us with very talented young men."

"That's true. Your previous junior associate pastors - Mr. Benedict, Mr. Mitchell, Mr. Jordan - they were all closer to seven feet tall. And their stays on your staff were relatively short."

"That's correct. They went on to other opportunities."

"Yes, I believe Mr. Benedict has left the ministry and now plays professional basketball in Italy?"

"I got a card from him a week ago. I think he's putting on weight over there. All that pasta. *Molto bello.*"

"Do you have any explanation for why you have such turnaround of ministers, especially when they're tall?"

"Would you believe that our church has very low ceilings?" He shifts in his chair and unbuttons his coat, glancing to see if she has taken his joke. She has not. Her face hasn't changed. A questioning look, almost childlike, and hard to inspire anger. But he feels angry, though he doesn't want to admit why. He tries not to look in the mirror for fear of what he might see.

"Now, as I understand it, Mr. Davis, Mr. Benedict, Mr. Mitchell, Mr. Jordan, all were graduates of one seminary?"

He clears his throat. "Were they?"

"You hired them, didn't you?"

"Yes, well, the church board did."

"But you were there during the decision making?"

"Well, yes."

"And that seminary would be Lake Perla Theological Institute, based in Kuhn, Kentucky?" She wants to sound as though she is reading the words, but she has obviously memorized them.

"If you say so."

"Rev. Naismith, would you be interested in knowing that there is no Lake Perla Theological Institute, based in Kuhn, Kentucky?"

Naismith registers a certain amount of shock, but he doesn't overdo it. "There isn't?"

"No. There's a website that hasn't been updated in several months that you can find by doing a search, but strangely enough, no admissions information is available for anyone who might be interested in applying."

"That so?"

"There's not even any mention of a basketball team on that website."

"Well, how do you know this place you mentioned doesn't exist?"

"For starters, there's no Lake Perla listed on any maps of the state of Kentucky. No theological institute listed on any educational registry with any of the major or minor American denominations. There's no Lake Perla listed among any accreditation organizations.

And finally, no Lake Perla Theological Institute in Kuhn, Kentucky. I know that because I drove there and walked every inch of it."

"You did?"

"Yes. There's a very nice gas station there and a fruit stand on warmer days. Not even a blinking light."

"That so..."

"Yes, and you'll also be interested to know, if you didn't already, that Mr. Davis, Mr. Benedict, Mr. Mitchell and Mr. Jordan all were standout athletes on their college basketball teams who, as far as I was able to learn, never exhibited even the slightly ambition toward the ministry. They did not, however, have the ability to rise to the professional ranks automatically."

"The call comes on us all rather suddenly."

"Yes it does. Which is why you may get a call yourself from the MUG, especially in light of this." She holds up a piece of paper.

"What's that supposed to be?"

"Well, it's just confirmation that the website for the Lake Perla Theological Institute was created on a computer that, I believe, is attached to the network of Everlasting Community Ministry. Wouldn't happen to be yours, would it?"

He smiles reflexively. "Miss LeFevere, this isn't the first time I've heard allegations of this sort..."

"I know. That's why I'm here. I've spent the last four months researching this."

"Four..."

"You see, Mr. Wilcox, the MUG commissioner, asked me without the board's knowledge, since he knew that three of the churches on the MUG board are former satellite congregations of your church. So it was assumed they would vote along with you against any investigation. And he wanted to handle this discreetly."

"That's a lie! Henry Wilcox would never do something like this behind my back."

The door opens, and Henry Wilcox enters the room. It occurs to Naismith that the mirror behind Miss LeFevere was a window, like in those cop shows. So technically, whatever he's been doing has been behind her back.

"What is the meaning of this?" Naismith asks.

Wilcox, the man Naismith has silently insulted for years with mock courtesies to his commissioner's office, the same office Naismith secured for him, is smiling. He looks, for the first time in a good while, satisfied. "I got you, Walter. I finally got you."

Now Naismith drops all pretenses, since there is nothing left that he can hide behind. He is appalled by the sadism of this, and he knows that Wilcox is not responsible for it. "I should have known you'd never do as you're told!" He stands up to face Wilcox, whom he expects to shrink away. But Wilcox doesn't. He is emboldened. So Naismith points to the desk. "To bring this girl in! What are you? Some high school newspaper investigative reporter?"

"I'm twenty-seven, and I investigate this sort of thing all the time. You don't think you're the only congregation that cheats at church league sports?"

Wilcox cannot hide his satisfaction. He gestures toward her as though she is a new car. "She cracked the Texas church volleyball steroid ring. We called her in because we were tired of looking the other way. We were afraid you'd find some ex-NBA player trying to rehabilitate his image by 'going into the ministry.'" His fingers supply the scare quotes.

"But think of what we did with that money! How much did it cost you to bring her in to find this out?"

"Nothing," she volunteers. "He offered. I told him I wouldn't take a cent. Not even for expenses." The satisfaction in her voice is unmistakable, as is the relish.

5

Whitlow Mountain sits in the back of the church. He always sits in the back, right corner, occupying the last portion on the pew as though he will be charged a fee for every square inch he occupies. No amount of coaxing from Alterman will ever convince him there is a better place to see the whole of a church.

At the altar, Father Livingstone Abayami is heading into the peroration of his homily. His sermon has lasted perhaps seven minutes. Whit is timing him, making a few notes for later. He doesn't intend on counting off though. Livingstone has paused in a few places in the sermon to make sure his congregation understands his careful Nigerian accent.

Father Abayami is Whit's special project, and he has been coming here to southwest Texas for almost a month to assist him. Tomorrow will be the Father's six-month anniversary at the church.

Whit came as a favor to Dietrich, the priest overseeing Father Abayami's entrance into the community. Father Abayami is just one of a few African priests the church has brought to America to minister at churches where priests are in short supply. His command of French, Italian, and his native dialect does him no good here. He had been a priest to twelve different congregations in his homeland, leading as many as four at the same time, but here in America, he is struggling leading one church with 700 members and a budget of several million dollars. Dietrich isn't worried that Father Abayami is in over his head - he knows Livingstone is a tremendous preacher and a good administrator.

But his brand of the faith is different from his flock's. He is the only black man in the congregation. He has a hard time ministering to people without a job in America because he doesn't think of them as poor, given what he has seen in his homeland. Dietrich senses his congregation wants to love him, but Livingstone is too remote for them to fully embrace. This American style of worship - where one needs to be gentle in places where Livingstone is used to force, and vice versa - is eluding him.

"It reminds me of a story," Abayami says from the altar. Whit feels himself tightening up as his African pupil begins the joke Whit rehearsed with him the previous night. It had literally taken two hours to teach him this. Not the joke itself, and not just how to tell it, but why he should.

"I don't understand this," Livingstone said, the day before, when they had been practicing.

"The joke?"

"No. I don't understand why all this is necessary."

"Tell me what you mean," Whit said. He is used to teaching young ministers this way. Let them get it out of their system.

"I've been a priest for fifteen years. People used to walk half a day to hear the Gospel preached. I held their attention for three hours once. And here, I get angry letters from a woman who doesn't want to struggle with her children through a sermon that's more than ten minutes long!"

The words made Whit smile. They remind him of the tent revivals of his youth, when cars would whiz by on the highway and his mother would pat the sweat from his forehead while his father taxed his voice to its outer limits, warning of a hellfire so imminent that Whit had to remind himself he had been baptized twice already by the age of ten.

"Part of that is the American lifestyle," Whit said. "People are used to things in a hurry."

"Yes, but it doesn't make any sense! People are in a hurry, but they don't seem to want anything more than a joke and a verse of Scripture. We used to *heal* people at our services!'"

Yes, that too reminds Whit of his childhood, in so many ways. His father, with his left hand on the forehead of a woman trembling under the weight of some sickness, his right hand in the air alive to the hoped-for stirring of the Holy Spirit. And here was this man from Africa, come to tell him that such a thing was still going on in the world. And in Africa! The home of Whit's people! When he was that boy in the tent, he heard heroic tales of missionaries across the sea, in villages with exotic names full of people hungry for the story of Jesus.

And now, that part of the world is sending men back to the place where those missionaries of old came from.

And they are being sent to tell jokes.

"And I have seen women give all the money they have to God with tears in their eyes. Here, we are not meeting our weekly goal for offerings. But I can't get these people to give by simply preaching the Gospel. How am I going to make them write a check by telling a joke?"

"I know it doesn't make any sense," Whit finally said to him. "It's like that other joke, why are people quiet in church?" He paused. "So …you won't wake up anybody."

Father Abayami did not smile. He didn't get it.

"Liv, you say you've been a priest for 15 years. And English isn't your native language, is it?"

"That is correct."

"Do you feel like you're compromising when you speak English?"

"No. That is presently the language of my flock."

"Then, this is part of their language."

Abayami pauses from the pulpit, as Whit watches. The priest is visibly trying to remember all that Whit told him the night before, about timing and pacing.

"There is a story about a priest who was trying to remind his congregation about what the church needed," Abayami says. "So he got up on Sunday morning, and he say, 'My people, I have good news. And I have bad news. The good news is that there is more than enough money to pay for what this church needs."

The pause that follows feels enormous, but Whit feels the tingle in the air. The congregation anticipates a punch line.

"The bad news, my friends, is that the money is unfortunately still out there, in your pockets."

The laugh that follows is loud and sustained. Whit studies Father Abayami's face, and the man grins a broad, generous, grateful smile. Whit can see the humility in his features, and the relief that seems to flood him. He can even see a few people reaching for their wallets and purses.

Whit feels the phone within his coat vibrate. It's probably Alterman. It's been awhile since he last heard from him.

What was it he had said to the Nigerian, just before he left him that night, just before they had prayer?

"Liv, why did you come here?"

"Because I thought this is where God wanted me to be."

"You wonder about that?"

"I suppose that here, I am tending to a garden. Over there, I was planting seeds."

"No, you're planting here too. The soil is kind of...weird, over here."

Father Abayami smiled. That word, *weird*, seemed to fit.

"You remind me of my old bishop," Abayami said. "He always had answers for everything."

"That's funny," Whit said. "You remind me of my father. I don't think he would have been very comfortable in this time. He was just like you. He was a maniac for the Lord."

"With a love so great, who would not be a...a maniac, did you say?"

Whit thinks to himself - perhaps when he is through with Alterman, he might make a trip to Africa himself. That is, if he ever feels better again. Do a bit of preaching like he used to. See what it's like, going off into a strange country with a word older than time itself. He hasn't preached a sermon since Gilda died, those seven years ago.

No, he can't do that. It's not safe to let Alterman go at it without him.

6

The morning meeting usually occurs at Templeton's house. There are several reasons for this. Alterman is cheap, and his staff believes this is due to his Wall Street background. But his frugality is only exceeded by his paranoia. Alterman would never trust having an office, either for fears of retaliation or espionage.

Templeton lives in a two-story house that he never could have afforded as a pastor. His wife Sharon has prepared a light breakfast of muffins that none of the men will touch, especially Alterman. Alterman fasts once a week. Sharon looks like a housewife in her warm hospitality sweater but anxiously clutches a cellphone in her right hand. If she doesn't hear from the couple who are due at closing that afternoon, she cannot continue to fantasize about what she will be spending her realty commission on. Her tenacity is one of the reasons she has occasionally been a mystery worshipper for the firm on commission. She even crossed a line once by handing out tracts at a busy intersection when one of the members of the church they were auditing collapsed from heat exhaustion. Alterman was impressed.

By snapping open his black binder, Alterman signals he is ready to begin. Whit clears his throat, and that is the reminder that they should open the meeting with prayer. Alterman never seems to remember this. "That's why I keep you around," he usually says to

Whit, though Whit has decided long before that Alterman does this on purpose. A healthy silence follows the "Amen."

Alterman asks Templeton what's in the mailbag by the hand-me-down stand-up piano in the corner. Templeton announces it's "fan mail" from his former church. Members still loyal to him who heard about what they have been calling "The Sting" have written, begging him to come back. "But I'm not even thinking about it," Templeton says, with a wave of his hand. He will not reveal to Alterman, unless asked, that he wrote a letter to the present pastor apologizing for what happened. Alterman does not ask. He seems to have already moved on to their next commission.

"What are you working on?" Alterman asks Ingersoll.

Ingersoll is not dressed for work. He is unshaven and wearing a dirty ballcap. His green T-shirt reads, in yellow letters, "You have been weighed in the balances, and are found wanting." His glasses reveal smudged lenses when he moves into the light a certain way. He still looks like a college student eyeing a box of cold pizza for breakfast after a night of cramming. He is a contrast with Cherie, who has on a classic fifties-style skirt and sweater combination that simultaneously makes her look older and almost like a schoolgirl. She takes a prim bite of a blueberry muffin and immediately looks for crumbs that might have slipped from her lips.

"Same thing as always," Ingersoll says. "You had me asking about Wydgate. By what I can tell from his returns, he made about $125,000 in profit last year, after taxes."

"Was that Wydgate's cut, or total?"

"Total, but he's the only employee," Ingersoll says. "I don't quite know what his salary is. Might be better than ours." A scamp's grin flashes over Ingersoll's face, as though he might polish his resume for a bigger paycheck. His eyes glide across Alterman's face and he quickly changes to a humorless look that correctly mirrors his boss. "Anyway, Wydgate wouldn't put that information out there, so I'm doing a little checking."

"Think you'll find out?"

"What makes you think I can't?"

"What's this about?" Templeton asks. "Why have you got Bobby doing corporate espionage? Why do you care what Wydgate's making?" Wydgate, of course, is John Patrick Wydgate III, the founder and president of their main competition in the mystery worshipper industry. Wydgate has made inroads into the lucrative Cumberland Presbyterian market, where Alterman hasn't yet been able to make any headway. Wydgate claims Alterman has spread the rumor that he's Unitarian. Alterman has no comment.

Alterman sighs heavily. "Turns out that he made an offer."

"Offer?" Templeton says.

"Wydgate offered to buy us out."

Whit, silent up to this point, whistled at the news and took a sip of his coffee.

"When?"

"Sent me an e-mail about a week ago. Said he wanted to talk to me about maybe consolidating our businesses. I'm not stupid. I know what that means."

"What, pray tell?" Templeton says, with a mocking smile.

"Oh, he'll make a big show, pay some money, and then he'll run us all off one at a time. Or he'll run me off and keep you jokers. That is, after he's taught you some manners."

"How much did he offer?" Templeton asks.

"What do you care?" Alterman demands.

"Just curious. Didn't mean anything. I'm loyal to you, *Sensei*."

"What about the rest of you?" Alterman asks. This is his obligatory poke for another undying pledge of loyalty.

"You think I'd want to work for Wydgate?" Cherie asks. "He has long nose hairs. You ever seen him up close? You want to just pull them out one by one, but you'd have to touch them to do it. Ewwwwwh!" Cherie squeals at the idea, like a high school anatomy student confronted with her first dissection worm.

"I work for you, Bossman," Whit says. *Bossman* is his usual term for Alterman, though he has a way of saying it at times that sounds like a putdown, as he does now. It's also calculated to make Alterman feel uncomfortable, as it carries overtones of the plantation overseer. Whit seems to relish making Alterman uncomfortable. But Whit's tone of voice has more to do with his mood. Whit hasn't been feeling well for some time, and it's been going on long enough not to be just another bug. Whit probably thinks nobody else has noticed, but he won't say anything. They've got an audit coming up.

Alterman waits a moment to see what Ingersoll will say, but nothing comes. The boy didn't get enough sleep last night.

Alterman reaches down, pulls his ballcap off, and slaps him over the head with it. "I don't care what you think, Cool Breeze." He then carefully replaces the hat. "One thing, though, is we might have a new client."

"Who?" Whit asks, rubbing his hands together, as though he has had a muffin and needs to divest himself of crumbs.

"This is a good one," Alterman says, without smiling. Alterman never smiles.

The rest of the people in the room, including Sharon, wait for him to identify the client. He's enjoying their anticipation.

"Well?" Templeton asks, tiring.

"It's The Sweet Lightning Church."

Whit again whistles, only this time for a much longer moment.

"That's Thomas Everhart's church, isn't it?" Templeton says.

"Yep." Alterman mouths the simple reply as though Thomas Everhart hasn't written two nationally best-selling books despite his current station as the pastor of what might normally be an anonymous 1,250-member exurban church. Not big enough to be a megachurch. One of the many legends that follow Alterman everywhere he goes is that he does not like megachurches. Another is that he does not like churches.

"Where did the name come from?" Templeton asks, as though he has long wondered this.

"The church is located on Sweet Lighting Road. Evidently bootleggers used the highway during Prohibition to run liquor, and the name stuck. The church used to be Sweet Lightning Road Church."

"One of those 'stealth' Baptist churches?" asks Whit. This is a sensitive subject for Whit. When the group audits Baptist churches that drop their denominational identification in order to attract more worshippers, Alterman has to make sure Whit doesn't deduct points.

"Actually, it's nondenominational. It's been that way since Everhart started it."

Nobody in the room needs to be told who Everhart is. His tanned, dimpled chin has jutted from the covers of several popular Christian issue magazines, along with his pristine wife and three pristine children. People are usually shocked to learn he is almost fifty years old. He was asked to deliver an opening prayer at a political convention. His two books have been an elegantly told autobiography that has sold well over a million copies and a recently-released self-help book that gives its readers a month-long course of devotions and Scripture readings. It is even now flying out of stores, garnering mention on talk shows and being brandished at leadership seminars. In the interests of modesty, Everhart recently had to refute a story that the President of the United States called him for advice and support. In Templeton's car is an audio copy of the pastor's autobiography, read by the author in a generous, deep, conversational voice. He is one of those remote personalities who somehow generate a satisfying scent, drawing casual strangers toward him.

"Anything in particular that they want us to do?" Cherie asks.

"The whole treatment."

"Yes!" Ingersoll says, rubbing his hands together. "Bonus money!"

"I wonder why he's hiring us?"

"Don't know. I'm supposed to go visit him sometime next week," Alterman says.

"What do you think?" Ingersoll asks. Now he's rubbing his hands together, as Whit did a moment before.

"He's probably angling for a bigger job," Whit says.

"That's what I thought," Alterman responds.

"Get a nice splash if we don't find anything," Whit says, waving his hand like a preacher making a point. "If we do, he can fix it. Then he moves on to a bigger church or something else. Speaking career. Consulting."

"Maybe he ends up doing *this*?" Ingersoll says. There's that grin again.

"No, we've already got one preacher too many on our staff," Alterman says, eying Whit.

"Right back at you, Ace," Whit says.

"Maybe we should look at this a bit less cynically," Templeton says. "He might just want to have a better grip on his church, you know?" Templeton is thinking about the book out in his car, and the impressions he has of Everhart. The voice he heard on the CD struck him as earnest and honest and Templeton suddenly feels protective of it. Just as suddenly, Templeton reminds himself that he needs objectivity if they're going to audit this guy. But he can't forget the voice.

"True. But we need to be sure before we step into something like this," Alterman says, clearing his throat. "Good thing we'll have another body."

"What?" Templeton says.

"I've got an interview this afternoon for another operative." Alterman calls the auditors *operatives*, as though they are spies. It's an affectation that makes Templeton occasionally roll his eyes.

Ingersoll shifts on the sofa. "You don't think we're doing enough?"

"No, on the contrary, you're all working very hard. You're doing *too* much."

"I don't think the work has suffered any," Cherie says, a little uneasily.

"People, nothing to worry about. We're not downsizing. We're upsizing."

Templeton, who is hearing all this for the first time, holds his tongue. Alterman formed the company. Templeton's a partner, but he knows who the boss is on these things. "Who is she?"

"She's Indian." Alterman reaches into his pocket and pulls out a piece of paper to read her name. "Rambha Jakkannavar."

"Gesundheit," Whit says.

"She's from Bangalore," Alterman says, ignoring the elder man. "Smart as a whip. Already talked to her on the phone a few times. Great record."

"What's she doing now?"

"She's fresh out of college."

"No experience. She must be *something*." Ingersoll's tone is wary, and everyone in the room can tell he is skeptical of this.

"What kind of experience, pray tell, do you think would make a person right for this job?" Alterman asks.

"I don't know," Ingersoll says.

"The Mafia," Cherie immediately chimes in, with her baby doll voice. There is a wave of suppressed laughter among them, except for Alterman. He winks at her.

7

"Good afternoon," she says, sitting down and shaking his hand in a gesture that looks calculated to expend the smallest amount of valuable seconds. Alterman doesn't even have time enough to get up from the table.

Alterman chose this particular restaurant because it is dark and he can sit and eat undetected. He is conscious of Wydgate even when his nemesis seems nowhere to be seen. There is no music and enough sonic peace in this place to conduct a job interview.

He is slightly surprised because Rambha Jakkannavar walks right up to his table and introduces herself. No preliminaries, no sideways glance, no hesitant question of his identity. She knows he is Alex Alterman and begins talking, as though they have spoken every day of their lives.

"I appreciate you giving me this opportunity," she says. "I have some definite ideas for this position and I realize you may feel you are taking a big risk in hiring me on - but I can assure you, you won't regret it because I will bring a great deal to this position."

She is carrying a large purse - the word that comes to mind is bag - that lands on the table, rattling the salt and pepper shakers together.

"I'm sorry - I carry a 20-pound weight in it - it helps with staying fit."

She speaks in dashes - just a quick, cursory intake of breath rather than a noticeable pause in-between sentences. Her words remind him, strangely enough, of telegraph sounds - she is modern. Her diction is slightly British and her conversation is manic and she sounds concerned that if she stops the flow of words, someone else's will intrude.

It quickly becomes apparent this is not a job interview. She already has the job, she appears to believe, already has plans for what she will do, and will occasionally solicit his appreciation.

She is quite beautiful. Alterman is smitten with her. Her hair is a lustrous black with dazzling curls. Her eyes are as black as stones collected from the ocean floor. If he did not know where she came from, he might be unable to tell what her nationality is. She is twenty-four, but her complexion and carriage make her one of those women who could be as young as their late twenties or in their forties. She wears a deep purple dress that reminds him of royalty. He can't decide whether she smells exotic or whether it's his imagination. He feels intoxicated, and slightly annoyed at himself.

He feels he is being played. Alterman always feels he is being played.

He is fascinated by her biography. She was born in India and educated in the UK. Her family has been Christian going back several generations. Upon immigrating to London, they were not fully accepted in British culture nor Indian culture because of their faith. That has made her an outsider for virtually all her life. Yet she can make herself home in any situation, she says. A lot of diligent prayer, she assures him, is why she has found her way to him.

"I am a member of one of the world's oldest Christian communities, Alex," she says, already adopting his first name. "The Apostle St. Thomas himself brought the Gospel to India and the Word took root there. There are more than 20 million Christians in India. Like him, our nation is still learning to overcome its doubts."

Alterman assures her that he's familiar with these facts, though she feels the need to elaborate for a few more minutes before moving on to the ideas she has. In seconds, her speech has lapsed into a learned American cadence, and he imagines that she sounds like her classmates in the graduate level theology courses she has been taking. He would like to ask her some questions, but he does not feel he will ever get the opportunity. And Alterman is afraid to do so, because it might expose his self-consciousness about never having taken theology courses. He hired Templeton and Whit so he might be surrounded by pastors and defer to them on such matters. He figures they sense his unease but they have never asked him about it, and he is grateful.

Rambha Jakkannavar, without realizing it, is frustrating Alterman's attempts to break into her monologue. She yawns even as she is talking, but the words do not pause. She explains that she was up late the night before, preparing to meet him. She begins a story about one of her classmates and then delivers a pitch perfect, absolutely believable impersonation of a person Alterman has never met. Rambha has probably never lived in an American inner city, but she can plausibly deliver the patois of someone who has spent her life there.

Alterman looks down at the card of questions he had scribbled out earlier. If she had wanted to, Rambha could have read them. Alterman's penmanship is impeccable. During meetings Alterman doodles on paper by drawing lines. The lines are so straight that one who didn't know Alterman would never believe he drew them without needing a ruler.

The first question, suggested by Whit, was what Bible verse best described her, or which one did she find herself trying to live by. He senses he will *never* find this out.

At first, Alterman doesn't think she is paying attention to him at all, but after a minute, he realizes that she perceives all too well what is going on. She senses that he is losing patience with her, and she is strategizing what she will begin talking about next. Just to test this theory, he very innocently moves his right index finger up to his temple and leaves it there for a second longer than normal. He could be scratching an itch, indicating a headache, or giving a stagy indication that he is thinking about something. Within a second, Rambha wants to know if he needs headache medication. She has her own.

So she *is* perceptive, he thinks. The other skills check out well. Her grades are awe-inspiring, and every instructor he has spoken with over the phone says she is something well beyond even the average overachieving student. There is something driving Rambha forward at great speed. Alterman remembers a comment from a professor - Rambha, for all her polish and intellect, is still emotionally quite childish and needs a taming that her studies have not yet given her.

But yet, there is her continuing monologue, closing in on twenty-five minutes by the time the food arrives. And still, she does not let up. She is obviously self-motivated, obviously ambitious, obviously intelligent and capable of intimidating anyone who gets in her way. Taming her might be a stretch, but he has something in mind for her, especially on this new client.

Then she takes a breath. The silence startles Alterman so much that he forgets to jump in, which is his downfall. The breath Rambha takes is only to fortify herself for what is about to come.

"But I really feel that it's imperative that I work with you, because what you are doing really speaks to me," she says, putting her hand up to her neck to indicate how close the idea of work is already intruding on her person. "I mean, I am in awe of what you have accomplished and how you've done it. You wake up one morning and stagger into the shower and you wonder if this is how you want to spend the rest of your life. After all, it is the only life that God will ever give you.

"I mean, I remember thinking about that one night. I was alone. It was the end of the day and I was about to do something and I happened to look out the window of my apartment and I could see the sun setting. It was a breathtaking sight. And what I thought of then was that it would never again be that particular day, and that particular hour, and when it was gone it would never come back again. And I felt like a fool because I started weeping, like I was mourning the death of someone from my family. And all I was mourning was this lost hour, this day that was ending. It did not seem fair. I know I am not the first person who ever had this feeling, but it felt like I was. And I wanted to go out into the street and shake everyone into their senses! 'Don't waste this!' I wanted to tell them.

"But Alex, you seem like such a perfect person to work for, and I have a good feeling about you to start off with, so that's good. But anyway, back to the sunset. When I quit crying, I told myself that I wasn't going to have that same feeling. I was going to do something. Something memorable. Drastic if I had to. And so, after much prayer, I am here."

Rambha gestures her fingers out, as if to indicate that she is at the endpoint of her long spiritual and conversational journey. Indeed, she pauses long enough to take several breaths, as though she had exhausted her stories, both about herself and others, and is ready to begin this career she has sought with the rays of a dying sun.

"So let me ask," she at last begins, "do you have any questions?"

Alterman figures she is the sort who would respond to a challenge, even an insulting one.

"Yes," Alterman says. "Can you be quiet for extended periods of time?"

"Within reason."

8

It is a week later. Alterman catches an early morning flight to Florida and rents a car to make the short drive to Thomas Everhart's church. The sight of it takes his breath away.

The highway Alterman follows bends along the coast until Sweet Lightning Church rises, unmistakable from a distance, like one of the high-rise resort condos that line the white sand beaches about a mile or two down the road on the coastal highway. It would be impossible for vacationers to ride past this building without knowing it is a church. Sweet Lightning is charmingly traditional in appearance - red brick with white columns, white steeple, stained glass with no images but moody colors that play in the light like a kaleidoscope as the sun rises and sets.

Alterman chose this particular day to come because he knew it would inconvenience Everhart. A little research revealed that this day, a Saturday, is Sweet Lightning's quarterly volunteer clean-up day. It gives Alterman a chance to see how diligent the congregation is, as well as its pastor. Sweet Lightning Church began in Thomas Everhart's living room almost a decade before, his first member the man who came to fix his plumbing. Everhart had no way of knowing the man had only just been paroled from prison on a murder conviction six months earlier. The church quickly grew on the hushed information that it would accept virtually anyone.

Getting out of his car, Alterman glances toward the road. A woman is standing across the street, shouting something he can't quite make out. She is a street preacher, hoisting a Bible at passing cars, straining to be heard. He waves at her, and waits for her to wave back. Then he pauses to see if she will get any louder.

Everhart is found in the foyer. He is standing with one hand on his hip, explaining to a group of fortyish women where the new cleansers are kept in the utility closet. In his free hand, he holds a scrubbing brush. There is enough clean tile for Alterman to deduce that Everhart has been here since before sunrise. Everhart turns to see Alterman in his white shirt and blue coat with matching bowtie and decide Alterman is irregularly dressed enough to be someone worthy of his attention.

When Alterman is finally face-to-face with Thomas Everhart, he is impressed despite himself. People he has seen on book covers are almost always disappointing in the flesh. Their faces have been photoshopped into perpetual youth or an erroneous health that reality mocks.

Everhart needs a new photographer. His images didn't do him justice.

"Brother Everhart," Alterman says, adopting the title the women gave him. "I'm Alex Alterman. I spoke to you on the phone the other day." The two men shake hands. Everhart needs no additional information to call Alterman to mind.

"Oh yes," he smiles.

"You're not supposed to be here until Monday," says a voice nearby. It belongs to a chocolate skinned woman barely five feet tall. She is not dressed as someone who came to clean.

"Got into town early," Alterman says, looking at both the woman and Everhart. "Just thought I'd drop by. Wasn't sure if you'd be here."

"On cleanup day, this is where you'll find me," Everhart says. He indicates the woman standing by. "This is Keysha. She's my new administrative assistant. Just got hired." She reluctantly takes Alterman's hand. Keysha then looks uncertainly at a broom that is being handed to her by another member.

Everhart continues talking. "To tell you the truth, I wouldn't trust these tiles with just anybody." His voice becomes conspiratorial on the last bit, and he smirks at his own joke. Alterman does not. This is one of his tricks. Since pastors use humor to break the ice, he long ago decided not to laugh at any of these comments, unless what the man says is genuinely funny.

"Did you want to talk?" Everhart finally says.

"If you've got time…"

"Sure. Just as long as I can get back to this. You know, it's something I've been looking forward to for weeks."

Again, no laughter. Everhart swallows. He gestures for Alterman to follow him. The two men walk silently through the church, past other work details. A few of the youth are repainting a patch of wall near a doorway. Some seniors are moving a table near the receiving hall for the benefit of vacuuming. Alterman pays attention to the number of lights needing replacement bulbs.

Everhart's study is tasteful and unremarkable, except for the number of books behind his desk. The few titles Alterman can see are noticeable in that they are not theological or concordances. At least one title he can make out is "The Master and Margarita." Alterman's eyebrows go up.

"What brings you here, Mr. Alterman?" Everhart says, sitting down behind his desk. Alterman can catch a whiff of the man's cologne and a trace of sweat in the air.

"Please. You can call me Alex."

"I read your book. 'Judas Iscariot, CEO.'" Everhart says the words like the man giving the answer to a trivia question.

Alterman is simultaneously impressed, and terrified. He doubts the book is still available except through Internet firms that search for out-of-print books. And Alterman thought he had bought them all up. How many times has Alterman told his coworkers to read his book? It's all in the book, he says. Templeton claims to have read it twelve times.

Alterman tries to move on, unfazed. "I should congratulate you. You've accomplished a great deal in a short time. My partner is an admirer of yours."

"It's not my doing. The Lord has been very good to me. I just happened to write a book at the right time for people to notice. I never dreamed they would want another, and I never dreamed it would take off worse than the other."

"Worse?"

"Bigger I should say."

"Got another one in you?"

"Yes. Meditations on the Ninetieth Psalm. The only one written by Moses."

"You have set our iniquities before you," Alterman intones, "our secret sins in the light of your presence."

After another moment of silence that borders just on the fringes of uncomfortable, Alterman speaks. "Well, you asked why I'm here. I would have thought you probably guessed why."

"I wouldn't be much of a pastor if I didn't at least know who you are. So I take it you're here to evaluate my church?"

Alterman looks Everhart over skeptically.

"I mean, our church. I say mine because I belong to it, not to imply ownership. I hope I don't get a point off on the final grade."

"Not to worry."

"Just what exactly is it that you do? I've heard explanations from those who have been through the process. I've also talked to the ones who wouldn't recommend it."

"We don't do the same thing every time. It depends on what we're asked to do. And we've never gone somewhere that we weren't invited."

"One pastor I talked to said Satan can say the same thing."

Alterman nods in admiration of the verdict, then ignores it. "There's the full treatment. We sit in on virtually every ministry you offer. Services, special events, outreaches, music, missions, benevolence. Even funerals. Or we can simply look over one aspect and see how you might be doing it better."

"I talked to one colleague who said there's no question that you made him a better pastor."

"I'm flattered."

"He also said that he needed counseling every day for six months after your visit. Said he felt like he'd wrestled with a fallen angel."

Hmmm. That would look good in an Internet pop-up ad, Alterman thinks. "You know what they say. God breaks you to make you."

"You've broken a lot of things, from what I've heard."

"I'd like to think they were clean breaks that were needed."

"But what about what some others say? That you're intentionally cruel, unrealistic, sneaky, tactless, mean-spirited, theologically shallow... Is all that necessary? From what I hear, you seem to enjoy your job a great deal."

"I do. But not necessarily as a way to 'break people.' For every story you've heard, I can show you the actual cases. You probably wouldn't think it so judgmental or intrusive."

As Alterman says the words, a spiel similar to others he's given in response to similar attacks, he feels the antennae of suspicion rising within his head. Surely Everhart knew he was coming, enough to check ahead. Even going so far as to read his book. But what is he afraid of? Usually pastors aren't nearly this belligerent in the beginning. It's only after they've had the report that they get this way. I wonder what he's nervous about, Alterman thinks.

He's hiding something.

Everhart opens his mouth to speak, but Alterman isn't finished. "We're not against you. We believe in the mission of the church. Not every church has the same mission. But every church should expect results. If people want us to be easy on them, they shouldn't ask us to look over everything and expect to enjoy all our conclusions. Jesus didn't say, 'Be perfect, but I'm not really not all that serious about it.'"

"Is that why you sometimes wear a bulletproof vest, like you are now?"

Alterman, who suddenly realizes he's sweating, shakes his head. Alterman never smiles, and for good reason. It's unconvincing. "This is a heavy coat. I'm used to colder weather."

"One of the pastors I talked to said that if you were a mystery patient in a hospital, you'd break your own leg to make sure your facts were right. Or you'd inject yourself with anthrax."

"Of course. The Lord could heal the sick. I don't have that option. I have to diagnose."

"I am curious about something, if you'll indulge me."

"Go ahead."

"What's the Biblical basis for your work?"

Alterman nods. He has heard this before, especially after the time Templeton and he faked an outbreak of cholera in a small town to expose a fraudulent faith healer. "You're familiar with Jesus' parable of the unscrupulous servant?"

"Yes. Luke 16:8." Everhart smiles, as though admiring a well-played card in a poker game.

"'The children of this world are in their generation wiser than the children of light.' Worldly people, dealing with worldly cares, are often more scrupulous about details than people called by the Lord. They say half the adults in America have switched denominations in their lifetimes, sometimes several times. There are more unaffiliated believers now than in memory. People are more fickle and more mobile. They don't care about the sermon sometimes as much as whether there's a shuttle bus for the people who have to park far out. It's a church's job to reach as many people as possible. We try to make sure there aren't a bunch of superficial flaws keeping folks from getting the message. What we do isn't superficial. What you do, what we do, is serious business. We're supposed to be servants. It's supposed to mean *something*."

"So you're here to judge us?"

"Actually, the professional term we use is audit. We're here to audit your church."

"Who asked you to audit us?"

Alterman, not wanting to act surprised at the question, nevertheless does. "A Mr. King did."

"Jonathan King?"

"Yes. Your chairman of deacons."

"Are you sure?"

"Yes. Sort of a high squeaky voice." Everhart's face never changes. "Something wrong?"

"Well, you may not be aware of this, but Brother King is no longer our chairman of deacons."

"Really? Why?"

"Because he died last week." Everhart's tone is not accusatory, nor shocked.

"Oh my. I'm very sorry. Sudden?"

"Actually no. He's been sick for some time."

"Yes. I spoke to him on the phone. He told me that the church was requesting this. He made it sound as though this was a leadership decision."

"He spoke to you?"

"Yes. At least, I thought it was him. I was a little surprised when he didn't meet me at the airport."

"Well, Brother King hasn't been in any state to talk to anybody in some time. You see, he was in a nursing home for the past four years. The last six months, he was in a vegetative state, you might say. You couldn't have spoken to him."

Alterman shudders, and his eyes dart down to the floor for a split second.

"Well, Jonny was my father-in-law, actually. He's so much better off, you see. He wouldn't have wanted to be that way. We kept the chairman's title for him out of respect. Sort of an emeritus thing."

"But *you* knew I was coming."

"Yes. We got your letter in the mail a few days ago, just before you called. I could tell that you had been requested to come here. I asked around my deacons, but nobody seemed to know who called you." A moment passes. "*Our* deacons. Excuse me."

So now, it all made sense. Thomas Everhart was nervous and combative because he didn't precisely know who had called Alterman here, but he *had* known the man was coming. So he had crammed as much information into a week as possible. And he had every reason to be suspicious since his long-sick father-in-law had finally succumbed to a slow and humiliating disease.

No need to replace one form of torture with another more calculated form, Alterman thinks.

"In that case, I won't take up anymore of your time." Alterman rises to leave.

And the strangest thing happens. Everhart seems disappointed. "Don't leave."

"No. It's obvious we were brought in under false pretenses. I can't do my job in that kind of environment."

"Are you sure?"

"Well, I mean…"

"Has this kind of thing ever happened to you before, Mr. Alterman?"

"Alex, please. No. We've been brought in during splits and power struggles and other unpleasant moments in churches, and we always refuse if it turns out one side is pitting us against another. But this is a first. Nobody's ever gotten us in by simply lying. Usually they start lying once we show up."

"I can imagine. And what did they say we wanted? This person claiming to be Brother King, I mean."

Alterman sits down again, and this seemingly pleases Everhart. "Full treatment."

Everhart has a look on his face like a man who gets a peek at the menu in an exclusive restaurant. "Did they say why?"

Alterman's eyes dart up at the ceiling to recall. "Just that the church would like to see if it's doing a good job, and how it can do a better job. I think that's the phrase I recall hearing."

"Hmmm…"

"But I've taken up too much of your time."

"Just a minute." Everhart puts up a hand, encouraging Alterman to sit back down again. "How much are we talking about here?"

"I can show you a fee schedule, but…"

"I mean, I have to admit I'm intrigued. It's obvious somebody wanted us to go through this. I'm tempted to see it through."

"Why?" Alterman says, against his better judgment.

"You think I shouldn't?"

"No, no, no! I mean, no it's not that I don't think you should. I mean, well, I don't know. I guess I'm used to pastors who.. Well I shouldn't say that. What I mean is, I would imagine somebody did this in order to potentially harm *you*."

"But the more I sit here and think about it, the more I think this happened for a reason."

"That's what I'm…"

"No, I mean, it was *meant* to harm us, but it *could* help us. We just have to see it as an opportunity."

"But…"

"Mr. Alterman, Alex. I can see this is the hand of God." Thomas Everhart stands up, and then thrusts his hand out, as if for a shake. "I want you to do your worst. We don't have anything to hide here. Give us your complete treatment. No stone unturned."

"I can't do that. It wouldn't be ethical, if we don't know who called us."

"Are you saying that all those pastors I talked to who raved about you were wrong? You're just an old softie at heart?"

Alterman is having severe problems controlling himself. He wants to help the man, and yet Everhart is saying things that anyone who knows Alterman would understand are bait. His first instinct is to leave right now and not entangle himself. But he also thinks about Everhart's celebrity, the chances a good job will directly impact his firm, and the chutzpah of the man in accepting a challenge from some unknown, unseen opponent.

"Anybody who would pose as your recently deceased father-in-law would have to be pretty low," Alterman says.

"They had to know we would eventually find out," Everhart says. "The truth will probably reveal itself at some point. It always does."

Alterman feels uneasy, but he's not sure why.

"Of course, that's what *you* probably say," Everhart laughs. "Now, do I have to sign anything?"

9

"He said what?" Templeton replies.

"He wants it. The whole thing."

"I realize you wouldn't have gotten us down here if we weren't going to go through with it, but he *wants* it?"

"All of it," Alterman says. "The full treatment."

Whit shakes his head. The rest don't say anything, but their feelings are the same. This feels like a challenge, like a playground dare.

It is another week later, and the team is readying its command center. Alterman has set up shop about twenty miles away from Sweet Lightning at a beach resort called Rendezvous. True to his reputation as an epic skinflint, Alterman has found a resort that is in foreclosure. They have rented several bungalows out for at least a month at next to nothing. Of course, there is very little support staff at the moment, which explains the knee deep grass, the non-functioning Jacuzzis, and the dim, murky green haze and odor of the unmaintained swimming pools. Weeds poke out from cracks in the tennis court.

Alterman, Templeton and Ingersoll are huddled around a table on the balcony of Alterman's room. Whit is perched on a bar stool against the sliding glass door, strumming on a guitar though he doesn't know how to play. Cherie is sitting on the floor in canvas shoes and shorts, smacking a stick of gum, looking like a disgruntled teenager denied her cellphone. They are crammed onto this balcony on the fifth floor because Alterman is anxious about being bugged. Within sight of the balcony is an adjoining golf course, the other buildings in the complex and a beach with only a handful of vacationers.

Out in the Gulf of Mexico, several hundred miles away, an oil well exploded weeks before and has been emptying untold gallons of oil - some estimate in the millions - every day for more than two months. News of the disaster has kept scores of tourists away at the exact moment this resort needs a buyer, at the height of the season. Alterman picked the place for this exact reason.

"Hey, we didn't open with prayer," Ingersoll says. He is wearing a shirt that reads, "Search me, O God, and know my heart; Try me and know my anxious thoughts."

"Whit, will you?" Alterman asks.

"Why does he always pray?" Ingersoll asks.

"Then you do it," Alterman sighs.

"I don't want to," Ingersoll smirks. "I just want to know why he always does."

"I'm going to send you to audit a snake-handling church one of these days."

Whit thankfully interrupts with his prayer.

"So what have we got here?" Alterman then asks Ingersoll, who has been researching Sweet Lightning for a week.

"We're talking about a suburb here basically. Edwards Crossroads is like a lot of these panhandle towns. They only recently started learning how to make money off the coast down here, so up until about 30 years ago, this was a sleepy little vacation town that existed on the road to some place bigger. Then Thomas Everhart showed up and started his church. The rest is history."

"Is the story they put out on him basically true?" Whit wonders, with a voice of fearful suspicion, like a child expecting a favorite athlete to be caught cheating.

"Yes it is, actually. Everhart started out as a bi-vocational pastor and got his degree working nights. He began his church in his own home and eventually got enough members that he moved into a theater. Used to pass around a popcorn tub as a collection plate. They met in schools, community centers, community theaters and the like up until about five years ago, when they finally got a sanctuary. He's built the congregation from practically nothing. Members have to take a class before they join and are required to do community service and tithe a certain portion."

"What's the rate of transfer to other churches?"

"Pretty low. And they don't have a lot of excess membership on the rolls. Seems they clear inactives off pretty quickly if they show a pattern of staying away."

"What's the congregation like?'

"If you mean their makeup, you're talking about a predominantly middle-class group, with a fair number of college-educated young professionals with families. Mostly whites. Typical suburb. Low mortgages, low crime, good schools. Not a lot of distance between the incomes. Just enough minority families to make some people congratulate themselves on their broadmindedness."

"Such a cynical boy," Cherie says sweetly.

"How does the congregation feel about him?" Alterman asks.

"Mostly from what I can find out, he's well-loved. Respected. The people who've been with him the longest are very loyal. He hasn't worn out his welcome yet."

"What about the church? What's its reputation in the community?"

"Impeccable. None of the usual stories about real estate gouging or bad karma over political stands. Most of the people in town seem favorable to it. They get high marks for their food drives. When they needed the real estate for their sanctuary, the Catholic diocese sold it to them."

"Not making any waves," Cherie says, with a barely detectible note of disdain.

"That kind of stuff is standard for a megachurch," Whit says.

"It's not a megachurch," Templeton corrects.

"Not big enough," Ingersoll says. "But it acts like a megachurch."

"What do you mean?" Cherie asks.

"Megachurches survive because of their small groups, as you know. You get 15,000 people in a church and everybody is more likely to feel like an outsider and alienated, and most people join churches to belong. To feel like they belong. To something. Sweet Lightning has lots of little groups. Study groups. Ministry groups. Volunteer groups. Sometimes as small as two or three members."

"Is that good or bad?" Cherie asks.

"Well, you do have churches that sometimes split off from these groups because they get too committed to an idea that their pastor doesn't dig too much. But these groups seem very loyal to him, and to the church."

Cherie asks again, as though she wants to engage Ingersoll a little more. "How much of that is Everhart's doing?"

Alterman raises his hand. "I imagine very little in this church isn't his doing. With the small groups though, they're independent, and their support is a sign of approval. You know the one thing that's constant when we do these. A church that's formed by a charismatic leader tends to mirror that leader - in its interests, its outlook, its temperment. Like draws like. We're liable to get into this and find out a lot more about Thomas Everhart than even his congregation knows. So keep your eyes open for it."

"What's he like? Everhart?" Templeton asks.

"People assume he's like the books - folksy, learned but not condescending, sort of small town but with big city sophistication," Ingersoll says. "Knows the big words in the dictionary and when not to use them. Still thought of as young even though he's been twenty years in the ministry. Can quote the Bible and the latest movies with equal felicity. There's a story going around that he washes the feet of his staff members every week, just like Jesus. They say he does this in order to keep him and them all humble."

Cherie looks directly at Alterman, and levels her index finger at him. "You are *not* touching my feet."

"So we do the usual?" Ingersoll says.

"No," Alterman says, and everyone looks at him.

Cherie suspiciously eyes her feet.

He points at Ingersoll. "First, you're not going to be the member this time." Ingersoll looks ruined at the words. His usual job is to be the one member of the group who joins the church. Ingersoll makes the profession of faith. He rents a house nearby. He attends services. He measures to see if the church makes outreach efforts to new converts. He measures what kind of response there is. How well the church does a job of plugging in someone to new opportunities. How friendly everyone is. Do they see if the newbie has any friends who want to join? And, if it happens in the early going, if the church tends to lose interest.

Ingersoll's mouth is open, even though he doesn't realize it.

"Cherie, your job this time. We'll give you the fake ID and the backstory to adopt. I want to make sure you know it in case you're questioned." The way Alterman says this, it makes Templeton think of border guards and secret police.

"But..." Ingersoll stammers.

"Just a second," Alterman continues, still talking to Cherie. "Part of the identity, you know, is that we'll give you a narrative to follow. Come up with your own variations. Your story will change as your identity develops, according to what we need to check. If we want to know about their singles ministry, then you'll be attending church to find a husband. If we want to know about their substance abuse counseling, then they'll need to smell alcohol on your breath."

Cherie Lefevere, offspring of career missionaries, scrupulous of her self-image, a woman who hates the taste of alcohol, shudders. All that Alterman says upsets her, for various reasons.

"Remember who you are, even if that isn't who you are." Alterman then turns to Ingersoll, who looks as though he might cry. "Don't worry. I got something for you."

"Was I...?"

"No. You've done fine. I have my reasons. I told you - Everhart did not call us in. Your job this time is to figure out who got us down here."

"That's all?"

"Did I say that? No, you'll be plenty busy. I expect you to find this out on top of everything else I have for you."

Ingersoll, for some reason, is pleased with this and chastened at the same time.

"Wydgate?" Templeton says.

"I thought of that, but what's his reason?"

"To embarrass you?"

"Doesn't sound like his style," Alterman says.

Ingersoll snickers. "What *is* his style? Does he have style?"

Cherie, probably thinking again about their nemesis' nose hair, shivers.

"What else is different?" Templeton asks, with no small amount of fear.

"We'll get around to that."

"What about the new girl? What's her name?" Cherie asks.

"Rambha is *already* working for us. You'll meet her in a little while. I think you'll like her. If you can get a word in with her." Templeton snickers at Alterman's words. He heard about the job interview and can only imagine how it was.

"Each of you will get a chance to check Everhart out on Sunday. I'll want your notes afterward. Any suggestions. Then Steve and I will go over everything and come up with everyone's assignments. Because this is important, be ready to do lots of stuff on the fly. Flexibility."

Cherie puts her hands together and begins moving her arms like a snake, winding them up and down. She stops when Alterman looks at her for a half-second too long.

"What about me, Bossman?" Whit asks, putting down the guitar.

"You're theology, as usual," Alterman says. "I want to know about how this church functions. Do they pray in a committed sense? Do they have people committed to doing it? If so, where? How often? Do they hook people into Sunday School? What are they learning if they get there? What percentage of his sermon is strictly Scripture, and how much time is he up there voguing?"

"That's a lot of information you're asking for," Whit says.

Alterman comes close to a smile. "On this job, we're going to have a lot of information. This next week, there's going to be a lot of maintenance work at the church. That will give us time to install some of our surveillance devices."

"How did we arrange that?" Ingersoll asks.

Alterman shakes his head. "You just keep track of the data we'll have coming in." He then speaks up over the sound of the waves, but not loud enough to be heard out in the condo's courtyard. "Remember - 89 percent of churchgoers think church exists to meet their own needs and those of their families. Think like they do.

"Churches have tried to make themselves worthy of their worshippers instead of worthy of their Lord. Chasing after what the audience wants rather than trusting that they want Him. The average worshipper isn't a worshipper. He's got time to binge watch whole TV series on Netflix, but no time to read ahead in the Sunday School book, if he can find it. He's got time to troll Twitter and post mean things on Facebook but no time to read his dusty Bible. He's got a closet full of clothes, the best car, and he's planning his vacation, but he's got no money for missions because he's maxed out on three credit cards.

"They're not thinking about evangelism. They're thinking about why the church toilets have rings in them. Not saying it's right. That's the way it is. But part of our job is reminding them of what it should be."

Alterman makes no comment when he realizes that half of his team are mouthing the words along with him, they've heard them so many times. So he is silent, as he hears them finish the words he has endlessly repeated:

"God has a right to be a member of His own family."

10

They all sit for the first time in the sanctuary separately, waiting for Everhart's sermon.

Alterman is wearing a bright red coat and tie, a ridiculous bit of deliberate self-advertising. The red coat calls attention to itself, and he is one of the few men in the church that morning with a tie. He wants to stand out, as Everhart preaches to his congregation, to see if this somehow rattles him. It's worked before. One pastor interrupted his sermon 12 times drinking from a glass of water he kept under the podium. Alterman swore he would never do that again, not wanting to impact the sermon to such an extent.

Driving into the parking lot that morning, Ingersoll's first thought is that the church is too small. Strange, he thinks. I know this place isn't a megachurch, but I still expect it to be bigger. He has to watch himself, Ingersoll thinks. Alterman hates preconceived notions.

Whit, however, thinks the place looks like a casino.

They never sit together. Ingersoll is regularly in a pew up front, as per Alterman's instructions. He is usually "the new member," meaning he makes the profession of faith and becomes enrolled as part of the treatment. But since Cherie is filling that role - and Ingersoll is at a loss to explain why she got the duty - he was given another seating assignment.

"Sit up in the balcony with the rest of the unclean," were Alterman's dubious instructions. Alterman always says churches with balconies are asking for some members to leave early. "Easier to slip out." Ingersoll isn't posing as anyone, which is why he is wearing a T-shirt with the words, "Unequal weights and unequal measures are both alike an abomination to the Lord."

Each member of the team gets a chance to evaluate their individual entry point. The firmness of the welcoming handshakes is measured. Whit is impressed that his greeter spots his white hair and begins speaking in a louder voice, just in case Whit is hearing impaired. The gesture shows forethought but also insults him slightly. He tries to return the death grip handshake but can't. The persistent tingling in his fingers, which he has tried to ignore for weeks, is getting worse.

Templeton notes the use of female greeters since one welcomes him, and he is impressed with her handshake.

Alterman's greeter needs a breath mint.

Templeton is the only one in disguise. He is wearing a leg brace that gives him a limp by preventing his knee from bending. He is convinced his fake mustache fools no one, but if that is the case, no one says anything or stares. In the parking lot, Alterman texted him to bend the frames of his dummy eyeglasses so they will look distressed. This is a classic Alterman touch. People might form a judgment about him based on such details, just as he instructed Templeton to rip one button from his shirt. On the one hand, an observant person might notice these things and conclude he is too poor because of his disability to afford new clothes and frames. That might cause someone to seek him out for charity, or ostracize him as an outsider. If no one notices, that too will be an indictment.

Cherie sits up front, three rows from the altar. Her body language is drawn in, as though she is hoping no one says a word to her once she sits down. Alterman's instructions were clear. "Don't invite any notice of you. Let them come to you and engage you, if they do. Make it hard for them." From the time she sits down, it is two minutes and thirty-seven seconds before a regular member extends a hand to welcome her. She notes the person is not a greeter, deacon, or minister, but a single mother toting a toddler.

Once the service starts, a strange thing happens to Cherie, something she's noticed several times in the past few months. The church is having a baby dedication ceremony, and once the opening hymn is finished, the new parents walk to the altar. Everhart is waiting for them. In one mother's arms is a newborn in a white smock. The child, a little girl, is named Eternity. Cherie notes the name silently to herself, striking an imaginary line through it. She will never name a child, should she have one, the same thing.

But just considering the idea for a moment sparks the feeling she has just recently started noticing. Cherie has begun to wonder how long she can do these church audits and hope to postpone the role she sees for herself *eventually* - wife and mother. She feels herself getting older. It is a ridiculous idea. She will not be alone. She will find a husband. She will hold a child of her own, from her own body, just like this woman is doing. She will not forever be the bloodhound sniffing out church athletic league cheaters. And at the same time, she silently resents Alterman putting her in this position. She knows that, somehow, he meant for her to feel this way. He's probably decided it's time for me to get married, she says. Typical.

Whit does not like the music, but he never does these days. The idea of "Amazing Grace" with drums drives him to distraction, even though the percussion is muted. These are digital drum sounds, which makes him shift uneasily even more. He's not sure what's more absurd – disliking the drums or disliking that they are artificial.

Templeton nearly falls when it comes time to stand during the fellowship portion of the service. An alert worshipper grabs his arm to steady him, and Templeton gives an embarrassed thanks with a sheepish grin. He feels the whole business is an utter sham. Templeton glances over at Alterman but knows he will never acknowledge him, even though Templeton is sure he saw him fall.

During the offertory hymn, another unexpected event happens. The offering plate passing by his face awakens Ingersoll, who fell asleep during one of the songs without realizing it. He has been up late the previous three nights researching Sweet Lightning, but did not realize this had taken a toll on him. He looks around at the faces, which do not acknowledge him, and wonders if he snored.

He wonders this because he sees a woman staring at him. He recognizes her as Keysha, Everhart's new administrative assistant. He saw the picture of her Alterman took with the camera hidden in his tie. She looks annoyed, much as she did in seeing Alterman. He senses she is already very protective of her boss.

Alterman, who is sitting in the exact middle of the sanctuary, notes that all the preliminaries - hymns, children's lesson, special music, offertory and choir performance - end so that the pastor has approximately 45 minutes to preach, assuming he ends at the top of the hour.

There is also a couple standing in the back looking out of place. Both appear to be in their twenties, the man with spiked hair and clothes a little edger than Alterman sees around the sanctuary. The woman with him has a short sleeved shirt that reveals a tattoo. The man is working a video camera on a tripod, the lens focused on the pulpit. The woman is making notes. Both of them have wry smiles on their faces.

Everhart strides to the pulpit when it is his time. "I want to talk to you today about a very timely subject," he begins.

> *Our text is Jeremiah 2:22. In the NIV, it reads: "Although you wash yourself with soda and use an abundance of soap, the stain of your guilt is still before me," declares the Sovereign Lord.*
>
> *You're probably sick of hearing about it. I know I am. It's the oil spill. Those of you out there who own your own businesses, you're probably so sick of hearing about the spill that you might just get up and walk out of here. Now, just listen to me. If I say something that doesn't hold your attention, or that you don't think I have the right to say, then you have my permission to just get up and walk right out of here, and I'll never think anything bad about you.*
>
> *Think about this. You've got this danger that everybody hears about, but nobody can see. I mean, let's just say*

there's somebody who went down to the beach one day with their family and sand pail and shovel, and they put down their towel, and here they are trudging out toward the shore, when all of a sudden, they see this little black thing there in the spray and wonder what it could be.

And let's just say you're standing there, ready to explain to them that that black thing is what's called a tar ball. And since they don't know anything about oil platforms or whatever, they say, in good conscience, what's a tar ball? Fair enough question. So you, well-meaning sort that you are, tell them that way out there in the water, beyond what you can see, there's this animal called an oil well, and it drills deep down under the water to the deposits of oil underneath. And that well is grabbing and pulling up loads and loads of oil, which is what their car eats, in one form or another, when it's hungry. And then you proceed to tell them that this tar ball is what's coming off a big leak, an oil spill that's right out there in the Gulf.

And they are suitably horror stricken, and ask, as they undoubtedly should, just how much oil got spilled out there? And you say you're not sure, but some people say it's millions and millions of gallons. Just an unholy mess. And it's got to go somewhere. So it's probably coming ashore. Could wipe out a whole lot before it's done. The water isn't safe anymore.

Now, you've done your duty. You've told your story. And you feel good about yourself.

And your friend doesn't believe you.

'I never heard anything so ludicrous in all my life! You expect me to believe that my car needs that black stuff? My car runs on clear stuff! I've seen it with my own eyes! I've smelled it! I know what my car needs.

'Give me a break!' your friend says.' You expect me to believe this little tar ball is the only evidence of millions of gallons of oil out there! I'm smart enough to see through this. All you're trying to do is get me worked up about

something that's not even true. It doesn't affect my life at all.'

How does that make you feel? What did you expect? Gratitude? You've spoiled this guy's trip to the beach!

Don't you see! That's what we're doing here! We're called to tell the world it's in danger! And the world can't see the problem! We tell them there's this terrible stain, out there! They should be able to see it, but they can't. They don't see it! Oh, they may see a little problem here and there, just a little speck, but it only seems small, easily swept away. And just like our friend here, who doesn't want to hear about a spill when he's taking in the waves, the world doesn't want to hear about something that's not here yet. Even if the oil should sweep in, there's still going to be some people who are going to stay out there, even as they get coated in it! This is their time! They're going to make the most of it!

You can tell people about the destruction of society! You can tell them about rising crime rates! Violence against women! Violence against children! Racism! A culture that doesn't value life! Corruption in high places! Corruption in the church! You can tell them all of that, and you won't be telling them any different from what crosses their minds. But as long as they don't actually see it, or won't see it, they don't think they're swimming in it! 'It's not here yet! I still have time!'

And what's worse! My friends, the spill isn't out there! It's here! It's all around us. They, and you, and me, and all of us - we are already black with the stuff! It's all over us! Already! Now! And no matter how hard we scrub, we'll never be able on our own to clean it off!

Alterman likes what he hears from Everhart's prodigious voice. He notices that for all the people in the congregation, there is not a lot of movement while the pastor is talking. The children who might ordinarily be jumping in and out of parents' laps are stationary, some staring directly at him. A few adults are leaned forward, as though they cannot hear the next word fast enough. The only time there are breaks in concentration is when someone uncrosses a leg and causes her pew to creak. The only other sound, besides the hum of the air conditioning, is the occasional sizzling rattle of hundreds of Bible pages when he directs them to seek out a verse of Scripture.

Everhart's voice is powerful, but not overpowering; a clarion, not a klaxon.

> *Now look over at Luke 1:77 through 79. Again, this is the NIV. "To give his people the knowledge of salvation through the forgiveness of their sins, because of the tender mercy of our God, by which the rising sun will come to us from heaven to shine on those living in darkness and in the shadow of death, to guide our feet into the path of peace."*
>
> *That's Mary, talking about the coming of Christ. Reminding us of why He came and what He was destined to accomplish.*
>
> *Because you see, the stain, the spill, is only half the story. You know, the oil company knows there's a problem out there. They're trying to solve it, even though it doesn't feel that way when it's a month later and they haven't capped the thing. But you know what the oil company is saying. They're saying that this problem can be solved. And solved by nature. One of the things is that there is marine life out there, microscopic marine life that will begin to break down the oil and consume parts of it.*
>
> *You heard me! Oil gets consumed in the ocean every day, whether there's a spill or not, and much of it by microbes you can't even see.*
>
> *But do you know what will do the greatest damage to that oil? You know there's something out there that chemically breaks the oil down further? The sun. That's right! The sun! Direct sunlight will make most of the chemical makeup of that oil evaporate. It doesn't seem possible, but it's true.*

Now some of you are probably saying, wait a minute, preacher. You had me with all this 'spill in the Gulf' part. I could see where you were going, but I think you've taken a left turn. Not at all. What I mean to say is this - Jesus makes a way. He makes a way to undo the damage inside us all. The light of the Son breaks us down, and rejuvenates us. You no longer need remain black with sin, coated and dirty. Can you believe it?

Do you dare believe it?

Don't leave here saying that the preacher told you the oil spill is just going away, like magic. You see, the problem is there. Even after the best work of nature, we're going to be feeling the effects. But what I mean is that God has made a way. It isn't clear to everyone, but it should be.

God is making it safe for us, but people are staying away. They'd rather not think about it. They'd rather not have to deal with what it means. Instead, they stay away. And so they do.

We need to convince them. And you know, I'm not talking about vacation resorts now. I'm talking about the church. Let them see what Jesus has done for you!

Alterman is walking out to the car. Around him are the many worshippers of Sweet Lightning, and he can tell by the looks on their faces that some of them are still considering Thomas Everhart's words, regardless of the arguments going on within each family over where to eat now that the service is over. It will only take a short time before he makes it back to the resort to debrief everyone. He too is thinking about lunch.

Cherie will be the last to arrive. When Everhart issued his invitation, Cherie stepped forward. Any misgivings Alterman might have had on naming her for this honor were promptly dismissed. She prayed with the staff member who held her hands and she wept copious tears as she was recognized by the congregation. She smiled gratefully to each person who lined up to shake her hand following the service. He had no doubt the tears were sincere, and he felt smug for having correctly foreseen this.

Alterman is almost to the car when he realizes there is someone sitting on the trunk of his rental. John Patrick Wydgate III is perched like a gargoyle, his feet on the back bumper. The look on his face would be expected - benign, brilliant irrelevance. Alterman feels his stomach start churning at the sight of the man.

"We meet again," Alterman says. "What are you doing here?"

"Hello Alex. Good to see you again." His tone is friendly and infuriating.

"What are you doing here, I said?"

Wydgate stands up and begins shaking his head. "I'll never understand why you're so hostile."

"The human drama of competition."

He gives off a self-satisfied smile that disgusts Alterman. Alterman never smiles. "Of course. But you know, there's plenty of business out there. We both want the same thing. We shouldn't be enemies, Alex."

"We're not going to be partners."

"I don't believe I said anything about that. Well, not business partners, anyway. But there's no reason for us *not* to be working together."

"You have your philosophy. I have mine."

"I know. I know. We've had this conversation a million times, Alex. I'm not here to argue which of our approaches is best for the client." Wydgate rubs a hand through his hair. He is wearing it a little longer these days. Alterman perceives it is the beginnings of a mid-life crisis, judging by the way his hair is less gray than the last time Alterman saw it. Wydgate's blond looks are unnaturally more vivid now. As Wydgate steps closer to him, Alterman sees that Cherie was right - he has a single, wiry hair winding out about four inches from his left nostril.

"Then what are you here for?"

Wydgate looks wounded at the question. "Your attitude Alex, if you'll pardon me for saying so, is not *Christian*." The words surprise Alterman. This seems a very harsh rebuke from Wydgate. He probably would never say something so direct to one of the churches that hire him. But then, immediately, he backtracks. "I'm not saying you're not a Christian. Just that I find this animosity off-putting."

Alterman is pleased to see his suspicions about Wydgate's milquetoasty demeanor justified. In fact, he hasn't taken his eyes off the single hair jutting out from Wydgate's nose. "I'm sorry. I get this way when I have a client." Alterman nods his head in the direction of Sweet Lightning behind him.

"Yes, that's why I'm here," Wydgate says. "I came to give you a bit of friendly advice."

"Which is?"

"Don't take this job, Alex."

"I'm sorry?"

"You heard me. Drop this job. Do yourself a favor and move on. Just tell him something came up and you won't be able to fulfill this contract." Wydgate's tone is surprising. His voice almost sounds menacing.

"You don't want me to do this job…"

"I know what you'll do with it, Alex. Thomas Everhart is a good man. God is doing great things through him. The Holy Spirit is alive in his ministry. The last thing that's needed is for your traveling circus to show up and put an end to all that."

"You think I'll hurt him."

"I know you will."

"How do you know that?"

"I know you, Alex. I've gone along with this rivalry we have…"

"We don't have a rivalry."

"That's correct. The only rivalry is the one that exists in your mind."

"You don't do what I do, and you don't do it half as well."

"Alex, you don't know who hired you, do you?"

This throws Alterman off-stride. "That's confidential."

"No need to play it that way. I know this job is big enough to appeal to your vanity. But you're making a mistake."

"How am I…"

"Alex, I'm just going on faith here. I have taken at face value the idea that you care about the work that goes on in churches. I am willing to believe that you really want the work of the Lord to go forward. Unlike other people, I want to believe that you are sincerely interested in how churches minister. I'm willing to ignore what you say about me, and some of the things that you've done. That business in Montana with the Methodists…"

"You know the court imposed a gag order…"

"I'm not here to argue that. I'm just telling you that if you keep going with this job, you're going to be doing a lot more harm than good. There are many, many people - sinister forces - who don't want this man to succeed. Think about it. Why else would they call you in?"

"I'm not aware of any *sinister forces*, as you call them, contacting me…"

"So you *don't* know who called you…"

"Listen, if you think I'm so dangerous, then why talk to me?"

"Alex, I am praying for you. I'm doing you a favor. I hope you know that. And right now, I'm praying that you'll not allow yourself to be used to break a good man who is doing God's will."

Before Wydgate has finished with his last syllable, Alterman reaches up and yanks the offending hair from Wydgate's nose. Wydgate gives a yelp of disgust.

"Sorry. Just doing *you* a favor." Alterman holds the hair out for Wydgate to see. Wydgate, for some reason neither man can explain, takes the hair. "Since you seem to know me so well, and for that matter, the will of God, then you shouldn't be worried. If God wants Thomas Everhart to succeed, then nothing I do can stop that. And while I don't have your ear for the Almighty, I do care about this job. I want *Him* to succeed, not this week's newly anointed prophet."

"Please Alex," Wydgate says, as Alterman turns to get into his car. "This is serious."

"Yes, it is. And I'm serious about it. Now if I were you, I'd get out of the way while I'm backing out. I'm not a very careful driver."

And Alterman sneers. "And while Everhart's a good pastor, he's not a faith healer."

II

The Origin of
Table Manners

1

Alterman rolls out the church floor plan. Without asking, he grabs everyone's cups and uses them to hold down the ends of the drawing. It's a good thing everyone's finished with lunch, Templeton thinks.

"Hook up your computer," Alterman says, pointing to Ingersoll. He hands him a scrap of paper with a few codes on it. "That's not your main laptop, is it?"

"No."

"Good. There's going to be a lot of data streaming in and it's going to eat up a lot of space."

"Where's the data coming from?" Ingersoll asks, tapping in the codes. He is wearing a T-shirt with the words, "For God shall bring every work into judgment, with every secret thing, whether good, or whether evil."

Alterman points to the floor plan. "All of these green dots are clocks. You can see they're stationed throughout the church – nursery, classrooms, common areas, kitchen, sanctuary, baptismal font, sound room."

"O-kay," says Cherie. There is creeping horror in her voice, Templeton thinks.

"There's a surveillance camera in every one of them," Alterman says. "Installed just a week ago. When he keys in the codes-" Alterman points to Ingersoll "-it will activate them all. They're also mic-ed up. The microphones aren't extremely powerful but they'll be adequate for what we need."

"The lighting's not so good in some of these areas," Ingersoll points out, as the images come to life on his screen.

"The cameras have night vision capability," Alterman says, indicating a function on the screen.

This is definitely something new for all of them. The feeling in the room shifts.

"The red triangles are church computers. They are equipped with keystroke loggers."

Templeton cringes.

"I'm afraid to ask what that means, because not knowing means I'm old," Whit says.

Ingersoll jumps in. "It records what anyone types into a keyboard. You'll know what messages they're sending, what web sites they're looking at." He looks at Alterman. "That *is* a lot of data."

"There's more," Alterman says, pulling out a sheet of paper. "Here's a manifest of cellphones. Every staff member at the church got a new cellphone last week. That code over there records where they are calling."

"What about the conversations?" Cherie asks, with fear in every syllable.

"We don't record them," Alterman says.

Her shoulders slump with relief.

"Yet," he adds.

"What's this camera?" Ingersoll asks, pointing to one image on the screen.

"That's the camera in the nursery."

"Where is it?"

"In a teddy bear," Alterman says. "Parents use those to spy on nannies."

Templeton raises a hand, speaking for the rest of them. He can see their nervous eyes, which seem to be pleading for him to assert some sanity. *You understand him*, their stares appear to say. "Alex, don't you think you've gone a wee-bit too far?"

"I told you this was a big one," Alterman says.

"I understand that," the partner replies.

"We're seriously looking at franchising after this."

"Just like Al Qaeda," Cherie chirps.

Whit steps in, sensing the mood. "Bossman, what are we supposed to do with all this?"

"This is way too much information to sift through," Ingersoll says.

"And it's an incomplete picture," Cherie says. "You're not going to be able to draw legitimate conclusions looking at this stuff."

"That's where you all come in," Alterman says. "Yeah, it's a lot of data, but you guys will be out there among them. This is no different from any other time we've done this, folks. This is a big audit, but it's still an audit. I'm going to listen to *you* more than any of their conversations."

"What are we looking for?" Templeton asks.

"We don't know what we're looking for. Just like usual. You're all getting the wrong impression."

"What about all this stuff? How long are we going to be bugging these people?"

Alterman waves his arms, as though erasing a blackboard. "We aren't bugging them. We're monitoring them. When the job is over, we erase the data, sever the links, take down the system."

"Or we sell it to the government?" Ingersoll says.

"I'll make inquiries," Alterman says. Templeton doesn't think he's serious. Not all *that* serious.

"Alex," Whit begins. He never calls Alterman by his first name. "I'm all for doing a job well. But why are we going to this much trouble? Why is this case special?"

Alterman doesn't look up. He points to the floor plan and motions Whit over. "Take a look at this." He indicates a room. "See that?"

"Yep."

"Know what it is?"

Whit shakes his head.

"Neither do I. You see, that room doesn't have an entrance."

"Doesn't have an entrance?"

"What I mean is that it doesn't have an entrance to any common area. It's hidden. There's got to be a way to get into it, but it's not on this floor plan. And I've walked the church, talked to a few people, and the existence of this room is a secret."

"What?" Templeton says.

"I'm serious. I don't know what this is, but whatever it is, it isn't mentioned anywhere."

The group exchanges puzzled glances at each other. Templeton is as intrigued as the rest of them.

"Maybe you ought to see this," Ingersoll says. He is holding up the wireless laptop, opened to a web page.

"You're supposed to be looking at the data stream," Alterman says, in a slightly annoyed voice.

"This got emailed to me," Ingersoll insists.

Templeton can't tell what the name of the site is. At first, he thinks it's "X-pose," but the X is actually a cross. He supposes that is the right name, but someone's trying to be too cute. It appears to be an atheist website devoted to posting embarrassing things about religion – meaning Christianity. In this case, the item has to do with Thomas Everhart.

"Celebrity Preacher Feeds Flock Junk Science!" is the breathless headline, with a grainy embedded image of Everhart standing in front of the flock at Sweet Lightning. The group then understands the identity of the young couple who stood during the service with a video camera. The story is credited to a Nathan Steeplechase and Tara Diddle.

Alongside the grainy image, the site quotes Everhart's statement during the service about microscopic sea life consuming part of the oil spill. While this is factually correct, the site points out that, according to scientists, it is a "gross overstatement" to conclude microbes would consume the bulk of the oil spill in the Gulf. Again, the site repeats, "according to scientists," the problem is much worse than has previously been stated. The story repeats the assurances of scientists like magical incantations.

"By spreading misinformation to the unfortunate people he has duped, Everhart does a disservice to science and to his congregation,"

Alterman reads aloud from the article. "Wrapping himself in pseudo-science will do him as much good as the superstition he sells between covers and on Sunday mornings." Underneath the article is a link allowing readers to contribute to the good work of the website, whatever its name is.

"This is quite impressive," Alterman says. "You realize, they're illustrating the need for us."

"Maybe, but even if you had a perfect service, they'd find something wrong with it," Ingersoll says.

"Takes one to know one?" Alterman says. He is joking, Templeton knows, with the same stone features as usual.

"Atheists? I think I've proven myself," Ingersoll said. "I'm still here."

Alterman says nothing.

"After all, you didn't make me give a profession of faith this time."

"I don't *make* you do anything at all," Alterman says. "And if I had any doubts about you, you wouldn't be working with me. Besides, it doesn't matter what *I* think."

"Well…"

"I'm joking. What do you care if I should think something like that, anyway?"

Ingersoll smiles. This is one of Alterman's games, like the Gestapo giving someone a pistol with blanks to test his loyalty. "You know how I came here, and what I'm interested in. You know how far I've come."

"Methinks you doth protest too much."

"You want me to recite the Apostle's Creed or something?"

"Spoken like a true apostate," Alterman says.

"What's it going to take?" Ingersoll demands. "St. Euplius was executed with the Gospels tied to his neck! He begged for the Romans to make him a martyr. Would that satisfy you?"

"Maybe, depending how big the Bible was."

"I believe, okay! If you want me to say it, I'll say it."

Just when Templeton thinks he should step in, the mood shifts. "Dude," Alterman says. He always calls Ingersoll "Dude" when he wishes to break down any formality between them. "I told you. If I had any doubts about your faith, I wouldn't trust you like I do."

"I'm sorry. I guess I'm more sensitive about that than I should be."

"*I* apologize. I guess I didn't realize that." Alterman pats him on the shoulder. Templeton thinks he sees Ingersoll flinch at Alterman's touch. "What do we know about these two?" Alterman says, handing the laptop back to Ingersoll.

"Nothing really," Ingersoll says.

"Check 'em out," Alterman says. "If they're as good as you, maybe we can use 'em." Ingersoll turns away so that Alterman won't see him roll his eyes.

Templeton has no idea what Alterman means by "use 'em," and he's terrified to ask.

Alterman's attention goes back to the floor plan. "And there's a mystery beyond this missing room," Alterman says. "Who got us here? We don't know. It could be somebody knows something's going on here and hired us to expose it. Could be they think we're the only ones who can."

"What about…" Templeton says.

"I already thought of him."

"Wydgate?" Cherie says, pinching her nose.

"If he is behind it, we'll find out from the equipment." Templeton sees through this attempt to get them going along with the idea of so much surveillance. Anyone else would have smiled.

Alterman never smiles.

2

A few hours later, Cherie stands outside the door of a three-story home in a very quiet, high-dollar neighborhood not far from the church. She is whispering two words to herself.

"Jennifer Mersault," she says. "Jennifer Mersault."

Jennifer Mersault is her cover story, her alias. She almost didn't remember the name when she made her profession of faith at the church. She knows all the details of the life that Templeton constructed for her – all its uncomfortable details - but for some reason, she can't remember her name. She reaches up to touch her bangs just before the door opens. Cherie has never worn bangs before, but this too is part of the cover story. She is to look *too* polished.

The door opens to reveal a woman in her forties. "Jennifer?"

"Yes," Cherie says. The woman, who has never seen her before in her life, hugs her and moves her in while the door shuts behind them. Cherie heard the woman say her name, but was so intent on remembering her cover that she didn't pay attention. All she knows is this woman is the coordinator of one of the church's small singles groups.

Inside, there are about twenty or so people who are standing up to meet "Jennifer." Each of them welcomes her, one at a time, with handshakes from the men and mostly hugs from the women. The crowd is largely made up of young professionals, men and women in their mid-twenties. She assumes from their clothing and manner that most of them are college graduates. A few of them look in their thirties, and maybe one or two are older. There seems to be a rough dividing line running through the midst of them, separating those who seem brimming with unnatural enthusiasm to those who look emotionally broken.

She has seen - and been a part of - enough of these fellowships to know that among them are people who have been divorced, jilted at the altar, the unlucky survivors of countless unfortunate relationships, or wildly self-confident and exacting people who haven't yet found the right person. The mood probably sways between the two dynamics. Cherie knows there is likely someone in this group who expected to be married by now and finds their continued isolation a great spiritual trauma. There is also probably someone in here who is hoping to learn what God wants for his or her life after the end of a marriage - a calamity that was beyond that person's imagination just a few years before.

There are plenty of lean, hungry looks here, as people have either staked out a possible mate among the faces, or are silently hoping for someone to seize the initiative. She notices the looks on the men and silently weighs each one, trying to keep in mind how a stranger would evaluate this as a ministry.

"Don't forget who you are supposed to be," Templeton told her before.

Templeton concocted "Jennifer Mersault" using the demographic information he and Ingersoll put together prior to the audit. Jennifer is a college graduate who has just come to town after a career switch. She has a background in law work but is currently employed in public relations. She has never been married, though she was briefly engaged until a few months before. These are the facts that Cherie can share about herself if asked.

The deeper story - the one the group will use for its snooping - is that Jennifer was fired from her previous law firm job because of her substance abuse problem, which she still needs counseling for. She is deeply disappointed because her fiancé left her after he discovered her addiction.

The suggestion of this as her cover story shook her when she first learned it. She wasn't sure how she should phrase any question about it. Finally, she hit on one. "What was I addicted to?" Cherie asked Templeton, when she saw the cover story folder.

"We haven't decided yet," Templeton replied. "You'll know when you sign up for their counseling."

She didn't expect that answer, and she felt something inside her relax. Whatever fear she had suddenly disappeared.

"What if somebody asks?" she continued, expecting more.

Templeton, apparently oblivious, shook his head. "Nobody's going to ask, because you're not going to volunteer that information. Remember, you're ashamed of it."

"Oh yeah," she said. When she realized nothing more would be coming from Templeton, she gained yet another appreciation for Alex Alterman.

Standing there in the middle of the room amongst the singles, Cherie needs little reminding that there is a part of herself that she is ashamed of.

The singles coordinator lady asks everyone to sit down. She explains once again that her name is Anna Sparrow. Anna has a good strong voice and a pleasant smile and it's obvious why she has this job. Anna offers "Jennifer" a plush easy chair while the rest of the group sits down on mismatched furniture, or for some, the floor.

"Is this your home?" Cherie/Jennifer asks.

"This? Oh no," she laughs. "This is a foreclosed house. One of our members is letting us use it for the time being, so long as we don't eat out here."

"It's a nice neighborhood," Cherie says.

"Most of these houses are foreclosed. Empty. It's quiet. Can get a bit spooky out here if we have night fellowships."

"The guys like that," says one of the women, a blonde with bright green eyes and a vivid tanned complexion. "They always offer to walk you out to your car." There is laughter around, some a little too loud. This girl won't stay single for long, Cherie thinks.

"So tell us a little about yourself, Jennifer," Anna says. "That is, if you feel comfortable."

Cherie smiles, embarrassed, silently wondering to herself if she can remember the complete cover story. What she recalls, at that moment, is the amused, slightly wounded expression of Bobby Ingersoll.

Ingersoll - the one usually tapped to join a church. Her getting the job this time has surprised and annoyed him. He seems to feel this is punishment of some sort.

"You never liked this," she said to him, when they spoke of it. "You always complain about it!"

"Yeah, but I never said I didn't want to do it!"

"You're such a silly boy."

She is thinking about him because in the middle of this singles meat market she admits to herself once again that she is annoyed he has never shown any interest in her. She is intrigued by his mild skepticism and attracted by his single-minded manner. She feels, in some way she has never admitted to herself, that she is the person to ease all of his doubts, whether they be about himself or the reality of the Almighty. She feels like she understands him, and wonders why he can't seem to look over at her during the staff meetings. Cherie suspects that perhaps he does realize her interest, but he either isn't going to return it for professional reasons or doesn't feel the same things for her. They are both the same age, and they obviously have the same core interests. She feels she is not spectacular looking but that he is ignoring her obvious virtues. Cherie looks younger than her age, an advantage occasionally on the job. She wonders how much of this within her is that annoyingly insistent biological draw of children and domesticity. She fears that the air around her reeks of desperation.

But none of this helps her become Jennifer Mersault, so she tries to put it out of her mind. Anna is talking to her.

"Now, when you joined, you put down on your card that you wanted to meet up with us," Anna said. "So I'll tell you what we tell everyone who comes in. We're interested in you. We want you to become not just part of a meeting, but part of a ministry. That means you get fed, but you also feed others. You follow me? This isn't just the usual singles thing where we get together and have a Bible study and snacks and then we let you figure out who you want to date and you all pair off or you sit alone and wait for somebody new to come in and all that stuff…" Anna's voice suddenly got very fast as she simulated the desperation of the rapidly aging single in a sudden explosion of words. The laughs of the others egged her on. "No, we *do* things. We're about helping people. We're about helping you. We volunteer around the church and the community. We feed the homeless at the shelter twice a week and we raise money for missions, for the sick, for whoever needs it. Once a year, we take a mission trip. This year, we're going to Bulgaria. Last year, we built a church in Paraguay."

Cherie nods. Jennifer would be impressed by this, Cherie thinks, and probably a little overwhelmed. Somebody fighting substance abuse might not want to commit that much time and effort, or risk the connections involved. She could make a very educated guess in that regard.

"But we realize you might not have signed up for that. You might just have wanted to meet somebody nice and fall in love and all that stuff." Here, Anna clasps her hands together and rests her cheek on them, batting her eyes like someone impaled on Cupid's arrow. Again, laughter. "And that's no problem. We like to help there too. Was there some reason you signed up?" Anna asks. "Not to put you on the spot in front of everybody, even though I know I just did."

Laughter again. Cherie/Jennifer laughs too. She thinks a stranger would feel coerced at this point, pressured into this group's definition of service and might not feel the impulse to ever return. Yet for the emotionally fragile Jennifer, still addicted on some level to whatever it was she was addicted to, she might see this as a welcome challenge.

"Well, I guess I was just sort of interested in meeting people," she says. "Not that what you said doesn't appeal to me, because it does."

"But you signed up…"

She pauses for a split second, as she thinks Jennifer would. "I used to be engaged. Just for a short time. Didn't work out." That's right, she thinks. Be vague. Just like someone in this position would be. She hears a few of the group say "so sorry" or "aww" with tones of recognition. "I guess I wanted to be some place where I knew I'd meet...you know..."

"Nothing wrong with that," Anna replies.

"We all understand how that is," says another of the women, a redhead with an empathetic smile. "You won't find anybody special among these losers." She looks among the men, who scorn her with comic gusto.

"Jennifer's probably realized she's the cream of the crop, looking at all of you," says one of the guys. More laughs among them. A few of the guys recoil, sensing some line was crossed by the joke. The women don't seem offended.

"Yeah, you know how it is," Cherie/Jennifer says. "It's so hard to meet good guys these days."

"Where do you usually go to meet them?" Anna asks.

And before Cherie can remember that she's supposed to be someone else, she replies, honestly, "Church."

3

Wednesday night, and Templeton stands near the church front door, checking his watch until he sees Ingersoll in costume pass outside in the parking lot. The two do not look at each other. Templeton has been here for some time, setting up, but now he is at the crucial stage where they can either proceed with the operation or abort. He has been busy counting the people coming in. Wednesday night services don't usually draw as many people as Sunday, and Sweet Lightning is no exception. Only about thirty percent of the Sunday crowd shows up at the churches they usually audit, but Sweet Lightning is flirting with forty-five percent, which is impressive.

Templeton could have had a job in mathematics if he'd wanted it, but he instead opted for the ministry. He is still able to count and calculate the numbers, and his instincts tell him that if the number of people coming into the sanctuary does not significantly slow down in the next two or three minutes, they will have to call it off. This is a sacrosanct rule of Alterman's - one that they repeat back to him constantly. *We do not disrupt a church that isn't broken. There's enough of that going on already without us helping.* That is why it is so vital that this part of the audit, which is absolutely necessary, must happen tonight if the number stays right. They would never try this on a Sunday. In a few minutes, though, Templeton notices a considerable slackening, and he feels they can go on. He sends a text to Ingersoll - *Jericho* - and off they go.

Templeton sits in the third row from the back as the service begins. Almost immediately, the trouble begins, as Templeton expects it to.

Most church sound systems, Alterman maintains, in staff meeting after staff meeting, are bad. The speakers are cheap, or the mixing board is cheap and doesn't sufficiently compliment the speakers, or something else. The operators, who volunteer and usually work as plumbers or nuclear inspectors or fishermen, don't pay enough attention during the service. There's no sound check beforehand. Someone always manages to put at least one open microphone too many on stage, usually close to a choir member who either knocks it over by accident or snores loud enough to be picked up.

Templeton has heard all of these gripes and a host more, which is why he got here an hour beforehand in order to set things up. At the Sunday service, he identified at least one choir member upon whom they could test things out. Templeton's years in the ministry have made him able to spot the one person in any choir whose voice clashes with the rest. This voice is usually the one that gets attention by the mics. After Templeton identified her, he had no trouble positioning one of the mics, when no one was looking, right in front of her. Like a dog sensing a mailman, Alterman always says, an obnoxious voice in the choir perks up at the presence of a nearby microphone.

When the singing starts, Templeton looks at his watch. The second part of the experiment begins, as the computer program projected the hymn lyrics onto a screen flashes up the wrong words. Now the question will become how long before someone spots this and tries to correct it.

Not bad, Templeton thinks, when the screen goes black for an instant. Then the picture resumes, but Templeton knows what he has done to the program before anyone came in, and within a second or two, the words are wrong again and the screen once more goes black.

The church's music director is in his late thirties, a big, gregarious tenor voice attached to an athlete's body named Craig Pride. After this second problem, Craig holds his hand up at the end of the chorus to bring the song to a halt.

"Folks, we seem to be having some trouble," he says, and the piano player, unbidden, begins some light fill-in notes behind his voice, in order to keep the service moving. "So I'm going to propose something radical. If you look down on the backs of the pews, you'll see this thing that might look unfamiliar to you. It's called a hymn book." The congregation responds with laughter. "Maybe you dimly remember something like it, but I can promise you they still work. If you'll turn to page 354, that's page 354, we can sing along together. Don't look for a button or a stylus, just turn the pages. Will you try that now?" More laughter, and now the sound of ruffling pages. "Let's do it. And let's all try to sing as though we know the words anyway! Page 354, let's go," and Craig brings his fingers down to begin directing the song, which is louder and longer and definitely has more life to it now. A good save.

At first, when the choir gets going, Templeton wonders if the obnoxious voice up there has laryngitis. He can't hear her voice properly, he thinks, and he studies her to see if there is something wrong. No, he can hear her, she's right there, but she's nowhere near as loud as she should be. By all rights, she should overpower the rest of the people up there. He fiddled enough with that particular microphone before anyone came in. They must have had a sound check beforehand, he thought, just to thwart him. Alterman would approve. Alterman always says that 90 percent of the sound problems in most churches could be solved with a simple sound check that wouldn't take more than two minutes before the service. And the choir sounds remarkably balanced. Templeton did enough snooping to find out that choir members who miss the previous practice can only sing during the service if they bring a written excuse.

That's one thing about this place, Templeton thinks. Everyone who serves has to give up something. They don't act grateful to have warm bodies here occupying positions. You don't just show up at Sweet Lightning and fill a pew. They *expect* something out of you.

Some of that has to be due to Everhart, he thinks, as the pastor stalks up to the podium to begin. With a barely perceptible movement, he reaches behind to switch on the mic he has attached around his ear. Immediately, a wave of feedback crashes through the congregation, and they respond like souls in perdition, clamping both hands to their ears for relief.

Everhart's hand darts back to cut off the microphone, then he looks up at the sound board in the balcony. His gaze is not accusatory, but simply a bemused "what was that?" expression. Templeton has seen lesser pastors forget the setting and lash into the person at the board. One even uttered a sulphurous oath from the pulpit that briefly landed him in trouble with the church board. Everhart stands for a second or two, waiting for a signal to switch it back on. It does, but the quality of the pastor's voice is not encouraging. His amplified tones sound strained through an old transistor radio. There is no resonance, no bottom register. The words are thin and pockmarked with white noise and not pleasant to the ear. He speaks for a few minutes, giving perfunctory words while he casts another eye up to the board, like a penitent looking for relief from the sky.

He has no way of knowing that Templeton switched the perfectly good batteries in the mic for nearly dead ones, just at the edge of effectiveness. Everhart flicks on the mic again, and begins reading his text from the book of Jeremiah. He does not have the screen above him to provide the words, so he takes up Craig Pride's joke about the unfamiliarity of books and directs those without Bibles to use the words provided in the books next to the hymnals on the backs of the pews. Templeton sees every pew has a Bible next to the hymnal. After an acceptable pause, Everhart begins reading. The words fade in and out. The noise is dispiriting, Templeton can see, from the way Everhart is very subtly rolling his eyes at the crackling sound.

There is something else too. Templeton has rigged the earpiece that Everhart is wearing. With each word he utters, there is a two- to three-second delay before the same words ring in Everhart's ear. No one in the congregation will be aware of this. It's an old trick of Templeton's. When this usually happens, the victims stutter through their Scripture readings and sermons, much like a public address announcer at a stadium dealing with echo. This slows down their preferred pace and tends to upset them.

Everhart switches the mic off again. He looks up at the board and points to the microphone on the altar, and not so subtly rips off the mic that was pinned to his clothing, the now ineffective one. The earpiece goes with it. He begins speaking into the altar mic, but Templeton has also fiddled with this one as well, and it now will not work.

This is the moment when even the best pastors usually lose it. It's a moment that gives Templeton a thrill he doesn't like to admit to, but he appreciates since he has been in this position before. Some pastors attribute a fit of technical difficulties like this to Satan, and are able to use the moment to their advantage. Others are notably rattled from the first word and quite simply unable to continue. One of the reasons the team saves this part of the audit for Wednesday night is the percentage of church members who usually attend then is underwhelming, and visitors are less likely. Alterman never wants one of these capers to prevent the sharing of the Gospel with someone who needs it.

Templeton catches sight of those two people from the earlier service - the couple who are standing in the back with a video recorder. They seem just as interested in how this turns out as he is, though Templeton is sure they have no idea what is going on.

But as always happens, whenever they do the sound caper, there is a sign - Everhart's sermon is about…perseverance. Whenever they test a church's sound, the sermon usually deals with this subject. Alterman interprets this as God's blessing on what they're doing.

Everhart is one of those guys who will seize the instant for its possibilities. Everhart grips his open Bible and waves off any concerns about himself. "I did this in smaller churches without a mic, and I can do it here," he announces. "Can everybody hear me in the back?" A few voices confirm they can.

And now Everhart begins to lay out his sermon points in a voice that seems eager for this latest challenge. Some of the congregation lean forward on the pews to hear better, but it isn't really necessary. Then the air conditioning kicks in with a dull roar that eats into the silence, and Templeton is silently amused because of this unplanned addition to the test. Still, Everhart soldiers on. In a few minutes, it is obvious that the sound equipment has been holding him back. His voice carries over them with the force of a nineteenth century open air revivalist. There is a richness in his voice, and in the words, that makes Templeton long for the days before air conditioning and sound equipment when the Spirit worked within the pull of the human voice by means more mystic than the control of Dolby sound.

And Templeton, without realizing it, begins chastising himself for the jealousy he feels against Everhart. He wonders what this eloquent man, still relatively young, a gifted writer and speaker, is doing in this church that is obviously too small for his talent or charisma.

Lord, I know your ways are inscrutable to me, he thinks in prayer, *but couldn't this man do so much more elsewhere, in some place bigger?*

But that thought inevitably draws him back down into something else - wondering not why Everhart is here, but what he himself is doing there.

Shouldn't our roles be reversed? I'm older than this man, and I think I'm more talented as a preacher. I'm a very good minister for my people. And yet, why isn't he out here evaluating me up on that pulpit?

God, why aren't you using me now?

Even as he thinks the words, he tries to tamp them back down into his imagination. There is no reason for him to be that negative. God is obviously using him, just not in the way he would prefer. The central mystery of Templeton's life at this moment is the same as it had been since just before he met Alex Alterman. The aim of his life had been preaching, only now he realizes that his present still involves the sharing of the word of God, just in a different way that the Lord has provided. But still that same question keeps dogging him: Why is he here? What is God up to with him occupying this place, the business partner of a man many people of faith call *the Scourge of God*?

Then Templeton snaps back to attention. Everhart has made a point - his voice loud enough that it echoes off the buffers in the rafters. Then he feigns surprise and scorn on the congregation. "That was a good place for an Amen! folks, and you just missed it!"

The voices respond, including Steve Templeton, with an "Amen!" Everhart is enjoying himself mightily up there, and Templeton wipes a tear in shame and looks around to make certain that no one is noticing him.

And just then, everyone in the congregation hears the squeal of tires.

4

Ingersoll has done the drill before, and it never gets old. He loves the play of it - getting into costume and using the hardware to get the work done. It thrills him, even as he sees Templeton inside, because he will relish each part of the experiment.

Ingersoll is wearing an oversize Army surplus heavy jacket, in spite of the temperature outside, which is hovering in the mid-sixties. He is wearing a wig and thick glasses and the extra heel in his shoe gives him a walk that is distinctive. Inside his pocket, if he is searched, is a copy of J.D. Salinger's "The Catcher in the Rye." His costume has been calibrated with every mug shot he's ever studied in acts of church crime.

There were 74,445 crimes reported on church campuses last year according to the FBI, Alterman says in their briefings. Of those, the overwhelming majority were cases of vandalism. But there's no way anyone on the team would stoop to such a thing. Instead, there are different ways of testing out a church's security.

Ingersoll enters through a side door and begins walking through the atrium, with his hands in his coat pockets, past the ushers. The heel addition gives him an ambling walk, but it also hurts his foot and makes his gait that much more clumsy. So he is bound to attract some attention. That is, if these men are paying any attention at all.

Alterman is clear. We're not going to disturb a service in any way that might not happen naturally, but we might as well see if a church has any contingencies for potential problems. Thus was born this page of Alterman's playbook – the random disruptor.

Ingersoll tends to stalk through church lobbies with a hurt look on his face, as though he only learned pain the first time he stepped through the church doors. He doesn't know if people notice him, since the disruptor's modus operandi is usually not to look at anyone just before an attack. The angry expression, the determined walk, matched with the coat, should be enough of a giveaway. The coat is big enough to conceal a gun, several guns in fact, or other implements of mayhem.

Alterman says there were 81 weapons law violations at churches in America last year. A man carrying just one firearm can harm scores of people, can destroy a single life. Ingersoll has heard the stories so many times he can mouth the words. He isn't carrying any weapons, of course. But he's testing reactions here, as he walks.

Or trips. When Ingersoll falls, as he always does, he tends to injure some part of his body. When they did the church in Texas, he broke his nose, but insisted on going through with the mission even after the ushers found him a cold compress and offered to call an ambulance. On some level, this church passed a test, but not necessarily the one they had meant for that day. This time, Ingersoll feels his leg pop and believes he might have torn a ligament. One of the ushers appears from nowhere to help him up, and he stands on the leg gingerly, like a running back whose knee has caught during a bad cut on turf.

All Ingersoll is waiting for is one key phrase to pop up.

"May I take your coat, sir?" he hears. An usher standing near him in a sport shirt and slacks reaches out a hand, as if he expects the coat to be handed to him.

Only about forty-five seconds since he entered the door. Not bad. And he even used proper grammar.

"Can I help you?" the man asks, once he realizes the coat is not being handed over. Only this time, there is a barely perceptible edge to his voice. It's obvious the guy suspects something. If he got a whiff of him, he'd know that Ingersoll hasn't bathed in three days. He's glad that Cherie is somewhere else.

"Yeah," Ingersoll says. "Where's your bathroom?"

The man softens considerably. "Right this way," he says, pointing in the direction of the door marked with the "men" sign. Ingersoll nods his thanks without making eye contact. They have successfully neutralized him, which is good for them because Alterman tends to be very unforgiving on the subject of pulpit security.

So it's time for Ingersoll to move to the next phase, which is parking lot security.

There were 1,248 motor vehicle thefts in church parking lots in America last year, Alterman says. Usually these happen because there is little or no parking lot security to speak of. But Ingersoll knows this isn't the case at Sweet Lightning. He did enough research beforehand to know that the church has mostly volunteer security provided by its deacons, but one of them is a retired FBI agent. That is why Ingersoll is wearing a bullet-proof vest, though he doesn't relish the possibility of using his mixed martial arts training.

It is already dark, which is why Ingersoll reaches into his pocket for his smart phone, which he dials as he walks out the door of the church. It only takes a moment of entering a few numbers before the parking lot lights are extinguished. They will stay off as long as Ingersoll wants them to, which should be long enough for him to fulfill his mission. Walking out the church's front doors, Ingersoll puts on his night vision goggles. He might not need them but he enjoys the thought of using them, as they carry the sinister glow of espionage.

He is serious about this sort of thing. Underneath his coat and a dirty costume T-shirt is another that reads, "I will stand on my watch and set myself upon the rampart."

Ingersoll staked out the cars when they drove in, until he found the red sports car driven by some teenage girl who got out in a hurry, possibly to meet her boyfriend. Not only is this car routinely cited as one of the easiest on the market to steal, the girl made it even easier by not locking the door. Ingersoll could see it from across the parking lot. She made it a little hard on him by parking so close to the main way out of the campus, but all he needs is about 90 seconds.

It will take that long to hot wire the car and drive it to the other side of the parking lot, where he will park it and leave, thereby proving that the security detail was lax. He takes a photograph of the license plate. If there is any damage to the car, a check will be sent to the owner.

Understandably, like Templeton inside, this isn't where Ingersoll saw himself either. When Ingersoll left the seminary to work for Alterman, he did so at the suggestion of Whit Mountain, one of his former professors. One wouldn't expect this slightly geeky, off-kilter kid to bond with a folksy ex-preacher, but Whit charmed him with his humor and seized his imagination with the way he taught the Pauline epistles. When Ingersoll was looking for a reason out of seminary, Whit suggested Alterman's work as a proof of the faith. Not that Ingersoll had to prove his own faith as much as prove the faith to himself.

Ingersoll entered his theology courses with what he felt was unshakeable devotion. The words on the pages of his Bible didn't suddenly fade or curdle in his imagination. What began to undo him were the attitudes of his professors. He was reminded of drill sergeants from movies about the military, who dehumanized their recruits in order to send them out into battle. Instead, these old men - and they were all men - treated the Bible with the same indifference as the directions that come with furniture to be assembled. The instructions were written in a badly-translated foreign language that no one could read, they seemed to be saying, and those instructions were just as easily discarded when they became too difficult. The tables and chairs could still be put together in any fashion. Leftover parts were understandable, but not needed.

And the attitude of other classrooms appalled him, where the teachers seemed to feel the Gospels were made of snow and these bright, eager, young minds would melt the stories into shadows of themselves, as though Jesus Himself might evaporate from too close scrutiny. Ingersoll remembered that his closest friends seemed more devout about science fiction movies and television shows than the Holy Word of God they were presumably spending the best years of their lives to learn.

But Ingersoll didn't dare tell Alterman - or anyone else - about his "Damascus Road" experience. It was such a transitory thing, it too felt like it might melt under the heat of his devotion. But he knew what it was, and he knew how it felt, and he was as sure of the agency of God in his life as a result because …the episode was so absurd.

He was at a party with some of his friends. With twenty people milling around an apartment, he sat brooding over a soft drink while the original "Star Wars" played on the television. It was a movie he genuinely loathed, but he didn't know too many people there and the girl he was interested in was too busy complaining to someone about one of her classes.

What am I doing here? he wondered. The question had come to him in seminary so many times he was seriously considering leaving. In some ways, he began to see his ambition for the pulpit as some kind of second-rate thing, that he was settling for something when he could be making money or finding something deeper.

And then, just as suddenly, the ideas fled him. There, on the screen, was the face of Darth Vader, pinching the air with his finger and thumb, using his powers to strangle a man who dared to question him.

"I find your lack of faith disturbing," he said.

The scene in his memory is so ridiculous that Ingersoll finds himself laughing at it, even today. The words are exactly what he should have been hearing, yet they were coming from behind the mask of a screen villain. He sensed many things all at once - the idea of God's unmistakable sense of humor, a grinning acknowledgment that, instead of speaking through Scripture, he must hide within the mechanisms of a pseudo-religious secular fantasy and emerge at the precise point when He would be recognized.

Of course, Ingersoll thought, sometimes God speaks from behind a black mask with the voice of a dark father. And when this happens, our reaction is almost always, "Well, this can't mean what I think it does."

Thinking back on it, Ingersoll wonders how his life would have turned out if he had been watching the Wizard of Oz, and his sudden epiphany had chosen to come with the famous line, "Pay no attention to that man behind the curtain." But instead, he left the party and the school and began serving this other dark father Alterman, a man who somehow felt the church would arise triumphant if it would only properly line its parking places.

It only takes about eight seconds for Ingersoll to check the lot just as he arrives at the sports car's door. He looks over his shoulder, opens the door and dashes in. Just as quickly, he pops the glove compartment open and Bingo! finds a spare key inside. The engine comes to life when he turns the ignition. Ingersoll recognizes a twinge of regret inside himself that he hadn't needed to hotwire the car. He knows how. Be as wise as servants and harmless as doves.

"Just a minute," a voice outside the car says. The voice is amplified, as if through a bullhorn, which it is. Ingersoll has enough time to see in the rearview mirror a golf cart with its driver holding a flashlight, glaring in the rearview mirror. Ingersoll squints as it plays havoc with the night vision goggles. "Step out of the car please." The voice is not genial and knows precisely that he is not the vehicle's owner.

Where did he come from? Ingersoll thinks. *How did he sneak up on me? Where was he? I didn't see anybody a second ago. Must be the FBI guy.*

Ingersoll ignores the queasy feeling in his stomach. This guy may have once been in the FBI, he thinks, but right now, he's in a golf cart.

Ingersoll floors the gas pedal and the golf cart disappears behind a sudden haze of burned rubber and the sound of his whistling tires. Ingersoll knows the parking lot well - he has studied its layout for just this kind of eventuality. There was that church they audited last summer where he was mistaken for a vagrant and pepper sprayed, right after they Tasered him. He lobbied hard with Alterman afterward to give the church a failing grade. Sure their pastor gave great sermons, he said, but they obviously weren't teaching the non-violent passages of the Gospels thoroughly. When Alterman suggested that Ingersoll should have turned his other cheek, Templeton had to separate the two of them.

But this golf cart evidently isn't just a golf cart, or there's more than one, because Ingersoll finds quickly that at least one golf cart is up ahead as he comes around one corner, barring his way. Ingersoll has enough time to back up and wheel out again, then down another row of neatly parked cars.

He can even now hear Alterman warning him, like a driving instructor coaching a nervous teenager with a learner's permit. "If you hit one of those carts, you're liable to kill the driver. Don't be afraid to give yourself up."

But Ingersoll feels insulted by the notion that he can be bested by a group of guys in golf carts, none of whom he's sure is equipped with night vision goggles. He will hear about this later from Alterman if he is caught, which is one of the reasons he doesn't want to get caught.

Ingersoll makes another turn, only this time he sees a woman up ahead and a smaller figure. He has enough time to register that this smaller figure is a little girl who is out far enough from her mother, and close enough to the path of his car, that the mother's immediate reaction is to lunge forward and pull her daughter out of the way. The woman is in her late forties. The girl is probably just shy of ten years old. The girl is wearing red pants.

He has enough time to step on the brakes hard enough that he fears his foot will go through the floor. The girl is in her mother's grasp now, and Ingersoll does not go until he is sure the two of them are out of the way.

Then he wheels out again, turning down another straightaway of car rows.

He has the insane idea that he is going too fast for these golf carts, but he is only going forty miles an hour for a few brief seconds, before he edges the gas down to make corners. He sees another golf cart, and he realizes that these guys have radio and are coordinating their response in some way to make sure he doesn't get away. They are going to be unlucky though, since they don't realize that Ingersoll has planned this, and not to escape with a car. Just to escape.

One of the carts is moving into position to cut him off. Ingersoll can't see the man driving it, but he sees it is taking a curve too fast and, before the man is able to compensate for his speed, it tips over and spills him out. Another horror grips Ingersoll – maybe this is a 60-year-old deacon who volunteered for the job and is unaware that the lining of the main arteries to his heart are clogged beyond measure, so that when his golf cart upends him, he will inevitably have the heart attack that will spell the end of Alterman's firm and Ingersoll's career.

But the man is actually in his thirties and appears well, even though he puts up a hand as he lies on the pavement, and the pose reminds Ingersoll of Caravaggio's painting of the martyrdom of St. Matthew the Evangelist. According to tradition, Matthew was murdered by the guards of the King of Ethiopia after Matthew preached against him for his lust. In the painting, Matthew lies before a guard, his hand extended over his head, not in horror, but to receive the palm branch offered by a waiting angel.

And Ingersoll remembers that Matthew is the patron saint of, among other things, security guards.

In his rearview mirror, Ingersoll sees the guards pour out of their golf carts and race to help their fallen comrade, who stands up just as Ingersoll rounds another corner, shuts off the lights, and parks right at the back of the lot. Then, he is out of the car, pulls off his rubber gloves used to prevent fingerprints, and sprints off. There is a wooded area adjoining the back, though Ingersoll briefly considers that he can make a run for the ocean and swim to safety, provided he's willing to swim the two weeks it would take to get from Sweet Lightning to the island of Cuba.

Ingersoll runs for the woods. He takes off his surplus jacket and reverses it, to reveal the inner design, which is the style of any other ordinary raincoat. He removes the rest of the costume apparatus, expect for the false heel.

He hears the shouts of the deacon security guards from halfway across the parking lot, but he feels prepared. If I were a car thief - he thinks, crafting the opening sentences of his report to Alterman - I would live in fear of the security at Sweet Lightning Church.

A chase in a church parking lot involving a stolen car and two golf carts, one wrecking? That might satisfy him.

But Alterman, Ingersoll reminds himself again, is never satisfied.

5

He wasn't going to stop at the church. He was going to keep driving. Everyone else was there, so it would be awkward for him to be there as well. But then he saw the couple. They were across the street, at the gas station, aiming a camera at the church. He pulled over and got out.

Alterman approaches the two with some nervousness, unsure of how to proceed. He wrestles with the twin impulses, equally attractive, of directly confronting them or drawing information out of them without revealing too much about himself.

The woman, Miss Diddle, speaks first, letting out a squeal as he gets close enough for her to make out his features. "You're Alex Alterman!" she says, pointing.

"Yeah," he says, now very uneasy, his feet stopping as though he expects a counter punch. But he is unaware that his hand is still outstretched toward them, as he had mulled over a handshake.

The two of them rush forward and grab it, pumping furiously.

"What are you doing here?" she demands. For a second, he thinks she might want an autograph.

"I...I have to be *somewhere*," he stammers out. "Just thought I'd come down and check the place out."

"Wow!" Steeplechase says, giving his partner a quick glance. "We lucked out being here at the same time."

"How do you know me?"

"Everybody in our field knows you, Mr. Alterman," she says, the *mister* making him feel 10,000 years old. Her voice, and her deference to him, is surprising. He expected her to be confrontational.

"You're the guys with the website."

"X-pose," she says. "Yeah, we've been working on that for months. Really taking off. Lots of page views."

"Six figures, right?"

"How did you know?"

Alterman wasn't impressed. He knew they were inflating the figures. He could tell by how they seized on the number. He'd seen churches do the same thing in stating the page views on their own websites. Everybody overestimates.

"You're one of us, aren't you?" Steeplechase says.

"One of what?"

"You don't believe," he says. "You're an atheist. Just like us."

"I knew it!" she says, as though he has confirmed it by the way his mouth is hanging open.

"You're going about this from the inside. You *want* to destroy churches," Steeplechase says. "You just make them think you're helping them."

"Why would you say that?" Alterman is surprised at him and looks wounded.

"You've got a bigger reputation than we do. Word has it you go from one church to another, trashing every one of them, sometimes for no reason at all. And they invite you in!"

"Don't churches do the same to you?"

"They invite us in, but they're trying to convert us. At least, that's what they tell us. Most of the time, they're trying to control the picture. They put us in the back, bad sound, bad lighting, all that. But they actually *pay* you! How do you do it?"

"It's a business," he says, unable to understand.

"We know, but still. There's your competition too. He's in town. I don't know if you know that."

"I always know where he is." Alterman isn't sure why he says this. Well, he knows, but he isn't sure why he said it *aloud.*

"We know *he's* a believer. But how do you get them to let you do this? I mean, we try to be as polite as we can, everywhere we go. And everybody's very nice to us. But you trash them and they keep asking for you. How are you able to do that?"

"They think what I have to say is valuable," he says. "What's your story? Why are you here?"

"He's the big news lately," Steeplechase says, pointing to the church, as though it was the same thing as a giant graven image of Thomas Everhart. "We figure Big Jesus will try to up his profile soon."

"Big Jesus?" Alterman says, before remembering what this means.

"That's our website code for mainline Christianity," Diddle says. "The corporations standing in for their Savior, who always demands a profit."

"You guys are serious, then, aren't you?"

"Of course we are," she says. "That's how we met. We were in a Bible study group in a fundamentalist college."

"Which one?" Alterman asks. They tell him. He nods his head knowingly. He was approached to audit them after the televangelist who founded the place died of a heart attack a few years back. After he had been imprisoned for tax fraud. And extortion. And other things.

"We got tired of the lies," Steeplechase says. "We got tired of having to explain things over and over to ourselves instead of just admitting the truth."

"Which is?" Alterman wonders.

"This is all a sham!" Diddle says, pointing again to the church. "All of it. The churches. The Bible. It's just preying on easily impressionable, uneducated people. Manipulating their hatred and ginning up their votes. Feeding them Bronze Age myths."

"Jesus wasn't Bronze Age."

"No, that's not when he was supposed to have lived, if he lived at all."

"Oh, he lived."

"How do you know that?"

"He lived," Alterman says. "He did it just to annoy you."

"Look," Steeplechase says, "you don't have to act with us. It's OK. What you're doing is needed. Somebody needs to expose the truth about what's going on in there." Again, he pointed to the church, as though a team of government scientists was dissecting aliens inside behind barbed wire fences.

"If only we were as dangerous as you seem to think we are," Alterman says, shaking his head.

"What do you mean?"

"I'm telling you. I look into these churches to tell them how to do their jobs better."

"But how can you get away with saying what you do to them?"

"I'm sorry, but you're dead wrong about me. I'm a believer."

"But some of the things you've done..." Diddle begins.

"They were necessary."

"Why?" Steeplechase asks.

"To get across the point."

"Which is?"

"You can't play at this kind of thing."

6

Obadiah looks skeptically at the teacher. He takes a step toward the woman dropping him off at the door to the classroom. A sign above the door reads "creepers and toddlers."

"It's all right," the woman says, in a sweet voice, picked up by the teacher. "It's all right," the teacher repeats, putting her hand out.

Obadiah's face has for a second or two hovered near tears, but his lip stiffens. The teacher's hand goes out again, and Obadiah takes another few steps and grips it. Not too much, but the grip is firm and sets them both at ease.

"See?" the teacher beams, putting her other hand behind the little guy and directing him into the room.

The woman lets out an audible sigh, presumably of relief. "Sometimes he doesn't do well adapting to new surroundings."

"I'm sure he'll be fine." The teacher looks reassuringly at Obadiah. "You will, won't you?" she coos, sweetly.

"I should tell you, don't expect him to talk too much," the woman dropping him off says. "He just doesn't talk. We're seeing a doctor about it."

"That's all right. He seems like a very good child."

"You'll call me if there's a problem?" the lady asks.

"That buzzer we gave you? It'll go off if we need you. Just like what they give you at a restaurant when you're waiting."

"Oh!" she says, as though she was a fool to just take the buzzer without asking what it was for. She hunches down, smiles, and waves at Obadiah, who has picked up a fire truck and begins pushing it along the ground. Obadiah looks up, smiles, and waves back at the woman, who is Cherie LeFevre. She puts the buzzer in her purse, as any other mother might, and walks to the sanctuary, counting her steps. It is necessary in order to determine how far the buzzers reach. She expects at some point Obadiah will give her reason to come.

It has been about a year since Alterman contacted Obadiah Falkenburg, the subject of a British documentary about his extremely rare condition. Obadiah is a 32-year-old man with a deep, commanding voice that occasionally serves him well working in radio. However, due to hormone deficiencies and a pituitary gland imbalance, Obadiah never grew beyond the height he achieved at the age of three. Except for a few more rounded features in his face, he appears to all the world as a toddler. His mere existence is one of the most closely guarded secrets of Alterman's organization.

Though rumors have inevitably leaked out, no one seriously believes that Alterman and Wydgate are able to spirit a dwarf into preschool classes at churches without some teacher being wise enough to figure out the ruse. The truth is that Alterman, while unable to sleep one night, saw a British documentary about Obadiah's plight and immediately set about contacting him. Alterman realized the value of having someone with a rare growth disorder on his payroll. "I knew," Alterman said upon meeting him, "that you'd be a devout man. With your condition."

Obadiah seemed offended at first. "What, you don't think I'd blame God for being a perpetual kid?"

Of course, he didn't. Obadiah is like that, though. He enjoys playing elaborate jokes on people, and that is why he likes working for Alterman. He has learned to keep silent so that his voice - and the British accent - does not give him away. Alterman has him flown over, on a private jet no less, in order to keep his existence as quiet as possible.

Obadiah knows the teacher is Margie Everhart, the pastor's wife. She is a lovely woman with immaculate hair and immaculate nails and a warm smile. Obadiah's folder told him that she is a child psychologist. We'll see how that translates into the classroom, he thinks. The file Alterman gave him on her is several hundred pages thick, counting a paperback copy of the book she wrote before she married the minister. She looked supremely confident in the author's photo. She seems different here - lost in her thoughts, preoccupied even. Obadiah wonders if he should mention this in his report.

Obadiah ambles over to the toy box. He has learned how to master the walk of someone for whom steps are still a new thing. The first thing is to look the toys over, see that they're not worn out or dangerous, and test the environment.

Then, the teachers. He doesn't expect a lot of trouble out of Mrs. Everhart, but there is always the volunteer with her.

Obadiah eyes the man coolly. He is a young father - probably a guy in his late twenties or early thirties, still getting used to the idea of kids. Or somebody elses' kids. The few times he sees the man interact with the children, it's usually through Mrs. Everhart. The guy reaches into the big box of Goldfish crackers but he hands them to Mrs. Everhart to dispense. Obadiah deems him *The Silent Partner.*

"Anyone want some fishys?" she asks, and a few of the children silently amble over to grab, some with smiles, some with a solemn, primal singleness of purpose.

"You want a fishy?" she asks Obadiah.

It has taken Obadiah awhile to learn that children don't usually respond with a shake of the head at first. He simply ignores the question, even when it is repeated. If he were to speak, he could fill a book with how much he despises these crackers.

Obadiah raises a chubby hand to receive a few, then he looks them over for a second before putting them in the pocket of his bright blue overalls. He has learned over time that this inspires a laugh from the teachers and not only helps establish his cover, but also disposes of the problem crackers. The teachers laugh to see how carefully he places the crackers in his pockets and assume this is something he learned somewhere.

"Okay, Obadiah," Mrs. Everhart observes aloud, "you'll have yours later."

Obadiah then walks back to the toolbox and looks for something he glanced at a second or two before - something at the bottom of the toolbox that looked like a toy gun. He is curious, because he usually counts off for violent toys found in the nurseries.

Obadiah angles his way down through the box, moving one toy and another out of the way. He knows that if he continues to do this, as a toddler would, he will lose his balance and pitch forward into the toy box. But Mrs. Everhart's friendly volunteer, the Silent Partner, is standing close by and grabs Obadiah at the waist.

"You don't want to fall in," he says, gently, before settling him down. There is a second's pause before the man adds, "You're a heavy one!" Obadiah blanches for a moment, but the Silent Partner doesn't seem all that concerned, so his cover isn't blown.

To get the job with Alterman, Obadiah had to sign a "loyalty agreement," which included, among other things, a proviso saying that Obadiah isn't allowed to do any more documentaries while he is with the company.

"Why not?" he asked.

"Because evangelicals watch documentary television 22 percent more than the normal population, surveys show," Alterman replied. "I don't want anyone recognizing you." Alterman then went to the trouble of creating an academic discrepancy with the film company regarding Obadiah's disorder so that the networks would pull the documentary. It would be better if fewer people saw it.

Alterman wasn't sensitive about it when they first spoke.

You and this church have something in common, Alterman said before one mission. You're both suffering from stunted growth.

Obadiah had to learn to restrain his temper after being hit in the face by two-year-olds unused to playing with others. Or resisting the temptation to say something when a teacher used excessive force in his judgment to subdue a problem child.

Still, these kids will drive you nuts. You know why they call them creepers? Obadiah asks. Because that's what dealing with them gives you. He still has the mark on his forehead from the girl at one church who threw a plastic toy tool box at him and connected. That church did not get a favorable rating, but the least of its problems was its nursery.

After a few minutes glancing around, Obadiah solves the mystery of the gun. Obadiah sees a little boy of about three holding a toy power drill in one hand. He is using the thing correctly too, as he fits one oversize plastic screw into the hole of a plastic imaginary steel girder. So maybe the church doesn't get points off for that, though he will keep his eye on the boy anyway. The drill is safe, in theory, but any toy can prove dangerous in the hands of the wrong child.

Obadiah looks up at the clock on the wall. After a discreet length of time, he approaches the Silent Partner.

"You okay?" the man asks, his voice modulating between kiddie talk and genuine concern. He can see something in Obadiah's face is not right.

Obadiah points to the bathroom.

"Oh, you have to go potty?" the man asks.

Obadiah nods. This is a crucial test, yet the ridiculous way the man talks threatens to make him blow his cover in a knowing smile. Children always turn adults into gibbering idiots.

For a second or two, Obadiah expects that the Silent Partner is slowly directing him at his pace to the bathroom, and in so doing, angling for points off. Obadiah knows the church policy is not to have a man taking any children to the bathroom.

The Silent Partner stays true to his calling. "Mrs. Margie," he says. "Obadiah here has to go."

"You do?" Margie replies, as though this is breathtaking news. "Well let's just go then," she says, reaching out to take Obadiah's hand on the short walk to the bathroom. Thus far, the church is doing well. Mrs. Everhart gets Obadiah to the door, where he provokes another round of laughter when he smiles and shuts the door on Mrs. Everhart.

"I guess he doesn't need any help," she says.

One thing operating in Obadiah's favor is that most church nurseries don't compare notes, just as most church nurseries don't expect toddlers to be smart enough to figure out how to escape. If they did, then they would know what to expect when Alterman is hired to audit a church. Because what Obadiah is about to attempt is the same part of the act that he has carried off successfully in a dozen or so churches.

Before he ever entered the church, Obadiah studied its floor plan and noticed that the nursery classrooms had shared common bathrooms, opening out to two different classes. So any child left alone in the toilet could walk out the other door and into another classroom. And Obadiah knew that, in this case, the other classroom was unoccupied. If someone had left the door to the other classroom unlocked, he was free and clear.

Obadiah gripped the door knob to the bathroom's other, opposite door, turned, and opened it into a darkened, vacant classroom.

The last time Obadiah did this, it took the previous church's nursery staff 45 minutes to finally find him, hiding in a storage closet digging into a box of chocolate chip cookies. At no time during his absence did they notify Cherie, who was sitting through the service waiting for her buzzer to go off. Instead, they cleaned Obadiah up and presented him back to Cherie at the appointed time, making no mention that he had been missing for nearly an hour. After all, he didn't talk, so they needn't worry about him squealing. The only thing that had kept that church's nursery from getting a completely failing grade was that the outside doors had been locked, preventing him from escaping.

Obadiah gets a nice feeling of vindication during each of these missions. All of his life, he has been underestimated. Even longtime friends occasionally act as though he is unable to think as profoundly or feel emotions as deeply as they do, simply because of his stunted size. Those who bother to find out are shocked that he once supplied the basso-profundo voice for a well-known cartoon villain, is a skilled auto mechanic, and has successfully parachuted more than 50 times. The poor people of this church, well-meaning though they were, don't know who they're tangling with. Before too long he'll wander into the sanctuary and disturb the morning service, he thinks, as he tries the doorknob to the classroom. Once out into the hall, they will be hard pressed to find him in a building so huge.

But the doorknob doesn't move. It is locked. And there is no way he can see to unlock it.

"Obadiah?" comes the soft voice of Margie Everhart, cutting through the darkness, just before the lights switch on. Evidently, she waited an acceptable moment before checking on him and finding the bathroom vacant.

In a split second, Obadiah tries to wipe the frustration from his face at being thwarted and replaces it with a benign look of toddler irritation at being unable to lock a door.

"Nice try," she says, patiently, taking him by the hand. "You need to come back in here with us. You're too crafty." What awes Obadiah is the quiet amusement he detects in her voice, as though she suspects there is more to him than is readily apparent, yet satisfaction that a potential embarrassment is easily disposed of.

As she walks him back to the rest of the children, Obadiah is deep in thought. He is trying to figure out if he can use the locked door to cite the nursery for a fire code violation.

7

"So how are you?" Alterman begins, cradling the phone.

He is standing up – Alterman carries a stand-up desk with him on trips because he doesn't believe in sitting down for long periods of time. He usually puts his phone on speaker but he doesn't like the way it occasionally cuts off what someone says on the other end. He always has the feeling he's being talked about nastily. And he's taking a risk, because this is Rambha he is talking to, and it's been awhile since their last communication. This is by design.

"Amazing, Alex," she begins. He can tell by her tone she is putting him on. Not in a joking way, he thinks, but in the way someone who has just been hired is trying to impress the boss. "I must tell you this is going much better than I anticipated. None of them suspect anything."

"That's what you think," Alterman said. "Just because you don't suspect anything doesn't mean they're the same way. Remember that."

"Yessir," she says, and he can almost see her saluting him on the other end of the line. The operatives in the field are always like this. You give them freedom to do something, and they resent you when you make the slightest suggestion of how they might do things.

After a moment of silence, he sighs. "What have you got?"

She snaps to attention. "Well Alex, the first thing I can tell you is that he seems very nonchalant about the whole thing. Brother Thomas, I mean. They call him Brother Tommy but I see no reason to be so informal."

"They always seem that way," he says. "It's a given."

"I wouldn't think so," she says. "Not how you might expect. From where I'm sitting, it's business as usual."

"You wouldn't know business as usual there as you've only been watching them for a few days, but I'll take your word for it." He knows he's sounding more dismissive than he usually is, but Alterman always sounds dismissive, even when he's praising someone.

"His only instruction that I'm aware of is that everyone is to proceed about their business in the usual way."

"And what sense do you get? Is everyone doing things in the usual way?"

She considers this question, judging by the millisecond of silence. "I would suppose one could consider it routine, but I do get the impression of everyone being slightly elevated, as you might say. On their toes somewhat."

"Afraid he'll step on them."

"Surely you don't think they're afraid of *him*."

"Who are they afraid of?"

"Why... you, Alex."

"Any special instructions you're aware of?"

"My perspective is limited, you must imagine, as I'm away from the rest of you."

"You have the best seat in the house."

"Quite. But no special instructions other than what I previously shared with you. He did say something about security needing to be better."

"I'm sure he did."

"He was telling the deacon in charge he was concerned more about worshippers' safety than whether we catch car thieves."

"Yes, I'm concerned about that too, actually..."

"I wasn't sure what he was talking about myself," Rambha says. "But that's the only thing I'm aware of. I would say that everyone I've talked to thinks he's under a lot of strain."

"Me again?"

"No. No, they say it's been going on a lot longer."

"I know how it is."

"Tell me," she asks. "How hard is it for you?"

"It's a lot of inside baseball stuff," Alterman says. He doesn't expect her to answer.

She does. "Tell me what you mean Alex. I'm interested to know."

"It's a long story."

"What is it? Indulge me, please."

Alterman clears his throat, somewhat put off by her insistence. "It's just that I'm not sure how to proceed with all of this. We're here, and I'm not sure why."

"Weren't we hired?"

"Yes, but we don't know who hired us. And now we learn that our main competition is here."

"Satan?"

"Not that competition. Another auditing service."

"They can't be as good as us. That's obvious."

"Good answer. But it strikes me as a more than coincidence that we are both here in this town at the same time. And then there are the atheists with the website. Something is happening here apart from us. Something bigger."

"Whatever it is should reveal itself soon enough," she said. "Better to let it come to you than force it."

He hadn't expected this. "Good work, eager young space cadet." He is almost ready to hang up, after he gives her the expected pep talk.

"Alex, while I have you on the line, let me ask: Is this a test of character?"

"You mean for Brother Everhart? No, it's the whole..."

She interrupts him with the tone of someone patiently instructing another adult in how to write the alphabet. "No, I'm sorry. You misunderstood me. I mean, is my part in this audit a test of character?"

"A test for who?"

"For me." She exhales in exasperation. "Seriously, I want to know."

"What makes you think that?"

"Well, you haven't denied it."

"Are you concerned that you might be failing this test?"

"No. I'm concerned that you aren't utilizing me to the fullest extent of my talents."

"As you say, we are both learning each other's routines. So your talents and their full scope are still in the process of revealing themselves to me."

"From this distance?"

"I may be closer than you think."

8

Cherie's next order of business is to ask Anna Sparrow if she wants to use the church gym. This will serve several purposes – she will get to know Anna. She can evaluate the gym. Alterman and Templeton have already put together a checklist for her. It will go toward her cover story of wanting to clean up her life. And lastly, they will need her to plant the microphone against the far wall of the gym. On the other side, based on the floor plan Alterman has, is the secret room.

They meet in the church commons area. Cherie again reminds herself that her name is supposed to be Jennifer, and notices immediately Anna's gym outfit. It manages to be flattering, stylish and modest at the same time, and she's not immediately sure how. Anna, away from the singles' group, somehow looks younger. Cherie knows she is in her mid-thirties, but the group seems to add a few years. Her figure shows some discipline. Cherie looks at her own baggy gym clothes and feels slightly embarrassed.

"This is terrible," Anna says. "I can't…"

"What?"

"Isn't this awful? I can't seem…I mean…I can't, you know, seem to remember how to get to the workout gym."

"You just haven't used it much," Cherie offers helpfully, in spite of the fact that the woman works here.

"I have used it, I promise. It's not *that* big a church, is it?"

Cherie points to a directional sign on the wall. "Is it near the regular rec gym?"

Anna snaps her fingers. "Yes! That's it. Let's go." A few turns and a few near misses down the wrong hall and they finally arrive.

Anna walks her through the gym rules. There is someone maintaining a desk at the entrance, but this person is only there in case anyone needs anything. Cherie asks if there's any ID needed to use the gym – the answer is no. All the church asks is that no one abuse the privileges. "They don't want anyone just showing up in the gym that they never see in Sunday School," Anna explains, in a whisper.

Cherie likes Anna, she decides. It might be interesting to really know her in a normal life, which Cherie doesn't feel like she has.

The two of them begin on side-by-side treadmills.

"This is nice," Cherie says. "I can't believe you don't need an ID card to get in, at least."

"That's Brother Tommy. He says this isn't a perk. It's a ministry. Anybody who comes in here using weights might have bigger problems than their waistline," Anna says. Cherie wants to correct her grammar, but it wouldn't be friendly.

Above their heads, painted on the wall, are the words, "My yoke is easy, and my burden light." Beneath it are the weight benches.

"Are you...are you liking things here?" Anna asks.

"Yeah," Cherie says, trying to sound mildly enthusiastic. Actually, she likes the place about as much as she likes Anna.

"I know the feeling you can get sometimes in a singles ministry. Like it's a meat show."

Cherie gives a knowing smile.

"Am I right? It's one of the things I don't like. It's a singles' ministry, but we treat it like that defines you, the fact that you don't have someone with you."

"Well, that *is* important for some people."

"Yes, but it shouldn't be *that* important. I mean, we've had a few people come through and you know they're only in it to find the guy, or the girl. Once they do, you might never see them in church again."

"I wouldn't… I mean, is that the way it is?"

"That's right. You're sort of new to all this. Well, I talk to a lot of singles. Usually, the really frantic ones are the ones a little older than you. They haven't been married and they start to feel the years creeping up on them. They figure if it doesn't happen soon, it never will. So they're ready to settle for whoever comes along."

"I can imagine."

"I know it's hard to be lonely, but all you have to do is look at the ones who are divorced. They aren't usually in on the meat show that much, because they're still smarting over what they've just gotten over and don't want to jump back in, just yet."

"Being lonely is scary," is all Cherie will say at first. "I mean, I was engaged, but it didn't quite work out. And I couldn't blame him all that much."

"You shouldn't say that about yourself. You're awesome, Jennifer!" Anna gives Cherie a smile and a fist pump, and Cherie stifles the urge to correct her name.

Cherie sighs heavily, with the weight of her fictional trials. "Actually, Anna, I'm in substance abuse counseling."

Anna's mouth unhinges, and her hand goes up to cover it.

"My fiancé and I decided – well, he decided – it wasn't going to work out because I couldn't give the stuff up."

"Oh," Anna says. "I knew you were …something had a hold of you. Or someone."

She keeps her head down. "I know I earned my way into it. But I'm trying."

Oh Lord, Cherie thinks, as she glances over to look at her – Anna is crying and is trying to wipe the tears from her eyes without smudging her mascara.

"Stop it! I'm fine!" Cherie protests. "And I know that. And I appreciate you coming here with me."

"That's…uh, that's nothing," Anna says, pinching her nose and wiping away the evidence of her crying. She clears her throat. "No, I'm happy to come. I try to get in gym time at least twice a week. Sometimes it's harder than others." Cherie can tell Anna is uncomfortable. The idea of Jennifer Mersault's former trials has made her uncomfortable.

"Twice a week? But you…"

"I know. I'm scatterbrained. It's a wonder I find this place at all." Then she begins slowing down, rubbing at her left knee.

"What's wrong?"

"Just a little twinge," Cherie says, and slows her treadmill down. "It's been happening more and more lately. I'm falling apart."

Cherie nods thoughtfully, and dials up a faster pace on her treadmill. She's guessed this equipment might have been bought used, but it's still in good shape. None of the machines look unsafe or obsolete.

"Besides, you shouldn't feel that way about yourself. I mean Jennifer, you started coming to Sweet Lightning because you knew you needed it. The thing is, everybody needs this. Some people just understand it more when they have a problem that makes it feel more pressing."

The words are the right tone, but something in her voice sounds mechanical, as though she's saying what she's expected to spit out at a time like this. Now Anna punches up the pace on her machine, and she's obviously ticked about something.

"It's like the whole meat show thing. So many people come to church for selfish reasons. They expect to get something out of it, rather than put anything in. I see so many who come in, and they ask questions like 'Why do I need church?' You start talking about things like communion with the saints, fellowship, the discipline of a community of believers, and their eyes just glaze over. I mean, you can't be the star of your movie forever!"

Cherie is now in a difficult position, because this sounds uncomfortably like something she might hear from Alterman. Or Templeton. She wonders, just for a moment, if she's being played. Does Anna know somehow who she is and why she's here?

Nah, she thinks.

But how should she react to this?

"What do you mean?" Cherie asks.

She smiles, and seems momentarily embarrassed by her opinion. "Guess I mean…I don't know. Like something Brother Tommy talked about last month. He was preaching about Cain and Abel. Cain killed Abel because God took Abel's sacrifice and not his. And he said that means that how we think we should worship God means nothing to God, because He expects us to worship Him the way He wants. But we don't like that – we don't like it so much that we want to kill anyone who gets it right. Because as long as they're alive, they convict us."

Oh boy, Cherie thinks.

"I mean, I don't want to sound like I've got all the answers. That's just the point. I need to know why I should care about these people. I need to know why their lives matter to God, just like mine. I need their correction, as bad as it may hurt."

And before she knows it, Anna is running, not walking, bad joints or not.

"I'm sorry. I must sound like I'm nuts or something."

"No. I think I see what you mean," Cherie says, still in character. "I guess I just never thought of it that way before."

"I mean, I'm here because I want to know Jesus. But you see some of these girls who come through here, and all they want to meet is their future husband, like he's going to come walking through the door any Sunday."

And as Anna pushes another button to increase the speed again, Cherie stretches her arms over her head. It's a motion that wouldn't normally gain any attention, and it successfully sends the mic pin she came with into the wall. That mic will be able to pick up, in some measure, any sounds that are going on behind that wall on the other side.

At the same time, she pushes the button on the device in her pocket, activating the mic. She can hear what it's picking up in her ear.

Sort of. What she hears are a murmur of unclear voices. She can't pick up any actual words. And she hears what she thinks sounds like phones ringing.

Then Anna resumes talking.

"I listen to what some of the girls in the group are talking about sometimes, and I think, am I ever like that? I mean, did I spend that much time talking about a man? And in church?"

Cherie interrupts her. "Well, if you get right down to it, we're still talking about a man in church, aren't we?"

Anna laughs at Cherie's joke, and she leans forward, enjoying the laughter, like she's preening. That's why Cherie slips on the treadmill and falls. In a matter of seconds, she knows that her old nemesis, the ankle she sprained years ago, is sprained again. She'll need to go to the hospital.

The shock that passes through her is familiar and defeating. She knows perversely that, in her pain, Alterman will be pleased.

9

Whit arrives at the corner at 9:15 a.m., checking his watch. He figures he'll have to do it several times, but within a second of raising his head, the bus comes into view.

It wasn't on any checklist, but Whit decided to take the church's Sunday morning shuttle bus service. Though none of the others believe he knows anything about the Internet, he got the idea looking at the church website. Whit was surprised no one else thought of it. The site said anyone could call the church Saturday or Sunday up until a certain time and request the bus make a stop for them.

But this isn't one of those comfortable, air conditioned shuttle buses like he's seen around the church campus. This is a surplus school bus that chugs to a stop with a whistling brake right in front of him. It says Sweet Lightning Church on the side, rendered in a paint job that is obviously in-house. There is a red, white and blue motif here also that looks out of place with the rest of the church's aesthetic feel. Lots of neutral whites and royal blues in their image, like those blue, square decals on the backs of the cars in the parking lot. This bus isn't like that at all. This baby has seen some action.

The folding door opens, and a smiling man at the wheel looks him over.

"You Mr. Mountain?" he asks.

"Depends who's asking? I finished school years ago."

"You never stop learning," the man says. "Hop on in."

Whit steps on and sees they will not be alone. He sees a lot of faces sitting in the back, some friendly, some still struggling to wake up. Some of the faces are Asian, some black, some look Arabic.

"This is our bus with the students from the community college," says the man. "I'm Richard Gates. I'm an associate pastor at the church."

Whit shakes the man's hand. There is a vacant seat behind him – in fact, there are many vacant seats toward the front. All the students, some of whom nod at Whit, are in the back.

Just like good little Baptists, Whit thinks.

"This thing gonna get us there?" Whit asks.

"If God is merciful," Gates says, and his voice wavers between parody and seriousness. "Truth is, I couldn't tell you how old this bus is. Our usual one broke down on the way before it left the church, so we had to get this dinosaur out of mothballs. To be honest, I'm surprised it started."

Just what you want to hear from your driver, Whit thinks. "You usually drive the bus?"

"No. I'm the guy in charge of transportation, but if anybody was going to take this out, it was going to be me."

"You're expendable," Whit says.

"Maybe, but the rest of you aren't." Gates smiles but doesn't take his eyes off the road. "Are you a visitor?"

"Yes. I'm just in town for a short time, but I thought I'd come see what all the fuss is about. I'm an ex-pastor. I hear y'all put on a good show."

"Oh, glad I dressed up for you," Gates says. "You'll like Brother Tommy. He's a fine preacher."

"You ever get a chance to preach, or you mainly administration?"

"Oh, I sometimes get to preach at the satellite sites," he says. "And I've played the Palace. I mean, I've preached here at the Main – we call it the Main."

"What's it like? Most of my experience is small church."

"Most of mine is big. This is actually smaller than I'm used to. I came here because of Tommy. He's in it, heart and soul. He knows what he's about. Got a great feel for things."

"What's he like to work with? Some pastors I know expect you to work for them."

"Oh, yes. Don't I know it." Whit has a feeling there's a story there, as though Gates has had a bad run-in with a pastor in the past, but he doesn't want to probe. You don't want people to feel interrogated, he can hear Alterman cautioning him in his head. "No, Tommy's not that way at all. Take this here, for instance. He gives me some latitude to get things done. Like this bus situation. Some pastors would be nuts about getting their OK to take an old rust bucket like this out and put it back on the road. But Tommy wants us to do whatever we can to get people to come to church. Just saying we're short a bus when there's an old one that still runs…"

"Lot of guys would be nuts about getting their lawyer on the phone," Whit chimes in.

They take a corner, and Gates wrestles with the oversized steering wheel as he pumps the clutch and eases into another gear. "Right. And see, this ministry here is very important to him. See these students. We have Bible study every Thursday night with these guys. They're from all over the world. Middle East. Africa. Japan. They come from all kinds of backgrounds. But when they get off the plane at our airport, we have people there to help them set up bank accounts and get settled. We don't say they have to come to Bible study, but they're curious why someone would want to help them. And a good many of them come to services. We can't just throw that away because a bus isn't working."

"Well, I think you're doing a great job there, Bob," Whit says. He has no idea of the man even enjoys being called Bob, but this is one of Whit's tricks – he assumes a familiarity in hopes of inspiring it.

"Couldn't do it without you, Mr. Mountain."

"Whit."

"How are you doing today, Whit?"

"Oh, it's been a good life, so far."

Gates laughs at his observation, which Whit makes routinely when anyone asks the question.

"Thing is, the bus breaking down doesn't surprise me all that much," Gates says.

"Why's that?"

"Well…it's kind of complicated, but Brother Tommy warned us about it."

"Bus problems?"

"Little bigger than that. Let's just say there's this group in town that's giving our church a little going over. I don't mean anything bad. It's like we're getting evaluated. See if we're doing a good job."

"I like your driving, if it helps."

"Appreciate that. No, I mean, Brother Tommy said it would be like this. If people are coming to town looking for things that could go wrong, you can expect things to go wrong. He said we may feel like we're under attack, but just to go about our business."

That's an interesting way of putting it, Whit thinks, especially since Alterman told him that Everhart welcomed them to do their best, or worst.

"What'll happen if they flunk you?" Whit asks, with a smile in his voice.

"Don't know. I don't think it's that kind of test really. I think it's more of showing how we can do our jobs better. I just know Tommy's taking it seriously. Very seriously."

"So you're worried?"

"No, not for me. I know how to do my job. I work with good people. If I'm worried about anybody, it's Tommy. He's headed for big things. Everybody knows it. And you being in the ministry, you know…when you're being groomed, the competition tends to notice."

"Yea, verily."

There is a buzz coming from the back of the bus. The students are chatting amongst each other, though Whit can pick out the various languages. Arabic and Japanese are being traded within the appropriate peer groups. It's funny to Whit that he can tell by the tone of their voices how tired they are. He knows nothing other than English, and yet he can hear a lack of sleep clearly in an unfamiliar tongue.

They are coming over a steep hill, and as they take the rise, he can see the tip of the steeple peeking out. The cross on top rises into view.

"Home sweet home," Gates says. Then he starts pushing the brake. He has to put his whole hip into the exercise.

But nothing is happening. Nothing good, that is.

"Uh-oh," Gates says.

Whit understands that the brakes are gone, just as they are beginning to accelerate. There are at least two traffic lights between them and the church, and both of those lights are red.

Whit also knows what to do when brakes fail, but for some reason, he can't open his mouth. His heart, ever a concern, is flaring up inside his chest, like a wounded animal, which it is.

"All right everybody," Gates says, as he tries to pick up the brake with his foot. There he is, pumping madly, as his voice rises. "Listen closely everyone. The brakes are out. I want you to hold on. And I want you to pray. Let's all pray that we get our brakes back and no one gets hurt." His voice has an unearthly, unsettling calm about it, though Whit can tell he is not calm at all.

And Whit would pray, but he can't open his mouth. His hands are gripping the bus seat and the bar in front of him. His jaw is clinched. And his heart doesn't seem to be pounding as much as it feels like one spasmodic beat that never contracts.

In this moment, for some reason, he thinks of Gilda. Whit's wife been dead precisely eight years, two months and twenty-six days, and the idea that her incandescent features are only a memory is still alien to him, though he has lived it every second since. He might never have become a pastor had it not been for her, and he would never have met Alex Alterman as a result. And he wouldn't be on this bus in the hands of the Very Right Reverend Gates.

But there was a moment in-between the moment Gilda left him and this – when he was lying in a hospital bed with his heart making virtually the same movements under the flesh of his chest. He was afraid to move a muscle that day, afraid to trigger another heart attack, the one that would kill him. But beyond that, he was weary and exhausted and numb and alone. But not alone.

He was afraid to even move his lips as he prayed: Dear Father, I realize that I can live or die right now. I don't know what you want. Whatever happens, may it be your will and not mine.

And somehow, he got better. He found his way into Alterman's orbit and discovered a rewarding career until he died when the brakes gave out on a bus careening down a busy city street on a Sunday morning.

Wait, Whit thought. There are no busy city streets in a Southern town this size on a Sunday. And even as the bus is halfway down the block, picking up speed, the light in front changes to green. There are cars in front of them, but Gates has turned on the bus' hazard lights and is blaring the horn. The cars in front are getting out of the way.

Whit can hear the students in the back of the bus, and their voices are calling on someone, at least. And by this time, Whit is praying, within his head. It's a very simple prayer, the only thing his brain can process:

Dear Father, help me make it to the bottom of this hill. Alive. As well as all the rest of these people. But especially me.

There's some hope, perhaps. Gates is pumping the brake. It isn't lifeless on the floor anymore, and though the bus is through the first light, the one ahead is still red. The bus nearly hits a Fiat – one of those new ones, emblazoned with a Sweet Lightning decal on the back.

"I can't wreck this bus," Gates says. "I'll lose my job."

Whit is suddenly back in the moment. He points to the curb. "Steer over there. Ride the curb. That'll slow you down."

Gates nods, and the wheel moves, even as he continues to pump the brake. He shifts down into a lower gear and they can all feel the bus jerking grudgingly, reluctantly slower. More cars angle out of the bus' way. There isn't the kind of traffic you might normally have on a street like this, but the downside is that their target – the church ahead - is the main reason for any traffic at all in this area. Most, if not all of these cars, are worshippers headed for the service.

They'll have a lot to talk about if we don't make it, Whit thinks.

But Gates is still unrattled, even if the bus is the opposite. Its shakes jostle the passengers at least two inches off their seats, and all hold on with the feeling that they will gladly walk to any destination in their future.

The light ahead changes, and even though there's been enough time for the lights to normally switch from red to green, Whit is convinced that there is a control room somewhere in the city with angels sitting behind it, pushing buttons before their wings spirit them to the point ahead in the street, where the bus will gently glide to a stop.

But it is not gentle when the bumper scrapes the side of a newspaper box, and it is not gentle when the front wheel hops over the curb, enough to rattle Whit's upper plate. But his heart is settling down, even in all the imperatives of gravity, because the bus is slowing down. By the time it's at a complete stop, Whit is too grateful to maintain any pretense of anonymity.

"Well, if it means anything to you Bob, I'll put in a good word for you," he says, before opening the folding doors himself.

10

It's time for the homeless trick.

Alterman worked for an hour on his facial scar. The clothes were purchased at thrift stores – carefully selected within a 50-mile radius of Sweet Lightning. He wears a single shoe.

Because it's so effective a gauge, Alterman is tempted to use the homeless trick for virtually every audit. But he holds off, because he doesn't want to run the risk of cheapening it as a resource. Besides, he can see someone putting a picture of him on Facebook and the image rendering him ineffectual forever.

That is why he never appears the same way, and he only uses the guise once a year. The details are scrupulously chosen, and Alterman will never tell anyone what he used to give himself a memorable body odor. Ingersoll might think his random stranger get up is convincing, but little does he know, Alterman thinks.

For Sweet Lightning, Alterman decides to visit the Sunday evening service. Sunday morning strikes him as too ostentatious. He ambles onto the campus from a spot he chose about a half-mile away. Alterman is always conscious of observers, even when there aren't any.

A white haired man, probably in his early fifties, approaches him. Usually, the crucial moment comes later. Alterman has been a homeless visitor at six churches, and five of them allowed him to wander inside, like an invading parasite, simply because no one felt comfortable approaching him. The other one spotted him immediately and forcibly ejected him. That church got roasted.

The white haired man surprises Alterman. "Hello, brother," he says, in a clear, honest voice. "Welcome." He sticks out a hand.

Alterman eyes the man suspiciously, nods his head, and shakes the man's hand with the wrong hand. This is crucial – this is the hand that smells the worst. He waits to see the man's reaction, which is immediate.

"You've never been here before, I can see," the man says, his tone never changing as he introduces himself to Alterman. His eye contact is devastating. Alterman is temporarily shaken, afraid his disguise has been seen through. "Do you need some kind of help?"

Alterman coughs, wipes his nose, and recoils at the smell coming from his hands.

The man doesn't wait for a response. "You look like you could use some food. We can scrounge you up something. The service doesn't start for fifteen minutes."

Alterman is flabbergasted. He had heard Sweet Lightning had a homeless ministry, but his understanding was that it was located downtown, not on the main campus.

The man continues, as he choreographs Alterman inside. "We're usually better prepared for this sort of thing in the morning, but it shouldn't be too hard to find something in our kitchen for you."

Alterman is seriously shaken by the man's attitude. For just a moment, he has the usual crisis of confidence during an audit, wondering if he has lost his ability to do the job. Something in him resists the idea that a church is doing well, especially when Wydgate is also personally consulting in the field.

"What's your name?" the man asks him.

Now Alterman realizes he is so shaken that he has forgotten the name he invented for this persona. Instead, he does not reply. He simply points to his mouth and grunts.

The man nods, as though he understands that this particular homeless man is unable to talk. "Well, I don't know why you're here, but I imagine you need help. We can feed you a meal, but I think you probably need something else. We can help you with that too."

Who is this guy? Alterman wonders. He isn't knocked out by the man's segue toward the deeper spiritual significance lurking within an offered meal. But he didn't shy away from it, the way other greeters do. So many people at the door act as though their job is to direct a visitor to the pastor or a staff member, and let someone else take care of any spiritual needs.

The two men snake through the church past classrooms and directional signs until they arrive at a kitchen and small dining area.

Sitting in a chair, in the middle of the room, is another homeless man. Alterman dies a little inside, realizes his timing is awful. No wonder Alterman didn't upset the man – he was merely the next in line.

This guy has a tangled growth of beard and a battered ball cap to distinguish himself, with clothes that smell of mildew. Alterman sits down next to him, and the man moves over slightly. Alterman smells worse.

"Here you go," the usher says, handing him a plate. There is a slab of sweet smelling ham, something that looks like a potato casserole, some steamed green beans, and a roll. "Would you like some coffee?"

Alterman shakes his head.

"Water then?"

Alterman shakes his head. He isn't going to make it easy.

"Coke?"

Another shake.

The man, inexplicably, smiles. "Diet?"

Alterman, flabbergasted, nods.

"Gimme a second," the man says, and in a ridiculously short span of time, returns with what he says is a diet drink. The food looks and smells delicious.

Alterman realizes this place is going to kill him.

The white haired gentleman assures the two he will leave them alone for a moment to eat, but will return in order to get them to the service. The other homeless guy thanks him in a voice that sounds amused.

Then the homeless man turns to Alterman. "Hi, Alex," he says.

Alterman, still in character, tries not to betray any kind of reaction. But he meets the man's eye.

"I told you it would be better if you weren't here."

It is Wydgate. His face is unmistakable beneath the beard. Alterman realizes if he stood up, Wydgate would tower over him.

"What are you doing here?" Alterman whispers in a grunt, trying to keep it down.

"Same thing you are," Wydgate says. "Doing a field test."

"No. What are you doing here? What are you doing at this church?"

"I got hired to audit it."

"Oh no you didn't."

"But I did. I got to hand it to you. I never would have recognized you. What do you think of the food?"

"I haven't tried it," Alterman says. "How did you figure out...?"

"Asking for the diet soda. That's typical. Going the extra mile."

"Right," he says. "I take my cue from Jesus."

"You saying I don't?

"I wouldn't know. If you think that, it's probably a guilty conscience."

"I sleep fine at night."

"But what are you doing here? Shouldn't you be somewhere writing a self-help book that insults the reader's intelligence?"

"Alex, you have no reason to hate me so..."

"We already covered this. I don't hate you. You're the competition."

"We *both* got served," Wydgate says, holding up the plate. "There's enough business out here for both of us."

"Maybe. You serve a vital function in the market. Making sure there's a cheap, less professional option in this profession."

"As opposed to you?" Wydgate chuckles, ruefully. "Maybe I don't need to include charges for dealing with my ego." Wydgate waits a moment, to let the words sink in. "So how are they doing?"

"Who?"

"Sweet Lightning. How are you grading them?"

"I can't tell you. I can only tell the person who commissioned the audit."

"Who commissioned it?"

"I don't have to tell you. Who commissioned you?"

"Alex, I told you. You shouldn't have come here. You shouldn't have taken this job. It's too dangerous."

"Dangerous for me, or you? If it's so dangerous, then why are you here? Somebody's hired you. Who was it?"

"I'll be honest with you," Wydgate says. "I don't know. And I know you don't know who hired you."

"And just how do you know that?"

"Because if you did, you'd come right out and tell me."

It finally dawns on Alterman that he didn't even ask Everhart if the church would be paying for the audit. Maybe he assumed it. Maybe he didn't even care. "So you think I'd come down here to audit a church not knowing who hired me?"

"Right."

"And you're telling me you took on a job not knowing who hired you?"

"Right."

"What makes you think I'd be as stupid as you are?"

"Because you're sitting here in this place, doing the exact same thing I am."

"Who says *you're* not copying me?"

"You can't stay away. You're here trying to figure out who hired you, and what it all means."

"Listen," Alterman says, his voice suddenly not in character. "Tell me something. Why do you do this?"

"What? Talk to you?"

"No. *This.* Auditing churches."

Wydgate looks slightly put out by the question, then embarrassed by it. He isn't used to talking about himself. Then he smiles, and Alterman wishes there was another hair he could pull from his nemesis' nose.

"Well, I guess, I joined the church when I was seven years old. My sister was eight, you see. She walked up to the front, and when she did, I said I wasn't going to let her beat me up there. I don't think I knew what I was doing."

Alterman waits for more words, but none come. "That's why you're in this business? What? Is your sister auditing churches too?"

"No," he says. "What I'm saying is I know I'm a Christian. That was how I got started. And that's where I stayed. For years. Didn't grow. Meant not a thing. Just fire insurance that I got simply because I didn't want my sister to beat me to Heaven. I didn't learn anything in youth groups, or choir, or summer camps or backyard Bible clubs. Or I didn't feel like I learned anything. That was my church's fault. It wasn't until later that I found out the nature of what I'd done. What I'd given up when I gave my life to Jesus."

"And you swore you'd get even with Him…" Alterman says, like a bad pulp detective solving an irrelevant mystery.

"I thought about all those kids out there who aren't going to be in the pews in years to come because there'll be nothing to keep them there. I didn't want to see that happen."

Alterman doesn't say anything at first. He swallows hard. "So why aren't you harder on them?"

"I don't want to hurt people, Alex. I don't have your talent for doing this, or as big a staff to do it, or your passion for wounding people. I just want to help."

"The Lord wounds people to turn them into what he wants."

"He can get away with that, Alex. He's the Lord."

11

"I was glad when they said unto me," Templeton says aloud to himself, "let us go into the house of the Lord."

It's absolutely dark where he is when he says these words, recalled from the Psalms, but he says them aloud and, in so doing, pinches his belly against the sides of the air duct where he has been for the previous two hours.

"I promise I'm working as fast as I can," Ingersoll says, into his ear, through the Bluetooth.

"Just seeing if I can still praise God as well as breathe."

"Can you see anything from there?"

"Not at the moment," he says. "I mean, I can see some light coming from a vent in front of me, and I think it's the room."

"Hear anything?"

"Not really."

Templeton wishes this were not true. If he could hear something, it might justify his dying in this air duct.

And how did he get here? It started a day before.

Ingersoll and he are brainstorming. Cherie is lying in a hospital and her attempt to find out what is going on in the secret room has been a muddle. They know there is some kind of activity taking place – the voices and the phones ringing. But they can't make out anything that's being said, and though they hear several voices, they have no idea how many. The mic wasn't good enough.

It's Ingersoll who mentions getting a camera into the room. They don't need anything other than one that could fit through an air vent. The challenge would be getting it in the duct work. Ingersoll is wearing a T-shirt that reads, "For nothing is hidden that will not be made manifest, nor is anything secret that will not be known."

"You wore that the other day, didn't you?" Templeton asks.

"No. That was Ecclesiastes. This is Jesus, from Mark."

"Oh. Well, how hard can it be to get a camera in there?" Templeton asked, with the confidence of the ignorant.

The two of them look over the floor plan, and Ingersoll has another layout of the duct work. They know this room shares its ducts with adjoining ones. The easiest entry would be through the choir room.

"Obadiah left town yet?" Templeton asks.

"Yeah."

"Too bad. He'd be perfect for that job."

"I'm not saying we'd need to climb into the duct work. If we could get someone in the choir room, they can snake the camera wire into the duct, then feed it through."

"Could you do it?"

"No. I'd need to be on the end activating the camera and troubleshooting. That could be done remotely, but somebody needs to be there to put the thing in."

Between the two of them, the imperative has already asserted itself. Templeton knows that Whitlow Mountain is not going to do it, and Cherie is in the hospital. And they can't ask Alterman because they can't ask him anything.

"You sure you can't tell me how to do this computer stuff?" Templeton asks, knowing the answer.

A day later, he is dressed as a maintenance man, since that was the arrangement Alterman already made to get the cameras installed in all the rooms. Templeton has on dark blue coveralls with a name patch that reads "Graham."

Ingersoll's voice in his ear instructs him once he gets through the door. The camera is all set to go in his work bag. He looks like yet another technician installing or repairing phone lines or a copier or satisfying some other vague electronic yearning.

"Take a right," Ingersoll says, after Templeton is around the corner in the main foyer. "Go up the steps and then take another right, and you'll start seeing the signs toward the choir room."

Templeton follows the path as Ingersoll talks him there, until he is standing in front of a large vent panel.

"Open her up," Ingersoll says in Templeton's ear, and Templeton uses a screwdriver. The panel slides out with only a little exertion and then Templeton fishes the video camera out. The camera is at the end of a coil of snake wire, which comes out of the bag at the same time Templeton draws out a mirror attached to a four-foot retractable pole.

He angles the mirror into the vent, clips on a flashlight, and looks up the vent to see what the mirror reveals. The air vent goes straight up, then turns above the ceiling tiles and extends over into what they believe is the secret room. The mirror shows light coming up from a vent, and the light source is most likely in that room.

Templeton flips a switch on a remote inside the bag.

"Is it on?" Templeton asks to no one close by.

"Yeah, we're getting an image," Ingersoll says in his ear. Templeton waves at Ingersoll with the camera pointed at him.

The hole where the vent panel had been is big enough for Templeton to step into it, which he does. He then begins feeding the camera and its coil upward. But the snake wire isn't cooperating. It isn't stiff, so he can't place it into the air vent where it bends. He can't throw it up into the vent without fear of breaking the camera at the end.

"Wait a minute, I think I'm going to have to get up there and push it to the vent."

Ingersoll says nothing, because he has no way of knowing whether this is a good idea or not.

It isn't. Because by the time Templeton positions the wire into the upper air vent, he is stuck inside at the lower part.

He doesn't think anything's wrong at first, because he can't see himself getting stuck. "Wait a second," he says. "Let me shove this thing closer."

But of course he can't, not without the mirror. And the mirror isn't cooperating because now he can't maneuver it inside the vent. He is taking up too much room. So he puts the mirror down and slowly begins to pull himself up into the upper vent. Now Templeton is becoming more conscious of his years and the sure hold of gravity upon him, because each inch he slides up the vent, the more impressed he is with how his midsection manages to squeeze into and fill up the vent.

But he's still not worried, because he can see that he is close to having the snake coil right where he wants it, and the camera positioned perfectly to reveal what lies beneath the vent. So Templeton, his body now face down and horizontal inside the air vent, begins sliding further inside to get the coil where he wants it. He wonders why he didn't let Ingersoll buy the stiffer kind of snake coil that could have been manipulated more easily, but Templeton was trying to stay in budget.

"I think we've got it," he says, just before feeding the camera right to the vent.

"See anything?" he asks Ingersoll.

"Yeah, the lights are on."

"Well?"

"There isn't anybody in…no, wait a minute. There's a few people. Yeah, we've got picture."

"Can you tell anything?" Templeton says, suddenly whispering and aware.

"It's hard to describe," Ingersoll says.

"What?"

"Looks like a bunch of phones. And a bunch of work stations, each one with a phone. But most of the phones are vacant. Just about two or three people in there right now. Heads are down so you can't really see their faces."

"Phones," Templeton says.

"What do you think it could be?"

Templeton doesn't say. His first thought is off-shore gambling, though he has nothing to base that on besides something he's read somewhere. Maybe it's a boiler room operation, or something like it, he thinks. Maybe it's some kind of call center for something maybe not illegal, but certainly not routine.

Templeton is fascinated though, that their scheme has worked. Except that he's in the vent.

"I think you can get out of there now," Ingersoll says.

Or maybe not, Templeton thinks. He can't move his mid-section. He begins to squirm a little, as little as he's able, and he becomes conscious of how hot it is. Maybe he didn't lose as much weight as he thought.

He tries to slide back the way he came, but it is harder this time. There is little for him to brace on, and he is worried that if he will bring the snake coil out with him because it's probably attached to him now due to the close quarters he occupies.

"You out yet?"

"No, I'm not," Templeton says.

"You really need to move," Ingersoll says helpfully.

"I know, but I don't think I can."

"You've got to."

"So far ... nothing's working." His voice is growing more exasperated as Ingersoll tries to suggest to him things that he's very aware of.

Templeton keeps it up, but he can't really move. When he tries to grope with his feet back down the vent, there is nowhere to gain a foothold.

"I'm not really sure how we're going to get you out," Ingersoll says.

"Prayer might be in order," he says, and he is not completely joking. "I cried by reason of mine affliction unto the Lord, and He heard me," Templeton says.

"What?" Ingersoll asks.

"Nothing. Just exploiting the situation."

"What?"

"Get over here. I'm not sure how you can get to me, but I need you to get me out."

"I'll see what I can do," Ingersoll says. His tone is not at all encouraging.

"Hey, before you go…"

"Yeah?"

"Have you got one of those martyr stories? Something appropriate?"

"Appropriate for being stuck in an air vent?"

"Try me."

"I don't know. St. Chrysanthus was tortured by being sewn up inside the belly of an ox, if memory serves."

"What happened to him?"

"He died. He was a martyr."

"Figures."

The next sound he hears is Ingersoll cutting off the connection. He can imagine several seconds of frantic movement to no purpose. Templeton waits a few minutes of silence, save for the sound of his cramped, strained breaths. *"Out of the belly of hell cried I, and thou heardest my voice. I am cast out of thy sight; yet I will look again toward thy holy temple."* The King James always has the right note of stately panic.

In a second, Templeton thinks on how many years he spent in seminary, the hours of study and the patient honing of his preaching, the prayer and the contemplation, the ministering, learning how to look into someone's eyes at the moment they feel incapable of self-sufficiency, unlocking the power of gesture, the patience bred by the Holy Spirit – and here he is stuck in an air vent posing as a technician in a church where he is not the pastor.

Is it possible he is doing something ordained by God? It is only a question he has asked himself every moment of his association with Alterman. And though he has been assured within and without that he is exactly where he is needed, he still feels the tug away. And he wonders why.

Judging by what Ingersoll tells him, they are going to have an interesting meeting with Alterman when it comes time to give up what they'd found out about this place. There isn't going to be much to the report, as far as the church itself goes.

Its programs, its staff, its outreaches – they all seem clean to an extraordinary scale. The cleanest he's ever seen.

The problem is all the information coming in from the cameras, the microphones, the eyes and ears looking down. They've all sifted through it, even as it continues to come in. It is too much. It is indecent. They can't keep their eyes away from it. And none of it belongs in the report.

On the tapes, they can hear a man and a woman in a hallway arranging a getaway. You can tell they aren't married – at least not to each other.

Ingersoll listened to a group of kids in one elementary Sunday School class room ganging up on another when the teacher was out of the room. There was a little girl with a stutter. Later, when the teacher came back into the room, the little girl wouldn't answer and got a mild rebuke. I wonder if she'll ever talk again, Ingersoll thought.

These are the sort of things that drive Alterman crazy – men talking out in the open about each other, gossiping about someone only briefly out of earshot. Conversations in the foyer about the soloist's children from another marriage, even while she was singing near the altar. A man shopping around an obviously phony business proposal, hoping to string in interested takers. A young man using a youth fellowship to set up something later in a storage room with an underage girl. Something that sounded like a drug deal between two middle schoolers. So many moments, hovering on the edge of disaster, voices that should know better dragging others down with themselves, even as they sink. He hears on the tapes the sound of hopelessness. There are hundreds of other moments, full of promise that there are good people in these pews who quietly magnify a Name with their actions, but he does not remember them as much as those others that make his blood curdle.

They unquestionably have more information during this audit than any other they've ever had. But Templeton's depressed about this. By their usual measure of an audit, this church is doing well.

But what about all this stuff going on? It isn't the church's fault, Templeton thinks. Any darkness is because of the people who are doing these things. The church can't make any of them into better people.

140

But, isn't it the church's fault if its congregation isn't learning anything? Here they are, in the temple of God. If this is how they act here, how are they out there? Isn't the church supposed to be the one place in the whole world where someone can go to get closer to God?

Immediately Templeton has another thought – You can't make people be Christlike. Even Christ couldn't do that Himself. That's the whole point though. You can't become these things without Him. You can't even be good. That's why you need grace. If we were perfect, we wouldn't need Him.

But still, thinking about it all depresses Templeton. And he knows it depresses Alterman. *You can spend your whole life in churches, and working on churches, and examining churches, tearing them up and putting them back together again, but the people in the pews are still fallen. You'd think it would get better, and then you look at yourself.*

Stuck.

Templeton shifts his foot. He has the feeling if he moves his hips or his arms, he might trigger a collapse through the vent. Beneath his feet is nothing. He has plenty of room to move them. His right foot has an itch, at the arch. He slides the right shoe off and starts rubbing it with the other foot, still wearing the shoe, to scratch.

Then he has plenty of room to scratch. He hears a sound like someone moving a piano, following by a wrenching and the scream of straining metal, and then he is falling through the vent.

Templeton closes his eyes and grimaces, his arms and legs curling up as he braces for the impact to come. But it happens much faster than expected. The vent has opened up and deposited him in the choir room, on top of wardrobe cupboards that hold the robes.

He has fallen perhaps only four feet. But he is afraid to open his eyes.

He needn't be. There is no one around.

"I guess I'm right where I need to be," he says, to Someone in particular.

Quicker than that, he suddenly thinks – we'll have to count off on their security. They should have already been on to us. That is Alterman talking inside him, and the thought of this frightens Templeton.

12

Cherie is going stir crazy. She has been lying in this bed for hours.

"Just think of the rest you'll get," Alterman had told her over the phone. She knew he didn't mean it.

Down the hall from her room, in an arrangement that still awes her, Alterman has gotten permission to set up Ingersoll. It is the weirdest stakeout she can ever remember.

Alterman's exultation, at least when it comes out of his mouth, makes sense. "Hospital visits are a vital aspect of a church's ministry," he tells her. "Jesus Himself commanded the disciples that they were to visit the sick, and to not do so was the same as not visiting Him. I can show you the statistics. There is no easier way to lose a member than to ignore them when they're sick."

It is a Friday. Since weekends are harder for churches to learn of someone's sickness, this is a prime auditing opportunity. The doctor who admits her needs some coaxing. He wants her to take a prescription and go home. She has the feeling Alterman would have appreciated it more, on some level, if she'd *broken* her leg. But it would have slowed the audit down.

And so begins the drill. They take her up to a room, where she's supposed to get all this sleep, and a nurse enters every hour on the hour to check on her vitals and occasionally hand out pills. If that isn't bad enough, there is Ingersoll. He keeps talking to her through an earpiece.

"You awake?" he asks.

"Yes," she replies, resigned, her words picked up by the wireless mic near the window. "If I wasn't, I am now."

"Have you gotten any sleep?"

"No," she says. "Just when I almost get to sleep, I have this birdie in my ear."

"Sorry. Listen, he'll be here in a little bit." *He* means Alterman.

"Why?"

"To check on you."

"To check up on me. Make sure I'm not taking it easy. This is so insane."

"You know him. He's got his reasons. No sign of anyone from the church. Not since your friend Anna."

Just then, there is a knock on the door. Cherie coughs loudly, as if to distract from anything anyone might have overheard out in the hall. She closes her eyes and opens her mouth as though she's been asleep. She has forgotten she is still wearing her eyeglasses.

"It's me, Jennifer," comes a voice. It is Alterman, walking into the room, dressed as a doctor. She opens one eye and strongly considers closing it again.

"You're my doctor?" she says. "No wonder I'm not healthy."

"I'm just checking up on you, Mrs. Mersault."

"That's Miss Mersault," she corrects him. This is one of Alterman's *how well do you know your cover?* tests. "Do we really have three people here covering this? You are crazy."

"This is no small thing," Alterman says, as he puts his stethoscope into his ears and grabs the business end. His voice is low and secretive. "This is a basic function of the church. We have to know how they do it, or even if they do it at all."

Cherie grabs the stethoscope suddenly and blows into it. She is partially convinced that Alterman may never hear normally again. Serves him right.

After he shakes his head and tests his hearing – it has survived – he croaks out, "Good thing I'm in a hospital."

"I've been here all day."

"And they still haven't come, have they?"

"This is such folly."

"You think everybody calls the church to let them know to visit? To pray? Some people intentionally don't call their church. But then they get indignant when nobody visits. They don't want anyone to visit. It's probably why they get sick in the first place. A church has to remember that."

"What are you doing here?" she asks. "You've got me..."

"Yeah, and Ingersoll's down the hall. Hey that rhymes."

"Insane. Just like I said. You just here to rap?" She flashes a mock gang sign.

"I'm here for the same reason I usually come to the field."

"Because you don't trust any of us to do the job right."

"I didn't say that."

"Because you don't need to." Then she remembers why she's really mad at him. "What's with the cover story?"

"Cover story?"

"You had me in my cover story taking pills before I came to this church?"

Alterman pauses. "That's Templeton. Sorry about that."

"And what's the idea of making me get involved in the singles ministry?"

He looks perplexed. "Because you're single?"

"Because this is one of your games. You're letting me know you think it's a good idea for me to settle down."

"You *are* in a hospital."

"You want me to get married."

"Absolutely. Then you can get on your husband's work insurance and cut down on our costs."

"Anybody you had in mind for me?"

"You're a big girl. You can find somebody. But that's your business."

"You ever notice that most of us working for you are single? We're all married to you."

"You're not moving in."

"A woman can be happy without a man, you know."

"Of course she can."

She noticed he could have said "you," but he didn't. "If the man is you, they can be very happy…" she adds.

"Going for Employee of the Month again, I see."

"I should get it. Sitting here in this hospital bed."

"How are you, anyway?"

"Okay," she says, without any humor. She realizes this is the most serious question he will ask.

"This is a vacation."

She shakes her head. "We never take vacations. Besides, this rates hazard pay. They just served dinner."

He nods to her. "Ingersoll is down the…"

"…down the hall…" she says, in unison with him.

"…down the hall so he can see if they come to visit. They do have actual members here. I've been installing bugs in their rooms."

Cherie stares at him. She didn't think he could inspire disbelief in her anymore.

He gets defensive. "I just want to see what they say when they visit. *If* they visit."

"What would be acceptable for them to say? In your book?" she asks, and then there is a knock at the door.

Cherie watches Alterman at that moment. His body hunches and he looks around awkwardly, as though he has been caught in the act of something distasteful. She is reminded of a silent movie villain, and all his costumed surgical scrubs need is a cape for him to shield his face. If Alterman was a vampire, he would be anxiously looking for a cross to run from.

A smallish man is walking into the room. He is somewhat unkempt, despite the fact he has a tie on. His shirt tail is untucked in the back and the collar is pulled tight even though the shirt looks too small for him. This man could stand to lose a few pounds. He looks to be in his thirties, but as awkward as a middle schooler. He obviously assumes that Alterman is her doctor, and by his body language, he wants to meld into the background until Alterman leaves.

"The doctor" motions him to go ahead. "I'm finished," Alterman says, sticking a finger in one ear, presumably to take away the persistent ringing brought on by Cherie.

The visitor introduces himself as a deacon from Sweet Lightning. "I just came from work," he said. "I don't believe I've met you."

She gives the cover story about her injury and feels Alterman is looking at her harsher than he is this visitor.

"You didn't have to come," she says. "I'm just surprised you found out I was here."

"Of course I had to come," the man says. "And we take hospital visits very seriously. It's a matter of pride for Brother Everhart. And for all of us. Is there anything you need?"

She gets the impression that Alterman would have her invent some need on the spot, just to see what he might be capable of doing. She has a craving for a roast beef sandwich, but she avoids the temptation to send him out on this errand.

Cherie gets the impression that this conversation is about to end. But then, the deacon sits down. "I realize you probably need your rest, but I'd like to talk to you for a little bit longer. Just to get to know you better."

"My, you're friendly," Alterman says, a bit scornfully.

"Wasn't always this way," the deacon announces, after a brief, awkward silence. "I used to hate hospital visits. All those sick people," he says, waving his hand. Cherie smiles at his little joke. Icebreaker.

"I know what you mean," Alterman says, fingering the stethoscope like he might presume a doctor would.

"But we'll talk for a bit and then I'll have some prayer with you before I go. If that's OK with you?"

"That's fine with me," Cherie says.

"It's not with me," Alterman says. "I still have to do an examination." Alterman's voice is withering. He is deliberately provoking the deacon to give up. He is posing as the unforgiving doctor with no bedside manner, perhaps because he's overqualified for the job, she thinks.

The deacon, after a moment's hesitation, smiles as he rises from a chair. "That's no problem. I'll go outside and wait until you finish."

146

The look on his face would make one believe there is nothing in the world he would rather do more.

"You don't have to stay," Cherie says. She thinks this is probably what Alterman would want her to say.

"I'll just be right out here," he says, in a saintly tone of voice suitable for one of Ingersoll's ancient martyr stories. And he shuts the door behind him.

"Why do you do that?" Cherie asks. "He thinks you're in here examining me, and all the while, you're examining him!"

"I'm sorry," Alterman says. "I thought that was our job here."

"You're making it excessively hard."

"To do what? To pray with you. To visit you. Once again, what makes you think any of this will be easy for anyone else? You want to serve? You have to be willing to be thorough, exacting. You want to call me later and tell me about his prayer?"

"Haven't you put a bug in here yet?" Cherie asks.

"Oh thanks," he said, and in one motion, Alterman flicks something she can't make out toward the wall behind her bed, like someone picking his nose and disposing of what he found there. "I'll activate that later."

His phone buzzes. Alterman looks at it for an instant, and his jaw hardens, as though he is about to pick up something that may break his back. He touches her forehead, like a doctor, making her wonder what he wants to do. Then he speaks, and any uneasiness fades away.

"I've got to go," Alterman says.

"Where are you headed?"

"Visit a sick friend," Alterman says.

But Alterman has no friends, Cherie thinks.

13

A week later, they are back at the resort. The lingering pain in Cherie's leg flares up at the sound of Alterman's voice.

"I've just spent the last two hours going over all your reports. And there are a whole lot of things going on here that have never happened before. It means nobody's doing their jobs."

"You okay?" Ingersoll whispers at Cherie, pointing at her ankle.

She rolls her eyes instinctively. She isn't sure why, or she doesn't want to admit it to herself. Not at first.

Then she glances over at Ingersoll, and sees he looks hurt. No, she knows why she rolled her eyes. She's taking her frustration out on him. She feels Alterman is pushing them closer to each other. She feels this even though she has no evidence of it, other than her own suspicions.

"I'm sorry," she finally croaks out. "I'm anxious. The cover story stuff is coming up..."

"Oh that's the best part," he says. "Don't worry. He'll show you what to do."

She isn't sure whether he means Alterman or God.

"Alex..." Templeton says, his voice correcting. He's never known Alterman to berate the staff before.

"How else can I explain it? Not one of you, not one of you has found anything wrong here."

"That's not true, Alex, and you know it," Templeton says.

Alterman is pacing, his hands wild and restless. "OK, let's go around the room." He points at Cherie. "I've got my spinster here who infiltrates the singles ministry and comes away disappointed that no guys hit on her."

"I didn't say that, Alex. I complemented them on it not being the usual meat show where every guy hits on you from the moment you walk through the door."

"That means you weren't paying attention to their theology."

"I was. I told you I didn't find anything wrong with it."

Alterman points at Templeton. Cherie cuts him off before he can continue. "And I object to the word 'spinster.'"

"What would you prefer?"

"You should be thankful we're talking about a church here and not *your* personal life. Can't see many women walking down the aisle toward that attitude."

"He's married to his work," Ingersoll says.

"When you got baptized, how cold was the baptismal font?" This is one of Alterman's foolproof tests. He usually nails every church on this.

"The body thermometer you made me wear said it was 82 degrees," Cherie says. "It was wonderful. I hated to get out."

Alterman grimaces as though shot at close range before his gaze falls back on his partner. "Then there's my theological assassin who's sat through the sermons and can't find a hole in any of them. Can't find a hole in the counseling. Can't find a hole in anything. Can't even rattle them with some good old fashioned audio hijinks." He then pauses. "How's your back?"

"Better."

"I was in the hospital," Cherie reminds him.

"I know you're better. You found more wrong with the hospital than you did the church."

Templeton jumps back in. "You were there during those sermons, Alex. You listened to the tapes too."

"Yes, but I rely on you to find at least some piddling little thing."

"Nobody's as hard on them as you are."

"That's my point. You're not doing your jobs." Before anyone can speak up, he moves on to Whit. "My softie here is interviewing people who don't belong on their rolls anymore. And let's be clear – most churches keep people on their rolls even in the most extreme cases – prison sentences, alien abductions, when they haven't come through the front door in 10 years. Half the church rolls in America are padded with whole cemeteries worth of people. Like a bunch of Chicago voters. And I could take all these interviews you've collected and make a commercial for Sweet Lightning Church."

"They mentioned a few things," Whit corrects him.

"We got the race car driver here," he points to Ingersoll, "who can't disrupt a Wednesday night service, and there's an event that's crying out for disruption at most churches." Ingersoll keeps his head down. He keeps expecting somebody to bust down the door and arrest him for the parking lot caper. He is wearing a shirt that reads, "For I know my transgressions, and my sin is always before me."

Alterman continues. "And do me a favor. Don't take this moment to tell me how St. Streptococcus of Dementia was killed after he fell off a golf cart." Then he reaches into his pocket and throws a piece of paper at Ingersoll. "Look that over when you've got a second."

Ingersoll glances down at the paper, which looks like a pamphlet. And Cherie sees him roll his eyes.

"I think that's our problem Alex," Templeton says, jumping in. "This isn't like most churches."

"Says who?"

"Says these reports," Templeton says. "What have *you* found?"

Alterman pauses. "Nothing." He looks defeated.

"Nothing?"

Alterman shakes his head. "I even gave them the homeless treatment."

Whit whispers to Cherie, sitting next to him. "He saw Wydgate."

"Really?"

Alterman shakes his head in disgust. "He was in costume."

"You both were undercover?" asks Ingersoll.

"Doesn't matter."

"So you didn't find anything? Neither of you?"

"I don't know about Wydgate. Not really interested in what he would be upset by." He waves his hand dismissively. "What about among the ministerial staff? Usually that's good for..."

"We've had keystroke monitors on every one – children's minister, associate pastors, youth ministers, even the janitorial staff. We hacked their phones. There was nothing."

Ingersoll shakes his head in disbelief. He remembers the church in California where one of the associate pastors was using Google's private browsing to search. They eventually hacked into his personal accounts and found he was looking at porn. The matter was handled quietly. Ah, the wonders of the associate pastors.

Templeton remembers. "What about the new girl? Is she even on this?"

"Yes."

"What's she doing?"

Alterman doesn't answer.

"She's the McParland," Templeton says.

"The what?" Ingersoll asks.

Templeton doesn't answer, and neither does Alterman. For a moment or two, Ingersoll looks in vain for someone to explain the term to him.

Templeton smiles. "Not even in the nursery?"

Alterman shakes his head at the memory of Obadiah's report. "Not even there. He was so mad. They practically smothered him with this annoying competence."

Templeton laughs.

"What's so funny? What are you laughing at?"

"I'm laughing at you, Screwtape. You're mad because this church is – horror of horrors! – not a vast kingdom of institutional despair."

"That's not it! We're not working hard enough. We're missing something. I know we are."

"How do you know that?"

"Because this has never happened before. And it's not a coincidence. What do you think it means when we're hired under false pretenses to come down here and audit a church, and we can't find anything wrong with it?"

"It's early," Whit says.

"No, and let me show you why." Alterman has had a laptop open on a table, but the screen was away from them. Now he turns it and holds it in his hands as he clicks on a video box. The screen is the homepage of X-Pose, the atheist site they had seen earlier.

The video plays, and Whit winces. Someone who had been on the bus with the nearly non-existent brakes recorded the ride and its near flirtation with disaster. There was the sound of the bus picking up speed, the shaking camera indicating the ride growing rougher, the expectation in the air of disaster. There is Brother Gates, calling on everyone to pray, and the resulting cacophony of voices. It looks like amateur video shot from a roller coaster.

Alterman plays the video, and then reads the accompanying text. "We previously documented the shoddy science being sold to the members of Sweet Lightning from its pulpit. And now we have evidence of the church's carelessness with basic safety. The students on this bus nearly died because the church relies on prayer to make sure its brakes work!"

"That isn't fair," Whit says. "That makes it sound like that was their usual bus."

Alterman holds up a hand. "Oh, they take that on a little further down. 'We should point out that the church has a fleet of modern buses. Was this bus specifically chosen for the nonbelievers? Or do they just not care about people who aren't 'real Americans?'"

Whit shakes his head.

Alterman puts down the laptop. "Folks, these are the atheists. They can be relied on to find something wrong."

Cherie stands up. "So you're saying we should at least be as good as the atheists?"

Ingersoll pounds a fist on one of the coffee tables. "They probably got the video off YouTube. I don't think they had somebody in there. This is bad, y'all. We've made this church look bad to other people."

"We didn't do that," Templeton says. "We aren't responsible for this."

Alterman points to Ingersoll. "No, he's absolutely right. This happened because we're here."

"How is that, Alex?" Templeton asks.

"Think about it. We came here, but we don't know who hired us. Wydgate is here. Coincidence? No."

"Does he know who hired him?"

"It doesn't matter," Alterman says. "At first, I didn't know if maybe, what? He hired us? He got us here just to show us up somehow? But then the atheists came. And this group is different. It's like they're doing the same thing we are, only for a totally different reason. I almost wonder if *they* got us here."

"So we're being used?"

"I'm used to being used. I'm OK with being used, as long as I know it's Him doing it. But this is different. It feels different."

"Alex, what are you saying we should do?"

"We can't go through with this. No sir."

"What? You're thinking about pulling out?"

"Yeah. We just leave town. Drop the whole thing." He points to the TV in the room. There is a tropical storm gathering force in the Gulf of Mexico, but its trajectory means it will probably strike another 200 miles further down the coast. "We might as well just pack up and head for wherever that storm is headed, be there to get blown away by it."

"We can't do that," Ingersoll finally says. "Leave town I mean, not go follow the storm.

"We can't do it now," Templeton says. "Word of this gets out and it sinks us."

"How does it sink us?" Cherie says. "That's your ego talking."

"No, he's right," Whit says. "You leave town and it'll blow up in your face."

Ingersoll sticks his hand up, as though he needs to be recognized to speak. "We could say we left town because of a scheduling conflict."

"That would be a lie," Templeton says. "Not a good idea for church auditors to lie. I seem to remember a commandment that covers that."

"You just say we were brought down here under a misunderstanding." Ingersoll shakes his head, as if to correct himself. "False pretenses."

"No, then people will want to know what happened," Templeton said. "And we don't know how this happened."

"Oh, yes we do," Alterman says. "It's Wydgate. It's got to be."

Templeton shakes his head.

"It's got to be him. I didn't want to admit it, but he got us down here just to embarrass us."

"Didn't you say he tried to warn you off the other day?" Cherie asks.

"That's just it! He knew by saying that what buttons he was pushing. I'm a pretty competitive guy."

Templeton is incredulous. "You? Nah!"

"He knew by saying that, the last thing I'd do is quit. He wants me here because he's the one who hired us."

There is a moment of silence. "You are insane, Alex," Whit finally says.

"Do I hear a second?" Cherie adds.

"Laugh if you want to. This could bury us," Alterman says.

"That's ridiculous," Whit says. Templeton knows this tone from Whit. He is the professor calling down the student from the ledge.

"How's it ridiculous?"

At this moment, the door opens. They hear a voice a split second before the man's face comes into view.

"I told you," says Wydgate, walking into the room. "I'm not the person you should be scared of."

III

From Honey to Ashes

1

"What are you doing here?" Alterman says. Though standing, he is suddenly even more alert. He looks poised to attack.

"I was listening." Wydgate appears pleased with himself. *You didn't think me capable of eavesdropping on you, did you?* he seems to be saying.

"How?"

"Check your belt, Alex."

Alterman, in one, frantic movement, unlatches his belt and slides it from his pants, wheeling it around like a serpent. The sight of it makes Templeton remember Alterman's earlier threat to make Ingersoll audit a snake-handling church.

There is a listening device on the belt. Alterman vengefully throws it to the floor and steps on it.

"Don't try to be clever," Alterman says, slightly winded. "It doesn't become you."

"Alex, you'd walk the earth to keep from admitting something you already know."

"What is it I'm supposed to be owning up to?"

"Who hired you? Who sent you here?" Wydgate's words aren't to Alterman, but to the rest of them. He doesn't wait for an answer. "The same thing happened to you that happened to me. We were both hired here by someone we don't know. They brought you all here and used Alex's ego to keep you here."

"That wasn't so hard," Cherie says, and Alterman shoots her an evil eye.

"The same person, I believe, hired me. They got me here because they knew I wouldn't want to leave Thomas Everhart in a lurch."

"Do you know him?" Templeton speaks up. He doesn't know Wydgate as well as Alterman does, but he still views him as competition. Templeton leans forward while seated, waiting for an answer.

"Only by reputation. The point is – and Alex will tell you – I came here because I was afraid of what you all would do to his ministry."

"What we would *do?*" Ingersoll asks.

"How you might tear him down."

"We don't go after people to tear them down," Templeton says, genuinely offended by the accusation. "We want the same thing you do. To help the Church grow. To see the Gospel preached."

"Yes, but *your* way."

"Just a second..." Templeton stands up.

"Wait," Alterman says, putting up a hand to stay him.

"...I don't have to take that from anyone," Templeton says, continuing.

"Wait..." Alterman continues.

"...don't care what you think you know..."

"Just a..."

"...former minister and I..."

"Your nose hairs are long," Cherie says, all at once. And the room is silent.

Wydgate is now the one who looks hurt.

"Way too long," Whit says, and Cherie nods at him.

Alterman jumps in. "Why are you still here? Why haven't you left? If you thought it was a bad idea before, when you thought we were here, why wouldn't you want to see us embarrassed?"

"I'm not interested in that happening to anyone, Alex. I told you, I'm not an enemy of yours. It's true. I don't always approve of your methods." Wydgate smiles, spreading his lips with knowing delicacy. "I've seen what you've done to churches. Ripping into the choir members like they're mezzo sopranos with the Metropolitan Opera. These people are accountants and janitors and teachers and lawyers. Their solo may be the only thing that gives their whole week meaning."

"So? The disciples weren't professionals either. They were fisherman and tax collectors. Most of them today couldn't even get into the churches that venerate them."

"All that is true. But I'm not aware that the Gospels ever mention how well they sang."

"What are we supposed to do, in your opinion? They want someone to tell them about the job they're doing, or supposed to be doing!"

"Alex, most of the people who go to church are nervous about even praying in public."

"Well that's the point. Jesus said go and make disciples of all nations. That's a command! It's not a suggestion! And it isn't just for 11 guys on a hill in Israel but for the whole Christian church! If they can't pray in public, how are they going to witness?"

"What are you shouting about?"

"Because this is *important!* Are you saying we should lie to them? Or sugarcoat it? What might the Lord say to them? Won't he hold us accountable if we're anything less than truthful?"

"I'm all for the truth, Alex. I'm just not up for saying to someone their entire worship experience is invalid."

Alterman pauses, and Templeton can see by his expression what is about to follow. All the members of the group have heard it themselves countless times. It isn't a rehearsed speech, even though it sounds that way, given the numbing number of times they've heard it. Alterman pounds a fist into the palm of his hand. The smack! resounds in their ears, and everyone winces, convinced it hurt.

"Churches aren't too big to fail! This isn't play. This is *real*. This is like pulling people out of burning houses. It's like nursing cancer patients. It's like rescuing storm victims from a deep, unforgiving ocean. This is the most important thing in the world! It isn't something you should endure for a couple of hours a week. You were *created* to worship. You were created to worship *Him*. You were made to glorify God. Everything that goes on outside those doors isn't supposed to matter as long as you're inside. We're supposed to carry Him out there. So what happens in a church should be worthy of Him. He didn't just purchase one hour of their time once a week by hanging on the Cross. *He bought them!*"

"I'm in the choir, Alex. You're preaching to me."

Alterman grunts under his breath, looks at Templeton, and nods. Alterman then turns and leaves the room.

Wydgate watches, then looks around, half expecting the rest of them to leave as well. But no one moves.

"What was that?" he asks.

Templeton stands up. "Give him a minute."

Wydgate still isn't satisfied. He waits through a moment of uncertain silence, then speaks again, this time to Templeton. It seems, despite their earlier words, Wydgate feels the most kinship with him. "I don't understand your partner."

Whit speaks up. "He doesn't make it easy." Wydgate is a bit startled. He hadn't expected anyone else to speak to him.

Now Wydgate looks defensive. Templeton sees it. For the first time, he looks like what Alterman has always pegged him as – an insecure, second-rate huckster who gives only a pale imitation of the same service they provide. Even his posture seems like an apology. Yet he continues on. "I'm telling you, I don't understand. It's like the other day, when we saw each other at Sweet Lightning. They offered him lunch, but he wouldn't eat it. I thought he'd at least take a bite to include it in his report."

"He doesn't eat lunch whenever we're auditing," Templeton says.

"Why not?"

Templeton tilts his head, as though the question is ludicrous. "Because he fasts whenever we do an audit. Just skips lunch each day."

"He does?" Cherie blurts out.

Wydgate looks astonished.

"He usually spends that hour praying."

"For what?" Ingersoll says.

"For you," Templeton says. "For all of us. There's a lot about him you don't know. He'll be back in a second."

"What's he doing?" Wydgate asks.

Whit speaks up. "He's in there praying, right now, I'll wager." Wydgate looks at Templeton, and he nods.

No one says anything. Not for the first time, everyone in the room seems to consider this man they have served and mocked, been frustrated and beguiled by, who has alternatively fascinated and disgusted them, as though they've not really grasped who he is or what any of his verbal tics or obsessions or calculated eccentricities mean. Alterman has altogether escaped them.

"Actually, he's probably in there listening to us right now," Templeton says, and Alterman reenters the room.

"All right," he says. He is putting on his coat, even though it's hot enough outside for short sleeves. "I have an announcement to make. My partner here…" he gestures toward Templeton "…already knows this, but I'm going to have to leave town for a few days. I'm going to New York, but I'll be back before the end of the audit. It's sudden. I'm afraid it can't be helped."

"What about the storm?"

"It's supposed to miss us here."

"What should we do?" Cherie says.

"Steve'll tell you," Alterman says, nodding again in Templeton's direction. "In the meantime, we're staying. We've got a job to see through, and we're going to do it. I mean, you are. I'll still be working, but not here."

Then Alterman turns toward Wydgate. There is no trace of the earlier animosity that has colored every word he has ever spoken to his nemesis.

"Tell me something," he says. "What do you believe? I know what you said the other day, but why do you do what you do?"

Wydgate's lips move, but no sounds come out. It's obvious he's not sure what he's supposed to say. Then the words come. "I…I believe…I believe in one God, the Father, the Almighty, maker of heaven and earth, of all that is, seen and unseen."

161

Then Alterman takes it up with him. "I believe in one Lord, Jesus Christ, the only son of God, eternally begotten of the Father, God from God, Light from Light, true God from true God, begotten, not made, of one being with the Father. Through him all things were made. For us and for our salvation he came down from heaven; by the power of the Holy Spirit he became incarnate from the Virgin Mary, and was made man. For our sake he was crucified under Pontius Pilate; he suffered death and was buried. On the third day he rose again in accordance with the Scriptures; he ascended into heaven and is seated at the right hand of the Father. He will come again in glory to judge the quick and the dead, and his kingdom will have no end."

Then the rest of them start talking, until they all take it up. "We believe in the Holy Spirit, the Lord, the giver of life, who proceeds from the Father. With the Father and the Son he is worshipped and glorified. He has spoken through the Prophets. We believe in one holy church. We acknowledge one baptism for the forgiveness of sins. We look for the resurrection of the dead, and the life of the world to come. Amen." When they finish speaking the words, which seem older than all time, everyone is quiet.

Then Alterman turns to Ingersoll and Cherie. "I'm surprised how well you all did that. I told you that would come in handy someday."

Cherie's voice is low and exasperated. "You quizzed us on it, like, *12 times.*"

Alterman speaks to Wydgate. "I want you to stay behind. Work with us."

"You do?" Wydgate repeats the words, unaware that all of Alterman's workers in the room do as well.

"Yes. I do. I don't have to worry about it. You'll know what to do."

"I will?"

"Yeah. You just said so." He puts his hand on Wydgate's shoulder, and watches Wydgate flinch. "That's the reason we do these things. The world can be a place of awful, endless desperation. When people come into God's house, they ought to find Him there. Not some gnawing sense of isolation, but the Spirit of God alive in people who know and love Him."

The air around them is weird, Templeton thinks. He's never seen Alterman like this. Not in a group. It's mystical, like those stories Ingersoll always springs on them to recall the saints. But this feels different. It is happening now.

"The truth is, I know you," Alterman tells Wydgate. "You exist to humble me. As long as you're here, I know I won't go too far."

"Do it your way," Alterman says to Templeton. "I'll be in touch." And then he's gone.

Nobody knows what to do or say at first.

Finally Cherie speaks. "What's he going to New York for?"

Templeton answers. "It has to do with what he did before this. Or maybe it has to do with the money. I'm not sure."

"The money?" Ingersoll says. They've never asked much about this. They only knew that as long as they worked for Alterman, they never had to worry all that much about a budget. He was willing to spend as much as needed to get the job done. Ingersoll always assumed they had a patron.

"You know how little we charge for what we do," Templeton says. "Who do you think pays your salary?"

Then Templeton starts to move, even though the rest of them don't. Wydgate still seems paralyzed.

"Maybe you understand now why he's that way. He understands judgment. You'd have to know where he came from to really understand."

"Where he came from?" Wydgate says. "Some little country church?"

Templeton shakes his head. "Wall Street," he says.

2

It is later. Ingersoll is outside Penobscot Elementary School, about six miles from Sweet Lightning. The last bell of the day has rung, and the car line has formed near the side entrance. A few of the children are walking off campus.

Not far away, the street preacher who had been at Sweet Lightning has moved her show across the street from the school. It seems odd for such a thing to happen coincidentally, Ingersoll thinks.

At the other end of the street, near a crosswalk, Ingersoll can see the two atheists, Nathan Steeplechase and Tara Diddle. They are dressed in bright, casual clothes next to a makeshift stand. They are giving out pamphlets to the children and little packages. The pamphlets are exactly the same as the one Alterman gave Ingersoll at their last meeting.

Ingersoll is wearing a shirt that reads "Then two bears came out of the woods and mauled 42 of the boys."

On the front of the pamphlet is a friendly, smiling dinosaur – a brachiosaurus with a mouthful of blunted, puffy cartoon teeth. He has on a lab coat and he is smiling. The picture is calibrated to entertain small children. The dinosaur, identified as Eli, gives a kid-friendly scientific lecture on the origins of the earth in a panel of cartoons.

"The earth is a big, wonderful place," Eli says, in a word balloon while holding a pointer in front of a picture of a globe. "It's even more wonderful when you understand it the way we can through science. It isn't magic, and you don't need to be afraid of somebody in the sky who made it! It's just us here, and we can explore it and understand it together!"

A talking dinosaur, Ingersoll thinks. Wow, that's original.

A kid walks past him and Ingersoll gets a look at the package in the hands of a girl with tiny dreadlocks. Whatever is in the clear package looks suspiciously like dirt.

"It's organic," Tara says. "It's a light snack with absolutely no preservatives, artificial sugars or animal products used. You see, we don't want to put anything harmful into the children at all, whether food or *ideas*."

"Not a fan of cupcakes?"

"Or fairy tales," she says.

The three of them are snapped to attention when they hear a child shouting. "This smells like your momma," says a little boy, and he throws one of the atheistic snacks at a girl. The grainy, gray substance smacks her in the face, and she begins to wail, her features coated in a black smudge.

"Don't talk about my momma!" the girl says.

"Hey let's not…" says Tara, sounding like a frustrated imitation of a kindergarten teacher.

Ingersoll looks down at the pamphlet. "My understanding of science, sketchy though it is, I grant you – dinosaurs didn't talk, that we know of. Unless we're talking about the Flintstones. How did you manage to create a tract that glorifies…nothing?"

"That's what's so great about it," Nathan says. "We racked our brains for weeks until we came up with Eli. He gets the point across. There's nothing else in life but what's right here in front of us, and that's enough for all of us."

In fact, that's the slogan across the top of the pamphlet.

"It's teaching the kids to think for themselves," Nathan says.

"Looks more like you're teaching them to think just like you."

"And you don't do differently in Sunday Schools? Vacation Bible Schools? Halloween carnivals? Christmas pageants?"

"It's not really free thinking though, in a literal sense, is it?"

"It's freer than your side of the street," he says.

"We're being more aggressive," Tara says. "It's something we're trying out, like the blog. If we're successful here, there are people who are going to take this national."

Ingersoll laughs inside. They are just like Alterman. Franchising.

"Let me get this straight," Ingersoll says. "You guys are atheists. You don't believe in anything."

"Anything supernatural," Tara says. "There's plenty we believe in. Just none of the god stuff."

"So you're hostile to faith?"

"No, we're not hostile to faith. We just don't believe."

"So this stuff with the dinosaur and everything? You lose a bet?"

"We're not hostile to faith. We just want kids to know there's more out there. And we had to sue to get this far. You won't believe how we fought in the courts just to be able to do what little we're doing now this close to a school."

"I'm sure your lawyer's kids are grateful for your efforts."

"We're not rich," Tara says. "You should see the place where we're staying. We can't take baths there. There's no running water."

Ingersoll smiles. "You should come over to our place. We have springs of living water…"

Nathan cuts him off. "No. Seriously. Look, I appreciate the offer, but I wouldn't want anyone to think we're associating with you. I mean seriously, I do appreciate it, but let's face it. You'll get me over there and try to witness to me."

"No. I can witness to you here just as well. What made you pick this place?"

"You guys," Tara says.

"What?"

"Your boss, Alex Alterman. I don't care what he says. Don't really care what any of you say. You guys are going around the country undermining churches, tearing them up. You know your reputation."

"Yeah, and your boss' main competition is here right now too," Nathan says. "Wydgate. He knows what's at stake, that's why he's here. So we're here too. We figure you'll get your foot in the door at Sweet Lightning, and we come into the community. While you do your job, we'll do ours."

"Which is to poison the well?" Ingersoll says.

"Hey, by the time we're both through – they'll be losing members and they won't be able to make new ones."

Ingersoll understands it all, in an instant. "And by that time, we'll be on to another church audit."

"And we'll be right behind you."

"Yeah, I wonder why anybody would think you guys were hostile…" Ingersoll says. "Except maybe the kids. I'd hate to taste those 'snacks.'" He inserts air quotes with his fingers.

"We're not," Nathan says. "We just want to lay out the facts and let people make up their own minds."

"No, I mean, you guys aren't exactly indifferent."

"Why should we be?" Nathan says. "We don't like seeing people misled."

"Did either of you guys have any church background?"

"Both of us," Nathan said. "But I don't see that makes any difference. All churches are the same. They're all filled with lies. Lies and good people who are somehow comforted by what makes the rest of the world miserable."

"Oh yes, it does matter if you had a church background," Ingersoll says. "Unbelief always has a motive."

"Could it be reason?"

"As reasonable as a talking dinosaur? Shouldn't your lawyer be worried about another kind of lawsuit?"

"What are you getting so out of joint about?" Tara asks. "I mean, you're a knowledgeable person. You have a background in unbelief, right?"

"Yeah, you could say that," Ingersoll says, as though she's learned something unpleasant about him.

"Doesn't it bother you where you are now?" she asks. "Don't you feel out of place?"

"Don't you ever get tired of praying to nobody?"

"Doesn't all this stuff about Jesus and everything seem dead to you? Doesn't it seem deader to you every day that passes?"

"I don't need enlightenment," Ingersoll says. "I already have that. Take away Jesus and you leave me with nothing but myself. But I already had me, and I traded that in for Jesus. He *is* light. If I give Him away, that leaves nothing. Nothing but darkness."

"That's nice," Tara says, as though she's doing him a favor listening to all this.

"And Jesus isn't dead. He's certainly a lot more comfort than a dinosaur peddling equations and bad granola bars."

"Maybe. But it introduces the kids to this. It reinforces what they'll be seeing in the classroom later. And in the real world."

"Talking dinosaurs."

"Science! Facts! The dangers of sweet fairy tales with blood and death in them!"

"They'll be seeing blood and death out there in the world," Ingersoll says.

"And most of it done by people who believe they have to satisfy a man in the sky by killing other people. Or keeping them from being what they want."

"Look guys," Ingersoll says, "I didn't come out here to argue."

"Then you came out to get a tract?"

"I certainly didn't come out to get a snack," he says. "I've consumed enough of that stuff in my life already."

Nathan says, "What I know about you – you could fit in with us. You're only doing what we're doing. From the inside."

Ingersoll is about to say something.

"I know...We heard your boss say the same thing. You're believers..."

"Yeah. And you'll have a hard time if you start following us around the country."

"Why?" Tara says.

"Well, for starters, you'll need a bath." Ingersoll turns and walks away. "Seriously, come see us if you need a shower." He names the resort.

"That's a nice place, that resort," Tara says. "How many old people did you fleece to get the money to stay there?"

"In my Father's house are many mansions," he says. "We've got soap too. Enough to wash away anything."

He wonders what he's going to tell Templeton when he gets back. This is not a good development, necessarily. Then he remembers what Alterman said about them earlier.

As he passes a public trash can, he sees a pile of the snacks, deposited by the children. They were at least careful with those. The pamphlets, however, litter the ground, bearing the imprints of scores of shoes.

"See you in church," he calls back.

3

Alterman surrenders his driver's license at the guardhouse. He submits to the patdown and hears the instructions before being led into the visitation ward.

The penitentiary has an alien smell about it, reminding him of a hospital of dubious cleanliness. There is no amount of industrial strength cleanser that can completely hide the character of the place. For some reason, he thinks of the men here, with unruly facial hair and tattoos and backgrounds so unlike Fixx that he can scarcely imagine it. This is supposed to be a "country club," but it's still a prison, and though there are white collar criminals throughout its halls, it's still a prison. He walks down a tiled floor with ruts and missing pieces toward the ward where he is told to sit down and wait, and all he can think about is that he will be able to leave this place in a short while and Fixx won't.

He has never visited Fixx before. They have exchanged letters but Fixx is paranoid about anything beyond that. He doesn't want his e-mails getting shared. He is afraid of the media, Alterman understands, but obviously not too scared since jailhouse interviews with him keep popping up in *The Wall Street Journal* and *The New York Times.*

It is hard for Alterman to believe it has been five years since he's seen his former boss. Even as he sits waiting, Alterman reminds himself that, under only slightly different circumstances, he could have been sitting in this place, and he doubts Fixx would have come down from New York to visit him. But there's no scenario in Alterman's imagination where Fixx wouldn't have gone to jail.

What would he have done in here, had he been imprisoned? Alterman can see himself auditing the prison kitchen, or the bathrooms, or organizing a laundry room sting. He can see himself with a dedicated band of cadres disrupting the prison chapel in hopes of getting better sermons. But he doubts he would have been as motivated. There is something soul crushing about this place.

Fixx shuffles in. Behind the glass, there is little of the man's legendary charisma now. He is like the rest of the inmates who file past, some with twitchy indecision and others scuffing their shoes as though they can't see beyond their eyelids, puffy with age and boredom and regret. Fixx doesn't know what to do with his hands. They stay close to his waist, then dart behind him like he's about to be cuffed. Then he grips them, and then he runs one through his hair just as he sits down. He is looking at Alterman, but he is looking past him, through him almost. He cannot meet his former employee's eyes.

That part Alterman expects.

Fixx picks up the phone, and Alterman follows. He is somewhat surprised that Fixx will sit and talk to him. The man's pride would never have allowed this earlier, he thinks. It's one thing to pontificate to a reporter over a phone and through an e-mail, but another to trade words after so long with a man you used to invite on your vacations.

"You look well," Fixx says. He says this though his eyes are still somewhere else.

"So do you," Alterman says. Neither man can believe the words. "What do you do in here?"

"You read the papers…"

"People don't read papers now, Boss," Alterman says. It's been awhile, but Fixx can still recognize one of Alterman's jokes. This is his way of saying, without saying, that Fixx never did understand the modern world.

"Enough of them do," Fixx says. "You should see my hate mail."

"You read it?"

"When you get as much as I do, you get curious. I give some away to the other guys in here – the ones who don't get any mail. It keeps them amused. They figure as long as they read mine, they know they've still got a chance of being loved."

"Who writes?"

"Mostly nobodies," Fixx says. "The people who only read about it and feel like they have to chastise the guilty. But about like you'd figure. I hear from the investors."

That too was Fixx. He could be so wonderfully dismissive of practically anyone. Alterman knew some of the people who probably write him faithfully, sharing their hate like reliable family recipes. They are the ones who had been enjoying their Florida condos, warmed at night by the thoughts of all the interest accumulating on top of their life's wealth – that is, until the depths of Fixx's depravity became known, and they found themselves embracing new careers past retirement age, standing in the doorways of discount stores greeting people who walk in.

"I've seen some of your interviews."

"I shouldn't do those," Fixx says. "I think I still talk to them in hopes of getting somebody to call and tell me to stop. Besides my lawyers, I mean."

"Bonnie calls, I'm sure."

"Bonnie doesn't call anymore. She probably won't call me ever again."

Alterman doesn't respond immediately to this. He keeps looking at Fixx's eyes, waiting for them to meet his. They don't.

He looks cornered.

"Listen," Fixx says. "Thanks for coming. You didn't have to…"

"Of course, I did. I had to see how you were. How you *are*, I mean."

"You know how I was. You better than anybody."

"I didn't know you any better than anybody else," Alterman says. He almost regrets the words immediately, but they're the truth.

"How are things in the cult, Alex?" This sounds more like Fixx. Alterman can't tell if this is his old boss' sense of humor, or if the man has somehow translated his career into something else.

"It's not a cult, and you know that."

"What is it then?"

"I'm more or less a consultant. How churches can better serve their congregations."

"Evangelical engineering, huh?"

"You might say that." He shifts in the seat. "The popular term is 'mystery worshipper,' you know, like mystery shopper. But that really does make us sound like we're a cult."

"We? You have people working with you?"

"Several, and I have a partner. Business is great."

"Sounds like you're literally doing the Lord's work."

"Feels that way."

"I'm proud of you. Probably always knew you'd wind up in something like that."

This surprises Alterman. "Why?"

"Because something else was always driving you. Not the same thing that drove me."

"What drove you?"

He ignores the question, as though Alterman already knows the answer. "Do you know anything? About Nick?"

"Nothing beyond what I read. Probably the same things you did."

Alterman sighs. Fixx says nothing, still staring intently at a place somewhere near Alterman's Adam's apple.

"How did you find out?" Alterman asks.

"My lawyers," he says. "They're the only ones who really talk to me anymore. The reporters wanted a comment but I wouldn't give it. I would have no hope of ever speaking to Bonnie again if I gave a comment now."

"You OK?"

"OK in what sense? I'm still eating. I'm still sleeping. If you wonder how I'm doing, the hardest thing for me to accept is why I'm *still* eating and sleeping. Why isn't this affecting me more? As it is…I'm just numb."

"People deal with grief differently."

"That what your cult believes?"

Alterman considers the idea of his company as a cult, and it revolts him. That would mean he had abnormal control over the smallest details of his employees' lives, and was able to superimpose his thoughts over theirs. He would be able to inspire fear in them, and command them to satisfy his whims. They would be sensitive to his mood swings, and instantly calibrate their own expectations to what they supposed his might be.

No, he decides. He doesn't want to consider that.

"You know, that's like the easiest scam in the world to get people to bite on," Fixx said. "The church thing. All you have to do is get people to invest money through their church in whatever you're selling. You get the preacher on board, and then the rest of them follow. When things go south, they don't want to admit something went wrong, because it's like their faith isn't strong enough. They don't want to go against the pastor. Then when the money's gone, they think God punished them for not having enough faith, or for putting too much faith in money. It's, like, foolproof."

"Did you learn about that in here?"

He nods. "Plenty of guys in here have tried it. A lot more have who'll never see the inside of this place."

"It's not a cult. It's not a scam. And if you're taking out your anger on me, I can take it."

Maybe Fixx wasn't mad a minute before, but he is now. "I don't need to mourn, Alex."

"Blessed are they that mourn, for they shall be comforted," Alterman says.

"Is that what you're here for?"

"I'm here to do whatever you need, Boss."

Fixx smirks a little, as though Alterman hasn't risen to take his bait. "Jesus said that, right?"

"Sermon on the Mount."

Then Fixx says, "You know, I didn't used to believe in hell, but I do now."

"This place that bad?"

"What? No, actually, this place is much better than I expected it would be. Food isn't that bad. I've lost weight, but that's good. Other prisoners more or less leave me alone. Some of them evidently don't have retirement accounts to worry about." Alterman laughs at his former boss' unexpected joke, in spite of himself. "No, it's up here." Fixx pointed to his forehead. "Where I am up here. Let me tell you how I spend my days and nights. I've got all the time to think, and some thoughts crowd out the others. How did I get here? I know how it happened, but *where* did it start? Where was the point of no return? When did I make a choice that made sure that no matter what I did, I was going to end up here? I think about things I did and how later I could have cleaned up the mess, and maybe no one even knows what happened afterward. What did I do? I can remember what I said in conversations from 20 years ago just like the one we're having right now, and I can't believe what I hear myself saying in some of them. I'm probably going to keep doing this when I get out of here, torturing myself. I'm always going to be doing it."

Alterman knows – as does Fixx – that he'll never walk out of this prison. The sentence is too steep and the public too unforgiving to allow anything less crushing. Nevertheless, he puts up with the fiction. "I think you may be a little hard on yourself."

"That's not what the judge said."

"You're not the first person who ever did something like this."

"But I'm the first person who ever did it on this scale. Alex, you're not my lawyer. And you're not naïve. And you know I can't promote you anymore. Why sugarcoat it? I won't believe it and you don't believe it."

"I didn't say what you did was right. I just said that you weren't the first. And you *are* being hard on yourself."

"Deservedly so. Alex, how many people did I ruin? That's like saying I'm just guilty of bad timing. I only picked the eve of the greatest financial disaster in the past seventy years to start a …criminal enterprise …that came to light when everything went south. If it hadn't happened, maybe I wouldn't have been caught."

"You always would have been caught."

"How do you know that?"

"Because somebody would have caught you."

"Like you?"

"I didn't say that."

The question in the old days was always the same whenever he ventured away from the office, to Hong Kong or London or Zurich. "What's it like to work for him?" No one ever believed Alterman when he said he never had problems with Fixx. No one asks anymore, and Alterman doesn't go out of his way to advertise.

Fixx smiles. "No, I know why they call it moral hazard. I lost all fear. No risk was too small for me. And I *enjoyed* it. I fed off it. I couldn't get enough of it. Every day I got up was me shaking my fist at somebody, but I have no idea who I thought I was taking on."

"Now you understand though. And you regret it."

He gives a short laugh, like a horse shivering. "I feel remorse that I got caught. But if I wasn't here, I'd probably be out there doing it again, rubbing my nose in it, patting myself on the back for how smart I was."

"You wouldn't be the only one."

How many times had Alterman asked Fixx to get in on his fund? He had lost count. He never asked at the office. It was on the golf course, or at Christmas parties, or on the one or two working vacations they took with their families. He would ask the question even though he was dimly aware of the risks, and the potential outcome. The answer was always the same. "Maybe some other time," Fixx would say dismissively, as though Alterman was the kid losing his teeth who wants to try a steak for dinner. Fixx's smile was benevolent and slightly condescending, and Alterman tried not to let it get to him, even when it did.

That's why now, when he thinks back on those days, he wonders if Fixx had always assumed he would be caught, and simply didn't want Alterman to go down like the rest of the people he dismisses, those pitiful suckers who had it coming, thinking there was anything like a sure thing in investments. As it is, Alterman prefers to think that all the time Fixx was putting him off he was really protecting him. And if he hadn't, then Alterman might be in a similar place, and wouldn't have had a cent when he needed it later, when he formed his own business.

"And if I hadn't been caught, maybe Nick would still be alive," Fixx finally says, as though all that was holding the boy on earth was his father's criminal activity. So it was the cops and the regulators who were to blame. Fixx winces and drops his head. "Did he really hang himself?" he asks, his throat catching on the words.

"That's what Bonnie told me."

"You going to the funeral?"

"Yes I am. Bonnie asked me to."

"Will you tell her something for me?"

"You know I will," Alterman says. His boss will not look up, will not meet his eye. Alterman can only imagine how he is, knowing that the funeral for his oldest son, who killed himself two days before, will happen tomorrow without the father there. What is it that Fixx will want to tell his wife, through all the silence and anger and regret? "What do you want me to say?"

"I need some new shorts," Fixx says, as though there is nothing that will rekindle his wife's love so much as his needs. "Boxers. I'll give you a list with the right name brands. I can't wear anything else. It hurts too much."

4

It's been ten minutes, and Cherie should have made the phone call by now.

But something keeps stopping her. It's the same uneasiness she's had since the beginning of the audit – the uneasiness with her role.

All the preparations have been made. Just a few days before, Cherie called the Century Rehabilitation Center and told them to expect her. As Templeton told her, she used Alterman's name and they immediately understood that she was to be admitted as an exercise. She would be accompanied by a friend, and they were to go ahead and admit her for substance abuse counseling. The story – away from home, still grieving over the loss of her fiancée and her promising career, Jennifer Mersault would fall back into her prescription drug habit and need someone to recognize it and get her help.

Her gym accident was, in some ways, a fortunate one. The hospital gave her pain medication, which was what tipped her back into old habits. Or so the story will go.

All she needs now is to call Anna Sparrow. As her singles minister, Anna will be the person she might ordinarily call, in hopes of getting help.

But she isn't sure how to make the call. She isn't sure how anguished she should be, or evasive. There are three sheets of instructions typed out in front of her, courtesy of Templeton, suggesting how she might use the cover story. But at the bottom of the last page, Templeton's instructions state: "You alone know your relationship with your minister. You must do only what you feel comfortable in hopes of seeing how she will react."

Cherie doesn't feel uncomfortable with the story, though. Whatever misinformation she gives Anna will be cleared up in the end. She's looking forward to that point.

What she can't get out of her mind is the innocent look on Templeton's face when he handed her the cover story.

Then the phone, intentionally ignored until now, rings.

Cherie recognizes the number. It's Anna.

"Hello?"

"Jennifer?" Anna's voice is weak, as if she is trying to be heard over some noise.

"Anna." Cherie's voice is also weak, because it has to be for the story to succeed. It's better this way, Cherie thinks. She'll have discovered my problem instead of me having to call her up. Maybe she thinks something is wrong.

"Jennifer, I'm sorry I haven't seen you in a while."

"That's OK… You were there when I went in. What's wrong?"

"Things are bad here. I just couldn't."

"What…"

"Jennifer, I need you," she says. "I'm afraid. I'm really afraid."

"What's wrong?"

"I don't know how to say it. I need you to come over."

"To your place?"

"Yes. Please, as soon as you can."

"Absolutely. What is it?"

"It's hard to explain. I just need someone to be here. See, I took them all. I don't know what's going to happen."

"Took them all?"

"It's my med.." Here, Anna's voice breaks down. There is no voice. Cherie thinks it may be the soundless weeping of someone unable to speak. Then, there is a ragged but sharp intake of breath, and it is obvious Anna is crying.

179

"Slow down, now. Just tell me."

"I can't…I can…Just come over." When the words finally come, they sound forced, as through a strainer. "I took some pills. I took too many pills. I'm not sure how many pills I took."

"What is it? What did you take?"

Anna says a name that Cherie doesn't recognize, though she can't be sure she heard the name correctly. She asks Anna to repeat it, but she can't tell a second time what it is. Her voice is sluggish and thick-tongued. Cherie has the picture of someone sinking.

"Listen, you're at your house right now?" She waits, but doesn't get an answer. "Anna? You're at your house?"

"Yeah. Yeah, I am."

"Stay on the phone with me. Should I call 911?"

"Just come here."

"OK, stay on the phone with me. Talk to me. Tell me what happened." Already Cherie is gathering up her things. She clutches the phone and pulls out her car keys. She can make it to Anna's in about ten minutes. She doesn't know what Anna has taken, so she isn't sure if this will be enough time to get her and get to a hospital before any damage is done. She is afraid to hang up on Anna. If someone else was here… then she realizes she can call 911 on the room phone.

"Anna, you still there?"

"Yes."

"Let me call 911, then I'll come. Tell me again what your address is?"

In the middle of all of this, Cherie is struck by how strange it is. What are the odds of this happening – a person with a prescription meds problem calling another person with a prescription meds problem, unaware of their shared bond?

Cherie isn't playing a role. That's the wonder of it all.

Six months before Cherie LeFevere began working for Alex Alterman, she was a youth minister in a Wisconsin Methodist church. When she didn't show up for Sunday services, a few of the kids' parents came to her apartment. No one answered. Police officers doing a welfare check forced her door open and found her unresponsive on the floor of her bedroom. She was nearly dead. The amount of opiates in her blood should have killed her.

It had all been too much really. She started in seminary, after she sprained her ankle the first time jogging. Then she began sneaking pills out of a friend's home. After a while, she found a few places, here and there, to buy them. Just as she needed them. The pressure of studies. Of finding a job. Of those teenagers needing her, wanting her advice, wanting some hope that there was something meaningful in life besides what they were seeing, even in their own homes. How could she let them down? How could she allow them to see what she really was? Besides, it wasn't anything she couldn't handle.

She finally did wake up. It took weeks of counseling for her to face anybody, but she couldn't go back to the church. Her old boss was the one who put her in touch with Alterman. He hired her, knowing what she had been through. She assumed it was pity, but she was willing to take anybody's pity. It was like she told him when she interviewed – she needed to see if the Lord could still use her.

So when Templeton handed her the cover story, she understood that Alterman had never told anyone else about her past. Alterman had simply allowed her to be the smart one, the perfect one, the A student who was always turning in her paper ahead of time. She nurtured this image for everyone, and most of all, herself. And he understood that she needed to feel this way about herself.

Which is why she didn't dare take any of the pain meds they gave her after the gym accident. The pain had been horrible. Her leg was slowly getting better, but there was always the itch.

The ambulance will be there probably a few minutes after she arrives, Cherie thinks. She runs to her car and speeds out of the resort.

"Are you still there, Anna?"

"Yes, Jennifer," Anna says. She is still crying - a ragged, exhausted, disgusted weeping. "I'm so sorry. I didn't mean for you to have to do…"

"Stop it," Cherie says. "We'll get you fixed up."

"I'm sorry to put you in this position."

"I'm your friend. You're there for me, aren't you?"

"I guess I'll lose my job now. Once this gets out. I don't figure you could keep all this to yourself…"

"Listen to me," Cherie says. "There's a lot you don't know. We'll get you help. You need help, that's the main thing."

"I just can't face it," she says. "I can't face what they'll say. They'll all be so disappointed in me."

"Listen to me. You're not the first person who ever made a mistake. It'll be good. You'll be helping other people. There are all kinds of people with all kinds of problems. What did He say? 'My power is made perfect in weakness.'"

"I feel so weak."

"Stay there, Anna," Cherie says. "Listen, I'm on my way, and so is an ambulance. So in case you're not ready, put some clothes on and get ready to leave. Get yourself moving." That would at least give her something to do.

She feels the temptation to keep all of this to herself. To help Anna overcome this problem and then to never say a word about it. But she knows what would have happened to her if someone had done the same thing for her. She'd be dead.

There's the audit, though. Alterman is sure to hammer a church with a singles minister popping pills.

He didn't hammer you, did he?

"Anna," she says. "Anna, say something."

"It's times like this I wish I was dead," she said. "I've felt like that for so long."

"Anna, I'm not just saying this. You've got to trust me. I *really* do know how that feels. It doesn't last forever."

"I just…it all seems so hard."

"I know," Cherie says. "I know."

"What made me think I could do anything for the Lord?"

"That wasn't your idea," Cherie says. "That was His. And He still can use you. That's why you're still here."

"No," Anna says. "No."

"Yes! Stay, Anna."

There is no answer.

"Anna, listen! There's a lot about me that you don't know. It'd take too much time to tell it all to you, but you have to trust me! The fact that you're talking to me now - it just proves there's more for you. I know. I know!"

Still no answer.

At last, Cherie can see the house. Her door is open. Anna is standing out front, holding the phone even as she clasps her arms to herself. She looks like she is standing against a strong wind.

"Jennifer," Anna says.

"Yes," she answers, even though it isn't really her name.

"Please forgive me. I need you to..."

5

Ingersoll is talking. He's back at the resort with Cherie, Whit, Wydgate and Templeton. Wydgate is holding an immaculately wrapped "welcome aboard" present from Cherie. When he opens it later, he will find it is an electric nose hair trimmer. "You'll know what to do with it," she says to him.

Whit has nodded to Wydgate, but he did not offer his hand in greeting as he usually does. There is very little sensation in the inert fingers of Whit's right hand. He grips them with his left, but the left hand only feels little more than a tingling. It comes and goes, though Whit tries not to think about what he will do when it does not come back again.

Ingersoll is wearing a T-shirt that reads, "Behold, I send you out as sheep in the midst of wolves; so be shrewd as serpents and innocent as doves."

"So they were saying how they're going to basically follow us out to churches as we do audits and pull stuff like this," Ingersoll says, waving the tract.

"And they'll undermine the church from the outside while we do the same inside?" Templeton says. Whit has heard the two of them work this out at least three times, just to make sure everyone understands. It all sounds so cockeyed.

"Yeah. They don't really take any of us seriously when we say we're doing this *for* the churches," Ingersoll says.

"Can't blame them," Wydgate says, giving a rueful chuckle.

"Laugh all you want, but this is worse than we thought," Ingersoll says.

"What do you think? Are they good enough to pull it off?"

"Who knows?" Ingersoll says. "You've seen what they were handing out. I don't think they could change many minds, but this is just the beginning. I get the sense that they're going to keep working at this until they find the right formula."

"Sounds like a soft drink," Wydgate says.

"If you package unbelief like a soft drink, if you make it sweeter, then everyone may want a sip," Cherie says. Whit watches the two of them. She winks at Ingersoll. Ingersoll smiles, as though he's not sure if her sudden chumminess means anything at all. The two of them have been dancing around each other like this for the longest, Whit thinks. He wonders if either of them realize how they look.

"Your situation okay?" Ingersoll asks her, risking a thaw.

"I think she will be," Cherie says. "Thanks for asking." Whit wonders who they're talking about, but he feels lousy enough not to care that much.

"It's about more than a talking dinosaur," Wydgate says, never taking his eyes off Ingersoll. "I can see your point. This isn't what concerns you. It's about what may be after this."

Ingersoll nods. "We need to call Alex about this."

Templeton cocks his head. "Why do they bother you?"

"I don't know," Ingersoll admits, cocking his own head, if for no other reason than to fit in. "Something different about them. Seemed to me more motivated. Sharper. More creative."

"And it depends on who's behind them."

"We need to call Alex about this," he repeats.

"No we don't," Templeton says. "Alex is incommunicado. He told us to handle things while he's gone, and he's gone."

Cherie protests. "He didn't say we shouldn't call him..."

Templeton meets her eyes. "We ain't calling Alex." He repeats the words for emphasis, only this time, she suddenly gets it and repeats them along with him. Whit mouths the words himself.

Templeton doesn't want to disturb Alterman, and Templeton doesn't want Alterman disturbing them.

"I can see what you're doing," Ingersoll says, "but Alex might know how to handle this.'

Templeton puts his index finger to his lips. "Shhh!" he says, short and emphatic. Wydgate chuckles, as though a thousand suspicions have been confirmed for him in a second.

Then Templeton's shoulders relax. "We know how to handle this anyway," he says.

All of them respond. "We do?"

"Look, we're all smart enough to figure this out," Templeton says. "We're looking at an outfit that could wreck our business, but that isn't the biggest problem."

"I probably need to say something to Everhart, just to let him know," Templeton says.

Wydgate raises a hand, as if he's afraid of being drowned out. "You know, we needn't look on them as adversaries, even though they are."

Whit nods. "He's right. They're just lost."

"That doesn't make them any less dangerous," Ingersoll says.

"Voice of experience?" says Cherie, supplying Alterman's standard heathen jibe at him.

Ingersoll nods. "I just wonder what…"

"What would Alex do?" Wydgate says, and the rest of them laugh.

The room is quiet for a few seconds. "You probably know better than anybody, coming from the outside," Templeton says. "What would Alex do?"

Wydgate rises. He folds his arms and starts to pace. It is hard to know whether he is doing this unconsciously or deliberately. It appears to Whit as though Wydgate wants to impress them somehow, wants to prove he belongs among them.

Then he stops and turns to Ingersoll. "Did you say they mentioned *me*? The atheists?"

"Yes. Have you had some contact with them?"

"No. I just saw them. Anything they know about me they probably got off my website." Wydgate is silent, and then something flicks on in his eyes, like a current. "They probably don't even know I'm working with you now."

Then something pops into Ingersoll's eyes, tangible enough to be seen like a bubble. "St. Inlex of Alucinatio converted to Christianity when he learned that another man who resembled him had been executed by mistake on suspicions of being a Christian. He was so taken with the idea that a man had died in his place that he embraced the faith."

Wydgate looks at Ingersoll, grabs a sheet of paper and a phone, and leaves the room.

"You know," Templeton says, "sometimes I can't decide whether you just know a lot of those stories or you make them up."

"They're true," Ingersoll assures him, getting up to leave. "Made up that one, though."

6

It has been weeks since Alterman has called Rambha. He keeps getting e-mails from her, but he wants to hear her voice. It's important that she hear his. He is standing up at his desk again, inside the hotel. He can see Central Park from his window, but he won't tell her that, though he is calling her to get something off his mind. At the moment, he needs her enthusiasm.

He doesn't find it though. Her voice is not as alert and cutting as it was last time. He has handled enough operatives operating alone to know that her mind is not totally occupied with the task. He wonders if she still feels underutilized. For her to be aimless is a form of torture.

"Anything come up lately?" he asks.

"Where are you now, Alex?"

"New York. Personal business."

"Is that where you are from?"

"No. But I used to work here. Doing a favor for an old friend."

"You sound morose."

"It's a funeral," he says. "In more than one way."

"Oh," Rambha says, her voice full of knowledge. "You mean *something* is dying with this person?"

"It's been dead for a while. This is the burial."

"All burials must be proper."

"Very true."

"Has this one been proper?"

"We'll see." He doesn't like the way this conversation is going.

"What does it mean, 'pulling a McParland?'"

"McParland was a man who worked for the Pinkerton Detective Agency in the nineteenth century. He infiltrated the Molly McGuires by posing as a miner. It was a long-term, heavy undercover sting operation." He doesn't know if she will know who the Pinkertons or the Molly McGuires were, but that is why God created Wikipedia. "So, do you think you could get the hang of this? Is this something you want to do?"

"I suppose so." Her voice does not sound ebullient, not like before.

"A ringing endorsement."

"I'm still at pains to understand why you sent me here, to do it this way?"

"You haven't figured that out yet?"

"No."

"And it's galling you, isn't it?"

"Yes!" There was the enthusiasm. "I don't feel you can fully appreciate what I can do from where you are, and over the phone."

"You're smart enough to figure this out, Eager Young Space Cadet. I dispatched you where you are as a loyalty test."

"A loyalty test? You mean loyalty to you?"

"Loyalty to the mission we have. Our objective. It's one thing to know beforehand that you want to do something like this for a client. But once you get there, you get the temptation to cut them some slack. Give in a little, be human. It's that attitude that gets churches in the situation they occupy when they call us. They cut themselves too much slack."

Rambha isn't saying anything, and Alterman detects a note of dissatisfaction, still there, unstated in so many words.

"If it makes you feel any better, I should tell you that this isn't where I saw *myself*." He clears his throat. "This job I mean."

"No?" she says.

189

Alterman begins. "I thought I'd just play with other people's money for 25 years or so. Take it and grow it, and harvest a little bit of my own at the same time. You know, it's easier the more you don't care about the outcome, at the end of the day."

"So you were in the financial markets?"

"Yes."

"What you're describing…it sounds too neat for you. Too boring."

"You think I wasn't ambitious enough."

"People can listen too closely sometimes to their own dreams. What made you leave? A conversion experience?"

"Not quite. Though finding out your boss is a crook can feel a little like the Damascus road. Blinding lights. A corrective voice from on high."

"Have you been getting my regular reports?" Rambha asks.

"Yes. You seem to admire Thomas Everhart. What do you think are his weaknesses?"

She does not hesitate. "The same as you."

"Really?" Alterman is amused, but he doesn't smile. Alterman never smiles. "This should be good. What are his weak-"

She doesn't allow him to finish. "The same things that make you both good at your jobs. Attention to detail. Single-mindedness. Obsessive concentration."

"Those sound like virtues."

"To you, they would."

"All right, since you've got me on the couch, enlighten me."

"It's him we have on the couch," she says. "Attention to detail is good as long as you don't miss the bigger picture. Single-mindedness is permissible as long as there is only one issue at hand."

"I see the pattern. So you're saying that he is ignoring something larger?"

"No," she says. "I'm saying you could be accused of paying too much attention to what you think are problems and not paying enough attention to what God considers the problems to be."

"Let's talk about Everhart first. What bigger picture might he be missing?"

"We are here, are we not, because there's a sense that he is a coming man? A potentially national voice? Or more?"

"No," Alterman says. "We're here because somebody asked us to come down. We don't know who, but.."

"My point is that he doesn't seem to care about the larger issues," she says. "He seems to care only about this church, this community, his sermons, *his* congregation."

"And this is a problem why...?"

"I don't know," she says. "I think it seems...suspicious."

"Should he be campaigning for something?"

"Not at all. It's the care of someone who knows he's being watched."

"Is he hiding from something? Do people write books if they're hiding from something?"

"Only if they want to be caught."

Alterman doesn't respond.

"So what's in my blind spot? Since you know me so well."

"I don't, Alex," she says. "I'm still learning you."

"But you have your suspicions."

"Don't worry about my loyalty, Alex. I still believe in this job. I just wonder about how it should be used. The power one has in rendering a judgment."

He nods, even though she can't see him. "You know, I think about it sometimes. What would have happened if we'd lived any other time in history? If we'd audited the Catholic Church, would they have needed Martin Luther?"

"Have you ever wondered if all these audits do is interfere in the divine plan?"

Alterman ceases talking for a second. "Think on this. If you'd been there for the crucifixion, it would have looked to you like a disaster. Soldiers mocking Him. The blood. The beatings. The tears. The taunts. It would all have been horrific, the most terrible thing you'd ever seen, the most terrible thing anybody had ever seen. And this is the culminating moment of human history! This is the reason for the Christ's coming! In all that darkness, God is as active as He has ever been before or since! So even when everything is lost, He is still there."

"So maybe what we're doing is wrong?"

"How?"

"Maybe we're telling them to correct something that doesn't need it?"

"They don't *have* to listen to us."

7

Templeton decides to come into the church without disguising his appearance. Ordinarily, Alterman would handle this, but Alex isn't here, and there's no sign of when he might be back. Templeton realizes his ability to conduct any part of the audit will be compromised once he introduces himself, but the need to make contact with Everhart is too important. He believes Alterman would see it his way, but you never can be sure with Alex. Sometimes the most common sense things are guaranteed to send him into a frenzy.

Templeton knows that Everhart is at the church. His car is out front, and the keystroke monitor shows that he's hard at work in his office. From the looks of things, he's been typing up sermon notes. Templeton feels the familiar tug of his preaching itch when he considers this, but he tries not to indulge that anymore. Instead, he is concerned about what he will say to Everhart. The news that Alterman is out of town might concern him. On the other hand, he might feel liberated. Alterman's reputation as Lord High Executioner is secure and well-publicized.

Everhart's office is not the church's main office. That is where one can find the ministerial staff. Everhart's office is "the study," hidden down several hallways among classrooms. Templeton walks indirectly to it, mainly because he wants to be nowhere near the choir room.

He has already heard stories about Everhart's new administrative assistant, Keysha. She evidently keeps close tabs on her boss and is very loyal to him. The idea seems to be that she is there to make sure nothing disturbs Everhart as he researches and writes his sermons. This can be a danger sometimes with new employees, Templeton thinks, though you'd be hard pressed to find a pastor who will fire a secretary zealously guarding his time.

She has already acquired a nickname around the church, Ingersoll says: The Great Wall of Keysha.

When Templeton enters the outer office, he forms a few opinions. The study is ostentatiously small – small in such a way as to call undue attention to itself. He knows the office beyond, where Everhart is supposedly toiling away, can't be much bigger than this one. He barely has enough room to open the door before he is standing in front of Keysha's desk. She immediately rises when he enters the room.

"Good afternoon. Can I help you today, sir?" Her voice is very precise, and she meets him in the eye immediately. If she were a peacock, Templeton thinks, her head would have a halo of bright feathers.

"Hello," Templeton says. "Is Brother Tommy in?"

"Yes, Dr. Everhart is here, but he's busy at the moment. Do you have an appointment?"

"No," Templeton says. "I was just wondering if I could have a few moments of his time."

"Have you checked with the ministerial staff? They're just as you come in the front."

"No, this isn't a pastoral problem. I know about the other office."

"And you're a member here?"

"No, I'm not," Templeton says. Barely the second word is out before she interrupts.

"If this is an inquiry about membership, they can help you at the other office."

"No, I'm not interested in joining. This is…"

"Like I said, Dr. Everhart is very busy today. He's preparing for Sunday."

"That's fine. Is there some way that I can see him?"

"If you could tell me what this is regarding?" She seems inordinately impatient, and he can see this might be an opportunity.

"Actually, I can't," Templeton says. "I can only tell you that it's very important."

"Dr. Everhart deals with very important things all the time. His time is very precious."

"So is mine," Templeton says. The Alterman he carries in his head reminds him that rude church staff members are yet another reason listed on surveys of why people discontinue regular attendance. In this case, he can also detect a snippy tone creeping into Keysha's voice. *Let's see how she does if I give it back to her,* he thinks. *Will she rise to the occasion?*

"Are you saying it's a personal issue? Do you know Dr. Everhart?"

"No, I don't know him," Templeton says. "But I think he'll want to know what I have to tell him."

She looks down at the desk, and her hands impatiently gravitate to her hips. "Maybe you could write it down for me?"

"No," Templeton says. "It's a private message for him."

"I wouldn't look at the message, if that makes you feel better."

"I should hope not," Templeton says, "but it's something I'd rather tell him in person."

"Really, I…"

"And I'd rather speak to him than someone who isn't even a minister," Templeton adds. He knows Alterman has never believed he can be appropriately nasty if required. But Templeton's worked in enough churches to know how the grammar of rude can be spoken there quite fluently.

Keysha's face looks as though he has just struck her. Templeton almost immediately regrets this. He realizes his bloodlust, in part, is inspired by the sudden opportunity. If he goads her into responding, this will finally be something they can report in the audit. But he doesn't want to go too far and entrap someone. That is one of Alterman's inviolable rules. Never push a staff member or volunteer to behave in any way which will pose a threat to her reputation or witness.

195

"All you would need," Alterman once told them, "is to hire a beautiful woman to see how faithful the pastor is, and you could easily shut down entire denominations. And that's just Protestant churches."

In a second, Keysha has gotten hold of herself. Her mouth flashes an insincere smile. "We're all ministers of one stripe or another, sir," she says.

She gets a point for that one, Templeton thinks.

"Yes," Templeton says. "But at this moment, I want to see Brother Everhart. It's imperative that I see him."

"Well you can't," Keysha says, and her smile doesn't change. "This is when Dr. Everhart prepares his sermon. And it's my responsibility to make certain that he isn't interrupted, especially by someone who doesn't seem to be a member and can't give a satisfactory answer as to why it's so important that he be allowed in."

"Do you believe in the Second Coming, ma'am?"

"Yes I do," she replies. "Are you about to tell me you're Elijah, or are you aiming higher?"

Oh yeah, thinks Templeton. She's going in the audit report.

"I can assure you I'm not the Antichrist."

"Neither am I. Sir, you may not be wasting Dr. Everhart's time, but you're wasting mine. Now if we don't come to some kind of resolution, I'm going to have to ask you to leave."

"Well I'm prepared to stand here until the Lord comes back, ma'am, and that's all there is to it. Once Brother Everhart finds out that you prevented me from speaking to him, he's going to rethink your position here. And then you won't be able to get another church job until the Lord comes back and forgives you!" Actually, Templeton couldn't take total credit for that speech. Templeton once heard a deacon use a variation of this on him.

Such is the Church, the institution that Jesus Himself said would stand against the gates of Hell.

"Whom shall I say is here to see him?" Keysha says, her lips tight, and her eyes shut a second too long.

"Tell him I represent Mr. Alterman," he says, and he looks at his watch.

By the time he glances up, Keysha already has her back to him and is opening the door. He doesn't hear any of the words, but he sees something inside her die when she has to turn to him and motion him inside.

Six seconds, he thinks, looking back at the watch. He suspects he could use Alterman's name to get an audience at the Vatican.

8

It is the 102nd floor of the Empire State Building, the observation deck. Alterman does not know why he is drawn to this place, infested with tourists as it is. He has paid an obscene amount of money for the view and waited too long in line. For all the years he lived in New York, he has never been here before. He always steered visitors in other directions, or managed to never make the journey himself.

The city is bathed in fog and dreary rain, and it looks like his soul feels. There is a stench about New York. He feels he shouldn't have come back here. There has always been an itch inside him to return for good, but he doesn't dare do it. He is reminded of the words, probably on one of Ingersoll's T-shirts: *No man, having put his hand to the plow, and looking back, is fit for the Kingdom of God.*

He hears several languages being spoken at once. A confusion of tongues is precisely how he feels. He is bewitched by the city and horrified that he once called it home. He longs for it and is repelled by it. Alterman feels that nothing has changed in him since he left, and that he is scarcely the same man who lived here.

It somehow seems appropriate to take the city in with one glance. He sees a boat cutting a path down the Hudson. He sees the cars beneath on the streets, as though he is seated at the right hand of God, and wonders about the people inside them. He sees a storm in New Jersey, comprehending that the entire weather system is contained in his vision. It makes him feel as though he has control over it, and no control over anything else.

He hears a few seconds of a woman speaking French. He wonders what might happen if he went down to JFK, boarded a plane for France, and never came back. Yes, it was a mistake for him to come here. Across the expanse of skyscrapers, he can make out Freedom Tower, newly finished. It took Alterman leaving New York for the city to finally get around to finishing it. The scar in the earth left by the terrorists of 2001 has healed, filled in by steel and concrete. Maybe.

"I didn't expect to see you here," a voice says, and Alterman turns around to see nothing. The voice is deep and British and familiar somehow.

"Down here," it says, and he looks in its direction. It is Obadiah Falkenburg, his nursery room spy. It takes a moment for Alterman to process it all. Obadiah is wearing a tailored outfit, so he doesn't look like a toddler who has wandered away from his parents amid the tourists. Even then, there is someone standing nearby – a woman with her arms out and an expectant look on her face.

"Is he yours?" she asks, looking at Alterman.

Obadiah wheels and rolls his eyes. "I've told you already ma'am, I'm a 32-year-old man."

She nods. She knew this, but still. "I'm sorry, I just…"

"It's all right," Alterman says. "I'm with him." This seems to satisfy her, and she leaves. "Sorry about that."

"I'm used to it," Obadiah says. "She just can't believe what she sees."

"Good for me," Alterman says.

"I know you're worried that someone will see me and you won't be able to use me for…"

"Stop," Alterman says. "I'm actually glad to see you."

"I've never been to New York," he says.

Alterman bends closer to hear. Though Obadiah has a powerful voice, he is still speaking from so far down that the other voices tend to drown him out. All Alterman can make out is a dull rumble. Still, in hunching down, he doesn't want to appear condescending. "Did you enjoy your time in Florida?"

"I most certainly did. It was quite good. I got some swimming in until someone thought I was drowning in the hotel pool." Alterman made very elaborate arrangements. He booked Obadiah and his family in a hotel hundreds of miles from Sweet Lightning. Then the tiny man pauses. "What's wrong?" Obadiah asks. "What are you doing here?"

Alterman looks away, out over the buildings. "I came for a funeral."

"I'm sorry. Here?"

"Here in New York. An old friend. An old friend's son. He was my friend. Too young."

"What happened, if I may be so bold?"

Alterman hesitates. "He killed himself. It's an awful business. His father couldn't be at the funeral, so I came."

"That is awful. I can tell you're shaken."

Alterman looks around, annoyed at the number of people. "Can we go somewhere? Somewhere else?"

"Of course!" Obadiah says. And the tiny man, whose every step seems a wonder, directs this man nearly four times taller than himself to the elevator.

There is an operator inside. He is a black man weighing about 350 pounds easily, the kind who probably has another job as a night club bouncer. He is wearing a light jacket and has a squawking radio on his belt. The doors close, and Alterman covers his face with his hand. "Oh, Nick," he says. He is not weeping, but Obadiah gets the feeling Alterman wishes he could cry.

"Nick?"

"Nick was his name. He killed himself because of something his father did. Because of several things his father did. Nick used to call me, at night, just to talk. His father stole money from hundreds of people. Millions of dollars. Billions."

"Fixx?" Obadiah asks.

Alterman nods, without thinking.

The elevator operator suddenly spits on the floor. "I lost my shirt because of him." The man calls Fixx something obscene. "Serves him right. He should kill himself."

Neither Alterman or Obadiah says anything until the doors open again. The two get off, even though they're not on the right floor. The operator says nothing, and the doors close.

"He's not the only one who lost something," Alterman says.

"I'm sorry. I only know what I've read about it."

"I don't blame him for being that way." Alterman takes out a handkerchief from his pocket and cleans the spit off his shoe. This allows him to look Obadiah in the eye. "Nick felt that way too. That's what's so bad. He used to say, 'I should have known, but I didn't. I knew nothing, and nobody will believe me.' I think that might be why he killed himself. Because maybe he thought they'd think he was...I don't know."

"What else did he say?"

"He kept talking about how his father lied to him every day of his life. How his father taught him ethics and fair play and how to conduct himself in business. And how he was lying the whole time, because even he didn't believe it. I know how he felt. I'm the same way. He was my boss."

"Fixx?"

Alterman glances away, and remembers that Obadiah knows very little about him. "Yes. That's what he said. 'He stole from me first. He took everything.' He would wonder if he could ever trust anyone again. His wife. His kids. Me. He didn't think there was anyone out there who wouldn't let him down. He couldn't even retreat into his memories. He had nothing to look forward to. You have to understand – Nick was the kind of guy who gloried in being his father's son. Before all that happened. He didn't mind living in that shadow. And in the end, that's what he's going to always be known for."

Alterman hasn't gotten up. He just sits down on the floor. It is cold stone and he sits awkwardly, letting his legs spill out in front of him.

"I asked him to come work for me. He would have been good at it too. He could have taught me so much. Could have learned so much. About going on. About allowing yourself to be forgiven, even when you maybe don't have anything to be sorry for. We all feel sorry. He said no. You know why?"

"Why?"

"He said he wanted to be close to his family."

Obadiah leans down and touches Alterman's leg. Even in this moment, Alterman realizes the tiny man is scared of approaching him. The way they all are.

"He hanged himself with his family in the house."

"How is his family?"

"I couldn't see Nick's wife. She didn't want to see me. I think I remind her of his father. But I saw his mother. She's gone on with her life. She changed her name. She had to."

Alterman leans his head back against the wall, and before Obadiah can say anything, he bangs it up against the wall – WHACK! WHACK! WHACK! – in a series of sudden, ill-considered, angry movements.

"Alex," Obadiah says.

"I should never have come back here," he says. "She wouldn't see me."

"It's like you said, Alex. You remind her of Fixx. She probably blames him for losing her husband."

"No," Alterman says. "Felicia. My wife."

"Your wife?"

"My ex-wife. She divorced me. I got the papers a week after they arrested Fixx. She's remarried."

"You didn't know she remarried?"

"I knew. But I never had to see it. It didn't really sink in until I tried to see her. I don't know what I thought. I suppose I thought that place in my brain where it's still 2008 was some place I could go if I wanted. All I had to do was step back into my life as it had been. Like she'd be there waiting on me. But that's all gone. She's gone to me."

"But you don't really want to come back to this, do you?" Obadiah gestures at the hall around them, as though it is indicative of all the world outside. Those skyscrapers in the fog, all those people frantic for the next subway stop, the millions outside teeming on the streets below them.

"No," Alterman says. "But it hurts to know I'm not a part of it anymore. I don't know why, but it does."

"Does it make you feel small?" Obadiah smiles at his own question. Alterman doesn't smile though. Alterman never smiles.

"You're saying I shouldn't feel that way. And you're right."

"No. You *are* small. So am I. As long as you remember that, then you'll know Who should have your attention."

"Some of us don't need as much reminding, I guess."

"Are you daft?" Obadiah says. "Didn't you see that woman up there wanting to take care of me? Don't you know how hard it is sometimes not to feel like a god? Alex, I don't age. People still think I'm a child, year after year. This is what eternity is. Inspiring love, being the center of attention. It's marvelous."

Alterman gives a short chuckle worthy of his counselor. And then he comes to himself, blinks rapidly and looks around, as though snapping out of a daydream. "I'm sorry. The old man, the sinful man in me, is dead. I just wish I didn't mourn him so."

9

In the entire history of his association with Alex Alterman, Whitlow Mountain has never "gone Josiah," as the group calls it – donning a disguise and entering a house of worship for an audit. There is something desperately silly and unseemly about the whole thing to him. "I'm too old to do something like that," he tells Alterman before each audit, which they both silently agree upon as the official story.

But the truth is that even Whit has his own disguise, the simplest and most effective one among them all. And they have arrived at the moment in any audit when his act becomes indispensable.

Whit enters Sweet Lightning through the front door. He is wearing the same short-sleeved flannel shirt he usually wears each day, a pair of dark corduroy pants that he insists on ironing before wearing, and the shoes he shined before leaving their temporary living quarters at the resort. He is wearing his windbreaker and he adjusts his bifocals as he enters the building. The air conditioning sometimes puts the lenses into a fog.

Whit will be …the old guy. Because of his age, the young people in church may suspect him of being judgmental, or friendly. The middle-aged members may expect him to be authoritative, or lost. The senior members will see him as a peer, or a potential adversary. But none of them will question his being there.

The only allowance Whit makes on these occasions is to mumble to himself, which may give someone watching him the impression that he's senile. He only employs this when he anticipates the pitter-patter of church security or the police. All of these make him virtually invulnerable, which will be key today:

Whit has resolved that he will find out what's happening in the secret room.

The other reason, unspoken, as to why Whit doesn't dress up like the rest of them is that he disdains the anxiety of undercover work. He can understand the allure of playacting, but one of the reasons he went into the classroom instead of climbing into the pulpit was his nerves couldn't handle the emotional demands of preaching after Gilda's death. He could if he had to, but he was sure there were better, abler people out there to heed the call than himself. They also serve who stand and teach.

His usual old guy act involves the occasionally heavy-footed shuffle, and a slower gait than usual. Today, it is no act. Whit awakened to find his feet still asleep. It took a few anxious moments, his heart mocking him unsteadily, before he willed them to start moving. Even the relief he felt when he finally rose was not enough to calm his stomach. The signs are becoming more insistent.

Whit's first stop is Room 92, on the first floor, where the senior adult Bible study is just breaking up. He's already been to one session and enjoyed it, but the first part of his act will be to arrive just at its close. *What, you mean we don't start at 4 o'clock? Oh, I must have gotten confused…* That way, if he is caught later, he can always have his confusion to fall back on, and a roomful of witnesses.

And sure enough, as he comes within sight of the room, he sees through the open door a cohort of about 20 graying men and woman nodding in prayer, amongst other reasons for having their heads down. Their leader, Mrs. Rosemary Anderson, is saying the prayer, but her eyes are open. She sees Whit approach and he can make out her beguiling smile.

Mrs. Anderson is a relatively new member at Sweet Lightning, but she apparently volunteered to lead this Bible study and quickly distinguished herself by asking each of the members their thoughts on the church. He gets the impression that this is a very outgoing, very talkative woman who is gathering information. He also believes that this woman's gray hairs are not real and that she seems artificially made up, which can only mean one thing – that she is the mysterious operative with the unpronounceable name that Alterman has inserted into the church. Whit can usually sniff out these things. He has deflated Alterman an untold amount of times by seeing through whatever disguise he uses on any occasion.

"I see you're right on time, Whit," Rosemary says. "That is, if we were meeting in Denver."

Whit puts on a confused squint, then grimaces, because that would be expected of him. "You mean y'all are just finishing?"

There is a murmur of gentle laughter in the room as the members rise from their seats. "You didn't miss anything," says one man, perched in a wheelchair wearing thick glasses. Whit can't tell if his tone is serious, and a jibe at Rosemary, or playfully sarcastic.

"Thank you, Georgie," Rosemary says, which clears up the mystery. Whit knows enough about this character that he hates being called Georgie, but he apparently will put up with Rosemary's doing it. "It's a shame you missed it, Whit. We had a wonderful time."

"What was the Scripture reference?"

There is another wave of giggles.

"'Behold, I come quickly,'" Rosemary says.

"Oh, well. I'm sorry. I guess I got frazzled about when we met."

"No worries. It's only been a few weeks anyway," she says, and Whit catches her smile. Yes, there's something there that seems familiar in her face, though there shouldn't be. He wonders if Alterman had introduced him to this woman before, only he can't recall it for the cobwebs. "We're all getting used to each other. Everything all right with you?"

"Yes, except that I'm obviously losing my mind."

"My wife tells me the same thing, that I should go see the doctor," says Georgie, who has been listening in on the conversation. He may be the only person in this room with good hearing left. "But when

I ask her which doctor I should go to, she can't remember his name, so I figure I'm still in good enough shape."

"Come back next week, Whit," Rosemary says. "I'm sure we have a lot of things to talk about together."

Whit nods and meets her eye. *Yeah, there's something going on there.* Of course, he thinks, I could be wrong. Maybe she isn't the McParland. If that's the case, maybe she's just interested in me. He'd only recently realized such a thing was possible. He had so completely closed off his mind to the possibility of contact with another woman after Gilda's death that he hadn't considered there being any interest on the other side.

Whit nods and heads in the direction of the men's room, because that might also be expected of him. He notes where it is, since he may need to use it later for other reasons. And he silently scoffs as he heads in the direction of the secret room because of the simplicity of his plan. All these young wackos and Alterman with his spy schemes, he thinks, when getting a bunch of people out of a room is the easiest thing in the world.

Whit remembers that the mystery zone is near the choir room, which is on his right side. On his left side as he stands in the hall is a long wall with no doorways. It stands out because of a long bulletin board with announcements of Bible studies, classes, trips and other points of interest.

If everyone in that secret room was suddenly forced out, they would have to come out of a doorway at the end of the hall, which leads to the stairwell to the other floors. There is a doorway in that stairwell, probably to the room, Whit observes. Once all the people are out, Whit theorizes, he will be able to enter and see for himself what is inside. The only complication will be figuring out if the room has totally emptied when he tries to enter it. He figures probably two dozen people might be inside, based on what he'd heard from Templeton's unsuccessful mission.

With a glance around in every direction, and satisfied that no one can see him, Whit walks over to the door nearest the choir room. He gives the area a last onceover to see if there are potentially any cameras, though he already knows there aren't. He then says the

Lord's Prayer under his breath, because he can't think of any other way to ask for divine help in this, and then he reaches over and pulls the fire alarm.

Almost immediately things go wrong. Whit has calculated that with the Bible study group breaking up, the only people in the church at this hour are staffers and the class, all of whom are already out the door by now. He will have a few minutes to duck into the men's room, where he will remain until any firemen show up. If they sweep the building and find him, they won't suspect an old man unsure on his feet who lingered too long in a bathroom.

But he hadn't counted on the tamper dye, which sprays out when he lifts the alarm lever. Whit doesn't realize at first what has happened. The sound of the alarm is much louder than he anticipated, and the light above his head begins flashing. But his right hand, which pulled the alarm, is now blue. Not the blue of someone losing blood pressure but an obnoxious, guilty blue.

Oh, he's going to have to explain *this*.

Whit panics, and he suddenly can't remember the direction of the men's room on this floor. He thinks of ducking into the choir room, but he remembers that someone might be in there still repairing after Templeton's surprise visit. He puts his blue hand into his jacket and looks down to make sure there is nothing guilty-looking on his coat sleeve.

His white coat sleeve.

Naturally, there is.

Whitlow Mountain probably hasn't moved so fast in a decade, not since heart surgery and Gilda's homegoing. He quickly starts down the hall, as fast as his betraying feet will allow, walking at a trot and looking around for any sign of eavesdropping eyes. He darts around a corner and sees empty Sunday School classrooms, but he will easily be discovered if he ducks into one of them, he thinks. His anxiety overtakes him though, and he bolts into one. He then shuts the door – too loudly – and stumbles over a table and falls. A coffee pot pays for his temporary blindness, shattering against the floor. If he gets out of this without going to jail or the hospital, he will remind Alex to reimburse the church for this expense.

It's moments like this when he wonders why he ever left the seminary. He begins reaching carefully for something to brace himself on as he rises, trying not to plant his hand in the middle of broken glass from the coffee pot. And again, his heart is pounding, as it was on the bus, as it was this morning. And he can hear Gilda's voice, accusing him in the darkness, for finding himself in such a ridiculous situation.

But it isn't Gilda's voice. It's the memory of her that's saying so, and that is why he chooses not to listen. It isn't really her, because she wanted him to stay in the pulpit. Probably the last woman born in America who was disappointed that her husband left the ministry to teach. There were things about Gilda that were even more radical than Alex Alterman. Something went out of the world, she used to say, when churches stopped disciplining their members. And she wasn't talking about for adultery or gossip. She was talking about profanity and going to theaters. That was why he still felt guilty turning on a television. They distracted people with lies.

No, Gilda would never get onto him for seeing after churches.

But she would if he managed to get caught like an old fool.

Then Whit's heart manages to right itself when he realizes there is no fire department in the world that can make it to a call in less than two minutes, which is probably how much time has passed since the alarm sounded.

Whit's back rebels as he gets up, and he glances outside into the hall. By now, he's managed to remember that the men's room is only around the corner, and he can get there easily once he opens the door. With his luck, the door will be locked or jammed, and he realizes he'll be relieved if this is the case, since it means he won't be acting when he claims to be a confused old man.

The door, surprisingly, opens, so Whit looks in both directions before walking out. The alarm is still bleating a steady claxon that he can feel beneath his dentures. Then, seized by a sudden suspicion, Whit turns on the light in the classroom and wheels around to see a vivid, accusatory blue handprint on the floor, surrounded by the remains of the coffee pot. In a second, he feels as guilty as Jack the Ripper.

Yes, he'll have to mention this to Alex.

Later.

Whit dashes out and continues his awkward walking gallop down the hall, around and into the men's room. Even in the act of motion, he checks twice to make sure his blue hand is safely concealed in his jacket pocket, and the blue on the sleeve is not noticeable. He assures himself it isn't, even though it most certainly is. It's about this time that Whit also realizes that, in his terror, he did not stick around to see if anyone came out of the stairwell door from the secret room, and any hope he had of getting in is now gone forever.

Whit is pushing the men's room door open with his shoulder when he feels it thud against something that sounds like a head. He has brained someone trying to leave the men's room, and he can hear the man's moan as he walks in. The man is holding his head with a yellow rubber glove, and Whit understands that, until the fire alarm sounded, this man was cleaning the toilets. There is still a scrub brush in his hand and he is just coming out to peek at what's wrong.

The yellow hand retreats, and Whit sees the pain-stricken face of the Rev. Thomas Everhart.

10

"Oh my," Whit says. "I beg your pardon. Are you all right?"

Everhart places his gloved hand up to his forehead again, then brings the fingers down. *He's looking for blood*, Whit thinks to himself.

"I'm sorry," Everhart says, even though there is no reason for him to apologize. He then looks up, annoyed at the sound. "Is that the fire alarm?"

"Yes, I think it is," Whit says.

"Well, that's awfully nice of you to duck in here and check to make sure no one was inside." It takes Whit a moment to realize Everhart is talking to him.

Whit feels obliged to shake the pastor's hand, until he remembers that his right hand is coated in blue dye. He also remembers Everhart is wearing gloves.

"What were you doing in here?" Whit asks. He positions himself on the pastor's right, and puts his left hand on the man's shoulder, as if to comfort him. It's awkward, but it keeps him from having to use that right hand.

"Cleaning the toilets," Everhart says. "I do it once a month." He shakes his head again, as if to snap any remaining fuzziness out of his skull.

"Really?"

"It's just something I do. Gives the janitors a break. Humility, or something like that. Funny about the alarm, you don't smell any smoke, do...?"

Everhart glances up, and it looks as though he's about to say something. Then his expression changes, and in a second, Whit can see surprise, confusion, and dawning realization. Whit is suddenly conscious of his facial expression, wondering if Everhart suspects something. How could he? He was in here cleaning toilets. Yet Whit feels he is giving away everything from his conscience stricken face.

Remember, if he asks you, you tell him the truth. You can't lie.

Finally, Everhart says something. "Aren't you Dr. Whitlow Mountain?"

"Yes, I am," Whit replies, astonished. "How do you know me?"

"Your book. I remember reading it in the seminary. 'The Phenomenology of Psalm 90: A New Hermeneutic.' You came and spoke on it at my school."

Now Whit *really* has to keep himself from shaking the man's hand. "That old thing? There isn't much new about it."

"No, no. It was quite a work. I'm actually working on my own book about that psalm."

"The title was the publisher's notion..."

"What?" Everhart winces, and looks annoyed at the alarm. "I really wish that thing would shut up. It's very hard to talk to somebody with it going on."

"Listen, we'd best get out of here just in case something is really happening," Whit says, ever the solicitous theologian, who just happens to drop in during a fire emergency.

Everhart tears off the gloves and throws them down. "Those ought to be OK there until we get this sorted out." He then looks up, smiles, and sticks out his hand.

"Arthritis," Whit says, nodding his head in apology, still concealing his hand. *This isn't a lie*, he tells himself, *since it has been flaring up lately. Probably that storm out in the Gulf.* That doesn't explain everything else that's going wrong with him, but he doesn't want to think about that.

In the evening it is cut down, and withereth. We spend our years as a tale that is told.

Within his mind's eye, Whit sees a glimpse of Gilda, after the ALS had taken everything from her, but had not yet taken her. He could still see her within her eyes. She knew what was happening.

But she was happy somehow. *How was that possible?* he still wonders.

Everhart's phone rings. He takes it out of his pocket and places it to his ear, putting a finger in his other ear against the cacophony. "What? Yes, I know. I'm near the Choir Room. I'm headed out." He pauses. "No, I don't see anything up here. Do you?" Another pause. "Well, when the fire department gets here, find me. I'm on my way out the door." Then he hangs up.

He gently takes Whit's elbow and they move toward the stairwell at the end of the hall. Not the one closest to the secret room entrance.

"Let me ask you something," Everhart says, as they move down the hall. The alarm sound has gotten less oppressive.

Whit stiffens. *He's going to ask me what I'm doing in his church.*

"You wrote that book when you were in your twenties. Isn't that right?"

"Well… maybe late twenties. Twenty-nine at the most. I think I wrote it while my wife was pregnant with our first child." He is trying not to shout out his answer, even though he has to. They are making their way down the stairs and he is trying not to trip. It occurs to him he is trying to conceal two things at the same time. Whit resolves to himself that if he gets out of this, he will never again do anything so reckless as this. Leave the undercover work to Alterman and the youngsters.

But that's assuming I ever have a chance to do anything like this, before I lose it all.

Will I look happy then? And who will look into my eyes?

"What made you want to write it?" Everhart asks, just as he opens the door to the stairwell. In there, the alarm sound is ten times worse. It is impossible for them to continue the conversation. Whit gives the stairwell a good look. There is no one else in it. Everyone who might have already been in the church has emptied out. *Well, that's one thing we can use in the report,* he thinks. *It's a safe church.*

The two of them move steadily down the stairs and out to an exit door, where the fire trucks are pulling up. Once the door shuts behind Everhart, the sound of the alarm is muffled and no longer so oppressive.

"I realize I've put you on the spot," Everhart says. "You probably wrote that book a long time ago. It's just..."

"What?" Whit replies, obviously relieved.

"Would you take any of it back? Is there something you've learned in your life that makes you look at what you wrote differently?"

Another line from the Psalm comes back to Whit – *our secret sins in the light of your presence.*

"Here, you go off and talk to the fire department, and that'll give me some time to think of an answer," he says.

Everhart nods, smiles, and looks genuinely pleased. Then he turns on his heel and takes out his phone. Presumably he is dialing his administrative assistant who is already assessing the situation.

Whit's ego chides him, but he isn't going to stick around to give his insights. By the time the fire department gets a look at things, it won't take long for them to determine the alarm was pulled on the same hall where the pastor was cleaning toilets. Maybe by that time, Everhart will associate the alarm with the sudden appearance of Whitlow Mountain, who will by no means be around for questioning.

And as he walks away, gripping his wretched blue hand to his side, Whit wonders... *is there anything I've learned that would change that book?*

11

It is October 2008, and it is raining. Alterman is riding in the back of a limousine to a hastily called meeting, and he is handing his boss a thick sheaf of papers and taking the man's dainty cellphone. Outside the window a cop directing traffic motions the limo into a parking garage beneath the ground floor of the Fed building. The wind is ripping apart someone's umbrella with the indifference of an earthquake.

These kinds of meetings are never good news, especially with less than an hour's notice. It is Friday.

Good Friday? Alterman thinks, bringing a smile to his face before banishing it.

Crucifixion is on their minds, but the Biblical reference is more final from the boss' lips. "It's the end of the world," the boss, Richard Fixx, says, but his voice is matter of fact, as though the world has ended every day this week and this is nothing new. He is right though. The company was at $75 a share a year ago. Three pennies will now buy that same share. Probably not the best time in history to work for a firm called Paneck Brothers.

A week before, Alterman had been in the stands at Yankee Stadium. They are tearing down the House That Ruth Built, but they are building a larger, more modern copy of the ballyard across the street. It hadn't felt final. This…this feels final.

"Armageddon," the boss says.

"There is life after Armageddon," Alterman chimes in.

"*Eternal* life," the boss says. "That's hardly a comfort."

Fixx is not a religious man, or at least, he wasn't until the moment of this meeting. Once inside, the Boss will meet his opposite numbers at the investment banks. Under normal circumstances, the only time these men would usually occupy the same room is at a Christmas party, with their invitations carefully staggered to avoid them being in the same room at the same moment. They are not alien to one another. They have, in fact, been on the phone with each other, independent of the government, for several weeks now, chatting as nervously as teenage girls over football players. But the Fed Secretary, like their anxious mother, has not liked the conversations going on without him. Those late night talks, those whispers about the plummeting value of all of their empires, don't change the fact that each deeply hates the other and would like to condemn all their fellows to financial perdition.

But there is a feeling in the car that something else, much more ominous than their own destruction, is about to take place. Alterman has seen the future, and believes he is in for a long night of cold pizza, the stale scent of flop sweat and endless video conferences.

"This is a crash," the Boss says. "A slow motion crash." He is referring to the stock market's steady needle which is no longer in decline but in free fall. "What are the odds, Alex? Cyclical recession or secular recession?"

Cyclical means the economy will go into a kind of hibernation for a couple of years before snapping back out. A secular recession means ... Armageddon. *It's funny they call this a secular recession*, he thinks, *because this feels very Biblical. Old Testament.*

They are out of the car and quickly into an elevator, none of them talking. Because Alterman holds the Boss' cellphone, he realizes this is some kind of baton. If this is a battlefield and the Boss falls, the cellphone will be transformed into the standard which must be carried forward. A more likely explanation is that if the Boss blows his brains out, Alterman will have the honor of telephoning his wife with the news.

There is a reason for their collective silence. Beyond the decomposition of the company's share price, that morning Paneck Brothers learned that it is now unable to borrow the necessary money to carry out the day's business. These credit swaps, which are standard procedure for every investment bank, have dried up. The firm is the alcoholic at the bar who had been told to pay up before another drink will be served. *We can't forgive this much debt*, the banks are saying. *No one is that forgiving.*

There is no credit. There is no trust.

Banks are withholding the lifeblood, Alterman thinks, and for some reason he seizes on the fact that holding facilities for plasma are also called banks.

And we are bleeding. And we are going to a meeting whether others intend to bleed us.

Alterman noticed this a year before. The computer models first started spitting out the facts one afternoon, and the reaction was a species of lazy skepticism. The computers, with their stubbornly literal interpretations of debt and risk and outcome, were insistent that Paneck Brothers was headed in a perilous direction. The company was loaded with debt that was becoming toxic and would eventually become lethal, if nothing was done.

On the company's ledgers were acres of real estate, home mortgages, loans and acquisitions bundled into packages and sold and resold, bought and rebought until the names of the original lenders and original borrowers were immaterial. Hidden in these acres were an untold amount of mortgages that were rapidly approaching foreclosure, which would eventually revert back to the bank. The result would be homes requiring resale, meaning the books weren't worth as much as the company thought. The computers were the unpleasant doctor holding the X-ray, with the patient's unidentified mass clearly visible and growing larger.

Alterman wasn't the only one who noticed, nor the only one who said something. Perhaps if he had been the only one, they would have listened to him. As it was, they ignored it all.

"Think of the Old Man upstairs," was one refrain. The Old Man was the senior partner who had seen everything since the Great

217

Depression. He had retired long ago, supposedly, but still came in because he knew he would die without the lifeline of the office. If the Old Man ever came down, then there would be trouble. He would presumably see the fatal flaw long before anyone else.

The Boss didn't seem worried. "We need more risk," Fixx would repeat endlessly. "More risk, more reward."

The breaking point came a few weeks before this Doomsday meeting, when the markets started tanking. Then the news started to emanate from the top floor. "The Old Man is coming down."

The reaction in the building was relief. When the Old Man finally arrived, they were waiting for him to bring the answer. The grizzled, ancient-faced oracle who remembered the Gold Standard asked for the numbers. He knew which ones he wanted. He seemed annoyed when he was pointed to a computer screen instead of being handed a bundle of tickertape.

It only took about fifteen minutes before he held up his hand. "You called me down here for this?" he said, and his manner was so matter of fact and amused that they all inwardly grinned. He confirmed in an instant why they summoned him. *He has, in fact, seen it all*, they thought, *and knows instantly how to fix this.*

The Old Man waved at the screen. "You guys are finished. You'd better sell now while you can still get something."

"No," the Secretary says.

The heads of the banks turn in his direction. His voice is the Voice of the Almighty, reading from the Book. "This is going to be solved this weekend. By the time the Asian and European markets open."

"Now just a second, you can't..."

"Gentlemen, I can't tell you where to go or what to do, but let me just say this. The government is not going to save this bank. That means it's up to you to come up with a solution, and if there's no solution, it's bankruptcy."

The Secretary doesn't need to remind everyone that Paneck Brothers has been in business for three-fourths of the Republic's lifespan. Paneck Brothers invested in cotton futures before the invention of the gin.

"I realize you are all competitors. But if you succeed in taking down this one bank, then the rest of your books probably won't be worth anything in a little while. The same thing that is happening to it could happen to you."

Alterman feels a silent thrill sweep over him at the Secretary's power and attitude.

"If this hits the world markets Monday morning, you're going to see chaos. A deluge. And there may be no ark for any of you."

Then they are back in the limousine, leaving the meeting.

"Will it work?" Alterman asks.

"It has to," Fixx says, and all of Alterman's earlier bravado – the lies he told himself about the Boss having it all figured out – deserts him.

"Do you want me to call Lowe Bank in Berlin?" Alterman asks. He takes out his phone, looking for the number stored.

"*Do* I want you to?" Fixx asks.

"Boss," Alterman says. "Relax. It's just the end of the world *this* week. They'll be others."

Fixx looks at him, his face totally devoid of humor...and understanding. It's as if he cannot comprehend what Alterman is saying.

"Relax, Richard. You're a billionaire. Even if the company goes under, you've still got your fund on the side. You know, the one you wouldn't let me in on..." This is an old joke of theirs now. It's been months since Fixx turned him down again, and Alterman has made his peace with the fact that the Boss, for whatever reason, won't let him in.

"Am I still a billionaire?" Fixx asks.

By the time the limousine makes it back to the office, Fixx has finally finished telling Alterman how his personal fund is basically a billion dollar Ponzi scheme, and that all of its members, all carefully chosen gold-minted rubes, are all basically destitute. Not even his son knows, Fixx says, almost sounding proud. Alterman realizes that if he calls Lowe Bank to bring about the merger, he will be bailing out his Boss and entangling himself in a criminal fraud worth billions of dollars. Yet if he doesn't call the Germans and offer up the company, Paneck Brothers will fold and hundreds of people will lose their life savings and their jobs.

"Why did you tell me this, Richard?" he asks, just as the car pulls up to the curb.

"So I could get some sleep," he says. "Call them when you get inside. I'm going home." Alterman gets out, the car squeals away, and Alterman wonders if his boss owns a gun.

Alterman still remembers the way it happened.

It is noon. Even though it's sprinkling rain, it's hot. This is the way it feels in summer, the way the sweat breathes through his heavy dress shirt and tie. He has put his coat on to walk outside even though he doesn't need it. It is the image that he feels he needs. There is dignity somehow in this gesture that only he can recognize, and only he would want to. He glides past the shoulders pressing him. Though no one will name it, there is panic in the air. Not the panic that propels investors from high rises, mourning the loss of paper fortunes, if they ever existed. This is the kind of panic that unseats empires, the panic of Visigoths at the city gates, the panic that these great buildings and kingdoms of wealth will not burn but evaporate, because they were all fantasies to begin with.

Alterman walks to the vendor in front of Trinity Church. He has picked this spot for the vantage point that it gives him. The tourists are shuffling by for their pictures of Wall Street. George Washington watches from his pedestal in front of the Old Federal Hall. Alterman hands his money to the vendor with the Middle Eastern accent for a

Polish dog and a sweaty bottle of water. Alterman's hand is soaking wet as he lodges the bottle under his arm to take the change in his dripping fingers.

Alterman smells the Polish dog as he looks over the faces flashing past him. He can spot the tourists, but he can spot the traders and the paper men and he can see the panic. He can see the debt that is stifling them all. They have convinced themselves for a long, long time that they were immune. They knew about the debt. How could they not? It was on their balance sheets, on the ledgers, in the annual stockholder reports. They couldn't run from it. They tried to disguise it and shuffle it and talk around it until the reports were wholly concerned with their debt. Then they ended up celebrating it. They were creative with it. They borrowed with the debt and married it to more debt, repackaged it into still more debt, grafted it into masses of even larger debt with limbs of debt and appendages of debt and faces of debt. Their debt walked like a man and spoke a debt-filled language that could be quoted for a price. Now it is all they talk about, and they are all paying a price and will be, except no one has any more money. The debts are being called and every fee they have run up is now being called in, every loan they still owe wanting everything. The debt had been nothing, but add twenty million nothings together and they equal everything. Those far off, ignored numbers are now rows and rows and rows of red zeroes that have no remorse and no mercy.

They are all in the grip of it, Alterman sees. All except the figure approaching from the midst of them.

He comes through the faces, through the swaying, walking figures, emerging as one might expect him to, in another time. Anonymously. Alterman at first thinks he is dying, and the sight of this man is the indication that his time on earth is over. Curiously, ridiculously, Alterman has a hot dog sticking out of his mouth and is taking a bite as he sees the man coming toward him.

I never saw it happening like this, he thinks to himself. *So it's true! This really is the end of the world!*

He is approaching, and time is drawing slower and slower until everyone moves with the speed of the continental drift. This is the day he will remember the rest of his life. The day Alex Alterman saw Jesus Christ Himself walk down Wall Street.

He is dressed as he has been in every storybook Bible or church window Alterman has seen in his life. His face has the impassivity of an icon. His hair is long and his beard is rough looking but not unruly. He has on a weather-beaten robe. He is carrying something in his worn, tanned, dirty fingers as he approaches. A few paces and Alterman can see that they are dollar bills. Jesus is offering greenbacks to the people around him. He looks them in the eye but they don't notice him. He is saying something in a clear, distinct voice, Alterman feels, yet the words aren't carrying. He holds the dollars out as though those passing need them, but they don't reach out. They don't see him or the money. They continue walking.

He looks like a merchant offering up a forsaken product. He looks like a parent in an amusement park who has lost track of his child. There is a quivering unrest in his heart, teetering on concern and beyond that, panic. Not the panic of the people. No. The panic on his face is that no one is paying attention to Him. Don't they realize what danger they are in?

"That's not a vision," Templeton tells Alterman, when Alterman finally has the nerve to tell the story much later of what he saw. "That's a daydream." His tone is that of an eager listener to a story who feels cheated at its end. This vision probably had more to do with the hot dog, he says.

"But he looked at me!" Alterman protests, as though his partner's skepticism is blasphemy. "It was Him! He had the eyes of burning fire! I felt like everything I'd ever done in my life was a sham! And if it took the rest of my life, I'd try to make up for it even though I knew I couldn't!"

And He does indeed look at Alterman. Alterman walks, at first, in a steady pace toward Jesus. Somehow Jesus is just as far away as when he started, but he keeps running toward him. Jesus is saying something.

Alterman runs and runs, but he traverses the whole of the street and cannot reach Jesus. He looks the ground over to see scattered, crumpled dollar bills, blowing in the wind and dancing among the moving legs. No one bothers to pick them up. He feels as though he should, but he is afraid that when he touches them, he will weep.

"This looks like it could be a secular recession."

For some reason the words stick in Alterman's mind. He knows what the words mean - this will be no garden variety 18-month recalibration of the nation's economy. No, this is something much longer.

In the defaults and foreclosures and failures and utter ruin that await them all, some people will turn to God to bail them out. He thinks of all the churches that will be unable to make their payments on new sanctuaries and family life centers and private schools and homeless shelters, and he realizes they will need something other than ready cash if they aren't strong already. If people can lose faith in the market, what is to keep them from losing faith in Someone much higher?

It was then and there, on the street, that Alterman took out his phone and called the F.B.I.

12

"You came!" Wydgate says.

Wydgate is in a booth in the dining room of a Mexican restaurant. He stands up from the booth and greets Steeplechase with a two-handed shake, as though they are two prime ministers at a summit meeting, observed by a gang of photographers. "Thank you so much!"

Steeplechase nods, uncomfortably, but returns the handshake out of politeness. Wydgate directs him to the seat to settle down. Wydgate notices Steeplechase's smell. He is sweaty and has about a week's worth of beard.

"Excuse me for a moment," Wydgate says, reaching into his pocket for his phone. In a second or so, he pushes a button. Then he sits down.

"Thank you," he says. "I mean it. I had no idea whether you would come or not."

"I felt like I should, on account of what you said. About Mr. Alterman, I mean."

"I meant it. I'm working with Alex Alterman now. It's just that not many people know about it."

"It's quite interesting to think that the two of you are partners."

"Not partners," Wydgate says, trying not to sound miffed at the suggestion. "It's more a marriage of convenience at the moment."

"More of a collaboration, you mean?"

"Exactly," Wydgate says. "It's a big job here at Sweet Lightning. Much larger than anything either of us has ever attempted. So we're trying to find our way clear to getting the job done."

"That's interesting," Steeplechase says. He reaches into his jacket pocket and pulls out a pen. He begins jotting something down on a napkin. Wydgate thinks there's probably a blog post being born here. That is, if Steeplechase is able to get back to the X-Pose website before Wydgate's plan comes to fruition.

"Wouldn't be interested in joining us?" Wydgate asks, with a wink. He can hardly believe the luck of having Steeplechase writing something down in his presence. This little act will make everything so much easier.

Steeplechase looks up at the words. He isn't sure how to react. "I don't think that's allowed," he finally says.

"Allowed?"

"No, I mean, Tara doesn't even know I'm talking to you."

Wydgate tries not to smile. He was counting on this being true. Suddenly, he understands why Alterman likes this part of his job.

"Of course, there's always room for one more on this side of the Jordan," Wydgate says.

"I can't swim," Steeplechase finally says. "Now why did you want to see me?"

"Ingersoll suggested it," Wydgate says. "He says you come from a Christian background?"

"Yes, but I don't see…"

"Tell me about it."

"I'm sorry, I'm…"

"Just humor me, for a second or two."

He sighs. "My parents were Sunday School teachers. But I can't say the whole thing ever really took hold with me."

"Why do you say that?"

"Because it didn't. I can't remember a time in my life when I didn't have doubts about it all."

"You too?"

He nods. "I've heard Christian people say what you're saying. It was different with me. The whole thing was an act. I wasn't the only one. I know I wasn't. There were probably dozens of people at my church who just went through the motions. If you sawed them in half, you couldn't have counted enough rings to make a Christian."

"Let's not talk about other people. Let's talk about you."

"What is this about?"

"Come, come, Mr. Steeplechase. Surely you don't believe a little conversation is going to send you back to Sunday School, do you? Now, do I understand that you thought other people's faith was vain, so you assumed your own was as well?"

"No, that wasn't it at all."

"I didn't think so. That's why I asked about you. You in particular."

"That's what I've been trying to tell you. Like the rest of them, you're not listening to me. You're trying to peg me. You're trying to figure out why I'm not like you anymore. Trying to find out how the devil got me." He waves his hands at the mention of the devil.

"Actually, they don't teach you how to read people's minds in church. I'm not trying to peg you. I'm actually trying to understand you. That's all."

"Actually, if you want to know the truth, I get tired of having this conversation. Religion isn't really all that important to me."

"That's why you go from church to church trying to debunk them? It's a hobby?"

"I mean it. It's not that important to me."

"Well, of course. You're an atheist, aren't you?"

"All right, you really need to cut out this passive-aggressive routine. You're sitting there questioning me, but you're trying to convert me. You may not admit it, but you are."

"I'll go ahead and admit it. I *am* trying to convert you. That's what I'm supposed to do."

"There's something else I believe in," Steeplechase says. "Waiters. Any chance we can get some food around here?"

Wydgate looks at his watch. It should be soon. "Let me ask you one other thing, if you don't mind," he begins. "Does it bother you that I'm trying to convert you?"

"Not really," he says. "You're not the first. I get this from my parents all the time. They think I don't believe anymore because I'm trying to get back at them. And honestly, I'm not. It's true, there were times when I looked at them and thought to myself, 'If that's what a Christian is…'"

"What happened? I mean, what made you think that?"

He smiles, and Wydgate realizes he's about to admit something against his better judgment. "It's just…I got tired of the act of it. All that talk about love. It's all lies. Nobody loves anybody. They just talk about each other behind each other's back. There's nothing different about them than anybody else. They want to act like they're special…"

"Not like you?"

"No, it's not like that."

"Well, obviously, you think you are different than them, don't you?"

"I am," he says. "Not better. Just different."

"But you *are* better, because you don't have all that God nonsense cluttering up your brain, right?"

"Did you deliberately pick this place so we wouldn't be disturbed by a waiter?"

"Listen Nathan," Wydgate says, "you've got a website. You're invested in this. It's part of who you are. You can't afford to believe, because then everything you're doing is a lie."

"I don't want to believe. *You* can't exactly abandon the church, can you?"

"But on the other hand, you aren't a passive critic of Christianity. You really care about this stuff. It's irks you, these Christians with their prayers and sermons and hymns."

"It should. Any kind of lies. Any kind of injustice. People should care about that kind of thing."

"But your problem isn't Christians. It's *God*. You were raised to believe in Him. You say you don't believe in Him. But for some reason, *He* won't let *you* go." Wydgate points at him. "He's still in there. You can't drive Him out. That's why you're unhappy."

"I'm happier with Tara and the rest of the X-Pose crowd. At least we're honest with each other. We stick with each other. We believe in something that's real."

Wydgate looks at his watch. "Are you sure about that?"

Just then, a familiar, expected figure walks up. Thomas Everhart stands at the booth. He has first spotted Wydgate, but then he glances over and sees Steeplechase. He shakes hands with the atheist first and seems to have no idea who he is, other than that his face is familiar. Wydgate nods approvingly.

"What is this?" he asks.

"Just talking a little heresy," Wydgate says. "Why don't you join us?" But he isn't looking at Everhart. He's looking at Steeplechase.

"I just might," Everhart says. "Actually, I was waiting for someone for a good while, and he hasn't shown up yet."

"Who is it?" Steeplechase asks. "Jesus?"

Everhart smiles. "Do you mind if I sit down?"

"I don't, if you..." Wydgate says, gesturing to Steeplechase. He says no, though he rolls his eyes.

Everhart sits down next to Wydgate. Then he does something unexpected. Wydgate pulls a pen from his pocket, slides the napkin over with Steeplechase's notes on it, and begins drawing the grid for a game of Tic-Tac-Toe. Steeplechase at first seems miffed, but Wydgate lets him win.

Within a minute, they are on to another game and another napkin. Steeplechase is anxious for the end of the earlier conversation, and Wydgate looks down to see a text message on his phone. Somehow, everything he needed to happen has occurred. He can scarcely believe it, and it satisfies him immensely. Answered prayers, he thinks.

13

Alterman rises and walks toward the podium. As he passes Nick's coffin, he pauses for a second, surprised. It is covered with an American flag. The reality of it makes him hesitate. He supposes at some point in the past he knew Nick was in the military, but the information must have gotten lost somewhere in his brain. He doesn't know if this is stress or the onset of age. He reaches under the flag with his fingers and lightly touches the coffin. It is an embarrassing, self-conscious gesture that makes no sense to him.

This knowledge, that Nick was a veteran, seems incredible in light of the fact that he is dead. How could he break? Didn't every drill he survived in basic training test his will? Didn't he gain any self-worth from having survived all that? Wasn't he equipped to kill or be killed? Even as he thinks about this, Alterman corrects himself. Nick hadn't served in war time. He hadn't needed to survive a conflict. His father alone had provided enough formidable action. His father was the most destructive thing he ever encountered.

Alterman hurries on to the podium.

From where he stands, Alterman can see Felicia. She is sitting on the left third row, close to the man she came with. She is looking down, perhaps at her rings, when he comes into her line of sight. This is a habit of hers - looking at the rings during unpleasant moments. He saw a lot of her forehead during the last months of their marriage.

She looks up, and they fix their eyes on each other, even as his words come. He doesn't know whether it is the occasion, or the fact that he doesn't seem to be showing any emotion, that makes her weep.

"I knew Nick, and I can say, like you, that it's hard to imagine a world without Nicholas Fixx. I don't want to, really. But the world is better because he was here, even if it was all for just a short time."

Alterman feels a tickle in his throat, but he is loath to clear it. He thinks of Nick, and of Fixx, up in his cell, and wonders what he is doing now. There was something on the news about him having a "private memorial service" that made some people snicker. How private? Just him in his cell? Who else might be invited? Alterman had offered to be there with him, but Fixx wanted Alterman here, as his representative.

"I knew Nick from his childhood. I knew him before *he* knew who he was. Nick lived in a shadow his whole life, and he shouldn't have. He was a decent, fine man. It's a shame that he never saw what others saw. It's a shame that he let things beyond his control determine the course of his life. Well, calling it a *shame* doesn't do it justice, really."

Alterman pauses, and as the flicker of an idea comes into his mind, he begins to chase it with words, even against his better judgment. "We all live in the shadow of a Father," he says. "But worse for us, this Father is perfect. And even though He offers total forgiveness, that offer is still too much for us to comprehend."

He looks out at the faces. The room is much like an audit. Some are getting it, and others are waiting for the words to end.

"We try to hold onto what we have," he says. "But are we holding onto something valuable? Whatever you're standing on, make sure it's unshakeable. Make sure it's true. Or else it will be swept away, and you will go with it. *Hold on*."

And then, at last, Alterman understands who brought him to Sweet Lightning. There is no one else it can be.

But first, there is the matter of the moment.

Well, if they think he's in a cult, he might as well indulge them.

"There is occasionally a sense, in life, that if something happened in the past, it might still be going on somewhere, that if we travel far enough in life perhaps we will stumble down the road that leads us back to places we've lost. I get that feeling sometimes, when I drive past a house where I used to live, and part of me thinks that a certain person is still in there, just as I left them once before. They're in there waiting on me to come through the door, and the years in between will vanish instantly. This feeling is behind the fear that grips us when we suspect that a particular year of hardship will revisit its horrors on us, or the promise we might find ourselves back in a night when love was long and lush. This feeling propels us on, with the hope that we will eventually round a bend in our lives and encounter that face long gone, or that if we keep moving past the remembered dark rooms of our lives, we will inevitably make it back to that moment when we were happiest, when we were most secure, and most loved."

Now they are all crying, and Alterman cannot understand why his voice is not clear. He knows precisely what he wants to say, but the words aren't as easy as they usually are.

"This feeling is an illusion, of course, but potent, even though we are in on the secret. What's gone is no more. But the kernel of it, the memory of it, is part of us that we want to believe is imperishable. And we may hope that the many mansions promised us at the end of time will have rooms crafted beyond comparison to everything that came before, beyond the expectation born of all our faulty memories."

He wonders if Felicia believes still, or did he take that too from her?

Alterman is finished, and he has no real reason to stay here any longer here. He walks to his seat and picks up his coat, and moves to slide discreetly out the side door of the chapel.

But before he does, he passes by the priest. "Top that," he says.

Alterman hears his own voice and wonders if this is a taunt, or an invitation.

14

They are back at the resort. There is a knock at the door. Ingersoll gets up to answer it. He is wearing a T-shirt that reads "Go out into the highways and hedges, and compel them to come in, that my house may be filled." Just before he opens the door, he knows who will be on the other side. He can smell him.

Steeplechase is standing outside.

"Why did you do it?" he demands.

"What?"

"Don't give me 'what,'" he says, barging in. "You know why I'm here. You all know why I'm here! You invited me to that lousy Mexican restaurant and they didn't even bring us chips until I'd been beaten 15 times by a preacher at Tic-Tac-Toe. And like an idiot, I sat there the whole time and even thought I'd pulled a fast one on you when you got the check."

"Brother Tommy got the check."

"Of course! I didn't even see that coming!"

"Didn't see what?" Templeton says.

"Don't play dumb with me! You invited me to that restaurant, a public place, and then you sent those pictures to Tara!"

"Pictures?" Cherie says.

"The pictures on the website!" Only a few hours before, X-Pose's latest post featured the headline "Megachurch Pastor colludes with spy!" Below the headline were photos of what looked like Thomas Everhart, John Patrick Wydgate and Nathan Steeplechase sitting in a restaurant booth, sliding pieces of paper back and forth as though exchanging notes. The photos looked to be taken with a camera phone and had a helpful shadow from a thumb in one, as though surreptitiously snapped. The three of them smiled in several of the pictures, as though they were happily plotting the conversion of scores of atheists between them.

"So what happened?" Ingersoll asks.

"What? You want me to go ahead and tell you? You know perfectly well!" Steeplechase, shaking his head, shouts at them. "By the time I got back, Tara has already thrown my stuff out. Said I was on your payroll. Said I knew too much."

"How are we responsible?" Wydgate asks.

"All you had to do was send a few pictures to my group and they'd get suspicious of me!"

"We didn't *know* that, necessarily," Wydgate says. "Might be better to say it was an experiment."

"Well, it was very cruel," he says. "I'd lived with those people for four years."

"You'd think that would count for s*omething,*" Cherie says.

"Yeah! But Tara says she wouldn't trust me now, no matter what I said. Says she has to rethink the whole strategy."

"Why?"

"Because it's *my* strategy! I came up with it! They loved it before."

"When they knew it wasn't tainted by belief!" Whit says, in mock horror.

"I mean it!" Steeplechase continues, still white hot. "This is unconscionable! Inexcusable!"

"The idea of you associating with believers! Some of it might rub off on you!"

Steeplechase pauses. "Yeah!" he bursts out. "As long as I've been with them, and it only takes one meeting and a few photos and all of a sudden, I'm the Pope!"

"How unforgiving…" Cherie says.

"How can you live with yourselves! This is so underhanded…"

Wydgate approaches him. "Explain to me what's underhanded about it."

"You knew! You knew this would happen!"

"Well, I did suspect that your partner's natural suspicion might kick in, given an opportunity. But I can't take credit for it all."

"I don't know what to do now!" Steeplechase says. "It's not like I can go back. This is a big deal! You have no idea how many people were looking to us! They wanted us to succeed! I was going to succeed too!"

"Nathan…" Wydgate begins. "You mind if I call you Nathan?"

"Don't talk to me!" Steeplechase says. "*You* can talk to me, but not him!" He points to Ingersoll, who steps forward. His finger again accuses Wydgate. "You're like a snake! Over here peddling your poisoned apples!"

Though they all want to, none of them are about to remind him that he's using a Biblical metaphor.

"What do you want to talk about?" Ingersoll asks.

Steeplechase sinks to the floor. He looks burdened by every frustrated dream nurtured in his lifetime. "And I was going to make money. Eli the Dinosaur. The merchandising. I could see a TV show. Stuffed animals. Concert tours." He pauses. "I could have hired somebody to wear the suit."

"Now somebody else will have to deal with the lawyers," Ingersoll says, in a consoling voice.

"That should be *my* lawsuit! They won't even go ahead with it now. It's all dead. I have nothing."

"You ever thought of working for us?" Ingersoll says.

No one makes a sound, but there is a definite tremor in the air. Steeplechase's head, defeated, suddenly rises. "What?"

"You say you've got no other place to go? It's hard for an atheist when nobody believes in him, isn't it?"

"That's all I need. I can't convert back to Christianity."

"Why not?"

"My parents. I'll never hear the end of it."

"Listen," Ingersoll begins. "You asked me how I do this. How I do belief. I couldn't. I needed to meet someone. Then I was convinced."

Wydgate smirks, expecting the answer.

"Who convinced you?" Steeplechase asks.

"The Holy Spirit," he says.

Wydgate realizes he still has a lot to learn about his new coworkers.

No one moves, not even Steeplechase. He looks exhausted, disgusted. They all realize his mind is playing out an endless array of scenarios he has steeled himself against for years. No matter how odious, he wonders if any of them are possible.

"What do you say?" Ingersoll asks, clapping his hands together. His tone is serious, but just quivering on the edge of it.

With a great sigh, Steeplechase asks, "Can I take a shower?"

15

It is very late. Alterman and Templeton are awake at the resort. Alterman has just gotten in from the airport. Laid out on a table in front of him is the paperwork that has accumulated in his absence. There are pages in a handwriting he does not recognize, but he says nothing. He seems satisfied with what he reads.

Templeton speaks, softly, so as not to wake the others in the adjoining rooms. "You OK? Rough flight?"

"No. I'm just fine. Was able to sort out a few things up there. Glad to be back though."

"Bad situation," Templeton says.

"Yeah," is all Alterman will allow. "Funny thing happened to me on the flight."

"What was it?"

"I got into a conversation with a man sitting next to me. We were talking about things, and then all of a sudden, he starts witnessing to me. Asked me if I understood what it takes to get to Heaven."

Templeton smiles at the thought. Alterman doesn't.

"I didn't know what to do at first. I thought maybe I ought to play along, see how he went about it. Audit him."

"Of course you did. How did he do?"

"Not bad. Not how I would have done it, but...I honestly think he was too easy on me."

"Knowing you, you're probably right."

"I let him know after a minute or two that I was just like him."

This amuses Templeton too. The idea that anybody could be "just like" Alterman. "How did he take it?"

"He seemed genuinely surprised. I didn't know how to take that. After a while, I wondered what it was about me that made him think I didn't believe."

"You never can be sure with some people," Templeton says.

"My mind was elsewhere, that may have been it. But it made me think about what we do. It's like something Rambha said."

"Who?"

"The McParland."

"Are we ever going to meet her?"

"Yeah. I've been keeping track of her. She's working out fine." Somehow, Templeton is going to have to be satisfied with this answer for the time being. "Anyway, I was talking to her over the phone and she asked if what we do really is accomplishing what we think it is. Are we making things better?"

"Little changes," Templeton said. "That's what you're always saying, isn't it?"

"I know. And I still believe that. It just got me to thinking. Made me wonder how God may be using us. I know He is, I just wonder."

"Hey Alex," Templeton says. "We're doing the Lord's work here."

"Yeah," Alterman says. He almost reluctantly nods his head in agreement, but he looks as though he has to be convinced. "Never hurts to make sure. How's Wydgate working out?"

"He'll do," Templeton says. "Surprising. He's not like you would expect."

"Good," Alterman says, sounding genuinely pleased.

"Anything happen while I was gone?"

"Not really," Templeton says, lying as brazenly as a hard luck card player with a lousy hand. "We got a convert."

"Really? About time we had one on this trip."

"Yeah. We still haven't figured out what's in that room."

"We will," Alterman says, clapping his hands together. "Won't take long at all. We'll probably be through with the audit before the end of the week."

"What about the hurricane?" Templeton says.

"Hurricane?"

IV

The Naked Man

1

"The situation," Alterman begins, "is dire."

The group is back together in the resort. It is two a.m., and the assembled are barely conscious. Alterman stands before them with Templeton close by. They all seem genuinely glad to see him again, yet their eyes are suspicious, as though they are students keeping some secret from the teacher, just returned from the office. Sitting nearest Ingersoll are Cherie on his left, and Steeplechase on his right. They have all introduced Steeplechase to Alterman, but Nathan remains quiet, Whit notices. He still seems ill at ease among them. Whit thinks, from conversations they've had together, that Steeplechase is probably struggling with the idea of what he is now, whether he ever was an atheist, or whether he really believes as the rest of them do. He seems grateful when Alterman makes no obvious fuss over him.

But none of this is on their minds now. Out in the gulf is Hurricane Luther, which until about six hours before had been a strong tropical storm seemingly headed another 250 miles down the coast. Then, in the space of less than an hour, it hit a very warm patch of ocean water. It turned like a boomerang, gaining strength while pivoting and pointing itself right at the panhandle not far from Edwards Crossroads. The evacuation area which had been situated two states away suddenly reoriented itself right on top of them. The storm is only 18 hours from landfall. If this was a larger metropolitan area, strangely enough, it would be easier to evacuate. The only question now is what category strength the storm might reach when it comes ashore.

"What we've got here is the worst possible scenario," Alterman says. "It's all happened too fast and too unexpectedly. We and most others in this community are stuck here. The roads are already jammed from the bigger cities, and they're going to get worse until the storm is right on top of us. I flew in last night, but you can't fly out today. They didn't expect the storm to do this, so now everybody is going to be looking for shelter."

"What do we do?" Cherie asked.

"I'm getting to that," Alterman says. "I've spoken to Brother Everhart and Sweet Lightning is going to be a shelter."

"Isn't it a little too close to the water?" Cherie says. Her voice quivers a little.

"It's close, but it's solid and it's built to withstand this kind of thing. We're not talking about a glass cathedral. This place has got shelter space built in. And he's adamant – this is what a church does at a time like this. It throws open the doors and invites everyone in to safety."

"Hello? Storm surge?" Cherie says.

Templeton jumps in. "Once again, this place was built for this kind of thing happening. And what Alex told you is correct. There aren't a lot of options here. They're closing this resort, probably within the next six hours. We can't stay here. What's more, there are people who are in the same boat who are going to need a place."

"Don't say 'in the same boat,'" Alterman corrects.

"Oh yeah."

"So we…?" Ingersoll begins.

"We are going to be helping Sweet Lightning get ready. We're going to carry their supplies, we're going to watch their kids, we're going to lock their doors, we're going to help cook their food, we're going to do whatever needs to be done. As long as this church needs help in this crisis, we're going to make sure nothing goes wrong."

"Nothing goes wrong," Whit repeats.

This is too much for Steeplechase. "Boy, bet that'll be different for *you guys*."

"How long have we got?" Whit asks. This is a question with many sides for him. Whit awoke that morning feeling worse than he has in weeks. He is surprised no one notices from the look on his face.

"Everhart wants to shut the doors of the ark by three this afternoon," Alterman says. "If the latest forecasts are right, this thing is getting faster which means we're probably looking at it coming ashore only a couple of hours later."

"Are you sure about this?" Cherie asks. She doesn't want anyone else to panic, her voice seems to say, because she's already got the panic situation covered.

Alterman nods. "First order of business is for everybody to pack your stuff." He points in the direction of their bedrooms. "Get all the computers. All the equipment. Everything. We don't want to leave anything. Turn off all the surveillance devices. We're shipping out of this place in an hour. Then when we get to Sweet Lightning, you're going to need to check with me on any immediate tasks that have to be done. Then we get everything together and prepare to ride out the storm. Everhart's told me there's plenty of room for us, provided we get there soon."

"There's probably extra space in the choir room," Whit says, eying Templeton, trying a joke to mask his condition.

"At least we know their fire alarms work," Templeton fires back.

"How bad does this thing look?"

"The hurricane? At this point, they're saying a strong Category 2 storm."

"So the audit's suspended?" Whit asks.

"Who said that?" Alterman says. "This is the ultimate example of what a church can do. This couldn't be better if we asked for it. This is..."

"An act of God," Steeplechase offers, his voice sarcastic.

"Well done, good and faithful servant!" Alterman roars. "This isn't some manufactured crisis, putting feedback into an overworked microphone. This is going to tax the abilities of everyone in that church to the limit, including us! It will be absolutely thrilling."

"Can everybody swim?" Cherie asks. Her tone of voice is somewhat frantic.

"You can't, right?"

"I can swim," she assures him. "But the whole 'high winds' thing tends to make it more of a challenge."

Ingersoll turns to Alterman. "I'm surprised you didn't sign her up for swimming lessons when you hired her, or advanced scuba. Or just throw her in a river and hope for the best."

Neither Alterman nor Cherie will say anything.

Ingersoll looks at Alterman. "You didn't, did you?"

"The swimming lessons were too hard. I'm scared of water."

"Which is why you're not a Baptist," Alterman says. "None of this is important right now."

"You should ask around," Cherie says. "I'm sure I'm not the only person worried here."

"All right. Show of hands. Who's concerned about being here in the storm?"

The arms shot up instantly. It's rare to see Alterman unprepared for an outcome, and for a brief instant, Ingersoll wonders if this news of a sudden hurricane isn't one of his eternally tiresome loyalty tests.

"When we get over there, the first thing we're going to need is some muscle," Alterman says. "The church has been using some of those foreclosed houses in the area to store supplies, and apparently they've got several filled with bottled water and other stuff that everyone is going to need."

"How many?" Ingersoll asks.

"I would assume several thousand bottles of water, for starters."

"I think I know where we can get some help," Steeplechase says.

2

"I can't believe I'm doing this."

Tara Diddle is talking as she unloads her fourteenth crate of bottled water. By now, she is drenched in perspiration from the escalating humidity and raindrops. Bands of showers from the storm are blocking out the rising sun.

It has been an hour since the group arrived at this house. It is a three-story job that looks similar to the other homes surrounding it, which are as unoccupied as it is. They were all built less than a year before the real estate market tanked. Since their foreclosure, the church got permission through some members to use them to store a few provisions in case of hurricanes.

Tara and Steeplechase are joined by Ingersoll and Cherie. The four of them are loading water onto the back of a pickup truck which will take the supplies to the church. A hot tropical breeze is hitting them all in the face, and the sky is filling up with purple clouds. Though the storm is more than a hundred miles offshore, they can feel a malevolent presence moving in, like a nightmare blooming in their minds with its worst portions still unrevealed.

At the same moment, teams of church members are going out into neighborhoods. Everhart has made it clear the church will be open to anyone who needs shelter, and he wants as many people as possible out inviting them. This serves two purposes – it opens the church's doors and gives those on the teams, who are staying behind, something to take their minds off the impending storm. Or so he says, but nobody can be that distracted.

Ingersoll is wearing a sweat-soaked T-shirt that reads, "The wind blows where it wishes, and you hear the sound of it, but you can't tell where it comes from or where it goes."

Tara drops the carton of water bottles onto the truck bed, the liquid bobbing up and down in each container. She lets out a strangled grunt.

"Tell me again why I'm helping you," she demands.

"Because you're an ethical person who believes in ethically helping people when they need help the most. Ethically." Ingersoll said this.

"And there are showers at the church," Steeplechase reminds her.

"They're going to be showers here pretty soon," she says.

She didn't have much choice. Steeplechase knew she would be as trapped as the rest of them, and since she came to the coast in his car, she probably wouldn't be able to find a way out quickly. Her misgivings about coming with them were overcome when she checked the latest readings on the storm's growing power. She scoffed at the offer of sanctuary even as she gathered up her things.

"How much are you charging people for their safety?" she asked.

"It's free. Like grace," Cherie said. Tara can tell Cherie doesn't like her too much.

"No. You'll ask for donations. Love offerings. And how many sermons are they going to have to endure about the mercy of God while that same God is presumably heaping down water and wind on them?"

"You want to stay here then?" Steeplechase asks.

"Of course not. But you've got your nerve. Coming and grabbing me up. Now I'm as compromised as you."

"We'll forgive you," Ingersoll says. He's interesting, Tara thinks. This guy with the shirt who so far has managed to carry half the number of bottles Tara has. She can also tell the girl who doesn't like her is possibly interested in the guy in the shirt, whose name she couldn't remember.

"It must not be that big a compromise, if you're coming with us," Cherie says. Tara at least respects her, since the girl is carrying as much water as she is.

"Look at him if you want to know how big a compromise it is," Tara says, pointing to her former partner. "He's batting for your team now. All he had to do was come running to you and you took him in. The only admission was refuting science, logic, common sense, independence…"

"We don't refuse anybody," Ingersoll says.

"You really believe that, huh?" Tara says. "You don't see that you drive away as many as you take in. Maybe more. You remake everybody in your own image. He doesn't even look the same."

She knew she had a point. He'd shaved since he left the atheist hangout.

"And besides, he never really was an atheist in the first place."

"I wasn't?"

"No," she says. "You came from this background. It was only natural you'd go back to it when you no longer belonged with us."

"You came from this background too. You're the one who cast me out."

"Sure. Blame the woman. It's what the church has done since Eve, right? Always works!"

"This isn't lifting any water," Ingersoll says.

"Yeah, and neither are you." She storms back into the house, where another carton awaits them all. "So let's get this straight. There are hundreds of people who are going to come to that church looking for protection, and I'm going to be right there among them. I'm doing this because I care about people and, if the opportunity presents itself, I'll remind them they don't have to surrender their minds in order to appreciate life."

"As long as we're all civil, it doesn't matter what you say," Cherie says.

"No, it's doesn't. Because we're all probably going to die anyway."

"We're all going to die," Ingersoll says. "But it remains to be seen if this hurricane is going to kill us."

"Have you seen how close that place is to the water? It's the best place to ride out the storm and the worst."

"You might feel it's a shame that it takes a hurricane to get you in a church," Cherie says.

"Look at it this way," Ingersoll says. "Most everyone is clearing out. Your atheist buddies won't know what you did to ride the storm out. What's a reputation in the face of high winds?"

"Is God going to stay His hand with me in the middle of the congregation?"

Ingersoll clears his throat. "St. Mary's Orphan Asylum was on the beach outside Galveston, Texas. There were 93 children and 10 nuns there when a hurricane hit on Sept. 8, 1900. The nuns tied themselves to the children and went up to the second floor. When the storm surge came, they starting singing "Queen of the Waves." Only three of the children survived. The rest of them were found buried in the sand on the beach. All of them were tied to each other, and it weighed them all down."

The only sound, for the moment, is the wind.

"You know, you really ought to memorize some happier stories," Cherie says.

He picks up a carton of bottles. "These things are heavier than all my sins."

"Shouldn't we be praying?" Tara asks.

"Who says you can't pray while you're working?" Ingersoll says, apparently trying to convince the rest of them that he is, in fact, working.

3

By the time they have all returned to the church, the building has already been transformed into a storm shelter. Crowds of people are waiting near the kitchen area to grab the supplies being brought in. A steady stream of families is walking through the door, being directed to the upper floors and the gym where cots have already been laid out with blankets. Those same families are being added to lists and the children receive tags around their arms to make sure no one gets lost. Once the families are settled, they are handed a hot meal and their choice of beverage. Others are directed to showers if they need one. In another part of the church, games for the children are being organized to take their minds off the storm. Over the previous two hours, the church has taken in roughly two hundred fifty families, with more expected.

The latest weather reports have the hurricane still steadily bearing toward Edwards Crossroads.

"And they came by twos," Tara says, shaking her head.

"Welcome home," Ingersoll tells her, with a smile.

"Don't think I don't realize what they'll do," she says. "Everybody comes in. You take down their names and addresses. Then they feel the need to give out of gratitude. Then you suck them in and they're on the mailing list, the membership roll, forever. Never mind if this is the only time they ever come into this place."

Once the group is inside, Alterman begins giving them jobs.

"You OK?" he asks Whit. "You don't look so good." Whitlow Mountain's pallor is ghastly, Alterman thinks, though it could be the light. He's either been outside in the rain or he's been sweating, and there's a good possibility it's both. He appears annoyed or fatigued - it's hard to tell.

Whit waves the question away, as though it isn't worth responding to.

After the morning's exertions, Ingersoll has again changed his shirt. The new one reads, "And suddenly there came from heaven a sound like a mighty rushing wind, and it filled the entire house where they were sitting."

"Okay, you three apostates," Alterman says, pointing to Ingersoll, Tara and Templeton, "they need you in the kitchen."

"Two apostates," Templeton corrects.

"Cherie, they can use you with the kids."

"The kids?"

"In the gym. The storm isn't here yet, so they're trying to give them something to do to distract them."

"Like they don't know there's a hurricane almost here," Cherie says. "What are they doing separated from their parents?"

"Before the storm gets bad, they'll bring them back to the commons area."

"Who is there with them now?"

"Everhart's wife, I think, is in charge."

"Why me?"

"Why not you?"

"Just a second," Tara says. "First of all, I don't work for you. Secondly, I'm not an apostate. If you want to get technical, I suppose *you* would refer to me as an enemy of the faith. And lastly, I'd like to point out that you immediately shove off the women to the kitchen or the child care."

"Being an atheist, I might expect you don't believe in cooks either. Food, like creation, just happens all by itself."

"Cute. I can't cook."

"There's dirty dishes too."

"The storm will get them," Ingersoll offers.

Templeton steps in. "Guys, we're only saying where labor is needed. You don't have to do anything if you don't want to. There's plenty of jobs to go around. But they can use all the help they can get."

Tara folds her arms. "If I do pitch in, it's only because I refuse to be labeled by any of you."

"Good. Go demonstrate in the kitchen," Alterman says.

"What about me, Bossman?" Whit asks. "Park the cars?"

"And just what are you going to do?" Tara demands.

"I thought I'd take a nap," Alterman says, daring her to say anything else. "You sure you're OK?" Alterman asks Whit again.

"I told you I'm fine. Now what can I do?"

"Mill around. See if anybody needs counseling. There's probably a few ill-at-ease people." Alterman pauses. "You might be one of them."

"You too," Whit says.

But Templeton hasn't left yet.

"We've got a real problem," Templeton says.

"Uh, yeah, it's out there," Alterman replies, pointing to the approaching water.

"No, this is a different problem."

"What is it?"

Templeton's eyes avoid Alterman's. That in itself is not a sign, but a clue. "You mean there's more than just the storm," Alterman asks.

"I've got to go get someone out of this."

"*You've* got to?" Alterman says. "Who is it?"

"It's a long story, but…" The mood lightens, because Templeton smiles. It is an embarrassed, chastened smile, like someone caught in a lie. "While you were gone, I had a job offer."

"Really?"

"From my old church. Shiloh Church at the Point."

It doesn't seem possible. "The one we just audited? The one that got to meet you again as Mr. Satva?"

251

"Yes. They came down here personally and asked me to come back. They were very nice. Offered me a lot more money. I was impressed."

Alterman, for once, is dumbfounded. "Wow."

"When we got through with the audit, the preacher they had immediately resigned. Said he couldn't work in a place like that. And evidently the audit caused a lot of soul searching."

"Church split?"

"No," Templeton says. "They said it didn't, and I've got to say, I believe them. They were as remorseful and penitent as you could ask for. Said they felt convicted for what they had done, came clean about the whole thing, said they had looked for a pretext to get rid of me last time, and they were willing, if I was willing to come back. The guy I had the most trouble out of, he was the one who made the offer. Had tears in his eyes."

Alterman, still skeptical, mentioned the name of the member he suspected. "Chaffey?"

"Yeah, it was him. And like I say, I believed him."

"And what did you do?"

Templeton's expression seems to be surprise that Alterman might think anything other than the obvious answer. "I turned it down. I told them I wasn't interested. I was flattered, but I wasn't interested."

Alterman is not amused. "When I came back, I asked you if anything happened while I was gone. As I recall, your response was, 'Not really.'"

"Well, that's the truth."

"We've got a reformed atheist working with us, and you got a job offer. Nothing happened?"

"I didn't want to bother you."

"You know, liars will have their part in the lake of fire, Steve."

"I didn't lie to you, Alex."

"No, you lied to *them*. You say you're not interested in going back to preach?"

"I'm not interested in going back *there*. There's no way I could, Alex. We didn't burn that bridge, we blew it up! No matter what they say."

"What did Sharon say?"

"It didn't matter what Sharon said."

"If it doesn't matter, then what did she say? Did you even tell her?"

"Of course I told her. She said she'd support anything I wanted to do."

"Of course she did. That's Sharon."

"Would I want to put her through that place again, Alex?"

"What does the Lord say?"

Templeton hesitates before answering. "That's between me and Him."

"But they're coming to you? They're coming with their hat in their hands!"

"And their shame in their hearts, Alex!"

"Didn't that feel good?"

"That doesn't matter now, Alex. The point is, they're still here. *In town.* I figured they would have left after I turned them down. But they're stuck here. I just talked to them on the phone. They called from the Conquistador, wherever that is."

"I know that place," Steeplechase says.

"I owe it to them to go get them," Templeton says. "I'm responsible for them being here."

"Well, they'll need a place to stay, definitely." Alterman turns to Steeplechase. "You know where this is?"

"Yeah," Steeplechase says. "It's not that far. Five minutes from here."

"Okay, you're coming with us." Alterman gestures at Wydgate. "You too. Come on."

Wydgate, barely conscious of what's being discussed, suddenly perks up. "Me? What did I do?"

Templeton says, "Alex, I'll go. It's my fault they're here anyway."

"Look, you're crazy if you think you're going. Besides, we'll need a guide."

"Alex..." Templeton protests.

Steeplechase also protests. "You don't really need me. You can use your phones. The map app, anyone?"

"Our phones could go out," Alterman says. "Besides, this kid knows the terrain, and he'll know landmarks in case something's blown over. And if something should happen to us, he's saved now." He lets the last sentence hang in the air for a second.

"Maybe I should mention…" Steeplechase finally breaks in.

"Too late now," Alterman says. "Time for your baptism."

"Alex, it's my fault these guys are here," Templeton says. "I can't let you…"

"Listen…" Alterman says, under his breath. "If I'm killed in a hurricane, I want you back here to take the company. If we're both out there…"

Templeton glances at Wydgate, the source of Alterman's decision. "But he's working with us."

"I know, but it's a matter of pride. I can put aside competition, but that's too much for me. If the Lord calls me home, he is *not* going to get my company!"

Templeton shakes his head at his partner.

"You got any problems with going out in the rain?" Alterman says to Wydgate.

"Maybe," he says. "Why do I have the feeling if anyone is going to get left behind, it'll be me?"

"Make sure you pray for him," Alterman says, as they go out the door.

4

Whit is sweating. There are more people in the church commons area than he might have thought possible, and their assembled body temperatures are stifling. But they have help from the weather outside. The windows are boarded up, but the light still coming in shows that the storm is getting closer.

He feels awful. He's supposed to be counseling, but if another person asks him if he needs help, he's probably really going to need it.

That's when Rosemary Thompson, the Bible study leader, sees him. He hasn't seen her since the day of the fire alarm caper, and he has taken a vow never to "go Josiah" again. The way he feels, the idea of him doing anything again seems unlikely.

He can't decide if it's the impending weather, or the inescapability of his condition. Whatever it is.

Rosemary smiles at the sight of him. She looks as perfect as before, and just as artificial. Whit thinks to himself that whenever the next audit rolls around, he hopes Alterman consults with her more closely on her makeup and wardrobe. This woman does not look like she is seeking refuge from a tropical weather system.

"Whit! Come sit with me here." She is seated on a cot. She pats her hand down in the space she wishes him to occupy. "You look like you could use it."

"I'm just fine," he says, though neither of them look like they believe him. "Just milling around to see if anyone needs anything. What can I do for you? You look lovely." Whit prides himself on his gentlemanly ways, and if they're going to be working together, he might as well ingratiate himself.

"I'm as right as rain," she says, then she seems to reconsider her choice of words. "How does it look out there?"

"Shouldn't be too much longer. I'm trying not to pay too much attention to it."

"This your first hurricane?" she asks, like an old pro.

"Can't say I've ever had the pleasure before."

"This is my…" she begins tallying a figure using her fingers as a guide. "Twelfth!" she shouts, when she arrives at the number. *She seems more smug than I would be,* Whit thinks.

"What's your secret?"

"Don't know. Just pure meanness I guess! I scare the storms off!" Whit can see how Alterman probably picked her. He guesses she has a background in theology, like him, and could probably take over most of his duties, if Alterman ever needed someone to step in suddenly.

"Oh, I can't believe that," he says, wiping his forehead with his open palm. "Sweet young thing like yourself."

"Such a charmer," she says. "Even if you do look like death warmed over."

Whit politely excuses himself. It's just about that time that Whit has the overpowering urge to get something, anything to drink. He looks around for a water fountain, even though there are legions of water bottles waiting for anyone to sample one. Those are for storm victims, he tells himself, and he instantly discounts the idea that he might be one.

Whit feels his left foot dragging against the leg of one of the cots, and he nearly trips. Luckily for him, he grabs the back of a chair and steadies himself. But even as he grips the chair, Whit can barely feel the sensation of his hand closing around the chair back. His fingers are numb.

When he is satisfied that he is still standing, he opens and closes his hand. He looks at it. The fingers still move, but he is convinced they are delaying, as though there is a snag somewhere in his nervous system. The more he moves the fingers, the less he can tell whether the feeling is returning to them, or whether he imagines it.

Then Whit is struck by the symmetry of fate. The last time he came to the church, he saw Rosemary, followed immediately by his reluctant encounter with Thomas Everhart. With Rosemary's tender concerns still on his mind, he again sees the preacher. Though this is his church, housing hundreds of people seeking shelter from a hurricane, Everhart looks as though his most pressing concern is Whit.

I must really look bad, Whit thinks.

"Dr. Mountain?" Everhart asks.

"Hey," Whit says, and offers his hand. It still has some patches of the alarm dye on it, but he feels confident Everhart won't see them. "Good to see you again."

"Probably not under these circumstances."

"I thought you might need some help here, so I came."

"Thank you. Thank you. I'm not sure how we're going to get through this, but I know we are." Whit smiles, until he hears Everhart's question. "Are you OK? You don't look too well."

The words roll effortlessly from Whit's lips. "Is it that obvious?"

"Are you ill? Is something the matter?"

Whit grimaces. He shakes his head. He can't admit the thing to himself, let alone anybody else. But there's very little keeping it back.

Everhart looks the scene over, and puts an arm on Whit's shoulder. "Come over here with me. There's a room in here where we can talk. Come on."

Whit shakes his head. He doesn't want to surrender to the man's charm, not with so much at stake. He'd rather keep to himself and endure it. That's what men are supposed to do, he tells himself, though he hardly feels worthy of being considered a man.

"Come on, hear me out," Everhart says. "You're here for a reason, and maybe not the reason you think."

Before they have made it to the room, Whit can scarcely believe he is weeping. His head is down and he has his hand over his face. He is sure somebody sees him, but it hardly matters anymore. Whatever has been keeping it all in check has now disappeared.

Everhart shuts the door behind him. "If there's anything I can do for you..."

"It's hard to say...I'm so afraid...I don't say things like this...I'm ashamed..."

"What are you afraid of?"

"Something's wrong with me. I've known it for a few weeks. I don't know for sure what it is, but I think I know, and it scares me."

"Is it something health-related? I mean, are you sick?"

"I'm afraid I am. I haven't been to a doctor, but I'm pretty sure I already know what's wrong."

"What do you think it is?"

"Brother," Whit begins. He was raised and has worked in an atmosphere all his life where a pastor is addressed as his brother, even if the connection is never felt. Yet he realizes if he had a flesh and blood brother, he's not sure he would have enough courage to reveal anything like this about himself.

"Yes?" Everhart says, still waiting.

"I feel weak all the time," Whit says. "I have pain in my joints. My hands have been numb. I've had trouble swallowing. This really has me shook up."

"Dr. Mountain, I'm not a doctor. What..."

"My wife has been dead several years. She had Lou Gehrig's Disease. I had to take care of her. I watched her die. How much do you know about it?"

"The disease? Not that much."

"You lose the ability to control your body. To move. To speak. You can't do anything for yourself. You just see yourself surrender, against your own will. I sat with my wife and she just slipped away. All I could do was watch. Watch her suffer, and watch her watch herself suffer."

"And you think you have that?"

"I'm sure I do," Whit says, his voice abandoning him. "And I'm terrified. I ought not to be. I ought to have faith, but I can't even concentrate. My heart is about to jump out of my chest half the time. I keep wishing I could just go ahead and die."

"Is that why you're here now? In the middle of the storm?"

"No. It isn't that."

Everhart gives a slight smile. "Because you're working for Alex Alterman?"

After a moment's hesitation, Whit nods.

"It's rare you have theologians show up at your church unannounced," Everhart says, breaking into a broad grin.

"Or that they trigger your fire alarms," Whit admits. Everhart nods his head, confirming that he made the connection. "I can't lie to you. I've thought about what might happen if I just walked out in the middle of that storm."

"Surely you've got more faith that that? The man who wrote that book?"

"You were right though. A young man wrote that," Whit says. "'Teach us to number our days, that we may gain a heart of wisdom...' I didn't understand what that meant then."

Everhart shakes his head. "You just understand it differently now, because you're older. Let me guess, you're probably disappointed in yourself. You feel like you shouldn't be afraid, but you quite naturally are. You've been around long enough to know..."

"You asked me if there was anything I'd reconsider about that book," Whit interrupts. "Moses wrote that Psalm. And he says at the end...he prays..." Whit's tender voice breaks at the idea that Moses, the man of God, would surrender his prayer to a scroll and the crude ink strokes that the Lord made immortal. "He prays that God will show His mercy and His great works. But I've been around long enough to know that sometimes He'll bring you face to face with the worst things you can imagine. I saw Gilda just disappear, as if she never existed. That was hard enough, but I never once thought I'd have to go through the same thing. And I'll have to go through it without her."

Everhart is close to him, but something in the man shakes at Whit's words. It is noticeable enough that Whit believes if he stands there long enough, he might hear the pastor give his own confession. But he doesn't. Everhart shifts his weight and clears his throat, as though denying something has issued a charge in the air.

"Dr. Mountain," Everhart begins, "Moses prays God will show His great works. Those works don't get celebrated in calm circumstances. Moses had to face the open water before he could see it parted. He had to hear the weeping of parents to experience the wonder of Passover. How else would He know the presence of God unless He was willing to endure it?"

Just then, even through layers of brick and steel and panic, they can hear a gust of whistling wind.

"Sounds like we may all see if before this is over," Everhart says. "Would you like me to pray about this with you?"

Whit gives a weary and embarrassed nod of the head. "Isn't there something I can pray about for you?"

Everhart shakes his head. "Your cross is already heavy enough."

5

Cherie isn't sure what's worse – being stuck in a hurricane, of having to watch somebody else's kids in the middle of it. As she walks down the halls of Sweet Lightning to the gymnasium, she starts to realize how awful this particular audit has been. From the beginning, when Alterman made her the "joiner" instead of Ingersoll, nothing has felt right. She doesn't know how to do the job, and she hasn't done it properly anyway, she thinks.

She hasn't been able to keep her mind on the business at hand. She hasn't even been able to keep a successful cover. Half the time when people call her "Jennifer," she doesn't answer immediately as she should.

Then there's this whole business with Ingersoll. Just thinking about it all makes her angry. And the anger is growing as she goes to help the pastor's wife with babysitting.

Margie Everhart is the first person she sees when she rounds the corner of the gym. There are about seventy-five kids in here of all ages. The teens are in a corner off to the side, with some helping watch the younger kids. There are adults among the mass, but most are women holding toddlers who by their tiny fidgets and whimpers evidently know something is wrong somewhere.

And in the middle of them, talking to a little boy, is Anna Sparrow.

It is the first time Cherie has seen Anna since that night when she arrived at her house. They went on to the hospital, and Cherie still hasn't caught up completely on her sleep since. Cherie already had a reservation at the rehab center, so Anna ended up talking her place. Cherie stood with her when she went to Thomas Everhart and admitted her problem. Everhart didn't know Cherie as anything other than one of Anna's friends. Cherie has been calling her and sending her encouraging text messages for weeks.

But Cherie's feelings on this score, as in many other facets of her life, are confused. All the time she should have been learning about the services the church offers for new members, she was dealing with Anna's problems. And somehow, in all of this, she hasn't managed to reveal to Anna that her name really isn't Jennifer and she isn't a new member and that Anna's problems might affect the audit that's being prepared for her church.

How long has she prayed over this? Should she even tell Alterman that one of the church's young singles ministers has a substance abuse problem? If she does tell him, doesn't it speak well of Sweet Lightning that they saw to it she got help, and paid for it? If Cherie kept it to herself, would she be allowing Anna to pick the habit back up the minute Cherie leaves town, as Cherie inevitably will? Cherie finally settled on honesty – she had to tell everything she knew. Her own experience had taught her that dishonesty always has wonderful reasons for its own existence, and it isn't obligated to be truthful in whispering them in your ear.

Cherie approaches Anna through the crowd in the gym. There is a frantic energy here. All of the children probably know or suspect what is happening outside in the sky above them. They don't have any choice but to stay occupied rather than think about what could happen. But where the adults feel a need to be reserved and stoic for the children's benefit, the kids are loud and manic and almost artificially happy. There are boys who look old enough to have a driver's license pushing others the same age against walls and laughing, while on the other side of the gym boys half their ages are doing the same thing.

Within a split second of seeing Anna, Cherie understands why she was sent to the gym. For the same reason she was made into the mystery worshipper – Anna Sparrow needs her. If there was no other reason for them to come to Sweet Lightning than to help this woman, that would be enough.

She looks better. That last time Cherie saw her, her hair, her clothes, her face, all indicated that she no longer cared about anything. Her body had become something she was encumbered with, and she was exhausted by its demands for sleep, food and peace. Every nerve was manic and worn, and every emotion overexposed and deadened.

Now she is muted. The colors of her clothes are muted. She doesn't want attention. She only wants to exist.

"Hey stranger," Cherie says, putting her arm around Anna. Anna stands up and embraces her. It is awkward, immediately.

"Jennifer? What are you doing here?" she says. Then, she quickly adds, "I was worried about you. I didn't know if you'd made it out…"

"No. I'm here. What are we doing?"

"I'm not sure," Anna says. Her voice assumes the tone Cherie remembers from their Bible studies – assured, confident. "I think we're just trying to keep them busy until things get awful. How does it look out there?"

"I'm trying not to know," Cherie says. "It's all I can do to keep going."

Anna squeezes her hand. "I know. That's the same way I feel."

"How has….it been?"

Anna nods. "It's been hard. It's been hard. Regrets. You know how it is. Regrets." The word, enigmatic, stands in for a thousand other emotions she doesn't want to enumerate.

"Have you needed anything?"

"No, you've been great."

"But what are you doing here?"

"They weren't going to keep the center open in the middle of all this, so I had to go somewhere. I figured this was the best place. I went back to my house and got my things and came here. I didn't have much choice."

"Why didn't you call me? I could have helped."

"Like I said, I didn't know if you'd be around..." For some reason, Anna isn't looking at Cherie as she says this. Though there are dozens of kids who could have caught her attention, Anna appears to be looking for something else to watch, rather than Cherie's eyes.

For no reason she can explain, Cherie takes Anna's hand. Instead of squeezing it, she holds it. No pressure, just the touch. "Is there anything I can do here?" Cherie asks.

"Noooo," Anna says, in an absent-minded voice, still looking away. Then after another second, she very forcibly takes her hand away. "I think it's all covered."

Then Anna looks at Cherie. Cherie doesn't know what expression she has, but she can tell that Anna has surprised herself. Cherie sees that Anna is just as disgusted with where she is, for several unspoken reasons, but in a way that only Cherie can understand.

"If I hadn't seen you..." Anna begins. Then she reaches into her pocket, and pulls out a bottle. Inside are three pills. They rattle as she places the bottle in Cherie's hands. Cherie slips the bottle into her pocket. "I had it all worked out."

"They let you go, so you knew where you had some?"

"I don't want to go through all this that's coming... aware," she says. "I'm not strong enough yet."

"If you hadn't seen me..."

"Get them away from me," Anna says. "You're here for a reason. Get them away. I know I can trust you. Don't take them yourself. I don't care what you do with them but take them away."

"Are these it?" Cherie asks.

"Yes, I swear."

"I'm here," Cherie says.

"I know. Thank God you are." Now Anna takes Cherie's hand. "Thank God I can trust you."

Now it is Cherie's turn to pull her hand away, but she grips Anna's tighter. "You *can* trust me. Listen to me, you can trust me. What was it you told me? Here, I'm not supposed to just be fed, but to feed others."

Anna smiles, but only for a second.

"My name isn't Jennifer Mersault. My name is Cherie LeFevere. I'm with a group doing a survey of this church. We were hired to come in and see everything that it does and see if it's working."

Anna's eyes roll and her shoulders sink. Cherie pumps her hand, to snap her out of it.

"As far as I can see, they've done everything right by you."

"You couldn't tell me this earlier?"

"Tell me when I could do that. I'm sorry."

"What does this mean for me?

"Nothing. After all, you are forgiven…"

"This time," Anna says. "But how long before I lose it again? These are opiates! I mean, I'm cramping, my eyes can't take light, I'm sweating all the time. How long before I give it up and they find me dead somewhere?"

"I know. Believe me, I have the same problem. I still struggle with it."

"It doesn't help being here, like this. I'm supposed to be helping people, and I'm a basket case! I can't take it!"

Just then, the two of them are conscious of someone else joining them. It is Margie Everhart. Cherie has never met her, but Anna knows her.

"Is everything OK?" she asks.

It obviously isn't. The eyes of both Anna and Cherie are red. It dawns on both of them how obvious they must have been, here in the middle of the gym.

Anna wipes her eyes. "Margie, this is…" she motions toward Cherie.

"I'm Cherie LeFevere," she says. In all that they have said, Cherie's real name is probably the least important fact, she thinks.

"What's the problem, Cherie?" Margie asks.

It takes a second for them to realize. Margie has been watching from across the room and believes Cherie is the one being counseled.

"I guess you didn't know," Anna begins. "I've been in counseling for several weeks. I've had some…dependency issues. I guess I thought you knew through Brother Tommy."

"Oh, no. No, I didn't. Tommy and I haven't spoken about church things in a few weeks," she says, and then, Margie begins weeping.

Cherie has done this so long that she isn't shocked when the problems of two people are suddenly exploded by the entry of another person to a conversation, shouldering her own shame. So barely a muscle of her face twitches when this woman she has never met before suddenly announces, "Tommy and I are probably getting a divorce."

6

"This is the reason we do this stuff," Alterman says, as they pull out of the parking lot. "This right here. There are moments in the life of a community where only a church can step in. The needs of the…"

"Hey, you might want to take a left at the light," Steeplechase says, interrupting.

"You say this place is five minutes away?" Wydgate asks, never taking his eyes off the storm in front of them.

"Yes. That's five minutes when the ocean isn't beating against the doors."

"Yeah, I can see where this could take a little bit longer," Alterman says.

The three of them can feel the car occasionally lurching in directions not dictated by the wheel. It is raining with a steady intensity that ensures they will all be speaking loudly the entire time they are on the road.

For a few minutes, the only sound, oppressive and insistent, is the wind and rain against the wipers. Murderous breezes move the car, and Alterman spots a power line hanging less than a foot above them from a snapped pole, but still far enough up to maintain the line for cars to pass under."

"How did you... get saved?" Steeplechase hesitates over the phrase. It sounds as though he bristles against the term because he was opposed to it for so long. It sounds awkward coming from him.

"You talking to me?" Alterman asks. "I don't remember."

"You don't remember?" Wydgate says.

"I don't remember when I accepted Jesus. My mother told me it was when I was six years old. I remember being baptized, but I don't remember walking an aisle or talking to a teacher or waking up in the middle of the night or anything like that. But I know I did. It's just always been a part of me. I wish I had a great story."

"If you don't *know* how or when you made a decision, then how do you know for sure you made it? How do you know your parents weren't trying to sucker you?"

"Yes, because my parents were, you know, just as deceitful and twisted as I am, right?"

"I didn't mean anything."

"You're built to be skeptical, because of what you've done, and that's OK," Alterman says. "You've been trained to believe that all those believers lie. They lie to you about how much they believe, they lie to the people they're trying to convert, they lie to themselves with this crazy, made-up God they carry around in their heads. I know, you didn't mean anything by it."

"Watch out there," Wydgate says, pointing up ahead.

But the storm means nothing to Alterman. "The way my mother told it, I was six. We never missed church. I asked why we went. My mother said to me, 'Because I'm a Christian, Alex.' So she says I told her, 'I'm gonna show you how it's done.'"

For a few seconds, the only sound comes from the weather. "You audited your own mother?" Steeplechase asks.

Now Alterman doesn't care about the past. There is standing water on the road before them. "How deep do you think that looks? Hey, heathen," Alterman says to Steeplechase. "This is your town, right? That pretty deep?"

"I didn't say it was my town. I've just been here longer." Steeplechase eyes the scene through the sheets of rain. "I wouldn't risk it. Take that side street." Alterman turns the wheel. A sound like a thousand fists buffets the driver's side of the car.

Then Alterman sighs, and speaks.

"What do you think happened?" Alterman asks. "With you, I mean. Why did you stop believing?"

"I don't know. Probably anger. Probably looking for something new. I guess I associated Jesus with my family. Don't get me wrong. I had a good childhood. Everything I ever wanted. Or could have wanted. But I guess I got tired of everything I wanted. I don't know. It was all too familiar to me. I wanted new." Then he points ahead. "Turn right here. The hotel is that big one on the right."

There is no standing water on the road, so Alterman speeds up a little.

Wydgate nods. He's either heard this before from others, or he knows the feeling only too well.

"Then I got away from my home, and the things I had trusted about my family – they didn't comfort me anymore. When I did think of the church, or what my parents believed, it just seemed dead to me. Like comic books. I had loved them when I was a kid, but I wasn't a kid anymore."

"What changed?" Wydgate asks.

"I would have said around that time that *I* changed, but I don't think that's right really anymore. I got tired of all that talk of faith. Got tired of always being wrong."

"Being wrong?"

"You know. The sin thing."

Wydgate nods.

"Meet other people and they don't think the same as you, and you don't want to say they're wrong. So you figure maybe *you're* wrong. You just try to accommodate. Get along. I don't know. If you want to know the truth, I was more of an agnostic."

"God's unknowable," Alterman says. "If He's unknowable, then I have no obligation."

"Yeah," Steeplechase says, recognizing a species of what he was.

Alterman is going to say something, but Wydgate goes first.

"You know that story about the woman in that country – I forget which – the one where her favorite portrait of Jesus is flaking and fading in her church? The portrait is hundreds of years old, but it grieves her that it's breaking down. So she goes there and paints over it, because she's trying to preserve it. – Alex, turn right there. It looks shallow." Alterman nods as Wydgate points to an area just ahead, in the hotel parking lot.

"That's the way a lot of us are," Wydgate continues. "We look at Jesus and we somehow think He needs *our* help, so we try to refashion his features in a way we think best. But we end up painting over the very things that draw people to Him. We retouch Him how we think He should be, and end up creating something unrecognizable. Ugly, even."

Not bad, Alterman thinks. He shuts the engine off after they've parked. Now they have to go inside. Steeplechase took down the names of the men and their hotel room number.

"Thiiiis ought to be fun," Alterman hisses, opening the door.

7

Templeton's church members are on the second floor of an open
motor court. Their room faces out onto a common balcony walkway
with a rail. Alterman finds the hotel room and pounds on the door.
The wind has grown manifestly horrible over the last thirty minutes.

Alterman grips the rain-soaked rail in spite of his innate fear
of lightning. It's a fact about himself that he doesn't dare reveal,
for anyone who's ever known him would be amused to find that he
fears what others might consider accusatory bolts from the sky. He
learned long ago to mistrust the feel of hair on the back of his neck
standing up. Still, he doesn't want to hold onto metal rails even on
clear days.

But he must. The wind, coupled with the rain-slick walkway,
makes anyone a risk to fall. Wydgate and Steeplechase have followed
him up here. Wydgate grips the front of his rain slicker to himself
and squints against the drops following horizontally. Steeplechase is
wiping his shirt front, pocked as it is by leaves kicked up in the wind.

Alterman again pummels the door, until it finally opens. The
face is familiar, for all the wrong reasons. He is a balding man
in a golf shirt with a bit of a paunch, and pinched features in the
elements.

"Mr. Alterman?"

"Yes. You're with the party from Shiloh at the Point?"

The man nods. "What are you doing here?"

"We've come to bring you to the church. Sweet Lightning. It's being used as a storm shelter, and it's a little further out of the danger of the storm surge."

"What?" the man shouts. Alterman repeats himself, over the wind.

"Do you want to go?" Wydgate asks. His tone is frantic, as though this cavalry will be heading back to the fort in a second's notice.

"Yes," the man says, though for a second, he looks Alterman over again, as though unsure of whether he should. The man then turns inside the room, shouts something no one outside can hear, and another man appears. He is very overweight, also balding, for some reason wearing a white dress shirt and tie. The tie flaps ridiculously in the wind.

"Follow us," Alterman says, and he does not wait. The larger man pulls the hotel door behind him, but the wind seizes it and pushes it back open. The man struggles with it for a few seconds, until the sound of it closing can be heard over the wind.

The men hold onto the rail, and a thunderclap momentarily loosens Alterman's grip. He continues on, and everyone follows him, taking ginger but purposeful steps down to the first floor and onto to the car. They arrive and, to their horror, find someone accidentally locked the doors.

"Sorry," Alterman says, embarrassed. He is a creature of habit, and his habit is to never trust any situation. What enterprising car thief wouldn't choose the coming of a hurricane as a golden opportunity to steal? Who would suspect it?

The five men file into the car once the locks spring, with Steeplechase taking the middle between the two churchmen. For a second or two, the men cough and sharply exhale from the storm, wiping the rain from their faces.

"All right, we're in a bit of a hurry," Alterman says, starting up the car.

"Just a second," the thinner man of Templeton's party says. "Shut the engine off."

"But..." Alterman protests.

"Shut it off. This won't take a second." As if prompted, the car shudders at another gust. Yet Alterman, recognizing the man's tone, does as instructed.

"I'm Fred Chaffey, Mr. Alterman," he begins. "This is Morris Beeks."

"I recognize you Mr. Chaffey," Alterman says, without looking back.

"I'm sure you do. I am the man who hired you to look at our church, after all. It's one thing to allow the devil to park on your driveway, but it's another when you invite him inside to supper."

"Amen," says Beeks, loud enough to be heard over the storm.

"Gentlemen..."

"I just want to say this is the first time I've seen you since you and Brother Templeton paid us a visit. And it would be wrong, storm or no storm, to ignore what's going on here."

"What is going on *is* a storm," Wydgate says, jumping in.

"No doubt you know why we're here," Chaffey says. As far as he's concerned, there isn't another soul in the car. "I have to say I owe you a lot. After you two pulled that stunt, I had to go back and look at myself and my Christian walk." Alterman winces at the phrase, which he feels is an overused church cliché. Christians don't walk, he often says. They either run to the Lord, or they run away from Him. But they can't escape Him.

"Alex, start the car," Wydgate says, but Alterman doesn't move.

"I owe you a lot, but I wanted to kill you. I mean that sincerely too. I'm confessing that I contemplated tracking you down and killing you, Mr. Alterman. It would have been a murder enough to inspire a song. But here I am, this storm bearing down that could end my life, and who do I find coming to save me but you. I tell you, that's the Lord. God obviously sent you to me so I'd have to make my peace with you."

"You can do whatever you want after we get to the church..." Wydgate says.

"I ask your forgiveness sir," Chaffey says. "I humbly ask for it. You made me a better Christian, Mr. Alterman."

Alterman, who was about to open his mouth when the man blurted out his plea, nods in recognition. Alterman decides he will wait at least to admit that he himself was about to ask forgiveness.

Instead, he turns around and shakes the man's hand.

"I'd say the same," Beeks says. "But they sent me down here with him to make sure he doesn't make good on his threat."

"Thank you, gentlemen," Alterman says. "But if the Lord wasn't interested in us making peace, He's made it easier for you to dispose of my body in this storm. Let's get out of here."

8

The kids in the gym have no idea what Margie Everhart has just said.

"What?" Cherie asks. In a second, she won't be able to remember exactly what they were talking about before Margie spoke.

"I don't know why I'm telling you this," Margie begins. "It's been going on for several months, ever since Tommy wrote his book. There's just been a lot of stress."

"What is it?" Cherie asks.

Margie continues talking, but she's looking mostly at Anna. That's the more familiar face to her. "It's been awful on us. I mean, you'll know what I'm talking about. Everybody *wants* Tommy now. He's getting offers to do other books. Other church offers. Television. There's even supposed to be this group that came in to look him over. They're all jotting down notes about this place. I have no idea what they're saying about me."

Anna glances directly as Cherie, who doesn't even twitch.

"Excuse me, Margie," says an imperious voice. It is Keysha, Everhart's assistant. "Have you seen Brother Tommy?"

Cherie has heard about Keysha, but seeing her is startling. She is very tall, and though everyone is dressed in sweats and clothes that can be slept in, Keysha looks dressed for a day at work. She has on heels. Her makeup is impeccable. She looks in charge of the place.

"No, I haven't," Margie says. Her face is a tight mask of impatience.

"Sorry to interrupt, but I know he was waiting to hear from the weather service."

"If I see him, I'll tell him you were looking for him." Margie appears to want nothing more from Keysha than for her to instantly disappear.

"Very good," Keysha says, and she leaves them with a too-perfect smile.

Once she is gone, Margie shuts her eyes. "It doesn't help when your husband has this new assistant who runs the place like clockwork and is a woman."

Anna looks crushed. "You suspect something?"

"No, but with all that's going on…" she says. She has the exasperation of a woman who is trying to ignore hints of something wrong while her mind is obsessing on them. "I just don't like it. I don't like any of it. I don't like what might happen. It's been a hard time. My father just died a little while back. I have a career. I made my life before I ever met Tommy. I love him, but I'm afraid of what'll happen to him. I just know it."

"What…" Cherie starts, but Margie cuts her off.

"He'll be gone somewhere, and people will pay attention to me. Waiting for either of us to make a mistake. I knew what I was getting into when I married him and he started this church. I knew he was good at what he does. And I knew it was what the Lord wanted him to do. But this, all this is different. I didn't count on this. I should have, but I didn't."

"You've told him you want to leave him?"

"No, that's just it. I *don't* want to leave him. He knows that. I want to stay here. I want what we have now. I don't want to lose this. And if I were to leave him, that would destroy his reputation. He couldn't do what he wants to do."

Cherie asks, "What do you think God wants him to do?"

"I'm afraid of that," she says. "What if I'm the only one standing in the way? But I don't care. I just don't care. I want my husband, and my life here and I don't want anything taking that away. I've prayed about this and nothing happens."

Then Margie looks into both of their faces.

"Except a hurricane comes out of nowhere. Now it may take everything away. Is that my fault?" Then this woman who doesn't want to be the center of attention looks around to make sure she isn't.

Cherie's first instinct is to let Margie Everhart keep talking. The woman isn't interested in solutions. She just wants to tell someone what she is struggling with. Maybe it was the sight of two women coming apart before her that made all this come out of her. Maybe she would have told anyone.

But in an instant, Cherie feels selfish, and wants to know something.

"How long have you been married?"

"Ten years. And don't think that isn't a sticky situation. We don't have kids. We both want them, but we don't want to sacrifice the time. But somehow it's my fault because I'm supposed to *want* kids."

"Is that what he says?"

Margie pauses. "No, that's not fair. He's never said anything like that."

"What has he said?"

"That he doesn't want to lose me."

"And you don't want to lose him," Cherie says.

"No. I don't."

Cherie surprises herself. "I don't need a man," she says. Anna starts, as though this admission is somehow an intrusion onto Margie's pain.

Then Margie's voice changes. For the first time, she sounds like a psychologist and not a broken person. "But you want a relationship eventually?"

"Not if it takes me away from the Lord. It's taken a lot for me to see that."

Now Margie's voice is totally detached. "What if that relationship gets you closer to Him? You can experience the Lord as part of knowing someone else. Would that be worth it?"

"Is that what happened to you?" Cherie asks.

Margie doesn't answer.

Anna, who has been quiet, speaks up. "Listen, you're distraught. This isn't the best time in the world to make decisions. Trust me."

"I'm sorry. You've got your own problems and here I come and hijack your conversation."

"No, no," Anna says. "What can I do for you?"

"I don't know. I feel so hopeless. I feel like whatever I'm going to do, it's going to be wrong. I don't want to disappoint anybody. They don't need to see what kind of person I really am."

"Excuse me," Cherie says, and she astonishes herself by leaving them, just as the lights go out.

Margie and Anna snap to attention and begin shouting for the children to carefully begin lining up to go back to their parents. Whatever they have all shared together is forgotten because something else is needed now by others. But Cherie walks right through the hall and out. There is someone she has to find. What she is about to do feels selfish, but she doesn't think they'll ever be a better time.

9

The water is deeper now. Alterman doesn't like the looks of it, gathering on the road from the direction they came. He instead pulls to the other side of the parking lot, and begins slowly navigating his way down a two-lane street across from the hotel. The Spanish moss in the trees is flagellating the branches it hangs from. Up a few lots ahead, the men in the car see a tree torn in half, the branches flying through the air until they come to rest in a yard across the road.

On this street, there are rows and rows of mobile homes. Alterman wonders at the placement of cheap real estate only a few miles away from prime resort land. These are probably owned by people who want a weekend getaway at the beach but don't feel like spending thousands on a time-share. Still, there are a few of these that look older than the Magna Carta. The water is pooling in the grass but the street is passable.

No one is talking. After the fervor of their pleas for forgiveness, neither of the emissaries from Shiloh at the Point will say a word. And neither Wydgate nor Steeplechase is in a theological mood. Because of this storm, everyone has the silencing fear of God in them.

Chaffey proves it finally. "Morris, now might be a good time to start praying," he says, in the nervously even voice of a man eying a lion.

Beeks' lips begin moving furiously and soundlessly.

Alterman turns down another street, seemingly on a hunch. He is afraid that somehow he has turned into a trailer park that has only one outlet to the main roads. The surroundings don't appear cut off, but in the wind and rain, it's hard to know precisely. Every few seconds, a new torrent of water buffets the car and renders everything before them a gray, watery mystery. Then the scene clarifies itself. The rain drops hitting the trailers sound like bullets.

Alterman's voice remains calm, though loud enough to cut through the bedlam. He is talking to Wydgate. "What do you think about auditing little churches? Ones that can't afford it? The small ones? The poor ones?"

Wydgate, who has momentarily forgotten what he does for a living in the face of the storm, is whiplashed back into clarity. "What?"

"You know, pro bono work, like lawyers."

Wydgate sees his point. "That's where the real war is being fought. The trenches. Tiny little churches with less than 25 people."

Alterman nods. "The churches are barely holding on. The people are the same."

"May the Lord have mercy on an unsuspecting Christendom," Chaffey says from the back seat.

Beeks' voice is now audible. "And Lord, be with the churches that Mr. Alterman visits, and their pastors, according to your abundant mercies."

Alterman finally sees another street open up that isn't lined by trailers. He speeds up, though they are only crawling still under the torrent.

"What about that up there?" Steeplechase says, pointing to a side street.

Without speaking, Alterman turns on it.

"No, not that," Steeplechase says.

"No, not what?"

"I didn't mean turn there. I mean look at that."

"Look at what?"

Steeplechase points. "See that building?" Steeplechase is pointing to a high rise that is right before them. If they drive directly forward, they will hit it. "That's the Captain's Island Resort," Steeplechase says. "It's on the beach front."

"Yeah?" Wydgate says.

"We've driven in the wrong direction," Alterman says. "We're headed straight for the water."

Then they all hear a rushing sound underneath the car. And water sweeps out around the car from behind.

10

Cherie knows that Ingersoll is in the kitchen. She knows where it is, even though the emergency lights are uncertain and by no means extensive. She can hear the rain beating against the roof and gusts of wind hammering the building. She knows he will still be there, doing whatever goofy thing Alterman dispatched him there to accomplish, because he is loyal and driven. She has worked with him long enough to know that isn't just his work ethic.

Bobby with his slacker T-shirts emblazoned with ironic Bible verses, his studious mannerisms and his head-shaking anecdotes of Christian history. Ingersoll, who manages to sound like an unbeliever with unshakable faith. Thoughtful, sweet Bobby, seemingly fascinated by her and enough to continually fascinate her.

But as she threads through the people and the hallways, she can feel the momentum in her waning. She wonders what that means. She felt so sure in the gym, listening to Margie Everhart. She knew precisely what she wanted and how she wanted to go about it, despite her words. She knew so well she left immediately.

And she's walked too far to stop now. Even now she is murmuring the Lord's Prayer because she isn't sure about anything, even its familiar words.

She stands in the doorway of the kitchen, and catches Ingersoll's eye. He walks to her. Cherie turns and starts walking, then looks back to make sure he is following. She opens a door to a Sunday School classroom. Even though it is dark, she motions him inside and shuts the door. Then together, they walk to the darkest part of the room. The only source of light comes from a narrow two-foot window in the door. But no one passing will see them, she is sure.

"What is it?" Ingersoll asks, even though he follows her. He doesn't suspect what is about to happen.

Ingersoll feels Cherie pull him close. Not totally, but enough that they are pressed together. She is embracing him. It's not the first time, but he can't remember it ever feeling this way before.

"Bobby," she says, her voice barely more than a whisper. "Do you like me?" She immediately feels sick at the words. This isn't starting out the way she expected.

"Well, yeah," he says. Hardly the type of endorsement she wanted. Sounds like he's saying, "Well, when you put it *that* way..." Maybe he isn't sure what her calling him by name means.

"I don't know if it's this storm. Maybe I'm going crazy. I just want to clarify a few things." She shakes her head at the inadequacy of her words. "For myself."

"Okay," Ingersoll says, unsure what he's supposed to say.

"Bobby...oh, I don't know what to say."

"You want to say something. I mean, I guess you do."

"Yeah, I...yeah."

She thinks she might kiss him, but she doesn't really want to.

"Bobby, I don't know what I want to do with you."

There are no words.

"That didn't sound right," she says.

"No, it didn't really."

"Man..."

"Are you OK?"

"Yes," she says. Now she remembers what she wants to say. "Bobby, I am OK. Thank you. Yes. That's the point. That's it. I'm... OK. Really. For like the first time in a while. I mean, a lot of things have happened to me, and I didn't handle them well and now I'm here. I mean, you don't know me. You think you do, but you don't. I'm not this perfect girl who's never had a moment's doubt in her life. And I don't know if I can't trust myself or if I want something or if I just...I don't know."

"I don't either," Ingersoll says, and he really means it. He has no idea where this conversation is headed.

"I'm trying to say it."

"Yeah?"

"I'm interested, Bobby."

"Yeah you are."

"I am?"

"Yeah, you're very interesting."

"No, I'm interest-*ed*. Interested in you."

"OK."

"I mean I'm interested in knowing you better."

"Oh," he says, and it all maybe makes sense to him finally.

"It's just...I don't know."

"Can I help?" he asks.

"Please do."

"You're interested in a relationship. You think you can handle it. You just don't know if you want to with *me*."

"Yes, that's it! Totally. Thank you. Wait! No, I am interested in you. I am. Really."

"No problem."

"Good."

"Yeah, and that's cool, because that's how I feel about it," he says.

"You do?"

"Yeah. I mean, I like you, and all that. You're really great. Great? I mean, you're awesome! And I have a bad way of expressing myself."

"You do? Look at me! I'm awful."

"Yeah, I noticed that."

"It's just...it took me time to figure all this out. I'm still coming out of something very bad. I mean, it's over, but it's not over, you know?" she asks.

"No I don't, but you know..."

"...no, you don't know..."

"...that's up to you what you want to tell me about it, whatever it is."

"Yes. Yes, you're right. I suppose I'll have to let you know about it some time."

"Whatever you want."

She smiles. "And I still don't think I've got all...*this*... figured out. I just couldn't admit to myself that I was..."

"Interested..."

"Yeah, interested..." Cherie repeats.

"Yeah."

"So..."

Just as Cherie speaks, she grabs him in a powerful embrace. For an instant it sounds like she has knocked the breath out of him. "Oh, I'm sorry."

"It's OK," Ingersoll whispers, as the door opens. Two people duck into the room and shut the door. It is a man and a woman.

It isn't necessary for either Ingersoll or Cherie to say anything to each other about keeping quiet. Neither can move. They just stand there, in a fierce and fiercely embarrassed embrace.

"It's almost here," says a male voice.

"I know. That's why I came to you. I didn't know if I'd get another chance."

"What's wrong?"

"Tommy, I'm sorry." Cherie places the voice – it is Margie Everhart. And the other voice is her husband.

"What are you apologizing for?"

"You know what it is. I'm so sorry. I know I've been hard on you."

"I deserve it," he says. "Everything you said was necessary. I should think long and hard about anything like this."

"I just thought about the storm out there and I didn't want you to hurt any longer. And I know I've hurt you."

"I've hurt you more," he says. "You know I want you to be what you want. Follow your dreams. Enjoy your life. I never wanted to stand in your way. I feel like I've done that."

"That's how I feel!" she says. "I keep thinking it's so unfair – it'll be so unfair – if you're prepared for something and I'm the one who kept you from it."

"Margie. We built this place, with the help of the Lord and a lot of people along the way. But we act like it's ours. I've been thinking about that because of this storm. What if it all gets wiped away? What if the storm is God's way of dealing with me about the way I've been?"

"I thought the same thing."

"You did?"

"I mean, I thought maybe it was God dealing with *me*."

Listening to them, Cherie wonders if one definition of love is the assumption of blame for anything on behalf of the beloved. Both of the Everharts seem determined to absolve the other. They probably both have considered a scene like this. Margie had only gotten there first.

"I don't know about that. Margie, I don't know if I'm going to lose this. But I know I don't want to lose you. If that makes me wrong, then I'm wrong."

"No!" she says. "I don't want you to choose between the Lord and me."

"You haven't done that. You made me ask myself who I was doing any of this for. And I really don't know. I don't. Maybe all of what you did is for the best."

"Tommy, don't give up on any of this. Don't give up on *me*."

"How could I?"

The room is quiet, but there was something going on. Cherie hears a discreet sound that can only be a kiss.

"This feels almost like high school," Ingersoll whispers in her ear. The words thrill her.

"I was home schooled," Cherie replies, in his ear. "I wouldn't know."

"I won't tell Alex about this if you don't," he says.

There is no sound, and the two of them wonder if they've been discovered. Then Cherie sneaks what feels like a kiss, but the moment is interrupted by a scream outside.

11

"That's not supposed to happen," Alterman says, to the rising water.

"Where is the church?" Wydgate asks.

"Mercy," Chaffey says, in a whine.

Beeks keeps up a murmuring prayer, devoid of coherent vowels but full of devotion.

"Which way is the church?" Steeplechase asks.

"You're the one who knows this place," Alterman says, his voice right on the edge of fury.

"Let me out!" Steeplechase says, stuck between the two Baptists. "I've got to see where we are. Get my bearings."

"Quick!' Alterman says. The water around them appears to be rising.

Steeplechase crawls over Chaffey, stepping on his foot as he opens the door. The rain instantly cascades in and Alterman wonders if this isn't a flood that will soon engulf the entire car. It is just the rain. He hears a splash that can only be Steeplechase stepping out into rising water.

"Ok, start backing up!" Steeplechase said. "Come on, come on!"

Alterman understands instantly. Steeplechase is motioning him backwards, standing outside, to direct him. He puts the car in reverse and prays he doesn't mow the kid down. The door is open, and the sound of rushing water continues. If they stay here much longer, the water will shut the engine off and they'll be stranded.

"Keep going," Steeplechase says. "Come on! Okay, now turn around back here." Steeplechase, his hands moving, is circling around the car, as he directs Alterman in the opposite direction. Alterman cracks the driver's side window so he can hear. Steeplechase is soaked, squinting against the rain, but his mood is lighter. He's figured things out.

"OK, now the church is in that direction," he says, pointing ahead. If Alterman wanted to, he could deceive himself into believing he sees the steeple. "Let's go," Steeplechase says, and Alterman guns the engine.

Except that Steeplechase is still standing out in the rain. "Hey!" he shouts.

"Sorry," Alterman says, in a voice the younger man outside can't possibly hear. He slows down and the door pops open for him, though the car never quite comes to a stop. Once he is inside, they continue.

But the problems continue. There is rushing water up ahead, but also another street they can turn down to avoid it. "What do you think?" Alterman says.

"Go," Steeplechase answers, before the other man has finished talking. Alterman turns to the right.

"I just want to say…" Chaffey says to Steeplechase.

"It was nothing." Steeplechase says, trying to cut off any thanks.

"No, I mean you're dripping all over me."

"Thanks for getting out and helping back there," Alterman says, feeling for once that someone is deserving of gratitude. He expects the others to say the same thing. They don't. The weather is too awful. He snorts to himself – it would figure that the repentant atheist would have better manners than children of God.

A little further on and Alterman sees they will have to turn again. There is a power pole down across the road ahead of them.

He doesn't want to stop, but he isn't sure whether he should turn left or right.

"Which direction is the church again?" he asks.

"To your left," Steeplechase says.

"To your right," Wydgate says.

"No, not to your left," Steeplechase continues.

"No, I mean look to your right," Wydgate says. On that side, the water is rising. It's the storm surge, coming from shore. It is steady and approaching, already sloshing against the side of houses. They have no choice – they have to turn left. They don't dare stop for anything at this point. They have to keep moving.

Alterman does. He is driving faster now, as fast as he dares.

Instead of houses on either side, they are now among quick marts and payday loan places – little strips of commercial buildings that are probably thirty years old and have housed all manner of beach-related businesses. The water is bunching up around them beneath the car. They can hear the rushing water sound from the wheels growing louder.

"How far are we from the church?" Chaffey asks.

"Not far," Alterman says, his eyes on the road.

"How far is that?" Chaffey continues.

"Not far," Alterman says.

"How far?"

"Why don't you start praying too?"

Then the engine cuts out, and the car jolts to a stop. Alterman shifts gears and tries to crank it. It won't turn over. A sloshing sound beneath the car is getting louder. But that sound is overtaken by another. The men in the car are aware of a change in the air, a drop in temperature moving around the exterior of the car. There is water on all sides, and it is growing, affecting the air inside. It has all happened so fast that before anyone can speak, they see brown, black water lapping against the windows.

"We've got to get out," Alterman says. "We've got to get out now!" He pushes the buttons to roll the windows down. "Everybody out!"

12

It has been two hours, and Whit has found his way to the kitchen. Templeton is there, with Tara and Ingersoll, and they are assembling hot dogs. Ingersoll pulls the wieners out of a broiler, and Tara and Ingersoll stuff them into buns and wrap them in individual sheets of foil. They are racing to beat the inevitable power outage. No one knows how long they have, and they want to make sure there is something for people to eat. Templeton can't remain still.

To pass the time, Ingersoll is telling them the story of Father Benito Vines of Cuba, who predicted hurricanes in Cuba decades ago without benefit of airplanes or radar. But it isn't the story (which he has heard at least three times from the man's lips in the past two days) that is making Templeton uneasy. It is the thoughts of Alterman out there and what might be happening to him.

Templeton sees Whit. "Alex and them back yet?"

"I haven't seen them," Whit says. He sits down on a stool at a serving bar.

"You all right?"

"Y'all keep asking that, you're going to give me a complex." He isn't good, Templeton thinks. He's still not going to admit it. When this is over, they're going to have to force him to go to a doctor.

Tara recoils. One of the wieners is hotter than expected, and she puts her burned finger in her mouth. Then she removes it.

"It really hurt?" Whit asks.

"I'm vegetarian," she says.

"Sorry," Templeton says. "This is probably nauseating for you."

"I said I don't eat meat. I didn't say I don't *like* meat."

"Resist the devil, and he will flee from you," Whit says.

The three makeshift cooks snort a collective laugh.

"You don't look so good yourself," Whit says to Templeton. "Something wrong?"

"I feel bad that Alex is out there, and I'm here."

"They'll be OK," Ingersoll says.

"They've been gone awhile."

"There's a storm outside, in case you missed it," Whit says. As if any of them need convincing at that moment, the power goes out. After a second or two, emergency lights kick on. They're not as bright, but the outlines of each figure reemerge from the darkness. Whit resumes talking. "That's not all that's bothering you."

Templeton shakes his head, but not in disagreement. "I just don't know what to do."

"About what?" Tara asks.

"He got a job offer," Ingersoll says.

"It's my old church, where I was pastor," Templeton says. "They ran me off, and now they want me to come back."

"Sweet," Tara says.

Templeton is amused. "Think so?"

"Yeah. That's gotta make you happy. Best revenge in the world."

"I'm not interested in revenge," Templeton says.

Whit laughs at him.

"What?"

"You're a fool if you don't see what's in front of you," Whit says. "You think you did this? You and Alex with that stunt you both pulled? This is one of those weird things that's got to be the Lord's doing. This is His way of showing He's in control. You can't ignore that."

Templeton doesn't say anything. This is why Alterman insisted that Whit be part of the firm. The spiritual enforcer. He is there to constantly test everyone's spiritual rigor. No, he doesn't look good. Maybe he's crazy.

"*You* think you should go back," Whit says. He is not asking a question.

Templeton is silent, but he isn't mulling the statement. He's already made up his mind. "Yeah," he says. "I miss it."

"I know you do."

"I understand now, after doing this, that I miss it. Just look at all these people. They came here for safety. They knew they could find it here. I want to be part of that," Templeton says. "I don't have to swallow any pride. That's already been done. I'd come back on my knees." Then he shoves another hot dog in the foil. "That is, if I make it out of here alive."

"That's a lot of faith you've got," Tara says.

"I'll bet," Templeton says.

"No, I mean, you guys look miserable. Both of you. All of you, really."

"That's just because I hate hot dogs," Ingersoll says.

"You all talk about light, but all I see in you is darkness," Tara says. "All the time."

Ingersoll will have none of it. "You guys went to beaches trying to convince people there's no God. The weird thing is that you didn't realize how doomed you were. That's like the worst place in the world to try and make that argument."

Tara considers this. "Yeah, you're right. People aren't thinking about God at the beach."

Templeton jumps back in. "They aren't thinking about Him because they don't have to. They can see Him in every direction."

Ingersoll, having made another hot dog, wipes his hands on the apron he is wearing and steps out, as though he has seen someone in the next room requiring his attention.

"What brought you down here?" Whit asks Tara.

"It wasn't hot dogs."

"No, this town. What brought you *here*?"

"I wasn't always like this. I mean, I don't think I've ever believed in God even when I was in church. But I wasn't hostile about it. Until

I started seeing people like you on TV all the time. I saw everybody taking sides. And I didn't want to be on your side. I didn't want to be on God's side if He was on your side."

"So you're saying there is a God," Whit says.

"No," she says. "I'm not saying that at all."

Whit has her focused on his eyes. "Listen to me. I'm just doing you a favor. *You know* there is a God."

"No, I don't. Actually, I …"

"Yes, you do. It's up to you to recognize Him. He's done everything else for you. What if you were to die just now?"

"It's a distinct possibility."

"What if everything came to an end? What would you do?"

"I'd end."

"But what if it all keeps on going?"

"You mean like you?"

"Seriously. What if the end isn't the end?"

"It's the end. Nothing happens after the end. Not for me anyway."

"You don't know that. You're just counting on it ending so you'll be right, and you won't have worry about anything. But deep down, you know differently. You just don't want Him to win the argument."

"You can't have an argument with something that doesn't exist."

"Every knee shall bow," Whit says. "Every tongue will confess. Even yours."

"So you would inflict your misery on me now," Tara says.

"I just don't want you to die without Him," Whit says. The old man, she sees, has a tear coming out of his eye. And though she can't believe it, the sight of him creates a tear in her own eye.

"Why should it matter?" she asks. "As long as *you're* covered. You don't even know me."

"I know what it feels like to be in pain," he says.

"With a face like that, I can believe it," Tara says, and winks at him.

Templeton finally throws one of the fully-wrapped hot dogs against a wall. "That's it. I'm going out there. They need me to find them."

"You *do* have a lot of faith," Tara says. "Give it a little longer."

"I can't. I'm going stir crazy here. There's more than enough hot dogs."

"What do you think you can do out there?"

"I don't know."

"You just feel like you need to get out. But there's a storm out there. It's already here, really. Do you think your friend would go out looking for you?"

"That's not a fair question. You don't really know Alex."

"I think I do," Tara says. "I understand him pretty well. The job is everything to him."

"It is, but not that way."

"Then how is it?"

"What Whit was saying, about what you'd do if you died..." Templeton looks over in Whit's direction, but the man is no longer seated there. "Whit?"

Tara puts down her latest hot dog and walks to the doorway, then she looks down. Templeton can't see what she's looking at, but he hears her words. "Nice try," she says. "It's going to take more than that to scare me into Heaven. And you're going to need help getting up."

"What is it?" Templeton asks.

"It's him," she says, pointing down behind the bar. Then she looks down again. "Get up."

Templeton at first is unsure what is happening, until he sees Tara place her hand to her mouth, and scream.

13

Alterman climbs out through the open window. The water pours in as he comes out, into the open air and the machine gun raindrops. One drop explodes in his left eye at an insane velocity – he thinks at first the eyeball is injured. He wipes at it while still struggling out.

He can make out Wydgate emerging on the other side. Now they have to make sure Chaffey and Beeks make it, which will be harder. Steeplechase is not going to wait. He is climbing out through the front seat and comes out the driver's side window. In a second, he is helping lift Chaffey out. Wydgate is struggling with Beeks. The men finally all are out of the car. They are standing in waist deep water, and it is rising.

"Which way?" Alterman shouts, against the rain and wind. The sound in his ears is all-consuming, and he feels as though he has yelled into a jet engine. But Steeplechase heard his words, or something, because he is pointing behind them. Squinting, Alterman can see the steeple this time. This flood, which has stopped their car, was a blessing – if they had continued driving, they would have again found themselves on the beach.

None of them feel blessed. Not even Chaffey, who is reaching back into the car for some reason. He pulls out a briefcase. Did he have a briefcase when they left the hotel? Alterman can't remember. It hardly matters. They have to get out of here.

The water around them is rushing, and it is filled with debris. There are chunks of trees and branches. Something that at first looks like a snake glides by, and Alterman feels his stomach curdle. Then he thinks it is a downed power line, and he again feels the same sensation. But it is likely a car's engine belt, and it is moving in the churning brown water. There are clothes and a scratched CD and a wet paperback book that has ballooned out in the water like an accordion. There are bits of tall grass and leaves, a candy wrapper and a real estate sign. The castoffs of civilization make a confusing stew all around them.

Alterman motions the rest of them on. They will have to get out of this water before it swamps them. There is a green, grassy rise up ahead the water is washing against, and if they hustle, they can make it up there. Alterman guesses that Wydgate and Steeplechase are in good shape. He is worried about their charges, the Baptists who are probably good candidates for heart disease after lifetimes of covered dish suppers. He has to submerge – should he use that word? – his instincts for self-preservation. He has promised Templeton he will retrieve these men.

He waves again. They are not moving fast enough. Now they see where he is pointing, and they pick up their pace. Alterman allows them to pass, and he looks up into the air.

The clouds, what he can make out of them, are boiling with tropical energy and pouring themselves out. This storm has now met the land and is determined to mow down as much as it can in its final moments. It does not want to go. It wants something on the land mass to pay as it saps the storm's strength. A branch flies past Alterman's face and hits the river of drainage around them, splashing water into his open mouth.

In the short seconds it has taken him to appreciate the storm, the four men with Alterman are making their way up the hill, and no one seems to be on the verge of collapse. Alterman sees Wydgate pulling Chaffey up. There is what looks like a drainage pipe to the right of them, and Steeplechase is directing Beeks away from it so he will not swept inside. Alterman steps to the right. He will go up the hill away from them, and probably be on top of it by the time everyone has gotten out of the water.

And then he steps, and there is nothing beneath him.

Even while his arms and legs whip around, groping for anything to latch on to, Alterman's mind continues to plot out the situation. He has obviously miscalculated. He thought there was solid ground beneath him, but this is a drainage ditch that he could not make out beneath the muddy water. Now he is sinking, and the water is pulling him under as he rushes toward that culvert he saw a moment before. He has no idea where he'll end up, but he has a good idea of what will happen before then, since he, in fact, cannot swim.

Alex Alterman, scourge of the evangelical Christian world, the bane of deacons and keen-eyed spotter of men's restroom filth in temples throughout North America, is going to drown in the middle of a storm that shares its name with the founder of the Reformation.

But Alterman's arms are strong, and as his mouth opens up to let the water in instead of air, his hand catches against hard concrete, and he opens his eyes. He has knocked up against the pipe of the culvert, and he is holding on. But the current behind him is going to carry him under unless someone grabs him.

The rising water from the storm surge continues on, but he is pinned against the concrete and holding on. He opens his mouth to try to get the attention of the others, but again, he can't even hear himself. He's not sure he's shouting anyway. He thinks he might be underwater. He is coughing, and the rain is coming down at such a pace that there is little difference between open air and flood. Alterman's other hand goes up to catch hold of the pipe, and his feet are carried inside. Yet he will not let loose.

Maybe I was meant to go out this way, Alterman thinks. *Going to New York was the Lord's way of letting me say goodbye to my old life. He has allowed me to start something, to draw others who will be able to do the job better. Now that I'm gone, they will carry on this work and all my imperfections, all the callous ways I have wronged men, will be forgotten in a haze of saintly remembrances.*

Except that Templeton still wants to be a pastor, he can't imagine Cherie remaining as an auditor, his death might drive Ingersoll back into disbelief, not to mention Steeplechase, which leaves Whit, who doesn't seem to be doing well for some reason.

And Wydgate?

Alterman holds on.

Then he feels a hand holding onto his. He grabs it, but pushes back against the pipe because he doesn't want to carry this person holding him down into the water with him. Alterman elbows up so he knows now that his chest is out of the water. Now this person holding him has both of his hands, and he opens his eyes slightly to see who it is.

It's Wydgate, and this man that Alterman has tortured and now embraced is holding on to him with every sinew. He can see the veins in Wydgate's neck as his one-time nemesis pulls, and for a second, Alterman wonders if he should just slip away.

This is what salvation is, he thinks. What it must feel like for Steeplechase. The waters are coming and the rain beats down on you, and the only way is to take the hand offered, but you do not trust the hand or the one who offers it. You realize you have to surrender a little of yourself, surrender to the humiliation that you need anyone, let alone this one, and if you don't take it, you will sink, and they may never find you, nor will they ever care to look.

Alterman can feel something slipping away, but he manages to wedge his legs against the culvert, and with Wydgate's frantic tugging, he feels himself slip out of the water and onto the land.

It takes all he has to realize, *I was drowning. I no longer am.*

Both men collapse against the ground as the rain beats their bodies. They know they must go on, but they need a moment's breath.

Alterman raises his head, and looks in Wydgate's eyes.

He wants to thank him. "Don't say anything to Cherie about me not knowing how to swim," are the only words that escape.

Wydgate says something, and it takes a second to register. "To whom much is given, much is required."

Then they hear something. It is the car. The water has completely engulfed it, and it burbles and sinks beneath the storm surge after a moment of floating.

"There goes my discount next time," Wydgate says.

"Oh yeah," Alterman says. "That was *your* rental car." He shakes his head, and stands up. Then he offers his hero a hand. "Things are looking up!"

14

Alterman never knew a human being could be so wet and still technically above water. For the past forty-five minutes, he has been out ahead of his rescue party, the church in sight but his group held in check by wind and rain, debris and water up to their waists. They have now made it to the church parking lot. He turns to usher them on. Steeplechase is the youngest of them, and he is still keeping a good pace. Wydgate is bringing up the rear, but this is out of caution. Beeks and Chaffey are slowly grinding toward the church. Wydgate has had to help each man to his feet after a fall.

There is a boat in the parking lot of Sweet Lightning, and they have heard the sound of it hitting a light pole with regularity for blocks. A car bobs on the opposite side of the lot, its nose beneath the water. They are all weary of the walking and the rain and ready to be out of it, and their relief is finally visible.

Alterman motions them onward, and he finds the door to the commons area has already been pried open by the water. Inside, the only sound is water being sucked into and out of the great hall, as though there is an enormous straw somewhere. Furniture floats on top of the water, along with pieces of sheet rock, ceiling tiles and bits of glass. Papers, programs and trash make a thick soup. The water has been here long enough that there is a layer of black slime coating the wall. Alterman hears a sound and looks up to see birds roosting on light fixtures along the wall. They were smart enough to seek shelter in the storm.

The hall is dark and quiet, except for the sound of the water and the rain, and Alterman guesses the power is out. Emergency lights are visible in places, but the yellow half-light gives everything an end of the world vibe. Alterman has had that feeling before, and survived. They have only to mount the last flight of stairs to the classrooms where Everhart said they would move once they learned the storm surge was coming.

The other four men in the party pause once inside.

"Just a few more steps, and we'll get you fixed up," Alterman says.

"Praise God," Chaffey says, sounding anything but holy. He can barely stand up.

"If this is the storm surge, it's deeper than expected," Wydgate says.

The men begin climbing the steps while Alterman races up, taking them two at a time. Steeplechase, almost half his age, is dumbfounded at how he can still have energy after what they have all endured. Alterman bangs on the door, which has been locked. After a few minutes, the door opens.

Wydgate sees it is Keysha, Everhart's administrative assistant, who answers the door.

"You shouldn't keep this door locked,"Alterman says, barging in. "There still may be people out there who need in."

Wydgate notices something as he walks in. He has already heard Templeton's tales of horror regarding his encounter with Keysha. The anger Templeton expressed is still vivid in Wydgate's mind, but he is not surprised to see Alterman calmly intimidate her, practically at a glance.

"Where is the food?" Alterman asks. "These men need to dry off and get something to eat."

His effect is so absolute, Wydgate sees, that she doesn't even speak. She merely points in the direction of the kitchen even as she shuts the door. Which she does not lock.

Chaffey and Beeks come in, and Alterman waves them on in the direction Keysha pointed out.

"How long has the power been out?" Alterman asks.

"Not very long at all," Keysha says.

"We've been out in the weather," Steeplechase says, as though he might need to point this out. He is dripping all over the carpet, his hair is a mass of wind-blown chaos and he cannot move without a sloshing sound.

"Hard to believe, isn't it?" Wydgate says, giving the younger man a good strong pat on the back, as if to excuse his needless observation.

"Brother Tommy will want to know you're here immediately," Keysha says, and she reaches for a radio clipped to her belt.

"Yes he will," Alterman says, as though she needs his assent. The expression on her face shows that she probably does, Wydgate thinks.

Then, everyone hears a scream. Wydgate looks at Alterman, who looks at Keysha, and in a second, they all take off running in the direction of the sound. It seems to be coming from the kitchen.

Only a few turns of the hallway, and they are there. Across the hall from the doorway, Everhart is standing with his wife, looking inside. They have emerged from a doorway opposite, and there appears to be someone behind them, still inside the room, Alterman observes. But the sound didn't come from that room.

Instead, there in the kitchen is Tara Diddle, standing over the body of Whitlow Mountain. His face is a ghastly pale, and he is not moving.

"Whit!" Alterman says, and his voice has a frantic quality that Templeton, standing nearby, has never heard before.

"He needs air," Alterman says, looking around.

Everhart dashes unbidden to Whit's feet. "You grab his shoulders and I'll grab his feet. We'll take him to the prayer room through that door." He nods in the direction he means, even as he takes hold of the unconscious man's feet.

"Honey, get the door," Everhart says to Margie, who has already moved the necessary distance to open it. Where Everhart and his wife had been standing a moment before, Alterman sees, is Ingersoll and Cherie. Ingersoll's mouth is wide open, and Cherie looks shaken. But she is looking at Alterman, not at Whit.

Alterman follows Everhart's lead, and in a second they are in the room, which Alterman has never seen before. They lay Whit down on the floor opposite a row of tables where phones are stationed. A flat screen above the tables hangs on the wall. There are already some people in here, but they look startled, as though they did not expect anyone to enter.

Especially not carrying a body.

Alterman pulls open Whit's shirt and listens for his heart. Templeton has joined him now and thumbs his wrist, feeling for a pulse.

"I don't get anything," Templeton says, his voice firm.

Tara, whose scream drew everyone, stands over them with her hands firmly pressed to her face, staring through disbelieving eyes.

Alterman, who knows CPR and has marked off churches where staff members do not, briefly wonders for a second if Whit is pulling one of his stunts. Alterman has posed as a man having a heart attack before just to see how trained the staff is in first aid. That was why he spent a week in the hospital a few years back for broken ribs. But Whit is not faking.

Alterman is rattled. This is his friend, his mentor, down on the floor, dying. If it was anyone else in the world, he would immediately know what to do and direct others to fill in the blanks.

He is lost now. Alterman is dripping water over Whit. He supposes he is probably already crying, but he doesn't know. Everything is chaos.

Alterman feels something he can't remember ever feeling. A hand comes out beside him and shoves him out of the way. Alterman catches himself before he hits the wall.

It is Keysha. In a few seconds, she has opened the automatic defibrillator kit. She pries open Whit's chest and attaches the pads. She wipes her hand of the water that came off Alterman when she shoved him aside. She presses the button in the suitcase attached to the electrodes. She shouts for everyone to stand back. She looks on as Alterman and Wydgate understand immediately just who is being put in his place.

Everhart is standing there now, and he is gripping Margie's hand. Everyone is watching what is happening, and no one remembers for the moment that there is a storm outside that could still kill them all.

There is a beeping alert and a prerecorded voice to tell everyone to stand away just before the electricity surges through the body of Whitlow Mountain, contracting muscles, lifting him up, and then depositing him down with a thud.

"Ooohhh," Whit says. He has only needed one charge to bring him back. Alterman, suddenly clear enough to realize his friend is alive, feels an inexplicable disappointment that it only took one shock. He would have expected Whit to be just a little more stubborn.

Templeton races up and removes the pads from Whit's chest.

"Talk to me, talk to me," Templeton says, and Whit's lips move.

"I'm here," he finally says, in the weary voice one would expect of a man who has just received an electric shock to his body.

"Can you breathe?" Templeton asks.

"Yeah," Whit says.

"Good work," Everhart says to Keysha, who suddenly looks up at him as if she forgot where she was.

"Yeah, good work," Alterman says, himself once more.

Keysha stands up, and offers him a hand. "Sorry about that, boss," she says to Alterman. "I knew I didn't have much time."

Alterman stands up. Both Templeton and Everhart, who have heard the words, say in unison, "Boss?"

For a second, Alterman is disappointed, then he remembers where they are and what is going on around them. He shrugs his shoulders, gives a nod of his head to Keysha, and looks at Everhart.

"Brother Tommy, this is one of my operatives," he says, gesturing toward Keysha. "This is Rambha Jakkannavar."

"What?" Everhart says.

"She works for me. She's been spying on you since before we got here."

Templeton, who up to this moment has been looking at Whit, becomes aware of what is going on. He whistles low and loud, shakes his head, and whatever anger he had at Keysha over their altercation is instantly transferred to his business partner.

Rambha, realizing that her cover is blown, smiles at Everhart, and offers out a hand. Everhart cannot explain why they exchange a handshake.

"So she works for you?" Margie Everhart asks, realizing in an instant who Alterman is.

"That she does," Alterman says.

No one is quite sure why Margie chooses that moment to tightly embrace her husband, but when she backs away, there are tears in her eyes and she looks relieved beyond measure.

"There's something I don't understand here," Everhart says, his face still in obvious disbelief. "I mean, how did you know I would hire her? I interviewed her! *I* picked her!"

Alterman, suddenly calm again, shakes his head. "Her resume was so impressive, how could you not pick her? If you hadn't hired her, I would have counted off on your evaluation."

"I see you made it back," Templeton says.

"Yes, and we brought your parachute," Alterman says, pointing to Beeks and Chaffey, standing to the side. They, like everyone else, are still shaken by Whit's near demise.

"They OK?"

"I think so," Alterman says. "We lost our car and had to walk the rest of the way. It was an act of God getting back here."

Chaffey, the water beading on his forehead, steps forward. Though he doesn't realize it, his hands are pressed together as though in a fervent prayer. "Brother Templeton, please. We made it through the storm. If we make it out of here alive, you owe it to us. You've got to come back. We want you."

"Even after all of this," Templeton says, his voice only barely skeptical any longer.

"I've just spent the past hour with your business partner," Chaffey says. "Surely you're ready to give all of this up?"

Templeton smiles. It's only a fiction that Alterman is his partner. He's my boss, Templeton thinks, and like his own Boss, Alterman can raise the dead.

"I suppose I don't have any choice," he says. "I accept."

Alterman, though, doesn't waste any time with congratulations. He immediately looks at Everhart. "I don't remember ever seeing this room before."

"This is our prayer room," Everhart says.

A weak voice from below chimes in. "I knew I'd get in here eventually."

Alterman leans forward. "What do you mean?"

"This is it," Whit says, pointing up. In a second, Alterman realizes that they are standing in the secret room that has eluded their prying eyes, all during the audit.

"This is it," Alterman says, unable to grasp it. "It's a prayer room. What are the phones for?"

"We take calls on our prayer hotline."

"I figured you would contract something like that out. Why the secrecy?"

Everhart smiles, as though caught in a lie. "I just thought it was kind of cool, like a conspiracy," he says. "A secret room. It's a shame, but Our Lord understood it. Sometimes the only way to get people to pray is to make them hide, feel like it's something truly special – which it is." Margie, still standing at his side, squeezes his shoulder, and then moves away.

Alterman grimaces at himself. There are days when he really overthinks this church thing. *In the end, the Lord's got it all figured out*, he thinks.

"Besides, I believe you know something about secrecy, Mr. Alterman," Everhart says, nodding toward his former assistant.

"Oh yes," Alterman says. "The Hindus believe the goddess Rambha was one of the most beautiful women in the world, but she was cursed to be a rock for 10,000 years for testing the virtue of a sage. To test your virtue, she was willing to answer your phone calls."

"And strong arm anyone coming in for a visit," Templeton adds.

"You didn't have an appointment," Rambha replies, her British accent revealed. She extends her hand to him. "A pleasure to meet you."

"She can't work for you," Everhart finally cries. "She's the best assistant I've ever had!"

Alterman, at last satisfied that he has calmed down, squats to look into Whit's eyes. For some unfathomable reason, he looks better now than he has in weeks.

"You saved me," Whit says.

"Not exactly, but you're still here. And we're very glad."

Somehow, he doesn't seem pleased. "I always wanted to die in a church," Whit says.

Alterman nods his head. "Well, there's always tomorrow."

15

It is several days later, after the storm has passed, after the flood waters recede from the church, after the boat had been removed from the parking lot, and after all of the members of Alterman's group, along with the contributions of one conscientiously objecting atheist, have put in significant time helping to clean up. With little fanfare Alterman texted Thomas Everhart and requested a meeting in his office that he said would last little more than fifteen minutes. He has to text the pastor since Everhart still has not found an adequate administrative assistant.

Everhart is waiting on Alterman's arrival. He sits at a conference table in the room outside his office. He has the look of the student who has waited on the principal all through lunch.

"How are you today?" Alterman says, entering calmly. He is carrying a yellow envelope and an iPad.

"Fine," Everhart says, thus lying in church.

Alterman sits down and slides the envelope over. "There's the final report, like you've been expecting. It's pretty self-explanatory. There's an executive summary. There's also a CD with videos that document some of our findings, plus a few other features. There's also a pretty thorough index."

Everhart eyes the envelope, suspicious to even touch it.

"I would have had it sooner, but I had to edit down some of Rambha's findings. She's very...verbose."

Everhart nods.

The pastor waits a moment, probably expecting Alterman to say something. He doesn't.

"Well?" Everhart finally asks.

"What?"

"What did you find? What are your conclusions?"

Alterman, used to this moment from so many previous audits, has learned to relish it. Finally, he unsheathes the dagger as he clears his throat. "The pencils in your pews aren't sharpened regularly." He says nothing more.

"OK?" Everhart expects more.

"That's it."

"No it isn't." Everhart says.

"Why not?"

"You were here for how many weeks? You observed everything. You...your...you planted one of your people in my office! I'm looking at this envelope and there's 300 pages in here."

"372," Alterman says.

"That's a lot of pages about dull pencils."

"You've got questions for me," Alterman says, "I've got questions for you."

"Very well."

Alterman, fixing his eye on the preacher, begins. "So why did you do it? Why did you decide to hire both my firm, and the firm of my biggest competitor, and bring us both here at the same time? And why did you tip off a group of atheists to come and take on your church simultaneously? I mean, that takes some planning, not to mention guts."

Everhart waits a long time before saying, "I'm embarrassed."

"You shouldn't be. Actually, I have to admit, it took me awhile to figure it all out. I had to get some distance between me and this place for it to become clearer. But I have to hand it to you – getting the atheists involved was a good touch. I may have another employee on my hands as a result."

"It was harder than I thought."

"They were probably more suspicious of you than we were."

"I baited them here, just like I did you. I'm sorry."

"Let me guess. You were nervous. You were getting more attention as the pastor of this church, as an author, appearing on television. You weren't sure how you felt about it. You thought you were being prepared for something much larger, and it flattered your ego. It was everything you'd ever wanted."

"Yeah, and it scared me."

"It scared you because you looked down the road a little bit and you began to see yourself a few years from now with a lot of money and a lot of attention and you wondered...."

"How I was going to mess it all up," Everhart says. "I mean, I know – you know – what they're saying about me. They're talking about me praying with the President and blogging and being a talking head on news programs. You hear that kind of thing and it starts to get into your skull. You see what happens to others who've been there before. A few months later they get discovered in an airport bathroom or in somebody's bedroom. I can't even conceive of that happening now, but you turn on that spotlight and..."

Alterman nodded. "Crucifixion isn't modern, but everyone knows what it's like to be crucified."

"If I mess all this up, I'm harming the cause of Christ. I'd rather you all reveal my inadequacies now, here, than have them revealed to me out there by somebody else. Right now, it's no big loss. If I took myself down, then maybe I don't deserve the attention."

"And you wanted to know if they were just paying attention *to you*, in the first place. You wondered if you were up to the task. So you recruited some nutcase and his merry band of upstarts here to set holy fire to your kingdom." Alterman gestures toward himself. "And you gave me just enough of a hint with your late father-in-law to know everything wasn't on the up-and-up."

"To find out if it's all real," Everhart says.

"Well, is it?"

"You tell me."

"Listen, who did you think was 'grooming' you for all this?" Alterman supplies the air quotes himself, tired of having everyone use the same word for Everhart.

"The Lord, obviously."

"What do you think now?"

Everhart sighs. "I don't know."

"It's still the Lord, Tommy. You know He's probably done some of this in your life already. Testing you. Putting you through your paces. Preparing you for what He has in store."

He nodded. "But I don't want to be wrong. Would it be so wrong to stay here? Just keep building instead of leaving it for...what? I don't know."

"What do you think the Lord wants you to do?"

"I don't know. Am I being faithless? If I reject what he wants from me?"

Alterman pyramids his fingers together and looks at Everhart with warm admiration. "Listen, I'm just the guy who gets called in when people want to know what's wrong with their church. The Holy Spirit wouldn't have called you if He didn't think you could do the job. And he wouldn't call you anywhere He wasn't willing to go first Himself. Anyway, I'm not here to give you peace of mind, Tommy. That's His department."

"I know."

"My guess is that, if it's right, you'll know. You've got a good thing going here. I can understand why you'd want to stay. And you probably don't want to put your wife through anything she isn't prepared for..."

Alterman looks at Everhart to show that nothing more needs to be said on this matter. He knows enough to have figured out where some of his anxiety was created.

"But if you really want to do what He wants, you have nothing to worry about," Alterman says. "And as churches go, there's less wrong here than most places. And believe me, I've seen some pretty messed up ones."

"I'll bet you have."

"But let me give you one word of advice, if I may," Alterman says. "You're trying to do the right thing, but you're afraid of making a mistake. You know you have to decide, but you don't want to make a wrong decision. Fear shouldn't cancel out your faith."

Everhart nods, but Alterman isn't finished.

"You know, Tommy," he begins, "when Pontius Pilate sent Jesus away to be executed and washed his hands of Him, that was a decision. It was indecision, but it was still a decision. That's the way people react today. They think there's something special about Jesus, but in the end, they just send him away.

"But that wasn't the only thing being washed that day. Jesus washed the feet of His disciples. He knew what they were about to do to Him, how they would all abandon Him. But He still made a decision. He went through with it all. Because they were His. Because *we* are His. That's why we'll always owe Him." '

Everhart smiles. "Why didn't you become a preacher, Alex?"

"I'm not merciful enough," Alterman says. "But in your case, I'll make an exception. As I told you before, this one is on the house."

"No, I put you through too much…"

"Nope."

"Alex, you were here during a hurricane."

"It was exhilarating," Alterman says. "But I did it for free. No trouble at all."

"Thank you, Alex," Everhart says. After a second, he shrugs. "I guess that means I can't bill you for the damage to the choir room."

16

When Alterman walks into Whitlow Mountain's hospital room, he is surprised at first. Sitting at the bedside, talking to the old man, is Tara Diddle. But she's with Whit, so he shouldn't be *that* surprised.

He had expected Whit to be in intensive care, or barely visible under a host of hoses and drip lines. Instead, he is laying upright in bed. A half-full cup of orange juice is before him. He has a slight growth of beard, but he smiles as Alterman enters. So does Tara.

"You finally checking in?" Whit says.

"I had to make sure your company insurance wouldn't pay for this," Alterman says, before glancing at Tara. "Just visiting?"

"Yes," she says. "You shocked that the heathen cares for others?"

"No, that's not what I meant," Alterman says. "I'm not antagonistic all the time, just to the people I work with, right?" His eyes shift to Whit, who barely grunts out a chuckle.

"She just came by to check on me," Whit says. "I have that effect on women."

"Obviously," Alterman says. "Rambha says hi."

"Who? Oh, my specialist who saved me. Is she coming by?"

"I'm sure she will. Since you never got properly introduced."

"Well, I'll work with her soon enough," Whit says. "I was sure I knew who the McParland was."

"You're not doing any work soon," Tara says. "You need some rest. Take it easy. You've earned it."

"For once, we agree on something," Alterman says.

"No, I've been here long enough."

"How do you feel?"

"I'm above ground," Whit says. "Not as good as I used to be. Definitely not as bad as I almost was."

"I take it that's you talking and not your doctor," Alterman says.

"If you two need to talk," Tara says, "I could step outside. I kind of need a snack."

"Here, let me give you some money," Alterman says.

"She won't take it," Whit says.

"You've been sedated," Tara tells him. "Yes, I'll take it." She extends her hand, palm out.

"I owe you anyway," Alterman says. "You were there when he collapsed. So many people, I'm not sure what might have happened in the middle of all that." He hands her a rumpled $5 bill.

"That's it?"

"All I've got."

Tara grimaces.

"The widow's mite," Alterman says. "Look it up. God smiles on small gifts."

"Probably laughing at this one," Tara says, wrinkling her nose, as she leaves.

Alterman nods in the direction of the door. "You witnessing?"

"She just showed up here," Whit says. "We've been talking for a while. She's a good kid. Reminds me of my granddaughter."

"She *is* good. What's the story with her?"

"Oh, the usual. She needs. She's not like what's his name though."

"Steeplechase?"

"Yeah. She's a tougher nut to crack. But she's got a good heart. She proved that coming here."

Alterman nods. "She must really want into heaven if she's coming to visit the likes of you."

"Amen to that," Whit says, scratching a whiskery patch on his chin. "You finished up here yet?"

314

"The audit?"

"Did you go easy on him?"

"Have I ever?"

"Yeah, you did," Whit says. "Even you have to cut some slack to a guy when a hurricane hits his church."

"Maybe he deserved it."

"You ever stopped to think that you were inside that church with him? Maybe he was in *your* line of fire."

"You were there too. And you're the one in the hospital," Alterman says. "Speaking of which, what *did* the doctor tell you?"

Whit glances away. And his hand goes up to his face. In a second his jaw is quivering. The whole thing happens so fast it takes Alterman's breath away.

"Whit," he says. "Whatever it is, you know I'm here for you. You know I owe you the world."

Whit's tears, pent up and running, descend down his cheeks in cascades. He turns his reddened eyes to Alterman, who feels his own moistened eyes overrun.

"Whit, I know something's been wrong, and you've haven't wanted to tell me. You know you'll always have a place…"

"Alex," he gasps, "it's all right. I didn't think it would be, but it is."

"What?"

Whit grabs Alterman's hand. "Lyme disease. I just had Lyme disease. They gave me something. They say I'll be fine in a week or two. I didn't believe them. I thought I had the same thing that Gilda had."

"Lyme disease," Alterman repeats. "You thought you had ALS?"

"I thought I was a dead man, Alex. I was so ashamed. I didn't have any faith at all. That's all it was."

"Why didn't you go to a doctor?"

"I was too scared to. I didn't want to wind up drooling in a bed somewhere and you coming by to talk to me when I couldn't give it right back to you!"

Alterman nods his head. "You couldn't have sat still, even sick." Alterman pulls out a Kleenex from a box on Whit's tray and hands it to him. "So just a few weeks, and you'll be well? What about your heart?"

"Be fine. My chest feels like I had a safe fall on it, but they say I'm..."

"Listen, Whit. Steve is leaving. He's going back to preaching. I'm not sure what's going on with Ingersoll or Cherie. This Steeplechase kid is good, but he's going to need some training. It might be a good idea to lay low for a while, in light of all that's happened here."

"What are you talking about, Alex? You giving up?"

"No," Alterman says. "Just saying you don't need to feel like you have to be back to work immediately."

"But you're saying I should give up."

"I'm saying maybe this ...would be a good time to retire. Get out."

Whit's stare is withering. "And do what?"

"I don't know. Reflect?"

"Reflect on what?"

"I don't know. That's what you're supposed to do, isn't it?"

"Alex, I thought I was dying. You think I want to retire now that I know I'm just fine? Now that I'm alive?" His grip on Alterman's hand is now painful. "I want to finish strong, Alex. You're helping me finish strong."

"I get it, you're strong," Alterman says wincing, wanting his hand back. "Did you really think you were going to die?"

"I had thought that. Ever since we came here. I kept thinking about Gilda. I didn't know why. Didn't want to think about it."

"Can I have my hand back now?" Alterman asks. He didn't think it possible, but the old man's grip was even tighter talking about Heaven.

"You're not going to get rid of me. I'm going to keep at it until the Lord calls me home. I don't care what happens. You hear me?"

"OK, great! Just give me my hand back and you can stay as long as you want!" Alterman snatches his hand away, flexing sensation back into the fingers. "Lyme disease, huh? You know how you got it?"

"Tick bite, probably."

"At the church?"

"I don't know, Alex. You already handed the report in. It's too late to hammer them on pest control."

The door opens. Tara is standing there, still holding the crumpled bill.

"The machine wouldn't take the money," she says, as though Alterman has pulled a fast one on her.

"Say you love Jesus and I'll buy you a meal," he tells her.

"Always for a price..." she says.

17

When Alterman steps from the hospital elevator at the lobby, they are waiting for him.

Templeton, Chaffey and Beeks are standing together. Not far away is Ingersoll and Steeplechase, listening to Cherie talk about something. No, Cherie is trying to talk over Rambha, who is setting them all straight on some point. He is surprised to see them together. He thinks something is wrong.

"What?" he says.

"It's nothing," Templeton says. "I came by to say goodbye to Whit and I thought you'd be here."

"We just came because we wanted to see Whit," Ingersoll says. He is wearing a T-shirt that reads, "It keeps no record of wrongs."

"And we were wondering what's next," Rambha says. She looks different now, dressed more casually and less in cover. Her earlier disguise was so convincing that everyone is having trouble remembering that she actually works with them.

"We don't have anything right now," Alterman says. "But I've got everybody's plane tickets. Head back home and I'll probably have something for you in a week or so." Then he turns to Templeton. "Except you."

Templeton shakes his head. "Don't worry. You haven't seen the last of me." Beeks, standing behind him, rolls his eyes. "I'm just going back to set up shop and then I'll start relocating. Sharon seems very pleased. Surprised me."

"You're sure about this now?" Alterman asks.

"Yeah. Thanks. I guess this proves how much I missed it."

"This is what you were made to do, brother," Alterman says, and Templeton swallows hard at the words.

"You know, you've taught me more about being a pastor than I ever learned in the pulpit."

"Don't give it to me," Alterman says. "Give it to them." He isn't talking about the two men standing beside his friend, who both look like they'd rather be on the other end of the planet. Yet Chaffey steps forward and offers his hand.

"Mr. Alterman, again, I owe you," he says. "You got us out of that storm. You about liked to killed us doing it, and I still haven't dried out from all that rain, but we're alive and we have a pastor."

"Yes you do," Alterman says. Then he grips the man's hand. "And I'll be watching very closely."

Templeton interrupts. "Let's get up and see Whit," he says. "Alex, I'll call you when we get there."

"Give my love to Sharon," he says, and then watches his partner until the doors close.

Alterman suddenly turns, aware that everyone is looking at him. "Didn't you all want to say goodbye?"

"We already did," Rambha says. "We've been standing here for a while."

"Got a better use of your time?" Alterman asks.

"You say you've got tickets?"

Alterman reaches into his jacket pocket and pulls them out. He looks at the locations and realizes the first belongs to Cherie.

"Here you are," he says.

"Thank you," Cherie says. "You know, I could have quit. I was *that* mad."

"Really?"

"Well, maybe not that mad really. But everything about this trip frustrated me almost to the end."

"Hurricanes will do that."

"You know what I mean."

"You didn't quit. But one of these days you might. I'm sure he's got other things planned for you." Cherie thinks for a second that Alterman glances at Ingersoll, but she might have imagined it.

"You know Alex, I wondered why you made me the congregation member this time, and I ended up helping someone who probably could only have been helped by me."

"Really? How is she?"

"She'll be fine, I think. I won't venture too far from her. And you helped me settle a few things in my head."

"Good," Alterman says, genuinely pleased for her.

"One thing," she says. "How did you know I needed to do this?"

"I didn't," he says. "I just prayed about it. The rest was up to Him. He knew."

"So He did."

Alterman hands a ticket to Ingersoll and then to Steeplechase. "I told you I would pay your way back to where you came from."

"Does this mean I'm working for you?"

"Maybe not for *me*," Alterman says. "You probably need to work out a few things with others before you consider that sort of thing. But I don't want you to think you can just walk away from what you saw here."

"Believe me, I won't."

"See that you don't. Not like this guy." He hands a ticket to Ingersoll.

Ingersoll turns to Steeplechase. "As far as he's concerned, I'm always going to be the guy that doesn't believe. He acts like any minute I'll go back."

"I'm not that bad, am I?"

"What about you?" Ingersoll says. "You ever think about going back to what you were doing?"

"Actually I don't," Alterman says. "Not anymore. But in case you do, I want you remembering all of this. Just like him. I don't want you to convince yourself this was all a mirage."

"Not even *you* could do that," Ingersoll says.

"You gonna watch out for these two?" Alterman says to Ingersoll, gesturing to Cherie and Steeplechase.

"Maybe," Ingersoll says, though it's obvious his hesitancy has more to do with Cherie.

"Good," Alterman says, and he leaves it at that.

"What about me?" says Rambha.

"I haven't forgotten you."

"I was wondering. There were times when I thought you had."

"No. I was just trying to." Rambha looks wounded at the words, until she realizes her boss isn't serious. "Do you really want to do something like this?"

"Yes," she said. "Yes, I do. This was very rewarding work. Even though I don't know everything we did, I know we did well here."

"It's not necessary you know everything," Alterman says. "Most of what we did wasn't even stuff we deserve to take credit for."

"That's why you gave me this job," Rambha said. "You made me blend in just so I would understand that the work was more important than I was."

"Did I do that?" Alterman says. "Go home, eager young space cade. Give me a call in about a week, if I don't call you first."

"Very good," Rambha says.

"And if this doesn't work out, use Everhart as a reference." By this time, she must know he's kidding.

Outside, Alterman finds his rental car. Wydgate is sitting inside.

"You were gone longer than I expected," Wydgate says.

"Yeah, I feel bad that you were out here," Alterman says. "Everybody was inside. You should have seen them."

Wydgate considers this. "You mean, to say goodbye?"

"Why?"

"I suppose this is the end of our partnership."

"Who says? I need a new partner, and there's plenty of work out there."

"Yeah, but how do you do this, Alex? There's no way you can be making money at it. You have a staff. You stay at a resort. Only you know how much this caper cost, and you didn't even charge a fee. I can't work like that, Alex. I love my job, but I *am* in it to make money."

"I know, I know," Alterman says. "And one of these days, I'm not going to be able to do this anymore. But it has to be done. And I'm the one to do it right now. It's a debt I owe, and I'll never repay it."

Then he offers a hand.

"And I'll need help," he says. "I've got a few more people working for me. Whit wants to keep going. And until I hear otherwise, this is what I'm supposed to do. So what do you say?"

Wydgate, for just an instance, realizes he will always be the target of Alterman's jibes, and that for however long they are together, he will forever be the competition who needed to be neutralized.

He considers this, and realizing he can live with it, takes the man's hand.

"You know, I'm glad I rented this car," Alterman says. "This is a good one. I'll hate to see it go."

"I know the feeling," Wydgate says. He knows this is Alterman baiting him, reminding him of his lost car, but he won't acknowledge it.

Alterman starts the car up and leaves the parking lot. The sun is brilliant and casts a clear sheen on everything they see. This renders all the chaos wrought by the hurricane in a perverse clarity. Debris still litters the roadsides, and they pass by signs stripped of letters, and large chunks of gaudy plastic. The road itself is covered in bits of vegetation, and everything still looks wet despite the heat of the sun.

Rounding the corner, they see Sweet Lightning. The church's steeple survived the storm, though the cross atop it is slightly bent. The electronic marquee still does not function, and there are windows covered by wood panels until their repair.

"Look at that," Alterman says, pointing.

Across the street, maintaining her former post, is the street preacher. She is once again dressed too well for the setting, and she holds her Bible open to the sky. Her finger exhorts the passing cars, and her voice is utterly lost in the mix.

Alterman pulls over.

"What is it?" Wydgate asks.

"Just give me a second," Alterman says. "The audit is never over."

Alterman rises from the car, and whistles loud enough to get the woman's attention.

"Hey you! Street preacher!" he shouts, loud enough to be heard inside any of the vehicles which continue on around them. "Speak up! You're preaching the Gospel! They can't hear you!"

She nods, as though a great truth has finally dawned on her.

"They *need* to hear you!" Alterman says. "It's *that* important!"

Alterman pauses for a moment, waiting for her to continue. When her voice is audible over the passing cars, he gives a thumbs up, nods and gets into his car.

And, as he drives off, Alterman smiles.

About the Author

William Thornton is an award-winning reporter and writer. A graduate of the University of Alabama, he lives in Alabama with his wife and daughter. His novel, "Set Your Fields on Fire," won the grand prize in the 2015 Aspiring Authors Writing Contest through WestBow Press and the Parable Group.

Read his blog, discuss this book and contact him at brilliantdisguises.blogspot.com.

Printed in the United States
By Bookmasters